I don't believe in love, that paltry, piddling emotion. Indeed, if love is ever going to find me, someone will first have to convince me it exists.

Chase St. John to his brother Devon,
while riding through Hyde Park

Does she dare?

To save her family from ruin, Harriet Ward invented a fiancé—a wealthy sea captain. But now the bank wants proof of the man's existence. Just as Harriet despairs, fate drops a mysterious stranger into her arms, who she believes has no idea of his own identity . . . Does Harriet dare mislead the disturbingly handsome stranger? And if she does, what will be the cost?

Will he win?

Chase St. John knows exactly who he is. While quitting London, Chase was waylaid by footpads and left for dead. Awakening in the care of Miss Harriet Ward, Chase is astonished when the tempting maid brazenly announces that he is her betrothed. Chase, ever a rogue, decides to play the part of adoring lover. But the price is rich, indeed, when it might mean losing his own heart.

Books by
Karen Hawkins

HOW TO TREAT A LADY
CONFESSIONS OF A SCOUNDREL
AN AFFAIR TO REMEMBER
THE SEDUCTION OF SARA
A BELATED BRIDE
THE ABDUCTION OF JULIA

If You've Enjoyed This Book,
Be Sure to Read These Other
AVON ROMANTIC TREASURES

THE PLEASURE OF HER KISS *by Linda Needham*
STEALING THE BRIDE *by Elizabeth Boyle*
TAMING THE SCOTSMAN *by Kinley MacGregor*
TO LOVE A SCOTTISH LORD: BOOK FOUR OF
THE HIGHLAND LORDS *by Karen Ranney*
A WEDDING STORY *by Susan Kay Law*

Coming Soon

MARRIED TO THE VISCOUNT *by Sabrina Jeffries*

KAREN HAWKINS

How to Treat a Lady

An Avon Romantic Treasure

AVON BOOKS
An Imprint of HarperCollinsPublishers

AVON BOOKS
An Imprint of HarperCollins*Publishers*
10 East 53rd Street
New York, New York 10022-5299

Copyright © 2003 by Karen Hawkins
ISBN: 0-06-051405-1
www.avonromance.com

First Avon Books paperback printing: December 2003

Avon Trademark Reg. U.S. Pat. Off. and in Other Countries, Marca Registrada, Hecho en U.S.A.
HarperCollins® is a registered trademark of HarperCollins Publishers Inc.

Printed in the U.S.A.

10 9 8 7 6 5 4 3 2 1

They say the St. John talisman ring was made by the fairies and given to the handsomest man in all England, one Sir Gervase St. John. The fairies spelled that ring so that whoever held it should fall madly in love. How I would love to find me a ring like that!

Madame Blanchard,
Lady Birlington's French dresser,
to her mistress, while doing m'lady's hair
for a ball at Marchmont

Chapter 1

Trust her? Ha! I wouldn't let that woman come within ten feet of me without first counting all my buttons and beads.

Lady Birlington to Viscountess Hunterston
after encountering Lady Caroline Lamb
in the hallway at Marchmont

Money, or the lack of it, haunted him. Oh, not because he had so little. He was, in fact, very wealthy. It was the beggarliness of his companion that caused him the most pain.

Chase St. John reached into his pocket and withdrew a folded stack of banknotes. He placed it on the table and slid it across the smooth surface. "There. As you *requested*."

Harry Annesley placed his fingertips on the notes, but then hesitated. "You know how I hate this. If only my father's solicitor could see clear of releasing my funds, I wouldn't be reduced to asking you for assistance." Annesley managed an embarrassed smile and lifted his shoulders as if to ask how he could possibly clear the way himself.

At one time, Chase would have believed the convincing lies. At one time, he might have even been

1

moved to induce his jovial friend to take the money. To insist, even. But those times were long gone.

And they were never to return.

Chase reached forward, his hand sliding over the table toward the money. "If you don't want the money, then—"

Annesley's hand closed convulsively over the folded notes.

"Well." Chase leaned back in his chair. "That answers that. And much too clearly for my liking."

Though Annesley's expression darkened, he quickly collected the notes and tucked them into his pocket. "You did offer."

"I always offer. And you always ask for more. It has become a bad habit between the two of us. One that must stop."

A small smile crossed Annesley's face. "We've been through a lot together." He looked at Chase meaningfully. "More than most people know."

It was a threat. Low and oily, as despicable as the man who uttered the words. Despite his disappointment, Chase managed to shrug. "I have to give you credit; you are a hell of an actor. At one time, I thought you were genuinely my friend."

"I am your friend."

"No. You are friends with my bank account. Not with me."

Annesley made a face. "I don't know what's come over you today, but you seem to think I've committed some breach of etiquette or—"

"I don't think anything," Chase said without rancor. "I know. I know who and what you are."

Annesley met Chase's gaze for a long moment. They were at White's, that most exclusive of men's clubs, and all around them buzzed an aura of respectability. Leather chairs sat scattered around heavy mahogany tables, the quiet clink of silver and the murmur of voices adding an air of unreality.

Chase wondered what fool had sponsored Harry Annesley's membership, then decided that he didn't really care. "I made a decision last night and I'm done. The next time you need funds, you'll have to look elsewhere."

"What do you mean?"

"I'm leaving London. And I don't plan on returning."

"Why? The season begins in a week."

"I don't care. And I'm not just leaving London; I'm leaving England." Chase reached over and signed the bill left on the table by the waiter before Annesley had even arrived. "I don't know where I'll go. Maybe Italy. Maybe not."

"Italy? What a foolish idea. Italy is far away, and everything you care about is here where—"

"Yes, Italy is far away. So far away that you will not be able to 'borrow' any more funds. You'll have to find another pigeon to pluck."

Annesley's shoulders stiffened. "I resent that."

Chase lifted a brow. "No," he said slowly, considering the man before him, "you don't resent it at all. But you should, for I meant it in the worst way possible."

For a moment, Chase thought Annesley would leap for him. Chase rather hoped that he would—it would give Chase the opportunity to pummel the rogue into a smear of blood, bone, and desolation.

But the bastard didn't even have the pride to do that. Instead, he clamped his mouth into a thin line, his lips turning white.

Chase waited, ready for anything.

After a moment, Annesley relaxed with a deep sigh, then leaned back in the brown leather chair and crossed his arms over his chest. "What happened, St. John? What has turned you?"

It was an admission, those simple words. Chase accepted them as such. "It's the strangest thing, Annesley. Last week, when I let you 'borrow' that thousand pounds, I did a little math. I realized that I've let you 'borrow' over five thousand pounds in the last two months alone." His gaze dropped to Annesley's pocket. "Make that six thousand."

The bastard's smile never slipped. Instead, he shrugged. "That's what friends are for, isn't it? To help one another."

"Before the accident, you never 'borrowed' anything. Oh, I put out more than my fair share for our amusements. But that changed after the accident. Since then, you've attempted to bleed me dry and you know it well."

Harry scowled. "What I didn't pay back in funds, I paid back in friendship."

"How? By encouraging me to drink? By gaining me entrance into all the worst gaming hells in London? By insisting that I forget who and what I am until I finally—" Chase clamped his mouth closed, a dull roar behind his ears. For a second, an image flashed before his eyes . . . of a rain-wet street. Of his carriage careening drunkenly out of control. Of the startled face of a girl as he rounded the corner, her large dark eyes widened in fear as his carriage—"No!"

God help him but he didn't want to remember that. Not now. Not ever.

Annesley motioned for a waiter to bring a bottle of port. As soon as it arrived, he poured some in Chase's glass and silently slid it forward.

Chase took a harsh gulp. Then another.

"I'm sorry, St. John. I'm sorry about it all. But . . ." Annesley filled his own glass. "I am not the one who ran over an innocent woman."

The words, said so softly, hung in the smoky room, lingering about Chase's head like a swirl of tepid air. Chase's chest tightened, and he had consciously to unclench his teeth before he could speak.

Harry waved a hand. "Nor have I forced you to do anything—not the drinking, the gambling, none of it. Everything that you have done has been of your own free will."

"I know," Chase gritted out. "I take full responsibility for my actions. It's my fault I drank too much. It's my fault I was driving my carriage at such a speed. It's all my fault. But it's your fault for blackmailing me ever since."

Annesley eyed him for a long moment. "Blackmail is such an ugly word. All I said was that I can't imagine what your brother Marcus would say if he knew about that particular incident." The man's gaze hardened. "That you *killed* that woman."

Chase's throat ached at the words. For all they knew, she wasn't dead. It was possible she'd survived, possible but—

No. The woman was dead. He was certain of it. And though he'd tried to drown his sorrow and hide from his responsibilities, the time had come to face facts. He was a St. John, and b'God, it was time he remembered it.

Annesley tilted his head to one side. "You will tell your brothers before you leave?"

Chase could almost see his oldest brother, Marcus, stern and forbidding, disappointment etched in his eyes. And for a second, Chase wavered. It would be so easy just to pretend he hadn't awakened to what his good friend, Harry Annesley, really was. If he could only pretend that nothing bad had happened on that night a year ago.

But he was through pretending. His stomach, and his sense of honor, would have no less. "I will send them a letter explaining all, once I have settled on the Continent."

It would be hell, writing that letter. But it had to be done; he owed his family that much. They cared for him, believed him better than he'd ever been.

He met Annesley's knowing gaze unflinchingly. "Not that it's any concern of yours."

Annesley looked down at his perfectly pared nails. "Isn't it?"

Chase's jaw tightened until it ached. He asked himself how the hell he had been so foolish as to believe that Harry Annesley was an amusing companion. Chase knew the answer—brandy. And more brandy. In the months since the accident, he'd seen the bottom of more decanters than he could count. "Marcus is a very intelligent man. I daresay he knows my sins already. I've never been able to keep a secret from him, even when I was a child."

Annesley suddenly smiled, a deep dimple appearing in his right cheek. "And you've had so many secrets . . . This, I think, is different."

It was all Chase could do not to grab the slimy bastard by the throat and toss him across the room. But that would just cause more talk, and there was going to be enough of that already. Most of society thought Harry Annesley a handsome, well-turned-out man, always impeccably dressed and perfectly behaved. If they only knew.

Chase shoved his chair from the table and stood. "It's done. I'm leaving tonight."

Annesley's smile slipped. "But St. John—"

"Go to hell. If you are going to tell my brothers, then do so. Here, I will even make it easy for you. Brandon is still on his honeymoon, but will return tomorrow. Marcus and Anthony were to visit Tattersall's. And Devon is at Gentleman Jackson's Boxing Saloon. Shall I call for your carriage? If you hurry, you might catch Devon, at least."

Annesley leaned back in his chair, a flash of contempt on his changeable face. "You'll regret this, you know."

"Considering all I have to regret, this is negligible. Good-bye, Annesley. And good riddance." Chase turned on his heel and left. The second he was outside, he stopped, lifted his face to the cooling breeze, and took a long, deep breath.

Around him, London trembled and toiled, carriages clattered down the streets, linkboys shouted, people scurried by, heads tucked against the swirl of dust and grit that lingered in the air. It was London in the spring, awakening after a long and bitter cold and shaking off the fetid fumes of a freezing winter held at bay with grim determination and tons of bleak coal fumes.

As ugly as it was, it was still home. Still where he'd grown up. It was a pity he had to leave it all behind. London *and* his family. His chest curiously tight, Chase turned and walked down the street, away from White's. Away from his lodgings. Away from everything and everyone he'd ever known.

And it was only the beginning. If he was to make this journey successfully, he had to face both himself and his past. And face it, he would. One way or another.

At White's, still comfortably seated at the table, Harry Annesley sipped his port and stared at the empty chair opposite his. Chase St. John was right about one thing—Harry Annesley was not what he seemed. Despite his fine clothing and his practiced ways, he was not a wealthy man at all. He was not from Wiltshire. He'd never inherited a house from his uncle. And his fortune was not tied up in a legal dispute. Nor had his father left him anything more than a pile of duns and a childhood of memories tainted by bruises and blood.

Harry had made his way on his wits and charm alone, watching with interest the rise of a man named Beau Brummel, the son of a tailor who'd breached the highest echelons of society with nothing more than his biting wit and impeccable dress. Harry thought that he could go one better, forging letters of introduction to gain entrance into places like White's and Almack's. He was accepted, but only because he was a personable young man and because he made it his business to know just how to dress and exactly how to act.

At first, Harry confined himself to married women who had access to their husbands' fortunes and were not averse, in exchange for certain favors, to making sure Harry's rent was paid and his wardrobe developed to the highest degree. Careful never to cross the lines of propriety, at least while in public, he became the preferred escort of half the married ladies of the ton, whose tolerant husbands would demand to know who their wives were going to the ball with, only to receive an airy, "Oh, it's only

Harry Annesley," which earned an indulgent, "Well, then, madam. You may go. So long as it's Harry and no one else."

The comments, though they allowed him access to places he normally wouldn't have been allowed, burned through Harry's heart, for they proved over and over again that he was not as important as he wished, no matter how he dressed. He became more determined to succeed in the society that only allowed him to stand at its edges.

But to reach those heights, he would have to establish himself well enough that he could marry the woman of his choice—someone wealthy, well connected, and desirable. Harry thought he knew such a woman, the daughter of a wealthy viscount. Harry had been flirting with her for a sennight, and he thought he detected some feeling in her gaze.

Not that it mattered. She was necessary only to cement his place in the society to which he belonged, and nothing else. He looked into his glass and sighed. It was one of the great ironic facts of the *ton* that wealth tended to marry wealth. And Harry, for all his scheming, didn't have the funds it would take to convince the protective papa of a tender young heiress that he was an eligible *parti*.

He'd considered an elopement, but that was too crass and could cause him to be ostracized from the very society he wished to enter. No, he wanted to be welcomed into the family he chose. Welcomed as an equal. And that would take some serious funding.

The desire had grown into an obsession. Harry ate, drank, slept, and dreamed of it. Though until he'd met Chase St. John a year ago, he hadn't known how to gain the entrance he so desired. How to get the large amount of funds he so desperately needed.

It was a pity Chase had suddenly developed a conscience. "Utterly inconvenient," Harry murmured into his glass.

A waiter stopped and quietly asked if anything else would be needed. Harry shook his head impatiently and waved the man away. The waiter bowed respectfully and reached for the bill that Chase St. John had signed not ten minutes earlier.

Harry's eyes were drawn to the bill. "Wait."

The waiter stopped, waiting politely. "Yes, sir?"

"Leave that. I may want something more after all."

"Of course, sir." The waiter bowed, then left.

Harry reached over and picked up the bill, looking at the flourishing signature for a long moment. Slowly, by barely discernible degrees, a smile touched his lips. Chase St. John might be leaving London, but his brothers would still be there. And for a while, at least, they wouldn't know the whereabouts of their beloved younger brother. It was just the opportunity Harry needed.

"Yes, indeed," he said, folding the bill in half. "I shall have to thank my dear friend Chase, after all." He tucked the bill into the same pocket he'd tucked the banknotes and, whistling softly, finished his port and called for his coat. Within moments, he had left the club and was making his way to his lodgings on 10th Street.

It took a lot to get a man like Harry Annesley down. He refused to give up hope. Thank God there was more than one way to pluck a pigeon. Especially one as wealthy as Chase St. John. Whistling absently to himself, Harry made his way down the crowded street, his hat set at a jaunty angle, no sign of his concerns on his handsome face.

Chapter 2

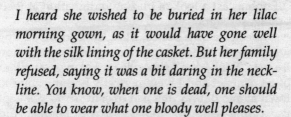

I heard she wished to be buried in her lilac morning gown, as it would have gone well with the silk lining of the casket. But her family refused, saying it was a bit daring in the neckline. You know, when one is dead, one should be able to wear what one bloody well pleases.

Viscountess Hunterston to Lady Birlington
while attending the funeral of
Lady Agatha Tallwell, who was neither
tall nor particularly well

"I am going to retch."

Harriet Ward cast a fulminating glance at her sister. "Sophia, if you retch in this cart, I will personally tell everyone we know about the entire experience. And I will spare none of the horrid details."

Sophia pressed a hand to her cheek and said with all the false tenor of a threepenny actress from Drury Lane, "I am ill, and yet you mock me. You are cruel."

"I am not," Harriet said, noting that though her sister tried to appear ill in the bright sunshine, she looked anything but. Sophia, for all her high-flown wiles and die-away airs, was amazingly healthy and

11

had never suffered more than a cold in her entire life.

"Well *I* think you are cruel, and so does Ophelia."

From where she sat on the backbench of the cart, Ophelia snorted. "Don't involve me, Sophia. I shall agree with Harriet, as you well know."

Sophia cast a look of blazing indignation at their youngest sister.

Ophelia calmly patted Max, an enormous dog who was a solid mix of working sheepdog and family pet. "Soph, don't shoot dagger glances at either of us. Harriet and I were perfectly happy riding to town alone. But no. *You* had to come. And *you* kept us waiting while you looked for your bonnet. And now, here we all are, listening to *you* complain. So I hope you do retch, only not in my direction."

Sophia gasped and opened her mouth to retort, so Harriet hurriedly said, "Enough, the both of you. I am in no mood to witness either retching or complaining. Besides, such commotion could upset the sheep." She glanced over her shoulder at the three ewes riding in the back of the cart, bleating piteously. It was a shame they had to be sold, but the Wards needed the funds to pay for extra help during shearing season.

"I don't care about upsetting the sheep. In fact, the sheep," Sophia said in a grand voice, "are upsetting *me*."

"How?"

"They smell."

"They're sheep," Ophelia piped up, adjusting her spectacles on the bridge of her nose. Younger and plumper than either of her sisters, she'd always been something of a bookish sort of girl. Though lately she'd discovered the wonders of the barn and had developed an unfortunate tenderness for the sheep, treating them as pets.

Harriet thought it was a good thing that they'd gotten sheep in order to collect wool and not to make lamb chops—Ophelia's soft heart would not have allowed for such a thing. Within two weeks of purchasing the flock, Ophelia had named them all and then, to make matters worse, had insisted upon tying ribbons around their ears.

Fortunately, Ophelia had ceased this unworthy practice when she realized that the other sheep were not only unimpressed with such vivid decoration, but thought of the ribbons as tasty treats. She turned to her sister. "Sophia, sheep can't help how they smell, but you . . ." She sniffed the air, then scrunched her pert nose. "What *is* that horrid odor? You smell like Grandmother Elbert, all musty and old and—"

"What?" Sophia's cheeks reddened. "I don't smell like Grandma Elbert! It's the *eau de cologne* Mother got me last Christmas, and it is very expensive."

"I don't know what it cost, but if it was more than a pence, she was sadly cheated."

"Oh!" Sophia said, twisting in her seat to glare at her younger sister. "At least *I* don't smell like a sheep, unlike *some* people I could name who spend all their spare time lingering in the barn as if they were a resident!"

Ophelia's chin jutted, her brown eyes flashing behind the round glass of her spectacles. "Just what do you mean by that?"

Harriet stifled a sigh. There was only one thing worse than driving a smelly hay cart to market, and that was driving a smelly hay cart filled with even smellier sheep, a large damp-scented dog, and two bickering sisters. "Stop it, the both of you! You're upsetting the sheep."

"What do the sheep matter?" Sophia asked, momentarily distracted from irking Ophelia.

"They matter a lot, and you know it. I want our sheep to look like the best, most pleasant-natured sheep on earth." Anything to get a good price. God knew they needed it.

Sophia looked over her shoulder and regarded the sheep with a dubious air. "I don't know how you could tell if they were upset. They all look the same to me. Very woolly and . . ." She tilted her head. "Perhaps they *do* look as if they have a mood. But it's not a good one."

"Nonsense," Ophelia said stoutly. "They're happy sheep. You can tell."

"How?" Sophia demanded.

Ophelia regarded the ewes for a moment, then suddenly broke into a huge grin. "Maybe you can tell they're happy sheep because they don't feel baaaaad."

Harriet winced as the other two giggled uncontrollably. "Ophelia, between you and Derrick, I've had more than I can take." Derrick was their younger brother, and at age sixteen bid fair to become the wittiest of the Ward family, a high honor indeed.

Sophia adjusted the pretty blue ribbons fastened to her old bonnet. "I'm sorry, Harriet. I shouldn't laugh, but Ophelia does that so *well*."

Ophelia grinned, twin dimples in her round cheeks. "I do, don't I? Sorry I made such a baaaaaad joke."

One of the sheep in the back of the cart lifted its head and answered.

Sophia chuckled. "You bleat even *better* than the sheep."

"You have your own gifts," Ophelia said in return, no sign of her earlier rancor. "You should be on a stage. No one can do Juliet like you."

Sophia's face burned with pleasure. She tilted her pretty face to the sky and placed her hand to her brow. *"What's here? A cup, closed in my true love's hand? Poison, I see, hath been his timeless end—"*

As if in great pain, a sheep bleated loudly while Max the dog shuffled in a circle, obviously anxious to get out of the cart. Ophelia giggled and even Harriet had to stifle a grin.

Sophia's face suffused with color. "I was not made for such conditions."

"None of us was," Harriet said dryly, hawing the horse to a trot. "I was not made to drive a smelly hay cart, either."

"I know what you were made for," Sophia said with a smug smile. "Captain John Frakenham."

Harriet stiffened. "Do *not* mention that name to me!"

Sophia and Ophelia exchanged amused glances.

"I don't want to hear another word," Harriet said firmly. "And if I do, you'll walk the rest of the way to town."

Ophelia leaned forward to whisper loudly to Sophia. "Harriet is always ill-tempered when Captain Frakenham is not in port."

"Indeed. She's pining for him. For his manly arms and his broad chest—"

"Enough!" Harriet frowned. "What *was* Mother thinking?"

Sophia sighed. "Oh, she was just trying to save Garrett Park. If she hadn't convinced the bank that you had a wealthy suitor on his way home from sea with trunks of gold, they'd have never allowed us time to gather the wool for the payment."

Harriet silently admitted that Sophia was right. Mr. Gower, the new officer at the bank, had unexpectedly arrived at Garrett Park one late afternoon with a rather unpleasantly worded demand for funds. Mother's usual good sense had been sorely muddled by a large dose of laudanum she'd just taken for an aching tooth, and with a sense of pure panic, she'd launched into a disjointed, but apparently convincing story of how the money would shortly arrive in the form of a wealthy sea captain, who would also claim her oldest daughter for his own.

Harriet was quite certain Mother had stolen the idea from a lending library novel. Still, the colorful fib had served its purpose; the bank had granted the extension.

Sophia clasped her hands together and sighed dreamily. "Captain Frakenham is the most handsome man in the world."

"And the wealthiest," Ophelia added with a mischievous grin. "From what I've heard, he has as much money as the Prince. Maybe more!"

"Piffle!" Harriet snapped. Mother's little fib wouldn't have been so bad had everyone politely ignored it. After all, the family only needed three more months and they'd have the last payment for the mortgage.

What Mother hadn't thought of—what no one had seen or planned upon—was that the bank officials, given the few details Mother had managed to mumble through her numbed lips, had gone home and repeated every word to their willing wives. And *those* worthy women had, of course, mentioned the matter to a few women at the Church Fund Meeting. And *those* women had mentioned it to their friends, neighbors, sisters, and daughters, and so on and so forth until the entire town came to hear of the mysterious Captain Frakenham.

As the story was told and retold, passing over the anxious tongues of every gossipmonger in town, actual details had appeared. Details like the fact that the captain was tall, dark, and handsome. And that Harriet was heartbroken if by some strange mischance he didn't write one of his weekly epistles. And that the worthy captain was an orphan who had raised himself by his bootstraps from the humblest of beginnings and had found untold wealth in sailing the seas of India and beyond.

Each new rumor added to the credibility of the whole, until Captain Frakenham was as real to the people of Sticklye-By-The-River as the butcher who sold meat from his shop on the corner. Except to the Wards, of course. They knew better.

"I wish there really was a Captain John," Sophia said, giving a blissful sigh. "He's absolutely perfect."

Ophelia nodded, her round face wreathed with a dreamy smile. "Thick black hair and the bluest eyes—"

"Blue eyes? Who told you that?" Harriet demanded.

"Charlotte Strickton. I met her in town the other day and she said she'd heard it from the parson's wife."

Blast it all, this whole thing was entirely out of control.

"I'm glad I'm not so shallow," Sophia said loftily. "I value the captain for his bravery and not his looks. When I think of all the adventures he's had, I feel faint with—"

"Oh for the love of—" Harriet snapped an exasperated look at her sisters. "There is no Captain Frakenham!"

"We know," Ophelia said, looking amazed.

"Of course we do," Sophia added with an innocent blink of her long lashes. "Really, Harriet, you are too serious."

"It annoys me the way everyone is treating me differently now that I'm supposedly affianced. I'm not affianced, and I never will be."

Sophia shook her head. "Nonsense. One day, the right man will come along, and you'll change your mind."

Harriet wasn't so sure. In all her twenty-four years, she'd never met a single man who had managed to make her feel anything more than acute irritation. It was a lowering thought, but not one she'd willingly share with her talkative siblings. "I, for one, was not born to become some man's wife."

Ophelia blinked owlishly through her spectacles. "What were you born for?"

"I was born to enjoy life, to lie in bed all day while eating bonbons and drinking hot chocolate. But somehow, fate has forgotten me, and so here I am."

Sophia eyed her elder sister with some awe. "Bonbons in bed. I like that. Anything better than these sheep, which smell even if Ophelia is too thick-headed to admit it."

"I know they smell," Ophelia said in an offended tone. "But they cannot help it and I, unlike you, am not about to berate them for it."

"What we really smell is not sheep," Harriet said before the two could start up again, "but profit. Extra funds that will enable us to replace Stephen for the shearing."

"Poor Stephen," Ophelia said, her eyes darkening in pity.

Sophia sniffed. "It was his own fault. I don't know what he was thinking, swinging from the barn loft on a rope like that. He's eighteen and far too old for such behavior. And he certainly has no right to upset Mother in such a way."

"He was trying to impress Miss Strickton," Harriet said. "Which I'm certain he did when the rope came untied and he went crashing into the barn wall."

Sophia giggled. "I wish I could have seen that."

"Me, too." Ophelia chuckled. "Perhaps we can get Charlotte to tell us the tale when next we see her."

Though Harriet understood her sisters' amusement at the thought of their pompous older brother's woes, she found that she could only manage a faint smile. That little rope trick had not only cost them precious time repairing the barn, but had also put Stephen out of service for the next two months, right when she needed him the most.

Harriet turned the cart down a narrow dirt road that was lined on one side by pleasant fields, a copse of trees on the other. They rounded a corner and Harriet hastily pulled the cart to a halt. "Goodness!"

"What is wro—" Sophia's eyes widened.

A beautiful black horse stood to one side of the narrow lane, head lowered, sides heaving, his hide flecked with foam.

"Good heavens," Harriet said, setting the brake. She gathered her skirts and climbed down from the seat, making the last hop into the dirt road. "Whose horse could this be?"

Ophelia stood, rising on her tiptoes, her bonnet sliding back off her head to reveal a collection of thick brown curls. "What a beautiful animal!" She clambered to the side of the cart and hopped down, her booted feet clomping pleasantly on the hard dirt surface. Max followed her from the cart, his large head coming to her elbow as he trailed along.

The horse shied at the approaching dog. "Oh, piffle," Harriet said. "Keep Max away."

"Sit," Ophelia said to Max. The dog reluctantly dropped to his haunches and didn't move. Max was a boon and a blessing to the Wards. He was a natural sheepdog, having been raised with the last batch of lambs. He made the barn his home just as they did. Even slept in the same stall when it rained. For this reason, the sheep trusted him implicitly, and it was no wonder; no stray dogs had ever managed to get a lamb or sheep that was under Max's care. For that alone, he was worth his weight in gold.

Sophia eyed the horse with an interested gaze. "He's beautiful. Whoever owns that horse must be mad to find him."

Ophelia snorted her disbelief. "Whoever owns this horse is probably laying in the mud somewhere. See how the stirrups are twisted? I'd say the owner took a rather violent fall."

Harriet took a step forward, then slowly reached for the reins. The horse shied, backing warily out of reach, head lifted, eyes wild.

Harriet dropped her arms back to her side. "Ophelia, you try. You've a way with animals and this one is horribly frightened."

Ophelia walked slowly toward the horse, talking in a low, quiet voice. Though he made a tired show of tossing his head, this time he didn't move when approached. Ophelia reached out and easily caught the reins. "There you go," she crooned, patting the animal's neck.

"I wonder if he's one of the new horses Baron Whitfield just purchased," Harriet said. "Tie him to the back of the cart for now, and we'll stop by there on the way to town."

Ophelia sighed. "I wish we could claim him. Wouldn't Stephen be so jealous if we found—"

BAM! The sharp sound cracked the air about them. The horse half reared, but Ophelia kept a tight grip on the reins. Max whirled to face the forest, his ears lifted.

"That was a gunshot," Sophia said into the silence that followed.

"It certainly sounded like it," Harriet said. "Someone must be hunting nearby." She climbed into her seat.

Max lifted his nose to the faint breeze and growled, his teeth flashing whitely. The sheep stirred uneasily.

Ophelia tied the horse to the back of the cart. "I wonder what's wrong with Max? Do you think he's caught the scent of a wolf?"

"Just keep him in check, for I've no wish to go chasing him through—" Before Harriet could finish the sentence, Max lunged forward, barking madly as he raced down the road. The sheep began to bleat loudly, urging him on.

"Max!" Harriet called, standing up and watching with a sinking heart as Max swerved off the road and disappeared into the woods. "Oh, *piffle!* We have to catch that silly dog before someone shoots him. From a distance he looks just like a large deer."

Blast it all, it had seemed a fairly simple project

that morning, to take three sheep to the market. Harriet tied off the reins and prepared once again to climb down from the cart, her irritation growing. "Come, Ophelia, you and I will gather Max. Sophia, you stay here until we return."

They were *never* going to make it to market. Never going to sell their sheep. And when the time to gather wool came, there would be no money to hire an extra hand, so they wouldn't be able to pay the bank, and Garrett Park would be lost forever.

"Not while I'm alive," Harriet said through gritted teeth. She marched toward the woods, her booted feet slapping forcefully on the packed-dirt road, Ophelia trailing behind.

It was a furious way to die, the cause of madness and broken dreams. And Chase St. John had suffered enough of both to welcome the impending blackness.

One moment, he was riding down a narrow dirt lane, a supposed shortcut to the main road to Dover where he was to take a ship to the continent. He knew this area only a little; his brother Devon owned a manor house somewhere nearby, and Chase had once come to hunt. All he could remember of the experience was that it had rained the entire time.

It was rather ironic that today of all days, the weather was unusually perfect—all blue sky and green, green hills. His new black gelding frolicked in the warm sun, a cool breeze lifted his hair, a bottle of good brandy at his lips. All told, it was a pleasant way to dull the homesickness that was already beginning to plague him at the thought of leaving his life in London. Of leaving his brothers and sister.

Trying to focus instead on the peaceful vista about him, he rode on, drinking more as the day progressed, his pain dulling. He'd just rounded a bend in the road when, quick as a wink, his brandy-soaked peace was shattered. Mayhem ruled as bullets flew. Coarse shouts assailed his muddled head, his horse bolted into the woods, then reared. A searing pain traced a fevered path across one temple.

He fell into alluring darkness. Sometime later, he slowly awoke to the sound of rough voices raised in disagreement. His assailants arguing over the rich contents of his purse and bags.

By tiny degrees, he became aware of the fact that he lay on the cool, damp dirt of the forest floor, left for dead if the blood that ran across his forehead and clouded his vision was any indication.

The earth chilled his cheek, the cloying smell of rotting leaves clung in his nostrils. He clenched his eyes even more tightly together and tried to move, gasping at the pain that flashed through his head, the heavy scent of brandy rising to meet him.

God, what he wouldn't give for more brandy. A keg of the stuff. Enough to dull the pain and halt the fear that was beginning to course through him.

The voices grew louder. Chase blinked through the haze of red, squinting against the bright sunlight that shivered through the leaves overhead. Brazen brigands, they were, to attack in broad daylight.

To one side, almost out of sight, he could just see them, two men hunched beside each other as they quarreled over his belongings. Chase tried to remember what he'd been carrying—several large notes, some guineas, a gold watch, a few cravat pins . . . nothing of real value. Not to him, anyway. He'd been on his way to hell, so he'd been traveling light. The last thing he'd wanted to do was load himself down with mementos that would only cause him more pain, more sadness.

One of the men stood, huge and hulking, lank brown hair that flopped in a greasy point over one eye. "There. Thet's thet."

The other man stood. He was smaller and dressed in a faded red coat, the bottom edges stained and ragged. " 'Ere, now! Ye got more 'n I did!"

" 'Tis me right t' get more. I planned this whole cull, did I not? Ever since we saw the gent come rackin' into the inn and demanding a bottle of the keeper's best. I knew he'd be bosky afore noon." The giant held something up to the sun, and a flash of sunlight rippled through the clearing.

Chase squinted through the sun-dappled leaves and for one instant, his vision cleared, the flash drawing his gaze. *Mother's ring. God, no.* He'd forgotten that he had the bloody thing, thanks to his brother Brandon, who had tricked him into accepting it. It was one of the few things of Mother's that they had left. And she'd prized it highly.

The rest of his belongings, he could replace. Everything, in fact, but that.

The man lifted the ring to his mouth and bit, then made a disgusted sound. " 'Tis not even made o' real silver. Do ye want it?"

The red-coated man shook his head sullenly. "Not me. I've enough worthless trinkets in me pockets as 'tis."

"And enough rocks in yer head, too."

The man gave a toothless grin as he tucked a wad of notes into his coat and spat on the ground. "If 'twere a gold piece, I'd be a-fightin' ye fer it."

"Ye'd lose." The larger thief curled his nose. "I

don't want this trinket, neither. Couldn't get a shillin' fer it on a Sunday. But 'tis a pretty piece fer all thet. There are carvings on it."

The red-coated man peered at the ring, but made no move to touch it. After a hushed moment, he asked in an awed voice, "Do ye think 'tis magic?"

"Magic, he asks. Thet's whot's wrong wid ye, Davy. Ye've got yer head in the clouds."

"I don't have me head in the clouds. I just asked if—" Davy clamped his mouth closed when the larger man burst into a guffaw. "Damn ye! Drop the bloody thing right there. It's nobut a trinket, anyways."

The other thief chuckled more, then casually tossed the ring to the moss-covered forest floor.

Chase watched, mesmerized as the circlet fell, end over end, sparkling in the lowering sun.

Every sound seemed abnormally loud, every smell overpowering. He watched the ring hit the ground, where it bounced once . . . twice . . . each move pinging loudly as if it hit a rock and not the soft, leaf-covered ground.

Somewhere in the back of his mind, he could hear his mother's voice. *It's a mystical ring, Chase. Whoever has it in their possession will meet their true love.* As silly as it sounded, she'd really believed it.

Chase, of course, had no such faith in magic. Or anything for that matter. Not anymore.

"Thet's thet, then," the large man said, gathering the items and storing them in his large pockets. "Let's be gone. I've a thirst on me, and there's nothing holdin' us here."

"What of the gent?"

"Leave him. As much blood as he's lost, he won't make it to nightfall."

Chase ground his teeth at the thought of dying here in the forest, his face pressed into the blood-soaked mud. By God, he'd live. He'd live if he had to crawl out of the woods on his hands and knees.

The creak of carriage wheels and the soft clop of horses' hooves lifted on the faint breeze, and Chase's heart leapt.

The red-coated thief whirled toward the sound. "What's that?"

Voices carried on the wind, a commingling of feminine tones.

"Bloody 'ell!" The red-coated thief scrambled to collect his loot, but the larger thief grabbed the man by his shoulder and shoved him down below the line of the bushes.

"Hold quiet now," he whispered hoarsely. "They can't see our horses from the road. Mayhap they'll pass on by and we'll—"

Grrrrrrrr.

An animal's deep-throated growl sounded unnaturally loud in the quiet glen. Chase took a deep breath, squinting through the brush.

The huge thief turned slowly toward the sound. There, standing behind the thieves, crouched a huge dog. Reddish brown with a thick ruff of hair about its blocklike head, its teeth glistened malevolently in the uncertain light.

"Don't move!" the large man said in a strained whisper.

Chase said a silent word of thanks to whatever higher power happened to be looking down on him right then. God knew that he didn't deserve divine intervention. Not anymore.

A voice called from the road. "Max! Max! Where is that blasted dog?"

The large thief's gaze remained locked on the dog. "Davy, we have to make a run fer it."

The dog took another step forward. A deep growl rumbled in the animal's throat, a froth of white dripping from its jaw.

"Ye mangy mongrel," the large man hissed as he stood. "On the count of three, we head fer the horses. One. Two. Th—" The man wheeled, crashing through the brush as he tore through the forest.

His partner gave a startled gasp, realizing he'd been left behind. For a startled instant, he and the dog locked gazes.

To Chase's fuzzy mind, it appeared as if the dog's grin widened even as he leapt, huge jaws open wide enough to close over the man's entire head.

With a horrible shriek, Davy took off, legs flailing wildly as he plunged headlong through the brush. The dog followed, teeth snapping furiously.

Chase wanted to watch. To see if the dog got the man, for he sincerely hoped so. But his head ached, and a thick fog was covering his mind. His eyes seemed determined to close on their own though he was curiously awake, his ears locked on every sound.

He was aware of approaching footsteps, of a surprised cry, then a soft feminine voice that issued orders in amazingly calm, stern tones.

If an angel administered heaven, ordering the clouds and sun hither and yon, she would have this same voice, Chase decided. A hint of honey dripped over cool, calm steel. He savored the silken tones, let them wash over him as he struggled to stay awake . . . to stay alive.

The fates, though, were cruel and capricious. A horrible thick silence dropped over him like a shroud, the delectable voice fading away as his senses released their tenuous hold on consciousness. Still fighting for his last breath, Chase St. John slid into an inky blackness from which there seemed to be no escape.

Chapter 3

That was Sir Royce Pemberley and Liza, kissing one another in his phaeton as if no one could see. And they are married, which is even worse! It will raise expectations all over town, and all hell will break loose.

Lady Birlington to her nephew,
Edmond Valmont, as that young man
followed her into the lending library,
his arms overflowing with her
overstuffed reticule, a large fur muff,
two pillows, a shawl with
Oriental fringe, three unread books,
and a very overweight pug

"**G**ood God," Harriet said, sinking to her heels beside the prone man, her heart thudding an uneven beat.

He lay on his back, an angry wound on his temple, blood smeared down one side of his face. The ground beneath his head was wet, a blackish halo about his head.

The brush crackled as Ophelia made her way into the clearing. "Did you find—good heavens!"

"He's injured, and there's a lot of blood." Harriet swallowed when she heard her own voice trembling. She pulled her handkerchief out of her pocket and pressed it to the wound. "Ophelia, go back to the cart and bring the bucket of water we brought for the sheep. Send Sophia to fetch help."

"How bad is—"

"*Now!*"

Ophelia whirled and ran, her feet flying over the path.

Harriet had never seen so much blood; her kerchief was already soaked and useless. *Blast it, but the man is going to bleed to death if I don't do something.*

She threw her useless kerchief on the ground and lifted her skirt to rip strips of linen from her shift. It was an old shift; all of her shifts were old. But it was very clean and made of good, serviceable linen.

Harriet formed a makeshift bandage out of the cloth, then held it firmly against the wound.

The bleeding slowed somewhat, but did not stop, the bandage swiftly turning red. "Hurry, Ophelia," Harriet muttered.

With her free hand, she dusted off a fringe of dried leaves and dirt from his cheek, absently noting the intricate tie of his cravat. The horse they'd found *must* belong to this man. He was certainly dressed in a manner that matched the animal's exquisite breeding. The man's coat was of extraordinary cloth and cut, his cravat of the finest linen, his boots of the latest style. Everything about him seemed perfection itself. In fact . . . her gaze drifted over the man's face, an involuntary sigh escaping her lips.

He was the most attractive man she'd ever seen. His jaw and lips were the carved perfection of a Greek statue. His skin a lovely golden color. Thick black hair, sticky wet with blood on one side, curled back from his forehead.

Harriet pressed the bandage more firmly in place, willing the blood to cease. The man's eyes fluttered, then opened, the thick lashes lifting to reveal eyes the blue of a cerulean sky.

Harriet's chest constricted. Good God, but he had beautiful eyes. Astonishingly so. Despite the awkward hammering of her heart, she forced herself to smile calmly. "You are injured, but help is on the way."

He seemed to understand, for something flickered in his eyes.

"Can you speak?"

He didn't attempt to answer, just looked at her as if he would never stop, his gaze so direct, so compelling that Harriet found herself leaning forward. She was pulled toward those eyes, toward his handsome, carved mouth. Drawn inexorably onward until—

His lips parted—perfectly formed lips that spoke of a sensuous nature and a firm resolve.

Harriet found herself watching his lips. "What's your name?" she whispered. "Who are you?"

His brow lowered, and he tried to form a word.

Harriet leaned even closer. "Yes?"

"I . . . don't . . . know." Then he was gone, his eyes sliding closed, his head turning to one side as his tenuous hold on consciousness slipped away.

"Careful, missus," Cook said, dusting her hands on her apron, flour drifting into the air in a shimmery cloud. "The water's hot, 'tis. I don't want you spilling it like that porridge you dropped all over the new rug."

Since the porridge incident had occurred over

twenty years ago when Harriet was all of four years old, Harriet was reasonably certain she was in no danger of spilling the hot water she was getting ready to carry upstairs to their patient.

They'd brought the poor man to Garrett Park. Though they'd looked for some proof of who he was, he didn't have a single paper on him—and no money either, which led Harriet to believe that he was the victim of a brutal robbery.

Harriet glanced up at the ceiling. He was upstairs in their guest chamber, still unconscious. A shiver of something amazingly like excitement traced through her. If he'd been handsome lying in the forest floor, covered in blood, he was breathtakingly beautiful lying in the large bed upstairs.

It really was a pity, but Harriet was certain that once the stranger awoke and opened his mouth, all vestiges of handsomeness would disappear. That's the way it usually happened, anyway.

Harriet caught Cook's admonitory gaze and adjusted her grip on the bowl. "I'll be very careful. I promise."

The old woman's narrow face softened a bit. "I know you will, Miss Harriet. It's a pity the gentleman didn't have no letters or nothin' on him when you found him. 'Tis a mystery, 'tis."

"The constable believes the poor man was attacked and left for dead."

Cook clicked her tongue. A thin, sparse woman with stern gray hair and a practical attitude, she possessed a quick smile and an iron-willed loyalty. " 'Tis not safe to walk out of doors anymore. Go on wid ye, now. Tend to the patient. The doctor's just left, and I'm certain yer mother will have some news fer us."

Harriet paused. "When did the doctor arrive?"

"When you went to the garden to gather some goldenrod fer the tonic. I was goin' to tell you, but I forgot it in the excitement."

"Thank you, Cook." Harriet turned and hurried out the door, carrying the bowl down the narrow hallway from the kitchen and into the main hall. Just as she lifted her foot to climb the stairs to the guest room, Mother swept into the landing and made her way downstairs, Harriet's younger brother following absently behind, his head buried in a book.

Harriet wondered how Derrick managed to walk up and down stairs while reading without falling and cracking his head, but he always seemed to succeed.

Harriet moved out of the way, careful not to spill the hot water. "How is our patient?"

Mother's brow folded in concern. "He hasn't yet awakened."

Derrick leaned against the wall, his eyes still directed on the pages of his book. He never stood upright anymore, lounging about like an overgrown stalk of wheat. "He's probably just sleeping."

"It's been hours." Mother sighed. Her hair, once the same soft brown as Harriet's, was now pure white and softly curled about her smooth face. "I do hope the poor man doesn't die."

Derrick glanced up from his book, disgust in his tone. "He doesn't look as if he's about to die; his color is far too good."

"What did the doctor say?" Harriet asked.

Derrick shrugged. "Not much. We put the patient in one of Stephen's nightshirts and found nothing more than a few bruises and that gash on his head."

Mother's soft brown eyes shimmered with concern. "The doctor said that there was risk of a brain injury."

"A *slight* risk," Derrick said inexorably.

Mother glanced at him reproachfully. "Any risk is too much when speaking of a brain injury. I hope the poor man isn't like Mrs. Billingsworth. She fell from her horse not two years ago and hit her head and died."

Harriet frowned. "Mrs. Billingsworth died just last month."

"Yes, but she never regained her memory." Mother leaned closer, and said in a confidential voice that was quite easy to hear throughout the entire foyer, "When she awoke, she was appalled to discover that she was married to Mr. Billingsworth, which would appall me as well."

"Lord, yes!" Derrick said, apparently finding this new conversation more to his liking. "The man never bathes and has the most peculiar habit of grinding his teeth between every sentence."

"My own memory is slipping at the mention," Harriet said, wrinkling her nose.

Mother nodded, her pretty lace cap flopping over one ear. "Had it been I, I would have pretended *not* to remember the husband, but maintained a *very* clear memory of the children."

"There you go!" Derrick opened his book. "If you ever decide to lose your memory, you'll know just how to act."

"Indeed I will," Mother said, smiling ruefully. She glanced at Harriet. "Derrick and I are going to the barn to see if Stephen has returned with the hay cart."

"I thought Derrick was going to fetch the hay?"

Derrick didn't look up from his book. "I was, but Stephen apparently wanted it done quicker than I was able to get to it. When I went to the barn, he had already unloaded the ewes and left."

Mother sighed. "And I daresay he's angry about it, too. Come, Derrick. He should be back. I hope he didn't injure his leg with such a prank." She crossed the foyer and out the door, Derrick slouching behind.

Harriet turned toward the stairs. She held the steaming bowl in one hand, then gathered her skirts and began the slow, steady climb up the narrow stairs.

That was one thing she'd change if she had the money, the main stairs. They were treacherously steep. The front hall was large enough to hold something more impressive, not to mention safer.

But that change, just like the others she dreamed of, would have to wait. Though hopefully not for long. Harriet paused halfway up and moved the bowl to her other hand, her fingers stinging from the heat. The door to the guest chamber was ajar and two soft voices trickled into the hallway.

"Well, *I* think he's handsome," came Sophia's breathless voice. "I don't know how *you* could think otherwise."

"I didn't say he wasn't handsome," Ophelia replied in a sulking tone. "I said he was *striking*, which means he's handsome, only a little more so."

"Oh. Well. That's all right, then."

Silence reigned as if the two were considering something. Harriet continued her climb.

"The doctor said he could awaken at any time," Sophia said finally.

"I hope so," Ophelia answered.

There was another second of silence, then, "Ophelia, do you think he might awaken quicker . . . with a kiss?"

Harriet, her foot over the top step, almost stumbled.

Ophelia, however, seemed intrigued. "Like in that play you did last year?"

"Exactly," Sophia said with obvious excitement. "Let's try it, the both of us! I'll go first. Then, if he does not awaken, you may try."

"Why should *you* go first?" Ophelia said, outrage in her now-ringing tones.

"I should go first because I'm older than you."

"By only eleven months! That hardly counts."

Harriet hurried down the hall to the first doorway.

"Ready?" There was a strained silence, then a smothered cough.

"Oh for goodness sakes, Sophia!" Ophelia burst out. "That's no kiss! Let the poor man breathe!"

Harriet shoved the door open. "*What* is going on in here?"

There, on either side of the stranger's bed, stood her sisters. Sophia hastily straightened, her face pink. She met Harriet's gaze and flushed darker. "Why . . . nothing is going on. Nothing at all. We were just . . . talking."

Ophelia stood on the other side of the bed. A fierce frown marred her round face. "Talking? You call that talking? It's a wonder he didn't expire!"

Sophia's hands curled into fists. "The problem is that you've never seen a real kiss."

"Neither have you! You nearly smothered the poor man!"

"Enough!" Harriet said. "Both of you!"

Ophelia eyed the bowl of steaming water in Harriet's hands, her eyes suddenly alight. "Are you coming to bathe him?"

Sophia brightened as well. "Oh good! Ophelia and I would be glad to assist you."

"I daresay you would," Harriet asked, setting the bowl of water on the side table, the china clinking loudly. "But I don't need your help. I am just going to wash his face and arms."

Ophelia's shoulders slumped. "Well. That *is* unfortunate."

Sophia sighed her agreement. "I suppose if you don't need us, we'll go to the barn. We're working on *A Midsummer Night's Dream*."

"I'm Puck," Ophelia said proudly.

Harriet eyed her sisters for a moment. "While you're down in the barn, why don't you see if Jem needs help with the milk cows. He was going to move them to the eastern pasture today."

Ophelia clapped her hands. "I'll be a real shepherdess!"

"You can't be a shepherdess for cows." Sophia's brow wrinkled. "You're a . . . Hmmm. What *would* you be?"

Harriet dipped a scrap of linen into the water and wrung it dry. "What you would be—and are—is a pain. Now off with you both. And don't come back until Jem says he's done with you."

Sophie nodded though she didn't move away from the bed. She trailed her fingers over the edge of the blanket that covered their guest, her blond curls framing the dreamy expression on her face. "Don't you think a kiss would be a perfectly lovely way to awaken a man? Just one touch of your lips to his and—"

"Sophia!" Ophelia cast a sharp glance at Harriet. "That's enough."

Sophia gave Ophelia a smug smile. "You're just upset because you didn't get to kiss him."

Ophelia stiffened, her glasses sliding a notch down on her nose. "I would have if you hadn't thrown yourself over him and practically smothered him until he coughed and—"

"He coughed?" Harriet asked, looking at Sophia. "I thought you coughed?"

Sophia tossed her hair. "He coughed a little. But I did *not* smother him. I mean . . . I suppose I might have leaned my elbow into his ribs a little. But only a little!"

Harriet closed her eyes. "You are both going to drive me mad. Go to the barn and help Jem."

Reluctantly, the two left the room, defending themselves as they went. Harriet waited for them to leave, then she closed the door.

Stifling a sigh, she approached the bed and looked down at the patient. He seemed sound asleep, no movement on his face, his breathing even and deep. "Sophia's being melodramatic." Harriet took the cloth she'd dipped in the water and sat on the edge of the bed.

If he'd been handsome before, he was dangerously handsome now that he'd been cleaned up a bit. She frowned again. Was he *really* asleep? She tilted her head to one side, leaned over and peered closely at him, her nose only an inch from his.

Nothing happened. She breathed a little harder, letting her breath fan over his mouth. Again, nothing happened. His breathing never altered, his lashes didn't tremble, nothing.

Oh, for heaven's sake, what am I doing? If he was awake, he would open his eyes, ask for something to eat, want to know where his horse was—something other than lie there dead to the world.

Relaxing a bit, Harriet straightened, though she found herself smoothing back the man's hair. Thick and soft to the touch, the black waves slid through her fingers. He remained deeply asleep, his lashes on the crest of his cheeks, his lips slightly parted . . .

Harriet looked at his mouth. Heaven had never made such a perfect pair of lips. Never.

Sophia had kissed those lips. Harriet wondered for just the barest moment what it had been like. Heaven knew she hadn't ever kissed such a beautiful man. She supposed she never would.

Harriet's heart lowered. It was a pity there was no real Captain John Frakenham. If there had been, she'd want him to look just like this man, with his dark hair and blue eyes . . . She sighed, admonishing herself for her silliness.

Still, somehow her fingers found their way through the man's hair, and then traced the line of his brow to his cheek. His skin was warm beneath her fingertips, his skin shadowed by a day's growth of facial hair.

If this really were the captain, she could kiss him with impunity. Kiss him because he was a man and because he was hers. The idea made her tingle, and, without another thought, she leaned forward and pressed her lips to his.

For an instant, a warm shiver shot through her, raising the fine hair on her arms and tightening her chest. It was as if she'd stepped through a blast of hot air, her body absorbing the warmth.

Then something happened. The heat intensified. Harriet opened her eyes and found she was right. She had indeed stepped into a blast of heat—one that emanated from his blue, blue eyes. The man was no longer asleep.

Just as in the story, Prince Charming had awakened with a kiss.

Chapter 4

*I found a four-leaf clover last week and sud-
denly women find me irresistible. Never believed in such nonsense before, but now . . .
just last Sunday Miss Hobbinton told me she
liked my hat and then on Tuesday Lady Dan-
bury "accidentally" dropped her kerchief right
in my path and I stepped on it. But the best
was yesterday evening, when I trod on Lady
Whistelsmithe's left foot while trying to waltz
and she didn't even yelp, just teared up a bit.
Lud, yes, I'm feeling quite the thing now.*

Edmund Valmont to the Duke of Wexford
at a chance meeting on St. James's Street

Chase wasn't sure what was fantasy, what reality. One moment, he'd been floating in a sea of
darkness, an ache behind his eyes as he struggled to
find his way to the surface. The next moment, he
was being summoned forth by a pair of soft, feminine lips.

His gaze dropped to those very *real* lips now. Full
and moist, they were amazingly sensual in a face

41

that was otherwise rather plain. Indeed, the little servant or housemaid who had just kissed him wasn't his usual fare.

For one thing, she was far too thin—completely without the beguiling plumpness and lush curves he usually sought. She had brown eyes, brown hair, even her skin was brown, as if she spent a great amount of time outdoors. Nothing about her appealed to him.

Still . . . she was close. Within reach, in fact.

He slid his hands up her arms and down again, the cap sleeves on her linen gown crisp against his fingers, the fresh sweet scent of lemon tickling his nose. Chase didn't hesitate—despite the nagging ache behind his eyes, he pulled her across his lap.

She gasped and struggled, her eyes widening in surprise, but he held her firmly. Chase wasn't sure who the chit was, but he had to admit that she affected him. His body was warming by the second, his manhood stirring as if he held a prime morsel in his lap and not a plain mouse of a maid. It was a lovely distraction from his rather annoying headache. He must have drunk too much port the night before.

"Let me go," she said, her voice pitched low, the sound both soft and unyielding.

Something about that voice tickled the back of Chase's memory. He wasn't sure where he'd heard it, but he had. All he knew was that if the woman now lying across his lap was half as seductive as her voice, he was in for a hell of a night.

Wherever he was, he might as well take advantage of all the amenities. He pulled the little maid against him, holding her imprisoned to his chest. Servant girl, daughter of the house, he really didn't care. He wanted to taste her and b'God, he would.

"You—what—" she sputtered. "Let me u—"

He kissed her. Hard. Pressing his mouth against hers, halting her words, and capturing her breath in his mouth. She didn't fight him, but lay stiffly in his arms as if suffering his touch.

Chase paused. Most housemaids pretended to resist, but only for a second. Most of them wanted to be romped as much as he wanted to romp them. But this woman offered no encouragement. None at all. In fact, she was unbending, stiff, anything but pliant.

His interest piqued, Chase deepened the kiss, covering her mouth with his. He ravaged, plundered, took, and demanded. She stiffened in his arms, and then . . . slowly, ever so slowly, she relaxed and let him do his worst.

And Chase's worst was good. Better than good— his efforts were masterly, and he knew it, had worked to perfect them. He might have failed being a St. John in many ways, but never in the bedroom.

He'd pleased and tormented, seduced and fulfilled more women than he could remember. And he took pleasure in their pleasure—took satisfaction in the realization that none would ever forget him or their time together.

He'd sampled beautiful women aplenty and usually found his delights in the more sophisticated connections. Yet here he was in the middle of the godforsaken country and a slip of a woman, this rather unremarkable housemaid, not only had an astonishing effect on his senses, but she also was not responding to his caresses. At all.

It was a challenge of the first order.

He applied himself with increased ardor, getting even more aroused as he did so. His head hurt like the devil, but that was nothing compared to the maelstrom of heat that swirled through his veins and pooled in his loins while holding this woman. B'god, he'd teach her a lesson or two.

Chase deepened the kiss, lengthened it, stretched it across time until he forgot all of his aches and pains and remembered nothing but the hot, sweet warmth of the woman in his arms. Of her taste and her scent and the heat of her skin beneath his fingers.

For her part, the little maid began to move restlessly beneath his ministrations. Soon, she was busy kissing him back, though not in a particularly satisfying way. She was hesitant, almost shy. As if perhaps she'd never—

Bloody hell, he was kissing a virgin! The thought cleared his muddled senses and iced his ardor. Chase would never know how he was so certain of that fact, but he'd have staked what was left of his life on it—the woman had never been kissed. Never been held in this manner. Never been anything.

Reluctantly, Chase lifted his head and looked down at her. For an instant, she remained where she was, a bemused look in her brown eyes, her lips parted and moist. She was a taking thing, he decided, mildly surprised to discover that she wasn't nearly as plain as he'd first thought. Up close, he could see that she was delicately made, her nose perfectly drawn, her eyes thickly lashed, her body whip thin, but gently curved.

She was, in fact, quite fetching. It was a pity she was a virgin. Chase avoided innocent women like the plague; they were far too prone to nervous twitters for his liking. He loosened his hold, and she instantly scrambled out of his arms and off the bed. Her feet thumped on the floor, and she whirled to face him, her eyes flashing fire.

She was even prettier mussed and upset, he decided. Her eyes shone with indignation, the velvety brown depths sparkling gold. Her skin, an unfashionable tan, was now touched with pink.

For some reason, Chase found himself grinning. "That's enough pleasantries for now. I am, after all, a wounded man."

"Pleasantries?" She sounded as if she was about to choke. "You call that a pleasantry?"

"Among other things." He nodded a greeting. "'Tis time for an introduction. Who are you?"

"I was going to ask you the same question," she said. "Who are *you*?"

"I asked first," Chase said gently. "So you have to tell me first."

She smoothed her skirts, the gesture amazingly calm, considering she was a virgin and had just been sitting in his lap. By his reckoning, she should be . . . upset. Instead, she eyed him with something ridiculously near disgust, even though her lips were still plump from his kisses. "I am Miss Harriet Ward. And you, sir, are in Garrett Park, my home."

So she wasn't a housemaid, after all. Garrett Park . . . the name meant nothing to him. "Where is this place?"

"North Walton. Near the coast."

The coast. His memory came flooding back. He'd been on his way to catch a ship. He'd left his home, his family, everything. Not because he'd wanted to, but because he'd had to. Because he'd lost the right to be a St. John.

The thought tightened his throat, and it was with

difficulty that he managed to say, "How did I come to be here?"

"We found you, in the forest." Her gaze flickered to his forehead and back. "Remember?"

Chase touched his forehead gingerly. It felt curiously tight, almost as if—his fingers found the bandage. He closed his eyes and let the thoughts flood over him. The attack. The robbery. The sight of Mother's ring falling to the ground . . .

He opened his eyes and found his companion watching him narrowly. What was her name? Ah yes. Harriet. Harriet Ward. *Miss* Harriet Ward.

Her voice broke his musings. "Do you remember?" she asked again, softly insistent.

Chase opened his mouth to answer, then stopped. If he told this woman who he was, considering that his brother Devon owned a house somewhere around here, word was bound to leak out. And the last thing he wanted was the sight of his brothers, all four of them, arriving to bundle him back to London. He'd made his decision and he was not about to waver, even with this little setback.

He glanced from under his lashes at the woman who stood beside the bed. She gripped her hands together, her body erect, her shoulders set. She looked as if she was ready for the firing squad, though he detected the faintest tremble to her soft lips. A smile tickled the corner of his mouth at the sight. Inexperienced she might be, but she possessed her own passions.

"Well?" asked Miss Harriet Ward, her silken voice edged with a shred of prickly lace. "What is your name? I gave you mine."

Chase leaned back against the pillows, aware that besides a great ache in his head and a general overall weariness, he really didn't feel all that unwell. "Miss Ward, I would tell you my name if I could, but I cannot."

A flicker of disbelief crossed her face. "You don't know your name?"

"I don't *remember* it."

"Oh. Do you . . . do you know where you came from?"

He paused a moment, as if thinking, then said, "No, I don't know that, either."

Her gaze narrowed. She was a tough one, he realized with a faint sense of appreciation.

"Do you remember where you were going?"

Chase pursed his lips as if he could almost remember that. But then, after a moment, he shook his head. "No."

"Are you married?"

"No! I mean," he added hastily, "I don't think so." *Damn, I have to be careful or she'll figure me out.*

She muttered something that sounded to his fuzzy ears like "piffle," if that was indeed a word.

"I beg your pardon?" he asked.

"Nothing. I was just thinking." She crossed her arms, staring at him as if he were a particularly nasty bug to be pinned to a display. "Do you remember being attacked?"

Chase frowned. Should he pretend to remember that? Or not? Perhaps the best answer was a nonanswer. "I suppose . . . I think . . . you said you found me in a forest?"

"Yes. Not far from here. By the way, your horse is fine."

He brightened, then caught her eye and realized his error. He forced himself to frown. "A horse? I must have been riding, then."

"And drinking."

Of course he'd been drinking. He'd been desperate to dull the pain of his homesickness. Still . . . that was not something he wished to admit to the little puritan facing him now—and he was quite certain she was a puritan. No one else could look so disapproving and for nothing more serious than a few gulps of brandy.

Chase opted for an innocent lift of his brows. "Are you *certain* I was drinking?"

"You reeked of brandy, and an empty bottle was found nearby."

"Perhaps it was in my saddlebag and just leaked out," he suggested mildly.

"Hm." She appeared unconvinced. Completely unconvinced.

Chase's amusement was quickly leaving, replaced by a sort of wary fascination. Miss Harriet Ward was obviously no fool. And she ruffled up like a wet hen when she was upset. For some reason, Chase found that he rather liked that outraged expression. Liked it a lot. Liked it so much that it made him want to reach out, scoop her up, and kiss her senseless.

He touched his forehead and wondered how hard he'd been hit. "I need to see a doctor."

She turned and picked up a cloth and dipped it in a bowl that sat steaming beside the bed. "Dr. Blackthorne just left. He said you'd be fine."

Chase had no doubt that Blackthorne was some sort of country bumpkin who knew more about torn horse ligaments than doctoring actual people. "What exactly did the good doctor say?"

As if she detected the sarcasm he'd tried to hide, Harriet shot him a look from beneath her lashes. She wrung out the cloth, then reached over and pressed it against his brow. "You can speak to the doctor yourself when next he comes."

The warm cloth worked magic on Chase. He closed his eyes, a strange lassitude weighing him down. The ache behind his eyes began to melt away.

Harriet, for her part, was having a difficult time remaining stoic. The man was so handsome, resting against the pillows, his black hair falling over the bandage in the most interesting way. His eyes had especially caught her attention. Bright blue and clear, she had the feeling that she could see all the way into his soul.

Heaven help her, but he was a beautiful man. And the realization that this bit of perfection had held her in his arms and kissed her madly, passionately, as if she were the only woman in the world . . . Harriet thought she would burst into flames at any second. Not from embarrassment, though had she any sense she would feel at least a little, but from pure hot lust.

Harriet was no stranger to kisses. She'd been kissed before. Twice, in fact. Once was three years ago, at the farmer's fair in Newmarket. She'd been walking along the stalls, a basket over her arm, when a lad had run by, grabbed her, and planted a firm kiss on her lips, then run off.

And then, two years ago, Colonel Hillbright's grandson, Mr. Landry, had come from London for a visit. Harriet later learned that Mr. Landry was actually in hiding from his creditors, but when she'd first met him, she'd thought him dashing and pleasant.

Indeed, they'd embarked on a three-week flirtation that had ended in the back garden of Garrett Park with a very brief kiss. He'd left the following day, his pocket stuffed with the draft for funds that he'd finally wormed out of his grandfather. Harriet was certain that he never again gave her or his grandfather another thought.

For her part, Harriet had been similarly disaffected. Still, she'd been glad for the episode as she'd thought it would be the only taste of passion she'd ever have—her only brush with the fires within. Apparently she'd thought wrong. Mr. Landry's kiss, which she'd managed to romanticize over the last two years, suddenly faded into insignificance. It was a mere peck on the cheek in the face of this new kiss.

A real kiss, she realized. From a real man. One who was obviously very experienced in such matters.

Harriet dipped the cloth back into the basin, noting that the patient's eyes opened reluctantly. He gave her a sleepy half smile, his lids lowered over his eyes. "That felt soooo good."

Harriet resolutely subdued the hot tingle that flashed through her. What was it about this man that ignited such feelings? Perhaps it was the mystery. Yes, that's what it was. She was a tidy person, one who liked all the chess pieces left on the board in their proper places. And this man, lying before her, was definitely out of place. She lowered the warm cloth to his face once again. "Better?" she asked in her most practical, efficient voice.

"Somewhat." His hand wrapped about her wrist, holding her hand to his cheek, his eyes shimmering with a surprising heat. "If you really wanted to make me feel better, you'd kiss me again."

She pulled back—as far as she could considering he held her wrist in an uncompromising clasp. "Really, Mr.—" She paused. "If you don't know your name, what will we call you?"

"Good question. We'll think about that while

we're kissing." His eyes twinkling up at her, he pulled her wrist to his mouth, where he placed a warm kiss to her bare skin, the wet cloth dangling useless. "I can do both, you know. Think *and* kiss. I'm quite talented."

She tugged on her arm, alarmed at the wave of heat that shivered up her spine. "I am in no mood to kiss you, and I have no desire to think up names for you either."

He tugged her closer, his lips curled into a smile that was as hard to resist as Cook's cinnamon scones. Harriet found herself wanting to smile in return, a response she firmly suppressed. Whatever else he was, the man was obviously a wastrel. The last thing he needed was encouragement. "Please release my arm."

"Once you kiss me." He wagged his brows. "You'd better do it. I'm injured, you know; I could hurt myself pursuing you."

He was so ridiculous that Harriet's smile almost broke loose. "Look, Mr. . . . whatever your name is, I—" She stopped and frowned down at him, a thought suddenly occurring. "For someone who has just realized that he has no memory, you are in a spanking good mood."

His gaze flickered just an instant, but his smile remained in place, as did his hand about her wrist. "That's because I know my memory will return soon."

She eyed him suspiciously. "How?"

He paused, and she could almost hear the wheels turning in his head. Something wasn't right here.

The patient pursed his lips, his thumb rubbing intimately along her wrist. "I know because," he said with great deliberation, as if trying to explain something to a person of lower understanding, "I remember *some* things. Like how to put on my boots. And how to kiss a woman."

"Useful talents."

He ignored her dry comment. "I know I'm going to get my memory back the same way I know that doing this"— he nodded toward where his thumb was rubbing a spate of delectable tingles through her entire body—"can make you do that." His gaze shifted to her arm, where gooseflesh danced across her skin. As warm as the cloth in her hand had been, it was nothing compared to the feel of his fingers clasped about her bared skin.

Heavens, what was wrong with her? She tried to free herself, but his hold tightened, and he looked up at her, his glance issuing a distinct challenge. "Afraid?"

"Of what? A man with no memory? Piffle." She cast about for something witty to say, but all she could find was, "So. You believe for some inexplicable reason that you're going to regain your memory. That's the most asinine thing I've ever heard."

He raised a brow. "Have *you* ever lost *your* memory?"

"No, but—"

"Then how do you know what it's like?"

"I know because—" She clamped her mouth closed, realizing she really had no idea why his reaction struck her as false. The patient's smug air irritated Harriet to death.

She opened her mouth to argue her point, when her patient tightened his grip on her wrist and yanked her to him.

Her legs hit the side of the bed, and she pitched forward, once again in his lap.

"There," he murmured, his arms holding her prisoner. "I'm feeling better already."

Harriet struggled to right herself, tossing the wet cloth onto the floor so that she could use both of her hands. "That is quite enough—"

The door pushed open, and Mother's soft voice said breezily, "Harriet dear! Dr. Blackthorne says— Oh my goodness!"

Harriet sent a glance of triumph at the infuriating man who held her prisoner as she waited for her mother to take him to task for his reprehensible behavior.

"Harriet!" Mother said in a scandalized tone. "What on earth are you doing to our poor patient?"

Chapter 5

Women are really simple creatures. Simply in-
decipherable, that is.

The Duke of Wexford to the
Duchess of Wexford, while driving home
from church on a Sunday afternoon

"**M**other, I—I'm not—he just—I didn't—Oh,
piffle!"

Elviria Ward blinked at her usually staid, calm
daughter—the very same daughter who now lay
red-faced and prone across the lap of their patient.
"Well!"

It wasn't what Elviria meant to say. Or even what
she thought she should say. It was just all she could
get out at the moment.

She was certain that later on, the perfect words
would come to her. Sadly, they always did.

Harriet's face flooded bright red as she struggled
to push herself back into a standing position, but it
was difficult given the softness of the bed and the
fact that the patient, though watching calmly, did
nothing to help. Harriet twisted this way and that, a
huge thunk echoing as she scrambled to her feet, followed by a muffled exclamation.

Elviria wasn't certain, but she thought perhaps that Harriet had uttered a rather *colorful* comment. Goodness, but Harriet was getting more like her father every day.

Finally back on her feet, Harriet glared down at the patient. "Oh! You made that as difficult as you could, didn't you?"

He crossed his arms over his broad chest and grinned. "If you'd wanted help, all you had to do was ask."

Harriet muttered something incomprehensible, then turned to face her mother. Elviria had never seen Harriet's face quite that shade of red.

"Mother, I know how this must look, but we didn't—that is, I was only—"

"Miss Ward fell across the bed, and I caught her," the patient said, a slightly imperious air to him even though he was dressed in one of Stephen's nightshirts, his head wrapped in a bandage. He did not appear the least bit regretful for what Elviria was certain must have been a gross impertinence of some sort.

She glanced at her daughter. Or *had* it been a gross impertinence? Harriet seemed flustered, but not precisely angry. Just irritated and infuriated and outraged.

How . . . unusual.

The patient slanted a lazy smile at Harriet, and Elviria's brows rose. Heavens! Even her heart stuttered a bit at such a smile. Poor Harriet's must be galloping like a hound-chased fox.

"Miss Ward," he said, a devilish glint in his blue eyes, "I hope you're not injured."

"Injured?" Harriet said stiffly. "Of course I'm not injured."

"Didn't you bump your elbow?"

Harriet's red cheeks puffed out a moment in pure indignation. "I didn't bump anything, thank you."

Frost chilled each word, though the air between Elviria's normally staid daughter and the handsome stranger hummed with definite heat. My, but this was interesting! Harriet never let her temper get the better of her. Even when she'd been a wee thing, unable to climb into a chair on her own, she'd never shown anything but calm good sense and reasoned judgment.

Which was why Elviria could only stare at her eldest daughter.

Harriet caught her mother's glance and colored even deeper.

Elviria's gaze drifted back to the patient. "I must apologize for not introducing myself. I am Elviria Ward, and you must be . . ."

No answer was forthcoming. Elviria glanced from the patient, to her daughter, and back. Neither one moved.

Finally, the patient sighed. "I'm afraid I cannot remember."

Elviria blinked. "You can't remember?"

"No."

Oh dear. How dreadful. "Not anything at all?"

"Nothing. It's as if the slate was wiped clean."

"A very small slate," Harriet said under her breath, but loudly enough to be heard.

"Harriet!" Elviria said.

"Sorry," Harriet muttered, though she smirked at the patient in a way that showed anything but remorse.

Elviria was hard-pressed to hide an unexpected grin. The patient, however, did not appear amused.

Instead his handsome face had taken on a distinctly predatory appearance, as if he was marking the comment for further retribution.

Elviria wasn't sure she liked seeing that look directed at her own daughter. Good Lord, the wounded man was turning out to be a problem, indeed. But not for long. Elviria had been on her own since her dear Randall's death seven long years ago. If there was one thing she'd learned in that time, it was to address problems as efficiently as possible. She wasn't always successful, but not for lack of trying.

Fortunately, this seemed to be a fairly easy puzzle to solve. She'd just get the man out of her house. Yes, that is exactly what she'd do. Perhaps the Langleys could be convinced to house him until his memory returned. The Langleys had only one child, a son about Stephen's age. That would be far more appropriate than housing a handsome profligate with three attractive, eligible females.

For some reason, Elviria was certain the stranger was a handsome profligate, whether he remembered his name or not.

As if to prove her point, the man never removed his gaze from Harriet. "Miss Ward, I'm certain your elbow hit the headboard. I heard a decided thump."

Elviria had to admit that Harriet gave the man her best "I'll-show-you-a-thump" look. "Was it a very loud, solid thump?" Harriet asked, blinking innocently. "Like a rock on wood?"

His smile froze, and his gaze became more shaded. "Perhaps. Why?"

"If it was rocklike, then it was your head against the board and not my elbow."

Elviria snatched her kerchief from her pocket and pretended to cough.

The patient's lips twitched, but he managed to say in an even tone, "No. It was more of an elbow sound."

"An elbow sound? What *does* an elbow sound like?"

"If you'll lend me yours for a moment, I'll show you what it sounds like," he retorted easily.

Well, thought Elviria. Now we know that the young man has brothers and sisters. Only a well-teased sibling would have responded so quickly. She wasn't sure why that information pleased her, but it did.

"Only," Harriet said, "if you will grant me use of your head for a like experiment—"

"Harriet," Elviria interjected, tucking her kerchief back into her pocket. "The poor man cannot possibly allow you to thunk his head against the headboard for no other reason than to ascertain what it will sound like. He's *wounded*."

Harriet eyed his bandaged head as if just seeing it. "I suppose you're right. But once he's better—"

"I'm certain he'll heal much quicker without you using his head for a drum." Elviria went to the bed, careful to place herself between the man and her daughter. "Please forgive Harriet. She has been under a strain lately."

"Oh?" The man's dark gaze flickered past Elviria, then back. "We all have. I'm sorry I've forgotten everything—"

"So you say," Harriet said from behind Elviria.

"He says?" She turned to look at her daughter. "You don't believe him? But why—"

"Mother!" Derrick stood in the doorway, his dark brown eyes filled with worry.

Elviria noted how his head barely cleared the doorframe. Though only sixteen, he was hands taller than she was. "Yes, dear?"

"It's Mr. Gower from the bank."

Elviria's good mood left her in a whoosh. Good God, surely it wasn't that time again. Her stomach began to knot. She hated owing money. If she had a pence for every night since Randall's death that she'd lain awake, wondering how she was going to find funds to keep Garrett Park for her children, she'd be a wealthy woman indeed.

Derrick ran a hand through his hair, his shoulder bumping the door. He was at that gangly stage, too large for his own feet. Elviria managed to smile reassuringly at him even though it was the last thing she felt like doing. "Please tell Mr. Gower that I'll be down soon."

Derrick frowned. "Are you certain? If you'd like, I can ask Stephen to speak with him."

Oh dear. That wouldn't do at all. Stephen might be older than Derrick, but he also possessed a much hotter temper and a tendency to think he was in charge of the world. "No, no. I don't wish Stephen to be made uncomfortable."

"Then I'll do it. I'll tell that old bag of wind to go and jump in the lake and drown—"

"No!" Elviria said hastily. "But thank you for offering your assistance. I'll take care of Mr. Gower."

Someone placed a hand on her shoulder. Elviria turned to find Harriet beside her.

Elviria managed a smile. "It seems as if we barely make one payment before another is due."

"It will be all right," Harriet said, giving Elviria's

shoulder a gentle squeeze. "I'll go and talk to him. You stay here with the patient."

"No. No, I'll go and—"

"Piffle! I said I'd go, and I will. Meanwhile, you stay here and tend the patient. Of the two of us, I think you have the more harsh task."

The patient made a dismissive sound, which Harriet promptly ignored. She gave her mother a quick wink and then swept out of the room as regally as any queen.

Elviria knew it was cowardly of her, but she did not wish to see a bank official, especially Mr. Gower. Younger than the other members of the banking board, he also possessed a tendency to be overbearing in the extreme. It was because of him that she'd been forced to make up that ridiculous story about Captain Frakenham.

It was a mess. A huge, tangled mess. Elviria had never meant for the seemingly harmless white lie to get so much attention. Attention that poor Harriet had to pay for.

Of course, it wasn't all Elviria's fault. Some little part of it she could subscribe to the laudanum she'd been taking for her aching tooth. Yes, she decided, a little relieved when she remembered the laudanum. That's why she'd made up that story. Because of the medicine. And *not* because Mr. Gower rather frightened her. She caught Derrick's inquiring gaze from where he stood lounging in the doorway. "I think Harriet can deal with Mr. Gower, don't you?"

Derrick nodded, his brown hair falling over his brow. "If anyone could, it would be Harriet. By the way, Mr. Gower was talking about the captain."

Elviria's heart thumped an extra beat. "What did he say?"

"He asked questions. A lot of them. I answered as best as I could, but I don't think he believes—" Derrick cast a glance at the bed and, finding the patient's gaze fixed upon him, clamped his mouth closed.

"Oh dear," Elviria said. "I don't like that."

"Neither did I," Derrick said. He pushed himself from the doorframe. "I'll be in the library if you need me."

Elviria watched her youngest son lope off. She had no doubt that he'd soon be lost in a book. She wished she could get lost in a book . . . or a deep, dark forest, for that matter.

There were times when life was just difficult. Elviria tried to contain the lump in her throat but couldn't quite do it. The lie that was Captain John Frakenham had served its purpose and kept the bank at bay for months, but it was apparent that the reprieve was almost over. Soon the bank would demand proof of the good captain's existence; and then where would they be?

Every year before this, the Wards had banked their efforts on corn. But with the prices falling so sharply, they'd had no recourse but to find another source of income. Harriet had studied various projects, contemplating everything from wheat to horses. They'd been handicapped by both the need to turn a quick profit and their limited investment capital.

So it was that Harriet, after much consideration, had purchased a large number of sheep. Her instincts had been correct—there was a huge demand for wool this year, and if they could just get the sheep shorn and the wool to Birmingham in time for the annual Wool Market, the payment would be made.

The patient cleared his throat. "I beg your pardon, but could I trouble you for a drink of water?"

Elviria realized guiltily that she'd been ignoring their poor guest. "Of course!" She crossed to the washstand and poured some water into one of the glasses. She took it to their patient and handed it to him. "There!"

He took a sip, his dark gaze on her face. After a moment, he said quietly, "I take it that Mr. Gower is a frequent visitor."

It was obvious he'd read the distress on her face. Elviria colored. "Mr. Gower comes to visit far more than we'd like. He's a banker, and we owe a dreadful amount of money, and—" She caught herself and put a hand to her forehead. "I'm so sorry! You don't want to hear of our problems. It's nothing, really."

He paused, his blue eyes narrowing. "It can't be nothing. You are all too upset."

Elviria took the empty glass and returned it to the washstand. She shouldn't tell him. But somehow it was a relief to utter all the worries that kept her awake nights. "My husband took out a mortgage on Garrett Park, thinking to repay it the very next year. But he grew ill and died. We were left with the payments. Every year Harriet manages to raise the funds, but this year, we haven't had time to shear the sheep. And then poor Stephen's leg—"

"Stephen?"

"My eldest son. He was to help with the shearing but last week, he fell from the loft and broke his leg. We cannot afford another farm hand and so . . ." She trailed off, her mind mulling the thorny problem. After a moment, she shoved it aside. She'd think about it later. Things might be clearer then. "That's neither here nor there. Come, you don't wish to hear our maudlin concerns."

"Perhaps I could help in some way."

"I wish you could, but the only way you could help was if you were—" Elviria looked at the man on the bed. *Really* looked. And what she saw sent her imagination flying.

He had dark hair, the way she'd always envisioned Captain John Frakenham, who was loosely based on a portrait she once saw at a private house in London. The picture had been of a pirate standing on the bow of a ship, the wind blowing his dark hair from his handsome face, his billowing white shirt open to reveal an exciting amount of chest, his hand resting on his sword as if he was ready to take on the world.

Now that she considered it, this man did look somewhat like that pirate. Elviria tilted her head to one side. The man's feet touched the bottom of the bed, so he was tall, with broad shoulders and tapered hips, much as one would expect from a sea captain. Of course, he didn't seem the nautical type, but with a little help—

Elviria caught her thoughts. Did she dare? If she could convince the man in the bed to pretend to be Captain John Frakenham for a short period of time—no more than a week or two at most—it would be enough to quiet the bank and gain the family the time they needed to get the wool to market.

But . . . would he? How could she even ask? She didn't even know the poor man, and he was bound to refuse, just based on the ridiculousness of it all. He didn't owe them a thing.

She sneaked a look at him and frowned. Beneath

his polite exterior, there was something hard about him, something implacable that boded ill for her idea.

Perhaps . . . perhaps she shouldn't ask him. Perhaps she should just *tell* him. Tell him that he was Captain John Frakenham.

The audacity of the idea held her frozen in place, her mind racing. How bold! And how . . . perfect.

The sudden thought of Harriet, who was even now in the sitting room with that horrid Mr. Gower, solidified Elviria's resolve. How difficult could it be to convince this man that he was the captain? He didn't know who he was, so what could he care? Perhaps, in a way, it would be a relief to the poor dear to know that he was *someone*. Someone important.

From the bed, Chase watched as a confusing flicker of emotions traced across Mrs. Ward's expressive countenance. Something was happening. She was astonishingly silent, staring at him as if he was undergoing some sort of transformation before her very eyes. He touched the bandage to see if his wound had reopened, but it was smooth and dry.

She smiled brightly. Too brightly.

An alarm sounded deep in Chase's head. He had a sister. He knew what that smile meant. Mrs. Ward wanted something. And from the degrees of brightness of her smile, it was something very uncomfortable.

She patted his hand in a maternal way. "I suppose you are wondering why my daughter, Harriet, seems so short of temper with you."

"I . . . ah. No. Not really. We didn't have the chance to be properly introduced, and I suppose I might have irritated her into an ill humor."

"Oh, Harriet is *never* in an ill mood." Mrs. Ward paused, then said in a meaningful tone, "But then *you* know that."

How could he know anything about Harriet Ward? He'd only just met her. Truly alarmed, Chase made sure his arms were free from the bed clothing. He might need both hands if he had to break free and make a run for it. "If Miss Ward was short of temper, it was because of me. I wasn't in a very pleasant frame of mind on waking."

"Whatever you said, it wouldn't have mattered. Harriet is upset because—" She swallowed, as if the next words were too hard to form.

Chase wondered if he should prompt her on. Perhaps he should just leave it as it was, tell the woman that he was tired and hope she forgot whatever it was that she wanted.

But somehow he knew that whatever she wanted to say, would be said. Either now or later. So with a sigh, he asked, "Why is Miss Ward upset with me?"

Mrs. Ward looked directly at him, then said in a great rush, "Harriet is upset because you don't remember her."

Chase touched his bandage. "Pardon me. My ears seem to be ringing. Did you say that your daughter believes that I should *remember* her?"

"Yes! That's it exactly! *You* may not remember who you are, but *we*, my dear sir, most certainly do."

The low ringing in his ears turned into a dull roar. "Who am I, then?" he heard himself ask in a dumbfounded voice.

"Captain John Frakenham. You are betrothed to Harriet, and you, my dear, kind sir, have come to save the day!"

Chapter 6

❧❧❧

*Love is best approached from the blind side.
That way, if you chance stumble upon it without meaning to, you might be able to get away
before it catches you in return.*

The Duchess of Wexford to
Viscountess Brandford upon supping on
broiled fish and calf's-foot jelly
at Brandford House

Chase was hallucinating. Yes, that's what had happened. He was dreaming. In truth, he was still lying in his own blood in the forest, the thieves arguing over his possessions. He was not at a mysterious place called Garrett Park, surrounded by raving lunatics who just appeared to be normal. Like the angelic-looking woman in a lace cap who had just announced that he was a man named Captain John Frakenham and was engaged to her daughter.

What was even worse was that Mrs. Ward was so maddened by whatever spell held her brain in thrall, that she didn't even know to look shamefaced at such a lie. Instead, she beamed at him as if she'd just conferred a great gift of some sort.

Chase caught her eager gaze and sighed. He

wasn't hallucinating. This was really happening. *Bloody hell, what am I to do now?*

Surely she didn't expect him to believe such a faradiddle. And even if he really had lost his memory and had fallen for her lame story, what did she think would happen when his memory returned?

When Chase had been ten, his younger brother, Devon, had fallen off his horse while taking a particularly brutal fence during a mad hunt. When Devon had awakened, he hadn't known who he was for almost a day.

For Chase and his older brothers, once they saw that Devon was fine, only confused, the incident had been cause for great merriment. Undetected by their parents, they had sneaked into the sickroom and attempted to convince Devon that he was, in fact, the illegitimate son of the head groomsman, a huge burly fellow with an askance eye and a horrible scar down his face.

There had been hell to pay when they'd been caught, and they'd all been sentenced to muck out the stables under the stern presence of that very head groomsman, but it had been worth it.

Mrs. Ward went to the window, where a low chair stood in the swath of slowly growing sunshine. She pulled the chair to the side of the bed, angled it toward Chase, then sat down, her skirts billowing about her, her gaze fixed on his face.

Chase wished she hadn't done that. The bed was rather high, and she was not the tallest of women. With the help of the chair, she was now staring him right in the eyes, her gaze wide and unblinking, as if she'd determined never to look away again.

He cleared his throat, wondering how to begin.

"Madam, I believe there has been some sort of mistake—"

"Oh, no! *You* are Captain Frakenham, though you don't remember it."

"Am I indeed?"

"Oh yes!" She nodded so hard her lace cap seemed in imminent danger of taking flight. "I've known you a long time myself."

Chase lifted his brows. "How long?"

"*Very* long! In fact, you might say that I've known you longer than anyone."

She seemed so secure in her belief that she could convince him that he was the admirable captain that Chase almost felt guilty for knowing who he really was. It was odd, but despite the fact that this woman was attempting to bamboozle him, Chase couldn't help but feel that she wasn't a truly untrustworthy individual—at least, not usually. She possessed far too serene a spirit to be anything other than guileless. And in all honesty, she wasn't a very good liar, either.

But what in the world did she hope to gain by this deception? "Madam, perhaps we had best speak plainly."

Mrs. Ward blinked once. Twice. Then she cleared her throat. "Plainly?"

"You say I am this . . . Captain Frakenham?"

"Yes."

"Who is engaged to your daughter?"

"Yes."

"Then why does your daughter act as if she's never met me before?"

"Oh, you know Harriet!" Mrs. Ward said airily. "She can be a bit stubborn at times."

Chase thought of the firm set to Harriet's mouth,

and he rather thought perhaps Mrs. Ward was understating the case.

Mrs. Ward placed her hand on his sleeve. "Captain Frakenham, I dislike placing this on your shoulders after your grievous injuries. But Garrett Park is in dire straits."

Chase leaned his head back against the pillows. Here it was—the reason she wanted him to be someone he was not. "How dire are things?"

She gave him an embarrassed smile. "Very. But we were doing well until Mr. Gower joined the board of directors at the bank. Even though I've told him of your existence and the funds you will shortly provide—"

"Funds?"

"Profits from your sailing. You're a very good captain, you know."

"That is reassuring to hear."

"I thought so," she said, unaware of his sarcasm. "Despite your existence, Mr. Gower continues to be an annoyance."

Chase's lips twitched. A rising wave of curiosity was beginning to tickle his sense of the ridiculous. "I take it that there is some question to the existence of the good captain's fortune?"

"Well . . . not a question exactly. More of an inquiry. And not just about the fortune." Mrs. Ward bit her lip. "You see, we mentioned . . . that is, *I* mentioned your existence to the bank officers—Mr. Gower in particular—thinking they might give us an extension on the mortgage."

"I hope they were duly impressed."

"Oh, very! You, my dearest sir, are in charge of a large ship! A very large ship. A very, *successful* large ship."

"That's also good to hear. By the way, what's the name of the ship?"

She blinked. "I—I don't—"

"Where was I sailing from?"

"I—we never—"

"And my crew? Will they be joining me here? Or am I to meet them somewhere else?"

"Oh dear!" Mrs. Ward pressed a hand to her cheek. "I—I'm sure I know the answers but not at this moment. I'm a bit distraught, you see. Mr. Gower is here, and that always muddles my thinking."

Chase regarded her steadily. Something strange was going on. Something stranger than he'd first realized. Not only was this woman telling him that he was someone he wasn't, but she didn't seem to have a firm grasp on who, exactly, he was supposed to be. It was almost as if this Captain Frakenham was a complete figment of someone's imag—

Chase's brows rose. Was that it? Had the Wards *concocted* the captain in an effort to stave off the bank?

He silently considered that, a glimmer of realization beginning to glow. "Let me see if I understand this; the bank was demanding their money, so you waved Captain Frakenham—"

"Which is you," Mrs. Ward interjected with a hopeful look.

"—which you *say* is me," Chase said implacably, "in front of the officers in an effort to gain some time?"

"Yes. And except for Mr. Gower, everyone has been quite satisfied. But now that you're here, we can set his pesky reservations to rest. All we need to do is let Mr. Gower see you—not for long because you are, after all, an invalid—but long enough that he stops asking so many questions."

"I take it you don't wish me to reveal that I don't remember who I am?"

"If you don't mind, it would be best if you'd just pretend to remember that you are indeed the captain." She clasped her hands together. "Oh, this will solve everything! Now we'll have time to get the wool to market and—"

"Wool?"

"Oh yes. Harriet bought hundreds of sheep. We're going to shear them and make the last payment; then Garrett Park will be ours."

Bloody hell, they're sheep farmers, the lot of them. That explained why Miss Harriet Ward had such a lovely, aristocratic accent, yet was as tanned as a laundress.

In fact, that explained quite a lot of things. For the first time since he'd awakened, Chase took stock of his surroundings. The chamber was large and square, with two huge windows that allowed sun to stream warmly into the room.

Perhaps it was the largeness of the windows or the warm red colors that decorated the room, but until that moment, he'd thought himself rather sumptuously housed. Now, however, he could see the threadbare spots on the rugs, the lack of decoration on the walls—as if all the pictures had been removed—and the overly soft, worn appearance of the counterpane.

The Wards might be from genteel stock, but it was rather obvious they were not well-off. And now, forced by penury to earn their way, they'd concocted a fictitious fiancé for Miss Harriet to keep the bank at bay.

It was a bold move. Chase eyed his hostess with a new respect. "You had some ill fortune."

"Oh, my, yes! My husband passed away several

years ago. It's just me, my three daughters and two sons. So far, we've managed on our own. But now—" She placed her hand on his arm, a genuine plea in her eyes. "Captain Frakenham, we need your help."

Chase looked at Mrs. Ward's hand, resting so innocuously on his sleeve. Good God, it was almost as if she thought him a knight on a white horse.

Unfortunately, Chase knew who and what he was. He was not a knight, and he felt anything but noble. "Mrs. Ward, I am not Captain Frakenham."

"No? Then who are you?"

Chase opened his mouth to answer. But a split second's thought made him close it. He was supposed to have no memory of who he was. If he wanted the Wards to believe that and not ask incessant questions, then he couldn't really argue about who he was *not*, could he?

Damn it all, perhaps he should just pretend to suddenly recall his name . . . but no. Word would reach his brothers within the day, if not the hour. Devon's house was only a short distance from where Chase had been attacked. His brothers would immediately ride out and attempt to talk him out of his decision to leave England.

Still, it was a shame to leave the Wards in such a predicament. Perhaps . . . he frowned. What if . . . Good Lord, he couldn't believe he was even considering this, but . . . what if he *did* agree to become Captain Frakenham? For a few days, at least. He could be a great help to the Wards, and he'd have a safe place to convalesce without his brothers being the wiser to his proximity to London.

The idea had some merit. The thought of traveling with an aching head held no appeal. Besides, as much as he didn't want to admit it, he disliked the thought of Miss Harriet Ward brangling with the bank official. He had no doubt she would hold her own, but at what cost? *Any* cost was too high. She was far too young to pay the price of her own father's shortsightedness. Chase had a sister who was almost the same age he judged Harriet to be, and the entire situation was untenable.

Chase eyed Mrs. Ward. "Tell me more about Captain Frakenham."

Mrs. Ward straightened her lace cap. "More? Of course! Let's see, your name is Captain John Frakenham and you have a large ship."

"That much, I know. Do I have any brothers or sisters?"

She bit her lip. "I'm not sure."

"Where was I born?"

"Devonshire, perhaps. Or maybe Yorkshire. No, wait!" She beamed. "The Lake District! It's lovely up there; I traveled through it with my uncle when I was ten, and it was just breathtaking."

"You don't know where I'm from."

Her smile faded. "Well . . . not really. No one ever asked." She caught his gaze and added quickly, "And you never told us. The topic simply never came up."

"Hm. How long have I been sailing."

"I—I—"

"And what items do I deal in? Tea? Silks? What?"

"I don't—"

"How old am I?"

"Old?" Her gaze grew somewhat glazed. "I'm sure I don't know. But it's not important. All you need to remember for your interview with Mr. Gower is that you're engaged to Harriet and stand to receive a large amount of money very soon."

Chase wondered if he should press the issue and force Mrs. Ward to confess her deception, but then he thought he caught the glint of tears in her soft brown eyes.

His humor fled. Not tears. He could never hold his own against a crying female; it was his one weakness. When he'd been growing up and his little sister Sara had cried, he'd always given in. Always.

Sara was married now, a countess in her own right and the mother of two children. But even today, if she were to come to Chase, a tear on her cheek, he would do anything she asked. It was one of the things that drove him mad thinking about the woman he'd run down with his carriage. Had she cried? Had anyone heard her? Helped her?

Or had she been left to die alone in the middle of a cold, rain-washed street?

His throat tightened, his head aching anew. How could he live with this? How could he expect his brothers to live with it? He touched his forehead where it ached. He'd figure out what to do. As soon as he felt better. "Bloody hell," he muttered, a surge of irritation washing through him.

"I beg your pardon?"

"I am sorry," he said quickly. "I didn't mean to let that slip."

A faint smile touched her lips. "That's quite all right. Mr. Ward was renowned for just such slippage."

Chase found himself regarding his hostess with a faint smile. It was hard to do else—the sun had shimmered her white hair into a lace-topped halo, and her eyes were amazingly like her daughter's.

"Captain John Frakenham," he heard himself say, as if he was trying the name on for size.

Mrs. Ward beamed and, once again, Chase was reminded of Harriet. Harriet who was even now downstairs being importuned by Gower. Though Chase had never met him, he had no doubts about the quality of man Gower must be. "I suppose I'll do it."

"Thank you! You will make an excellent Captain Frakenham!"

Chase looked at her.

"Oh—I—that is to say, you *are* Captain Frakenham so *of course* you'll do just fine."

"Hm. Well, if I'm to meet Gower, you'd best tell me everything you know about the good captain. Or rather, what everyone here knows of him."

Her brow lowered in thought. "Well, Captain Frakenham is very handsome."

He waited, but no more was forthcoming. After a moment, he said, "And?"

She pursed her lips. "You are also very wealthy, but I believe I told you that."

"Numerous times."

"Only because it is very important."

"Indeed. What else?"

Mrs. Ward tapped her chin thoughtfully. "Oh! I know! Lucinda Carleton has said that the captain earned his money from sailing the Indian Seas, which I thought was very interesting because—"

"Lucinda Carleton?" He frowned. "Who is that?"

"A friend."

"Of the captain's?"

"No, she's never met the captain. No one has. Except," she added in a rush after sending him a guilty glance, "Harriet, of course, has met him—I mean, you, quite frequently. And all of us here at Garrett Park know him—I mean, you—very well."

"How is it that this Lucinda Carleton heard that the captain—pardon me, I mean *I*—gained my fortune in such a way if she's never met me?"

Mrs. Ward paused. "I'm not certain. She just seemed to know."

"I see," Chase said, though he most definitely did not. "Is there anything else?"

"Well . . . I heard from Lady Chudrowe that you've a bit of a limp caused by an injury sustained during a pirate fight." Mrs. Ward's smile lit the room. "Apparently, you are very brave."

Chase regarded her flatly. "Tell me, Mrs. Ward, how many people know about the captain's existence?"

"Why, the whole town, to be sure! Everyone has been talking about you for weeks."

Bloody hell. It would not do to assume the identity of a well-known personae, even a fake one. That could cause undue attention. "I don't know if this will work. Too many people seem to—"

She stood in a rush, the chair scraping the wood floor. "Everything will work just fine, Captain. Trust me. Now we really must get downstairs. I hate leaving Harriet a second longer than necessary."

Harriet. Alone. Chase could see the very real distress in Mrs. Ward's eyes. He supposed that he could just stay near Garrett Park while he was here. So long as he avoided town, he should be well hidden.

With a sigh, he straightened and, holding the blanket over him to keep from embarrassing Mrs. Ward with a glimpse of her guest attired in her son's nightshirt, he swung his feet over the side of the bed. "We don't want your daughter to suffer from the importunities of—"

"Oh no! It's more the other way around." Mrs.

Ward bustled to the wardrobe. "Harriet has a bit of a temper. Mr. Gower will be burned to a crisp if we do not rescue him soon."

Chase almost smiled at that. Yes, the little brown wren had a flash of fire in her. He'd seen it several times already. He pictured her lying across his lap and he was surprised to find that the image stirred him.

Mrs. Ward's voice emerged from the wardrobe, where she was busy stirring through the neatly hung clothes. "Derrick collected what he could find of your clothing from the forest. The thieves apparently tore through your cases, looking for valuables. Two of your shirts were beyond repair, but everything else seems fine."

"I'll trust that you'll choose something appropriate."

She looked over her shoulder. "Appropriate?"

"For a limping, wealthy sea captain from the Indian Seas." Chase flashed her a grin. "I've got an interview with a banker."

Chapter 7

Pride is the most persistent, most stalwart, most infuriatingly stubborn passion of all. But then you St. Johns already know that.

Viscountess Brandford to her friend,
Mr. Devon St. John
while playing a game of billiards
(which her ladyship promptly won)

Harriet rushed downstairs, her heels slapping the worn wooden steps. She was glad to get out of the sickroom. The handsome stranger was certainly sure of himself, the braggart. Harriet hopped off the bottom step and glanced at herself in the mirror.

Good heavens! How had her hair gotten into such a tangle? An instant image of herself sprawled over the lap of their guest flashed into her mind, heating her cheeks. Harriet met her own gaze in the mirror as she tugged out a pin and tried to fix her curls where they stuck out at odd angles.

"Blasted man," she muttered aloud. It was all his fault. Had he been a gentleman and not treated her as if she was a flirtatious upstairs maid or a loose woman intent on seducing him, then Mother never would have found them in such a compromising position.

Not that he'd cared. He'd seemed rather amused by it all, the wretch. What was worse was that Harriet had almost been swayed by his wide smile and mischievous blue eyes.

But as much as Harriet resented the stranger, she preferred his company to Mr. Gower's. Harriet didn't like the man one bit. Only slightly more advanced in years than Harriet herself, Mr. Gower acted much, much older. He'd first come to Garrett Park three years ago, when the bank had employed him. He'd been rude, demanding, and thoroughly annoying.

Mrs. Maple, the housekeeper, came out of the sitting room, an empty plate in one hand. "Ye'd best get in there afore he asks fer another scone. I've none left, and there'll be naught fer it but to give him the Sunday loaf if he requests more. He's already eaten all of our apple tarts, too!"

Wonderful. Not only had the unpleasant banker come to disrupt the entire family, but he was nibbling his way through their pantry like some huge, overstuffed mouse. Harriet wondered if perhaps that was why she always felt so uneasy around Mr. Gower—he seemed inordinately greedy. The man was a swine; there were times when he looked at Harriet in such a way that it made her feel as if she was a particularly fat acorn and he a huge pig.

"I'll make certain he leaves soon," Harriet said firmly, hoping it would be that easy. She smoothed her skirts and patted her collar back into place.

Mrs. Maple's face softened, and she reached out to smooth a bit of Harriet's hair from her forehead. "Ye look fine, Miss Harriet. Shall I announce ye?"

"No. I will announce myself." She flashed a grin

at the housekeeper. "It will save us at least half a minute of his time."

The front door opened and a loud clomping sounded. Harriet turned to find her brother Stephen making his way through the front door. His left leg was heavily wrapped, his crutches barely long enough to allow his feet to clear. He came to a halt when he saw Harriet. A distinctly guilty look flashed across his face before he managed to clear it away. "Oh! There you are! How's the patient?"

"He's fine except that he says he doesn't remember who he is."

"Says?" Stephen's brows shot up. "What do you mean 'says'?"

"Just that I wonder about him. He seems far too at ease to have forgotten his identity."

"You always did have a suspicious nature, Harri. The man's head wound seemed rather grievous to me, so 'tis entirely possible he is telling the truth. Besides, what reason could he possibly have for telling such a whopper?"

Mrs. Maple sniffed. "Mayhap the man plans on dallyin' about and eatin' all our food, like Mr. Gower."

Harriet shook her head. "His clothes are very well made and his horse alone is worth a fortune. He could afford more mutton than our entire flock could provide."

Stephen brightened. "I just saw the horse. What a prime piece of blood and bones!"

Harriet had to smile at his excitement. Like Sophia, he had father's more golden coloring, and his hair curled over his ears just the slightest bit. He was dressed in rough clothing, and Harriet suspected that he'd been working in the barn.

She glanced at his injured leg. "You aren't sup-posed to be up on that leg more than a few moments at a time."

Stephen gave an impatient shrug. "I'm fine. I just fixed the broken door on the grain bin."

"If something needs done, have Jem do it."

"He's out with the cows. Sophia and Ophelia rode out in the cart with him."

Mrs. Maple snorted. "If I know Jem, he's fast asleep under a tree and the girls are doin' all the work. If ye needed help, ye should have asked Mas-ter Derrick."

An impish sparkle entered Stephen's eyes. "Der-rick did give me a hand. A very well served one, in fact."

"Did he? I just saw Derrick but he didn't mention helping you, he just said that Mr. Gower had ar-rived."

Stephen's sudden grin had a wolfish tone to it. "It's a pity Mr. Gower couldn't stay, but something of great urgency called him away."

Harriet frowned. "Stephen, Mr. Gower is in the sitting room."

Stephen's smile disappeared. "*Our* sitting room?"

"Of course," Harriet said. "Why would you think he'd left?"

"I wish he *had* left," Mrs. Maple huffed. "Instead o' eatin' all our scones. Cook made them special fer Mrs. Ward, she did."

"Stephen?" Harriet asked again. "You and Der-rick did something to put Mr. Gower into a rage, didn't you?"

"Us?"

She narrowed her gaze. "What did you do?"

"Nothing."

"Nothing at all? Or nothing you want to tell me about?"

Stephen shrugged. "You'll have to ask Mr. Gower that question. Only be forewarned, his temper might be a little ragged."

Harriet didn't wonder at that; from what she'd seen of Mr. Gower, his temper was never good. "I asked you two not to play your tricks on him. It was all I could do to soothe his spirits when you poured glue in his hat. He had to have his hair cut just to get it off."

Stephen grinned. "That was Derrick's idea. Rather clever, wasn't it? But never fear, what happened this time was purely an accident." His lips twitched. "A humorous accident, but an accident nonetheless."

Wonderful. Yet more joy to brighten an otherwise frustrating day. "I'll go and see what Mr. Gower wants," Harriet said with a heavy sigh. "If he's already in an ill mood, he will take exception to being left to cool his heels in the sitting room."

"You do that," Stephen said pleasantly. "Meanwhile, I'll go upstairs and see if Mother needs any help with our visitor. Oh, and Harriet?"

"Yes?"

"Enjoy your visit with Mr. Gower."

There was a definite tremor of humor in Stephen's voice. The wretch.

"That boy," Mrs. Maple said with a disapproving shake of his head as he made his way upstairs, the crutches scraping the wood steps.

"That boy is exactly like Father." Harriet managed a reluctant smile. "Father couldn't resist a good joke either."

"No, he couldn't. He was a good man, was your father."

"I know. I miss him every day." Harriet sighed. "I had best see to Mr. Gower before he starts gnawing on the furniture."

"Very well, miss. And if he dangles fer a dinner invitation, tell him he's already eaten it all and there's none left."

"I shall." Harriet flashed a bright smile at the housekeeper and then made her way down the hall and let herself into the sitting room.

As soon as she shut the door, a large man turned from the window to face her. Dressed in a plain coat of brown worsted with a sober waistcoat of yellow kersey, Mr. Gower was a handsome man, if somewhat florid. Or he would have been handsome if his hair hadn't been cut in quite such an extreme fashion.

Harriet had to bite her lip to keep from grinning at the sight as she dipped a curtsy. "Mr. Gower."

He made a ponderous bow. "Miss Ward."

Despite Mrs. Maple's charge, Mr. Gower was not as fat as the Christmas pig. He was, however, of a rather beefy appearance.

"Miss Ward, might I say this is a pleasant surprise. I had thought Mrs. Ward—"

"Mother is rather busy today. I told her I'd come and visit." Harriet pasted what she hoped was a pleasant smile on her face and held out her hand.

Mr. Gower hurried forward to press a rather damp kiss on the back of her fingers. As he did so, a wave of odor rose about him, so thick Harriet would have sworn she could see it had the light been stronger.

She blinked, forcing herself not to react to the rancid smell. What *was* that? Normally Mr. Gower smelled of tonic and hair treatment. But this odor was more . . . sheeplike. As if he'd rolled in the barn.

Harriet retrieved her hand and stilled the impulse to wipe it on her skirt. "Mr. Gower, how pleasant to see you. Please take a seat." She sank into a chair closest to the door, cautiously edging it away from the one nearest to it.

He smiled at her as he took the seat opposite, the odor wafting with him. "I must say that this is an unexpected pleasure, Miss Ward. Usually, you aren't present when I come to call."

"I've been very busy lately." She pressed her hand over her nose a moment, her gaze falling on the desolated tea tray and empty scone plate. "I see you've already had tea."

"Indeed I have. Your cook is exceptional."

"I will tell her you said so. Mr. Gower, to what do we owe the pleasure of this call?"

"I just came from a meeting." He looked at her in a meaningful way. "At the bank."

Where else would he have been at a meeting, she wondered with some irritation. "Indeed. How nice for you."

He waited, apparently expecting her to ask for more information.

Harriet easily withheld the impulse. "Perhaps you came today to see about Stephen's injured leg. That is quite nice of you, and I—"

Mr. Gower's smile disappeared. "Your brothers are—" He caught himself, coloring heavily. "I don't mean to say anything untoward, but I must tell you that your brothers would be the better for Mr. Ward's presence."

"We would all be the better for Mr. Ward's presence. Unfortunately, his death makes that an impossibility," Harriet said dryly.

"I beg your pardon. I didn't mean to offend you. But your brothers need the steady influence of a man, someone who could deflect their high spirits. But you are right in saying that you could benefit from having a man about as well." He glanced around the room as if assessing each piece of faded furniture. "It's such a pity how everything has gone to ruin."

Harriet bit the inside of her cheek to keep from saying something very unworthy. The man oozed certainty, and it annoyed her no end. "We all miss my father. He was a wonderful man."

"So I've heard. I was most impressed to find that he was listed in Debrett's. That is quite an honor."

Debrett's was a book that listed England's peerage. There was a very dusty copy of it somewhere in the library, though Harriet hadn't seen it in years. "His brother inherited the title, of course, but Father was always pleased to be mentioned."

"You are mentioned as well, Miss Harriet." Mr. Gower beamed, as if she'd accomplished something of great merit.

"Yes, though they spelled Harriet with only one 'r.'"

"That must have stung," he said earnestly. "To make the pages of that hallowed book, then be robbed of its true glory by an error."

Harriet could find nothing to say to this, so she settled for nodding in as cool and impersonal a way as her uncertain temper would allow.

Mr. Gower slid closer to the edge of his seat. The horrid odor that clung to him seeped closer to Harriet.

She pulled her skirts closer and scooted away. What *was* that smell?

Mr. Gower smoothed his uneven hair in a nervous gesture. "I can't tell you how delighted I am to have this unexpected pleasure of speaking with you."

"You've already said that." Harriet wondered how she could draw their meeting to an end. She supposed she could say she was overcome by fumes.

"Yes, well, there is a reason I'm glad you're here. Especially alone. Miss Ward—Harriet, I was going to speak to your mother today, but perhaps—"

"I don't believe I've given you permission to use my Christian name," she said quickly, an uneasy feeling arising. Goodness, surely this pompous oaf wasn't on the verge of making an overture? Surely he wasn't—he couldn't possibly think—she met his gaze, and her heart sank in her chest like a ship smashed on a jagged reef.

Good God, she should have been protected from this sort of thing—the entire world thought her engaged to the dashing, though absent Captain Frakenham. Her gaze narrowed on Mr. Gower. But perhaps Mr. Gower hadn't been as gullible as they'd thought?

"Harriet . . . my dear Harriet," he said with that odiously superior smile, "I have known your family for far too long to stand upon feeble conventionality."

Harriet had to breathe through her nose since her teeth had clenched so tightly together that air could no longer pass between them. And breathing through her nose made the odor only worse. Her eyes began to water, and she coughed a little. "I'm sorry. There's a smell—"

Mr. Gower's superior smile disappeared, his face reddening in an instant. "Can you smell—Damn it!

Of course you can. I thought I'd cleaned my shoes, but—" He grimaced. "Yes, well, that is because of your brother."

"Stephen?"

"The other one. He picked up a bucket of ... something just as I dismounted. I'm afraid I didn't recognize him, and I asked him to see to it that my horse was taken care of. And he, apparently offended by my request, poured the contents of the bucket on my shoes."

Harriet looked down at Mr. Gower's leather shoes. They were dark and stained. Her nose wrinkled. "I'm certain Derrick didn't mean to do such a thing."

"I'm sure he did, though he claimed it was an accident and the handle slipped."

"If he said it was an accident, then it was," Harriet said, though she had an instant image of Stephen's mischievous grin.

"He meant to do it, the little—" Gower clamped his mouth closed.

"Perhaps he did," Harriet said, lifting her chin. "He is not a servant to take your horse at your demand."

"He was dressed like a servant and so I thought he was one. Besides, my error does not excuse his behavior."

"No, it doesn't. *If* he did indeed sully your shoes on purpose, he is in the wrong. But so are you, for being so remiss in the attention that is due him."

Mr. Gower's mouth thinned. "I gave him a shilling for his trouble. Considering the sad case of your family affairs, one would think he'd be glad for the—"

Harriet stood. "Mr. Gower, thank you so much for coming to visit."

He reluctantly climbed to his feet, his brows knit. "Miss Ward—Harriet, I only meant that your family is in a very poor situation—"

"I don't care how poor my family's situation is. It was an insult to Derrick and to everyone under this roof that you tossed a coin to him as if he was a common linkboy. You are just fortunate I wasn't in the barnyard, for I would have poured the bucket over more than your shoes."

"You—how can you say that? Look at these!" He held out one foot.

Harriet pressed a hand over her nose. "Indeed. I'm very sorry you wore them into the house because now I'll have to have the rugs cleaned."

He lowered his foot, a mottled red traveling up his neck. "After all I've done for your family—"

"Done for my family? Endlessly tormenting us about the payments?"

"It's my job to—"

"Exactly. It's your job. So don't come here, mewing about how you've had our best interests at heart. All you've had at heart is money. Our money. And nothing else."

He straightened his shoulders. "At one time, that may have been true. But now—Harriet, I do not pretend that I find your family's sad financial plight to my liking. I do not. Though I've admired you and your determination for many months now, your situation has caused me some hesitation in speaking my mind."

"How unfortunate for my family," Harriet said with a burning look.

"So it is," he responded, missing her sarcasm altogether. "Most men would never willingly overlook such things. But however much I deplore the state of your finances, I have to admit it is gratifying to see that you've only one payment left before Garrett Park is your own. Of course, I realize that there is nothing else to be had. Neither you, nor any of your sisters, will have a dowry, will you?"

How dare the man even ask such a question! Harriet was so angry that she wasn't sure whether she could make it out of the room without saying something she was sure she would regret. "That is none of your concern."

"Oh, but it is," he said gravely. "For all my hesitations about your lack of a dowry, there is no denying your good breeding. Your father is in Debrett's, your mother was a Standish. I daresay no other family in this area is as well connected as the Wards."

"Mr. Gower, where are you going with all of this?"

The pompous ass smiled down at her, completely unaffected that she was glaring back at him. "Simple, my dear. After much thought, I've decided to make you my wife."

Chapter 8

The first time I fell in love, I was sixteen years of age. The second time I fell in love, I was also sixteen years of age. But then I grew older and wiser and I did not fall in love for a very, very long time. In fact, I almost made it to my seventeenth birthday before I experienced that wretched state again.

Mr. Devon St. John to Lord Kilturn,
an antiquarian with an unfortunate penchant
for dressing the dandy
and dangling after much younger women

Devon St. John tossed his cards on the green baize table that stretched before him. "I lose," he said in an affable voice.

Through the swirl of smoke that permeated the card room at White's, his opponent, Mr. Lawrence Pound, sighed languidly. Renowned in polite circles not only for his close connection with the Bessingtons, but also for his polite manner and impeccable dress, Pound tossed his own cards onto the table and said in a rather plaintive voice, "It is insulting how well you take defeat."

Devon quirked a brow. "What do you wish? Sighs and laments? Wild cries of unjust hands and a threat to put a period to my existence?"

Though the two men were both lean and well built, Devon St. John had the broad shoulders and well defined hands of his family. That along with the unmistakable combination of black hair and blue eyes, proclaimed his breeding as clearly as if the St. John coat of arms were embroidered on his pocket.

Pound took a thoughtful sip of port. "I rather like the last scenario, but then I've always been rather fond of gun play. Perhaps next time."

"Perhaps. If I lose again, which I doubt."

Pound sighed wearily. "I should have known better than to toss the cards with a St. John. Winning is devoid of pleasure when one knows it is but a temporary lapse in the alignment of the stars."

Devon leaned back in his chair and grinned. "You were the one who insisted on playing. I merely wished to talk."

"Yes," Pound said in a meditative tone, "it is a common fault with my family, to rush toward their own demise in a most hodgepodge manner. Quite ill-bred of the lot of us."

"Nonsense. You didn't rush at all. At times, it took you so long to play your card that I worried you had expired but were too polite to fall over."

Pound's thin lips twitched. "I was struggling to maintain the lead. You play a difficult game."

"You are too severe on yourself. There were several seconds I was unsure of the outcome."

"Seconds? Considering we played for over four hours, I find that statement positively vile."

Devon chuckled. "You find everything vile. Everything but port. Come, let me procure a new bottle for the winner—"

"Devon St. John!" came an urbane voice to their right. "Just the man I was looking for."

Devon lifted his glass from the table, his gaze still on his companion. "Shall we play one more round?"

Pound opened his mouth to reply, but the insistent voice intruded again. "Mr. St. John, you don't know me, but I'm—"

"How rude," murmured Pound. He lifted the quizzing glass that hung from his waistcoat by a ribbon and regarded the man who now stood beside their table.

Devon finished his drink. "Well?"

Pound's eye was hideously magnified by the quizzing glass. "No. I do not recognize him." He dropped the glass and picked up his port once again. "They are not nearly particular enough at this club. Perhaps I shall join Watiers."

"Mr. St. John—" This time the evidently annoyed individual moved to stand in Devon's line of vision. "I need but a moment of your time."

Dressed in the height of fashion, Harry Annesley appeared like any other pompous young ass of fashion. His shirt collar was starched to points so high he could not bend his chin a normal height. His cravat was a complex mess of knots and twists, fastened with a huge, gaudy ruby of questionable authenticity.

Devon decided after a moment's inspection that there was something . . . unsavory about the man. Something unrefined, as if despite the polish of his boots, a whiff of common breeding seeped through. "Well? What do you want?"

Annesley flushed at the curt tone.

Devon was well aware of Annesley's acquaintance with his brother Chase. He wondered that Chase would countenance such a man. His brother was usually far more fastidious in his choice of friends, but that had been before Chase's descent. Before Chase had cut his family from his life as thoroughly and ruthlessly as a surgeon.

The thought caused Devon's chest to tighten.

Harry smiled, a seemingly casual, self-deprecating smile, though Devon could sense a hint of superiority behind it. "Mr. St. John, I am indeed sorry to bother you and your acquaintance, Mr. Pound, but—"

"It knows my name," Pound murmured. He arched his brows. "Should I be honored?"

In Devon's opinion, Chase's downfall was somehow tied up with this man. "No," he said to Pound, setting his glass on the table with a snap. "You should not be honored at all."

Harry's face turned bright red, his mouth thinning for an instant. But he quickly regained control and plastered his usual false smile on his face.

Devon rather thought he preferred naked anger to the tight smile. He flicked a glance at the man. "Well?" he prompted shortly. "What do you want?"

The smile grew tighter, but remained firmly in place. "I wonder if you could assist me. I have been looking for your brother, Chase. Have you heard from him lately?"

Devon managed to keep his face expressionless, though it was difficult. The louse wanted something; his kind always did. What was truly unusual was that Chase was normally in the pocket of this man. If Harry Annesley didn't know where Chase was, who would? A knot of disquiet began to form in Devon's stomach. "I haven't seen my brother in almost two weeks. Not since our brother Brandon's wedding."

"No?" Harry's practiced smile faded and was replaced with an equally fake expression of concern. "I wonder where he could have gotten to?"

Devon shrugged. "I daresay he has found yet another amorata. He flits from woman to woman like a bee."

"With a stinger, no doubt." Pound shook his head sadly. "That was poorly done, St. John."

Devon managed a genuine smile. Pound's dry wit perfectly suited his own. "I shall try to be more subtle."

Harry placed his hands on the table and leaned closer, his cologne drifting over Devon like a fine cloying mist. "I hesitate to say anything because . . ." He broke off as if too embarrassed to continue.

Devon's gaze narrowed. *What the hell did the shyster want? More to the point, where the hell was Chase.* Devon continued to shuffle the cards, then dealt them into two neat stacks. "Out with it, Annesley."

"I didn't wish to say anything, but your brother . . ." He paused, sending a side glance at Pound. "Mr. St. John, perhaps we should discuss this in private."

Pound's gaze lifted from his hand of cards. "Ah! A secret, is it? Pray do not attempt to dismiss me then. There is little I like more than a secret."

Devon hesitated. Pound, for all his dissembling humor, was something of a gossip. But there was nothing for it now. Annesley had said too much already, and any attempt to keep Pound out of it was long gone. "Speak, Annesley."

"Very well. Mr. St. John, I'm sorry to bring this matter to your notice, but it is unlike your brother to miss a meeting." Annesley paused, casting a quick look toward Pound. "*Especially* when that meeting was a matter of honor."

Devon cursed to himself when he caught the interested gleam behind Pound's bland gaze. Whatever Annesley had to say, it would be all over town before dawn. Devon forced his attention to his cards. He carefully selected his discard before answering. "I'm sure there must have been some sort of misunderstanding. Perhaps he had the wrong location or time."

"I hardly think it could be that." Annesley pursed his lips. "To be blunt, your brother owes me a considerable amount of money." Harry reached into his pocket and withdrew a note. He placed it on the table. Devon glanced at it, then frowned. The note promised twenty thousand pounds to Harry Annesley and was signed with a sloping flourish that Devon immediately recognized as Chase's.

A stirring of unease filtered through Devon. Something wasn't right. Still, he forced himself to leave the paper on the table though he longed to snatch it up and rip it in half. "If it's a matter of honor, I'm certain my brother will answer it to your satisfaction. And he will no doubt be chagrined he missed your meeting."

"I hope so," Annesley said ruefully. He tucked the paper away. "Chase was a little upset when last I saw him."

"I daresay he'd been drinking. Heavily. It seemed to become a habit with him once he began to converse with you."

"Touché," murmured Pound.

With a noticeable thinning of his mouth, Annesley patted the pocket where the note lay. "I only hope your brother isn't gone too long, or I shall begin to wonder—"

"Annesley," Devon said with deadly calm, "what will you wonder? Surely you are not maligning the St. John name."

Silence filled the small area. Pound watched, an amused expression in his sharp gaze. Annesley seemed to be searching for words—though it was difficult to tell whether he wished to retract his statement or reassure Devon.

Devon turned away. "That will be all, Annesley. I'm certain that whenever my brother returns to town, you'll get your funds."

Annesley's expression was a frozen grimace compared to the wide smile he'd once had. There was nothing left for it but to bow and make his way to the door.

Devon and Pound played in silence for several minutes. Though Devon's mind was elsewhere, luck favored him and he won.

"Ah, the St. John luck returns." Pound picked up his port. "What do you think of Annesley?"

"Who?"

Pound's eyes shimmered with appreciation. "Annesley," he repeated gently.

"I don't think of him at all."

"Hm. I wonder where your brother is? He has been a bit of a loss of late, hasn't he?"

Devon didn't answer.

"For the last six months—maybe longer—Chase St. John has not been acting like . . . well, a St. John."

"My brother is fine. And he is as much a St. John as I."

Pound wisely did not say a thing and they had soon resumed their game.

But Devon found that he could not pay attention, a strange sense of unrest flickering through him. Where *was* Chase? And what did his recent disappearance have to do with Harry Annesley?

Devon stifled a sigh. Over the last year, Chase had become something of an enigma, disappearing for days on end, usually in the company of an actress or some other equally unworthy female.

Except, of course, when he'd taken up with the Viscountess Westforth. That relationship had proven itself to be something different—a foray into true friendship—although no one had realized it until they'd sent Devon's older brother, Brandon, to buy off the lady.

Something had happened in that meeting and a short time later, Brandon himself had married the woman. Devon thought about his sister-in-law, and smiled. Verena was as strong-willed and intelligent as they came, and she was every bit as in love with Brandon as he was with her. All told, the marriage promised to be as interesting as it would be lasting.

It was a pity Chase had not found such a bride. Of course, since Brandon had tricked Chase into accepting the infamous St. John talisman ring, chances were high that Chase might find his own true love. Or he would if he didn't leave Harry Annesley kicking his heels all over town, hinting to whoever would listen that Chase St. John had not honored a debt.

Such a thing had been known to ruin a man. To his surprise, Devon won yet another hand. He tossed his cards onto the table and called for his coat and horse.

Damn it all, where the hell is Chase? And why did he leave town after signing a note to Annesley?

Chapter 9

Starch makes the man.

The rather decrepit Lord Kilturn
to his valet, Hobart,
while standing before the mirror
adjusting his cravat
the evening of the Brookstone soirée

Harriet could only stare at Mr. Gower. Surely the man didn't mean to suggest that—he couldn't possibly mean to say that he and she could—that they would one day—"You must be jesting!"

Mr. Gower's smile never wavered, but his eyes narrowed unpleasantly. "I meant every word. I have carefully considered all the available choices, and I have decided that you would be the most beneficial bride for a man in my position. Your connections could be just the thing to help my career."

Harriet couldn't believe what she was hearing. "I don't wish to—"

"Please. Don't answer yet. I can see that I have startled you. But once you think about it, I believe you'll agree that a marriage between us would be beneficial."

"Mr. Gower, I do not wish to marry!"

Mr. Gower raised his brows. "No? What about the supposed Captain Frakenham?"

Oh piffle! Harriet'd let her astonishment freeze her brain into a block of useless ice. "I meant to say that I don't wish to marry *you*," she qualified. "Captain Frakenham is another matter altogether. Of course I wish to marry him; I'm engaged to him."

"Indeed."

It was one word, but the disbelief Gower managed to impart with that one word made Harriet pause. Oh dear no. If Mr. Gower suspected that there was no Captain Frakenham, everything was lost. For all that Harriet deplored Mother's invention of a suitor, the thought of losing Garrett Park just before the last payment was too galling for words.

Harriet smoothed her skirts nervously. "Speaking of Captain Frakenham, did I mention that he sent some silk to Mother?"

Mr. Gower lifted his brows. "Did he? How nice for your mother."

"A very nice length of it. He sent me some pearls and two strands of shells for Sophia and Ophelia, as well."

"Hmmm. I would love to see these items. Could you fetch them?"

Blast it, what was she to do now? She hadn't expected him to be so rude, but something seemed to have come over Mr. Gower.

Harriet managed a shaky laugh. "Of course you may see them! I'm not sure where Mother put the silk, and the pearls are safely locked away. Perhaps when you come to visit another time, I will have them all out for your perusal and—"

The banker shook his head, smiling. "Harriet, you should know that I have wondered about this Captain Frakenham from the beginning."

She tried to swallow but could not. "Oh? Wondered what?"

"I do not believe that you are indeed engaged to a Captain Frakenham *or* that he will arrive with a hold full of gold and save your family from further embarrassment." Mr. Gower's smile bordered on the insulting. "The other officials at the bank may believe what they will, but I am not so gullible."

"Mr. Gower, I assure you that I am indeed engaged to Captain Frakenham. How dare you insinuate that—"

"Nonsense. Harriet—Miss Ward—let us be plain. There *is* no Captain Frakenham. As far as I can ascertain, there never was."

"Are you calling me a liar?"

"I believe the falsehood began with your mother. I was curious from the first, so I wrote to London and made inquiries. There is no record of Captain Frakenham or his ship."

"Your research is incorrect, for I can assure you that—"

"You can assure me nothing." Mr. Gower captured her hand in his, his grip more than firm. "Harriet, I have been very patient with you and your family. You may rest assured that I have encouraged my superiors to accept your preposterous story about the good captain, and I will continue to do so." His thumb stroked a path over her knuckles. "For now."

Harriet barely contained a shudder. "I don't know what you are talking about." She tugged on her hand, but he held it firmly. She wondered what he would do if she were to scream, jump out of the window, and make a mad dash for freedom through the garden below.

"Harriet, listen to me." He stepped closer. "I may not have been born a gentleman, but I will be one before I die, as will my sons. I am asking you to marry me. You have everything to gain in this bargain."

"What? After next month, Garrett Park will be ours."

"Yes, but what will you do then? How will you provide for your family?"

She tried again to loosen his grip, tugging futilely. "Please, Mr. Gower—"

"You have the birth and connections I need to truly establish my name. I am willing to overlook the fact that your family is not financially responsible and that your brothers behave deplorably."

She stopped tugging on her hand, her irritation fanned into pure anger. "What about my sisters? Do you have anything ill to say of them?"

Mr. Gower regarded her gravely. "I'm certain that with a little guidance, they will learn some proper decorum. In time."

Harriet thought she would explode. How dare this man come to her home and insult her and her family in such a way? Especially after he'd spent the last year demanding payments and being such a nuisance that the sight of his carriage rolling down the drive made poor Mother ill with apprehension.

Harriet gave her hand one last yank, freeing it from his damp grasp. "Mr. Gower, I didn't wish to say this, but you have forced me. Sir, you are a pain in the a—"

The door opened and Mother bustled in, a rustling of silks and lace, her cap plopped unceremoniously on her head. The second her gaze fell on Harriet, she said in a breathless voice, "There you are, dear! I've been looking all over for you!"

Harriet frowned. "You knew where I—"

"Yes, yes, of course!" Mother paused just inside the door. "And there is that sweet Mr. Gower with you."

Sweet? How about rude and overbearing? "Mr. Gower was just telling me that he had to leave."

"Before meeting Captain Frakenham?" Mother said, all smiles. "Surely not."

Harriet opened her mouth. Then closed it. Captain Frakenham? Goodness, had Mother gone stark, raving mad?

Harriet stole a peek at Mr. Gower and noted with some satisfaction that he looked as thunderstruck as she felt.

"Captain Frakenham," the banker said slowly. "Mrs. Ward, there is no Captain Frakenham."

"No?" Mother asked, blinking in apparent astonishment.

In that instant, Harriet knew where Sophia had gotten her passion for acting.

"Mr. Gower," Mother said with some asperity, "you are sadly mistaken! There is indeed a Captain Frakenham. In fact, here he is now." With that, Mother stepped aside.

A broad-shouldered figure filled the doorway to the sitting room. Harriet's heart pounded an extra beat. There stood their patient. He appeared pale, the bandage still wrapped about his head. Harriet's gaze moved slowly over him, noting the way his coat hugged his wide shoulders then tapered to a narrow waist. His waistcoat was an understatement of elegant simplicity, his snowy white cravat tied in a fascinating array of twists and knots. She had to admire his taste; it was impeccable.

Harriet tried not to look directly at him as he walked forward, every step holding a liquid grace that was somehow salaciously delicious.

If he'd been dangerously attractive lying prone in bed, he was lethal striding across the room, moving with all the grace of a very large, very masculine cat. Harriet found that she could not look away. Could not help but notice the way his powerful thighs moved beneath the material of his breeches. Could not help but feel a little breathless when his deep blue eyes rested on her, and her alone.

"My dear," he murmured, on reaching her side. He took her unresisting hands in his and brought them, one at a time, to his warm lips. "How is my lovely fiancée this morning? I trust you slept well?"

Heat shivered up her fingers, through her arms, and directly into the pit of her stomach. Her whole body tightened in response.

She blinked up at him. "Captain Frakenham? But—"

"Harriet!" her mother said firmly. "Pray ring the bell for some tea. I'm certain Captain Frakenham is in need of nourishment."

"So I am," the captain easily agreed, smiling down at Harriet. Though his expression was schooled into a mild greeting, Harriet was all too aware of a devilish gleam in his eyes. He was laughing at her. He knew she had to respond to his overture in front of Mr. Gower. And the wretch was enjoying every minute.

Harriet pulled her hands free, then, for good measure, tucked them behind her back. For a mad moment, she wondered what would be worse—having to pretend to be on an intimate footing with the peacock who stood before her, grinning as if delighted to have the opportunity to torment her, or listening to more of Mr. Gower's asinine declarations.

"Oh dear!" Mother said. "I am so horrid at making introductions. Captain Frakenham, this is Mr. Gower, an officer from our bank. Mr. Gower, this is Captain Frakenham, Harriet's betrothed."

As Mr. Gower reluctantly took the captain's hand and the two exchanged greetings, Mother gripped Harriet's arm and whispered in her ear, "It was the only thing I could think of."

"How did you convince him to help?"

"I didn't. I just . . . told him he was Captain Frakenham." At Harriet's astonished look, Mother blushed. "He doesn't remember who he is, so what difference will it make?"

Harriet blinked. "But . . . what if he remembers his real name?" *If he doesn't already know it. Blast it, what is Mother thinking?*

Mr. Gower looked as if he wasn't sure if he was upside right or upside down. He kept shaking the "captain's" hand, over and over as if unable to stop.

Chase didn't know what he was enjoying more, the obvious shock the banker seemed to be experiencing or the look of pure chagrin on Harriet's face. It was amazing, but Chase was beginning to believe he might actually get a little enjoyment out of this charade.

Truly, there was much to be said for assisting the Wards. For one thing, he was no longer a sanctioned member of society. He was free for once of the onerous St. John name. For this instant, he was a sea captain come to visit his beloved. An earthy, common sea captain, full of tales of excitement and derring-do, as far away from the confining restraints of what Chase St. John really was.

Chase's heart took flight. He was going to enjoy this very, very much. He grinned at the banker. "Mr. Gower, I've heard quite a bit about you. I'm delighted we finally meet." Chase looked down at where the banker was still mindlessly shaking his hand. "Would you mind releasing my hand? I may need it sometime in the near future."

Gower reddened and stepped away. "I'm sorry. It's just that you—Captain—I cannot believe—that is to say, I didn't think you—"

"Didn't think I what? Would return for my Harriet?" Chase reached over and slid his arm about Harriet's waist, grinning when he heard her sharp intake of breath. She was a tightly made little bundle, he realized with some pleasure as his hand grazed her hip. "How could I leave such a tasty morsel alone?"

Dead silence met his pronouncement.

Mrs. Ward laughed a little uncertainly. "Captain Frakenham, the things you say!" She fanned herself a little. "The captain has been at sea a very long time."

"Indeed," Gower said, his jaw set, his brows lowered. His gaze roamed over Chase a moment, then stopped on the bandage. "I see you are injured."

"A mere scratch."

"How did you get it?"

"Pirates," Chase said blandly.

At his side, Harriet stiffened, and he was hard-pressed not to laugh. Instead, he nodded safely. "A battle with pirates off the coast of India. Nothing serious, of course. We routed them in thirty minutes and captured their cargo."

"Cargo? Was it a rich prize?"

"Mainly slave women."

Harriet pinned him with a hard glare. "Slave women?"

"Harem girls, actually." He held Harriet a little tighter, then winked over her head at Gower. "A healthy prize indeed, a hold full of slave women."

A sound suspiciously like a snort came from Harriet, who was still being held prisoner against Chase. He blinked innocently down at her. "Did you say something, dear?"

"No," Harriet said flatly, her brown eyes sparkling with indignation. "Not yet."

Mother leaned toward the banker. "You'll have to forgive Captain Frakenham's boisterous spirits. He's been at sea for months and months and—"

"Almost a year," Chase agreed, tugging Harriet a little closer until her hip rested against his. "And I thought of nothing but you, my little flower."

That seemed to raise some hackles. Harriet's smile, already patently false, grew more strained and she said through her teeth, "It's a pity you'll be returning to your ship so quickly, Captain Frakenham."

"Return?" Chase said, feigning bewilderment. "Oh no, sweetheart. I have no plans for returning to the sea for a while yet. In fact"—he released her and went to the settee, where he lay down, crossed his ankles on a small pillow and tucked his hands beneath his head, and said, "I plan on enjoying your hospitality for weeks and weeks to come."

His gaze found the empty tea tray and he frowned. "Speaking of which, I am famished. Harriet, my love, bring me something to eat, would you? But no tea. I prefer stronger spirits. Some brandy would not be amiss."

A choked exclamation came from Harriet.

Mrs. Ward quickly intervened. "I will be glad to ring for a nice light luncheon. Meanwhile, I daresay Mr. Gower must be on his way. He's a very important man and cannot linger for hours on end."

From his position on the couch, Chase gestured magnanimously. "Of course he can't! Anyone can look at him and see that he is not your average banker, by any means. Mr. Gower, I wish you good speed on your tasks today. May you foreclose on at least three separate properties."

Mr. Gower tried to smile, but failed. "I do not think I will be foreclosing on anyone today."

"No? Perhaps tomorrow then. Good day."

Mrs. Ward opened the door. "Mr. Gower, let me walk you out. Harriet can take care of the captain."

Gower did not seem to like that arrangement. He looked meaningfully at Harriet. "I will speak with you again, Miss Ward. Soon."

Chase watched closely. Something passed between the two . . . irritation on Harriet's part, and something else on Gower's. Had that been a warning? Chase frowned, determined to question Harriet the second he had her to himself.

Gower turned from Harriet to bow in Chase's direction. "It has been a pleasure meeting you, Frakenham. I hope I get to see more of you before you leave again. When *is* your ship due to sail?"

"Not anytime soon. It is in port with repairs."

"Is it? Do you mind my asking which port?"

Chase didn't even pause. "Whitby."

"Ah yes. I've been there. And the name of your ship?"

"Really, Mr. Gower," Harriet said, an air of tension

clinging to her. "There's no need to question our guest as if he—"

"Nonsense," Chase said easily. "My ship's name is *The Tempest*. She's a three-masted rig, just returned from India."

Gower managed a more genuine smile, his eyes narrowed. "Thank you. Good day, Captain."

"Good day, Mr. Gower."

Gower bowed once to Harriet, then followed Mrs. Ward out the door. And for the first time since he'd assumed the role of Captain Frakenham, Chase found himself alone with his fiancée.

Chapter 10

His lordship tells me the other day that starch makes the man. But let me tell you, 'tis silver that provides the starch. And that's where my heart lies.

Lord Kilturn's valet, Hobart, to Ledbetter,
the Earl of Greyley's valet after
a chance meeting at the tailor's

Harriet eyed the man lying on the settee. He hung over both ends, his arms behind his head, his ankles crossed on one of the good cushions. Not that he seemed to care. He was too busy watching her through narrowed eyes, tension evident in his biting blue gaze.

Harriet sniffed. "You, sir, were impolite."

"I wouldn't say that."

"I would. There you were, acting as if I was your—"

"Fiancée," he said smoothly. "Which you are, according to your mother." He lifted his brows. "Isn't that what you are? Or did I miss something?"

She choked. "That isn't what I was speaking of. You don't remember who you are, and yet you came in here and . . . and . . . took liberties!" Yes, that described what he'd done. He'd stepped far over the bounds of propriety. Even now she could feel where his hand had rested on her hip, his fingers warm through the thin material of her dress.

That touch, so simple and yet so possessive, had caused a reaction that lingered still. She smoothed her hands over her skirts, wondering if he'd felt that same flare of heat. If his body had also shivered with sudden—

She caught his gaze and colored, certain he could tell her thoughts. "Your actions were totally unnecessary."

"You may not have needed a visible reminder of the fact that you are supposedly betrothed to me, but it seemed that Mr. Gower did."

"He didn't believe there *was* a Captain Frakenham."

A faint smile touched the stranger's lips. "Yet here I am."

Harriet eyed him a moment. Oh yes, there he was. Six-foot-plus of whipcord muscle and solid sinew, of hard blue eyes and breathtaking handsomeness, all wrapped into one unknown, yet very dangerous, man. Even lying on the couch seemingly at his ease, he emitted a sharp-edged, almost lethal quality. "Tell me, sir, do you still not remember who you are?"

"Not clearly, no." He touched the bandage that wrapped about his head. "But your mother says I am Captain Frakenham, so . . ." His eyes met hers. "Who am I to question such a thing?"

Harriet opened her mouth, then closed it again. As mad of an idea as it had been to convince the stranger that he was Captain Frakenham, they were stuck with it for the moment. Especially since

Gower had met the man and would be looking to prove him false.

Harriet clamped her teeth closed over a rather unladylike expression. What a horrid tangle.

The stranger raised his brows. "Now that I think about it, the fact that you and I are engaged to be wed puts our relationship in a whole new perspective."

"A whole new perspective?" she said pleasantly enough, though it was difficult to keep her teeth from clenching. She didn't care for the way he was regarding her, as if he thought her a specially baked pastry.

He pushed himself upright on the settee, his coat stretching briefly over his muscled arms. "And since we are to be married, then we are free to act as couples who are to be married do."

"Oh piffle! What nonsense is that? Before you knew we were engaged, you hauled me into your lap and kissed me. What would you ask for now?" She held out a hand when he opened his mouth as if to answer. "No. Don't say a word. Just know this; I will not tolerate such inappropriate behavior."

His lips quirked. "You'll have to excuse my earlier behavior. I didn't have my memory, nor did you attempt to enlighten me of my true identity." A frown rested on his brow. "As a matter of fact, why *didn't* you tell me who I was and what we were to one another?"

Mainly because she didn't have one-tenth of her mother's imagination. "I didn't tell you who you were because I thought it would be nice if you remembered it yourself. Not that it matters. Whether we are engaged or not, you do not have the right to be overly familiar."

"Overly, no. But as your fiancé, I would assume I'm allowed certain liberties."

"Liberties?"

The braggart waved a hand. "Touches, kisses, and such."

She didn't like the sound of that "and such." But the other two . . . the touches and the kisses, those caused definite reactions in her traitorous body. "I want no touches, no kisses, nor any 'and suches' from you, thank you."

His brows rose thoughtfully. "You know, I wouldn't think a sea captain would be a timid lover. Yet somehow, you have the air of an untouched maiden."

Harriet stiffened. She took exception to his tone, to his expression, to everything about him. But she could hardly protest his calling her "an untouched maiden."

Piffle! This entire situation was untenable and it was all Mother's fault. First she'd dreamed up the too-handsome Captain John Frakenham, then she'd given him life and made him into a walking, talking nightmare. But her worst act had been to leave the lout stretched out on the sitting room settee for Harriet to deal with.

She pressed her fingertips to her brow. She had no time for this. There was shearing to worry about, and then packing the wool for market. And then the actual selling. If they didn't get a good price, all would be lost.

All would be lost, too, if "Captain Frakenham" recovered his memory at an inopportune moment. Harriet had little doubt the man would be furious—and who could blame him? *If*, of course, he'd really lost his memory to begin with. She eyed him suspiciously but could tell nothing from his guarded expression.

Heavens, it was a complicated coil! And it was probably all for naught—if Gower hadn't been suspicious before, he was now that he'd seen Mother's horrible rendition of Captain Frakenham.

For lack of an acceptable target for her frustrations, Harriet rested her gaze on the supposed captain. "If you're waiting for me to bring you your luncheon, you'll starve."

A sudden smile crossed his face as he pushed himself upright, his boots hitting the rug with a muffled thud. "You are a prickly thing, aren't you?"

"I'm just far too busy to wait on you hand and foot."

He stood, stretching as he did so. "What you are, my love, is difficult." His gaze flashed over her, lingering on her face. "But tasty, for all that."

Harriet couldn't help but note that he was amazingly trim, power emanating from his every move. With his dark hair falling over his brow in startling contrast to the white bandage, his blue eyes shadowed by long, black lashes, he almost took her breath away.

Almost. She still had enough calm, orderly logic to remember that just because he looked like a prince, he was probably anything but. "I'm not trying to make anything difficult. You simply do not understand our position."

"Ah, but I do. Your mother explained everything. The bank is breathing down your family's collective necks for the final payment on Garrett Park, and the only thing that has kept them from being even more demanding is the hope that I, the good captain, will arrive with a cargo of gold coins."

"One good coin might do us. We don't need that much," she lied.

"That's good to hear," he said dryly, clearly unbelieving. "Your mother told me how important it was that Gower didn't suspect anything was wrong. So I simply pretended that I remembered things. Frankly, I thought I did a damn fine job, considering how little I had to work with. Your mother was none too forthcoming with any useful details about, ah, my past."

Harriet sighed. "Mother is rather vague about most things."

"So I've gathered."

"And I suppose . . . I suppose I owe you a word of thanks for your efforts."

He grinned, sexily impish. "Not if it's going to cause you to rupture something."

Oh, piffle. Why did he have to suddenly become so engaging? She preferred it when he was being an asinine jackanapes and her irritation could find an outlet. "Thank you for your efforts, but did you have to make up so many details? The name of your ship, the port where she's berthed?"

Chase shrugged. She was a sharp one, Miss Harriet Ward. He hadn't meant to say anything so specific, but Gower's pompous certainty had needled him. "Details make the lie all the more believable."

"You seem to know a lot about lying for someone who has no memory to lie about. In fact, you do it so well it seems to be a natural-born talent."

"Don't all sailors tell sea yarns?"

Her eyes narrowed. "I wouldn't know about all sailors, just one. And that one is one too many."

That did it. Chase was hungry and his head ached abominably. Worse yet, he was being harangued by a tiny sprout of a woman with a mouth so soft and full that it was all he could do to keep from tasting her then and there. "You don't seem to hold me in a very loverlike esteem. Did we argue like this before I hit my head?"

"I can't think of a time we didn't argue."

"How depressing."

Her lips quivered, then widened into a grin, a deep chuckle tickling the air between them. It was the most sensuous laughter he'd ever heard. A heated shudder raced through him and he vowed to hear that chuckle more often.

Her gaze drifted slowly over him. "Did Mother show you all of the clothes we gathered from the forest?"

"Yes."

"Did you recognize anything?"

"Recognize?"

"Your belongings."

He opened his mouth to answer when he remembered that he wasn't supposed to remember who he was. "No. Of course I didn't recognize anything. Not that there was anything of value left other than my clothing. The thought rankled, and he had a sudden memory of his mother's ring, flashing in the sun.

His heart sank. How could he tell his brothers that he'd lost Mother's most prized possession? Perhaps he could return to the spot of the attack and look for it?

"Did the thieves take everything of value?"

"So it seems."

A flicker of a smile touched her lips. "Wait here a minute."

She spun on her heel and left the room, the sound of her skirts swinging around her filtering back through the open door. Chase listened as her footsteps crossed the hall. A door was opened; silence followed, but only for a moment until she returned.

"That was quick."

"I had this in the library. I almost forgot about it." She walked toward Chase where he stood by the settee, her hand held out before her.

Chase glanced down, then froze. There, lying in the center of her palm, was the St. John talisman ring. The silver circlet gleamed as if it had been polished.

His heart thundered in recognition. His mother's ring. Safe. It was more than he'd dared hope. Thank God it hadn't been lost. Chase reached for the ring, but then he caught Harriet's knowing gaze.

He paused. "Oh. Isn't . . . isn't this mine?"

She lifted her brows, daring him to make a claim. "*Is* it yours?"

Damn it! She was playing games with him. Chase dropped his hand back to his side. "I thought it must be mine, or you wouldn't have offered it in such a manner."

Her fingers closed over the silver band, a faint smile on her lips. "We found it near where you were injured. It could be yours, I suppose." She regarded him from under her lashes. "But then again . . ." She lowered her hand and dropped the ring into her pocket.

Chase had to fight to keep his expression blank. The little minx! Well, there was more than one way to get something out of a woman's pocket. If he had to, he'd divest the prim Miss Ward of her entire dress, pocket and all.

Yes, he decided, two could play at this game. And who knew? Maybe they both would win.

Harriet's face creased. "I suppose I'm not being very gracious. You . . . you did help us."

"Nonsense. I did nothing more than come in here, allow that imbecile from the bank to gawk at me, say enough to assure the man that I was indeed a real person and in charge of all my faculties, and then made certain he knew you, my love, were off bounds."

Her gaze caught his. "Off bounds?"

"I saw the way he was looking at you." Chase realized he hadn't liked it at all. Funny how just pretending something could make it seem real. "Your mother didn't tell me the banker had a liking for you."

"She doesn't know. In fact, *I* didn't know until today."

Chase frowned, noting the downturn of her mouth. He had a sister, himself, and his protective instincts leapt to the fore. "An unpleasant shock, was it?"

"Just . . . unexpected." She caught his gaze and colored. "Not that it excuses your behavior one bit. There was no need for you to be so . . . . earthy."

"I like earthy." And he had. He realized that in some way, living in London and being a St. John had removed quite a lot of earthiness from his life. "Perhaps I let myself get a bit carried away. I cannot remember what it was like to be a sea captain, much less an engaged one. I had to improvise."

"For your information, Captain Frakenham would never have made such a spectacle of himself."

"No?"

"Never. He is a real gentleman."

"He?"

She colored. "I meant, you."

"Perhaps this bump on my head has loosened my inhibitions."

She gave an inelegant snort. "You're incorrigible. You do realize that Mr. Gower will try to disprove all you told him. And when he discovers it's not true—"

"Then I will tell him I was mistaken. It's not inconceivable that I might misremember something."

"Something, perhaps. But for a captain to forget the name and location of his ship?"

She had a point. He touched the bandage. "But I hit my head. Very, *very* hard."

"Yes, but we cannot afford to raise his suspicions where the captain is concerned or he'll guess—" She clamped her mouth closed and glared at Chase as if he'd done something horrid.

Chase straightened. She'd almost said it . . . almost. He closed in on her, wondering if perhaps he could get the truth out of her yet. "Gower will guess what?"

Her jaw tightened. "Nothing."

From his superior vantage point, he couldn't see into her eyes, so he placed his finger on her chin and tipped her face up. "Miss Ward, why do I keep getting the feeling that neither you, nor your mother, is being honest with me?"

She took a step back, breaking his contact, her brow lowered. "If you feel that way, 'tis most likely because of that bump on your noggin. I daresay you've addled your brains a touch."

He took another step closer. She matched him move for move, backing away, her expression guarded. Her gaze flickered to the door.

"Don't even think about it," he said softly. "Running away will solve nothing."

She stopped moving then, standing firmly in place, her chin in the air. "The Wards never run," she said with a decided air of hauteur. "Though if I *was* thinking of making a dash for it, you couldn't do anything about it."

"Couldn't I?" He advanced again, only this time, he moved slightly to one side. She responded by stepping in the opposite direction—and ended up backed against the edge of a small table, hemmed in by a large chair on one side, and Chase on the other.

"Piffle!" Her full mouth thinned. "Please move out of my way."

She had the most engaging eyes—large and appealingly shaped, with a delicate sweep of lash and brow. "Tell me something, Miss Ward, am I *really* Captain John Frakenham?"

She didn't even blink, the little jade. "Yes. You are." Harriet leaned forward then, her gaze narrowed, an earnest expression on her face. "And you cannot disagree, unless . . ."

"Unless?"

"Unless you believe you are someone else." Her brows rose. "*Are* you?"

It could have been funny. And perhaps it was, in a way. She didn't believe him when he said he didn't remember who he was. And he didn't believe her when she said he was Captain John Frakenham. In order to prove her wrong, he'd have to admit his falsehood. In order for her to prove him wrong, she'd have to admit to her falsehood.

It was a quandary of the highest order.

Chase, of course, knew damn well who he was, but he couldn't tell this woman. Not without potentially causing a maelstrom of gossip that could possibly alert his brothers to his location. This was a small community, he reminded himself, thinking of all the tales that had apparently gone 'round involving the nonexistent Captain Frakenham. He could only imagine what they would say about a real, live, flesh-'n'-blood St. John.

He simply couldn't risk it. All he really knew about Harriet Ward was that she was very, very good at lying. Almost as good as he was. "If both you and your mother say I am Captain John Frakenham, then that's who I am."

Some of the tension left her frame, and she nodded approvingly. "Indeed you are."

Chase didn't know whether to laugh or shake the wench until her teeth rattled. She was a bold piece, this little sparrow who dared cage a lion. It was possible . . . extremely possible that Miss Harriet Ward might make for a very delightful dalliance despite her prickly exterior.

He rubbed his chin as he considered her from head to foot. "Hmmm."

"What?"

"You are a curvaceous thing, aren't you?"

She flushed. "Stop that!"

"Surely you're used to me looking at you. And touching you, too." Urged on by some imp of madness, he threaded his fingers through one of her curls where it lay against her shoulder, having escaped her bundled and bunched hair.

She immediately jerked away, and the soft silk tress slid from his fingertips. Unbound, he thought it would drape over her shoulders and down, curling possessively along the taut lines of her back. She was so small, without an ounce of plumpness to her except for the seductive curves of her breasts and hips.

He eyed her breasts for a moment. They were small, but well-rounded. They would just fit in his hand. His fingers curled at the thought, and he had an instant image of her naked and pliant beneath him—

She plopped her hands on her hips. "Look, Mr.—"

"Captain," he corrected softly, forcing himself to meet her gaze.

Her cheeks stained bright red, her eyes flashing. "Whatever you are."

"Don't you mean *who*ever?"

"No," she said flatly. "*What*ever you are, you are being quite rude, staring at me as if I was a cow you were thinking of purchasing."

"I was trying to remember you, of course. I keep thinking that there must be something"—he deliberately glanced back at her breasts—"that might trigger my memory."

She crossed her arms over her chest. "I can assure you that you've never seen that much of me."

"Never?"

"Never."

"Hm." He pretended to ponder this a moment. "You're certain we've never—"

"*Never!*"

He pursed his lips and regarded the wall opposite as if in deep thought.

She stomped her foot, the heel making a solid thump on the rug. "*What* are you doing now?"

"It's just that . . . well, I can't remember a lot of things, but I do know that . . . I know that . . ." He shook his head. "I'm sorry. I can't say."

She huffed.

There was no other word for it—a sigh would have been softer, and a hiss would have been

sharper. No, Chase decided, it was a definite huff.
He lifted his brows. "I beg your pardon?"

"Tell me."

"I would, but I don't want to shock you, and I definitely don't want your mother to think that I—"

"Mother has nothing to do with this, and I don't shock easily."

"I suppose . . ." He regarded her for a short time, then nodded. "Very well, then. I was thinking that it was strange that I should remember how a woman's naked body would look, but not remember yours."

She stiffened, outrage in every line. "That is because you've never seen my body."

"That's very strange. I hate to ask this, but ah . . . is there something wrong with you?"

Her mouth dropped open.

He placed a finger beneath her chin and closed it.

She snapped back to life. "What possibly could be wrong with me?"

"I don't know; you'll have to tell me." He tapped his bandaged head. "I'm the one who can't remember."

Her chin lifted another notch. "Look, Mr.—"

"Captain."

She closed her eyes for a long moment, her jaw clamped tightly. "Captain," she managed to grit out. "You and I were engaged, but not . . . not anything else."

He sighed as if disappointed. "I see."

"I believe we've said enough on this topic. Mr.—Captain, if you will excuse me, I have things I must see to. Please make yourself comfortable. Mother should return shortly."

Chase didn't want to move, but he could tell Harriet meant business. There was a definite glint to her eyes that told him she'd reached the end of her rope.

He moved out of her way and with that, Miss Harriet Ward gave him an infinitesimal nod, then swept from the room.

Chase had to stifle a grin. She really was a bundle of fire and sparks, this seemingly meager woman. He wondered how her barely contained passion would translate in his bed. The thought hung in his head, tantalizing him with images of what could be, what might be.

At that moment, something clicked into place. It was as if the stars had aligned themselves for this one moment. Chase had been on his way out of the country, leaving behind all he held dear. Yet here he stood, cast in the guise of a carefree sea captain, arguing with a blessedly logical female about his own identity.

Perhaps he wasn't meant to leave England yet. So long as no one in this little community knew he was a St. John, his brothers would never be the wiser. The thought of his brothers made his throat tighten . . . he had to leave. Had to spare them from the scandal his actions had caused.

All of his earlier amusement fled. He would stay long enough to help the Wards convince the bank that there really was a Captain Frakenham, and then he'd be on his way.

After all, what difference could a few days make?

Chapter 11

I thought I was in love once. Turned out it was just some bad mutton. Unfortunately, by the time I'd ascertained the true cause of my distress, I was already wedded, bedded, and headed for the worst ten years of my life.

The valet, Ledbetter, to his employer,
the Earl of Greyley while helping that
stalwart individual into his new coat

Harriet retired to her room. Located on the second floor, it was pleasantly, if somewhat sparsely, furnished, the bed old but serviceable, the dresser and washstand faded from so much waxing, the wardrobe mismatched. But the rug was thick and warm, and the curtains on the windows were new, presents from Ophelia and Sophia from a Christmas not long past.

Normally, Harriet took comfort in her room. But this time her heart was beating too thunderously for her to do more than stomp across the floor, drop onto her bed, and fall back against the coverlet.

Captain Frakenham—or whatever his name really was—was the most exasperating, overbearing, and arrogant man she'd ever met. He was also, she

129

had to admit, a remarkably good actor. He'd taken to the part of Captain Frakenham with astonishing ease. Almost with joy.

Oh, he'd overplayed certain parts. Rather like Sophia would do. But overall, he'd been quite believable. Harriet sighed, threw her arms over her head, and stared up at the ceiling. The stranger might not be Captain Frakenham, but he certainly looked the part. Tall, black-haired, broad-shouldered . . . for some reason, she'd pictured the fictitious captain just that way. She remembered the "captain" lying on the settee, dwarfing the whole room with his presence.

It was so perplexing! Whoever he was, she was certain he was not common born. His accent was impeccable and his clothes made by a master tailor. He also sported an unconscious air of command, as if he was used to people obeying his every whim and whimsy. That air of command hung about him, an almost visible cloak of authority.

Drat it, who *was* the man? There had to be a clue somewhere. Harriet reached into her pocket and pulled out the ring.

She'd thought for a moment that the captain had recognized it. There'd been an unmistakable gleam in his eyes. But had it been an unconscious reaction? Or had he indeed known the ring as his own but not claimed it?

She fingered the smooth silvered surface, squinting at the decorative runes cut along the edges. It was certainly an odd piece, not at all the sumptuous bauble she'd expect of a man like him.

Did he know who he was? Or was her skeptical imagination interfering with her usual calm logic?

She sighed. All she knew for certain was that she and her family desperately needed him to continue being Captain Frakenham, at least for a while.

Harriet slid the ring over her finger, the metal strangely warm. Her hand tickled as if a feather had run along it starting at the ring and ending at her wrist, where her pulse beat a steady rhythm. How odd.

The light from the window sparkled on the circlet, and Harriet found herself smiling. It was a pretty piece for all its simplicity.

Well, it would look very good locked in her jewelry box, for she wasn't about to leave it out where it might disappear, especially not if the "captain" suddenly regained his memory and decided it belonged to him.

She pursed her lips thoughtfully. She couldn't quite decide if he knew who he was or not. There were times when she was certain of it, but then other times he seemed somewhat . . . lost. Alone. Perhaps he had indeed lost his memory. Why else would he have agreed to assume the captain's identity? It was a puzzle.

She rubbed her thumb along the ring, turning it so that it sparkled. She supposed she'd better find Mother and see what was to be done with the stranger now that Gower thought the man to be Captain Frakenham. They needed only one—perhaps two—weeks. Surely the stranger could play the part for that length of time.

Harriet supposed she'd better remove the ring. She tugged . . . but nothing happened. The ring wouldn't budge.

Harriet pulled harder. Still nothing happened.

Sighing, she pushed herself upright, shoving her hair out of her face. Wonderful. She held her hand before her, grasped the ring, and tugged—*hard*,

wincing as she yanked. For a second, she thought it
was slipping, but just as it moved, the ring seemed
to tighten, to cling to her finger as if hanging on with
all its might.

"Piffle!" Harriet said, alarm sifting through her.
She rose and went to the washstand, rubbing soap
on her finger, then pulling yet again.

Still nothing happened. A half hour later, after
much tugging and muttering, Harriet realized the
impossible—the blasted ring was stuck. She sat back
on the edge of the bed and stared at her reddened
finger. The ring didn't *seem* too tight. Indeed, it
turned easily right where it was. But every time she
tried to pull it off, it seemed to tighten as if by—

She curled her fingers closed. "Nonsense," she said
aloud, as if to reassure anyone who might be listening. "My finger must have swollen a bit. That's all."

The words comforted Harriet some. That made
perfect sense. Still, she couldn't help but stare down
at the runes that collected the light and wonder at
the way her life seemed to be going lately. First she'd
found the stranger, who had promptly kissed her,
followed by Gower's unexpected declaration, then
the "captain's" infuriating attitude . . . and now this.
Stuck with a strange ring on her finger.

A ring that just might belong to that infuriating
jackanapes.

The ring seemed to warm at the thought. Harriet
narrowed her gaze at it. "Enough of that."

She stood. Perhaps Cook would know how to get
the blasted thing off. With any luck, a touch of butter
would do the trick.

Muttering to herself, Harriet made her way to the
kitchen, wondering as she did so where her brothers
and sisters were—things seemed strangely quiet. As

soon as she got the silly ring off her finger, she'd see what everyone was doing.

Harriet pushed open the door to the kitchen. The warm afternoon light streamed through the open windows and mingled with the scent of dried herbs.

"There ye are, miss!" Cook labored at a large wooden table in the center of the room, flour liberally dusted over her red apron. "I was just thinkin' bout ye, I was."

"Were you?" A rich aroma caught Harriet's attention. "Mmmmm. What is that?"

Cook grinned, jerking her head toward a half dozen steaming pots. "Nothin' but dinner."

Harriet counted the pots. Seven. Last night, they'd had mutton stew and peas and some of Cook's special crusty bread.

But this . . . it looked as if a feast was in the making. Harriet went to the pots, aware of Cook's covert gaze.

One after the other, Harriet lifted the lids. The entire kitchen filled with a rich aroma that made her mouth water. "Dumpling stew, roast saddle of mutton with mint sauce, plovers' eggs in aspic jelly, peas and asparagus—goodness! It's not Christmas again, is it?"

Cook chuckled delightedly and gave Harriet a meaningful look. "Don't ye be teasin' me, Miss Harriet! Ye know what day 'tis. Or will be soon! And 'tis not Christmas. Not with the weather warming so every day."

Harriet closed the lid of the last pot, the clang echoing pleasantly amid the burbling sound of the dumpling stew. "I know what it is. The new rector is in town, and Mother has asked him to dinner."

A sly smile crossed Cook's lips. "You'll have to ask the madam about thet. I was tol' to fix a sumptuous dinner and so I am. Ye should be pleased as pork, Miss Harriet."

"I should be? What do I have to be pleased ab— Oh. I see. The captain."

Blast it, she hadn't thought about the fact that the servants, who had not been privy to the fact that the captain was a figment of the Wards' collective imagination—only because it was suspected they might leak the truth—would believe the farce her mother was even then encouraging.

"Of course the captain!" Cook exclaimed. She beamed at Harriet. "Who else would I cook good mutton for if not your intended? I must say, 'tis a handsome man. I'm just a little miffed ye didn't tell me who he was right away."

Harriet's jaw tightened. "Oh yes . . . well, I didn't want to ruin the surprise for Mother."

Cook sighed happily. "I've heard so much about the captain that 'tis almost a wonderment to meet him."

"That's what I thought, too," Harriet muttered. "Where is the good captain now?"

"In his room. The missus thought he should lie down a mite. I must say 'twas a good idea, fer he looked a bit snookered after meeting with the banker."

Cook wiped her hands on her apron. "There. All done. Do ye think the captain'd like a maraschino jelly with his dinner? I saved a bit fer a special occasion and, well, there aren't many more special than this."

Harriet managed a faint smile. "I don't know what he likes. I'll have Mother ask him."

"Ye'd best be findin' out, miss. Ye're the one as will be marryin' him," Cook said cheerfully, scraping dough out of a bowl and rolling it as though her life depended on it. "I hope yer young man likes lemon tarts. Fresh and crisp they'll be, just the way ye likes them."

"I like them any way I can get them," Harriet answered truthfully. Even if they had been made in the captain's name. "I thought we were saving the lemons for the Ladies Auxiliary Sewing Committee."

"So I was. But the missus said to make them tonight and so I am. I always do as I'm told."

That was a blatant lie. Harriet couldn't count how many times she'd asked Cook not to give Stephen quite so many pastries between his meals, a request that was actively ignored by all parties concerned.

Still, what concerned Harriet the most was that *Mother* had requested the tarts. That was not a good sign. At all. "Where is Mother?"

"In the library, workin' on the accounts, I suppose. That's what she said she was goin' to do, anyways."

Harriet nodded and made her way to the door. "Thank you, Cook."

She was halfway to the library before she remembered the ring. She glanced down at it and scowled, giving it a sharp tug. The blasted thing still wouldn't move. It would just have to wait until she finished talking to her mother.

Harriet shoved open the door to the library. "Mother, I wa—" She halted. Not only was her mother in the library, but the entire Ward family, as well.

Mother looked up from where she sat at the oak escritoire, calmly penning a missive. "There you are!

I was just going to send Derrick for you. We are having a meeting about the captain."

"Glad you made it on your own," Derrick said. He opened the book he held and settled farther into the large, plump chair, sprawling comfortably. "I was almost finished, and I didn't want to leave."

"Oh, Harriet! Mother just told us about the captain!" Sophia gave an excited whirl, her skirts flaring out about her ankles. "Nothing could be more perfect! It's as if an angel sent him to us. And now, Mother says we're to act as if we are all in a play!"

Harriet looked at Mother. "A play?"

"Indeed," Mother said calmly, dipping her pen into the inkwell. "We must make everyone believe that the stranger is indeed Captain Frakenham, at least for a week or so. Especially the staff."

Harriet pressed a hand to her temple. "Surely it won't be necessary to take things that far. So long as Gower believes that the captain—"

"Harriet," Mother said, gentle reproof in her voice, "you know how things got out of hand last time. I merely made mention of a fiancé, and, before you knew it, I was being hounded for details, which I imprudently made up on the spot."

Harriet sighed. "I know."

"I thought the story would remain contained within the confines of the bank, so I did nothing more to ascertain the rumor I'd begun. This time, things are going to be done in a more thoughtful, timely manner."

"What do you mean?"

"Before, because there *was* so little information on the captain, people began to take it upon themselves to make up things. This time, we are going to grasp the rumor mill firmly by the horns."

Stephen nodded. He stood leaning against the mantelpiece, his crutches momentarily idle against the wall. "Mother's right, Harri. Gower will run back to the bank and tell all. The next thing you know all mayhem will break loose; people will be streaming in, asking hundreds of stupid questions and trying to steal a look at him."

Ophelia plopped down on the small leather settee placed to one side. "It will be just like when Mr. Wilkers told everyone he'd had twin calves off the same cow. Even old Mrs. Crumpleton came to see, and she hadn't left her home in over two years, claiming her knees were bad."

Harriet opened her mouth to protest, but then closed it. Her heart sinking, she realized they were right. It wouldn't be long before the doorway darkened with all manner of people, all coming on some seemingly innocuous errand, but really thirsting for a glimpse of the captain. "Good God."

"I know," Stephen said. "I don't like it either. But I've thought it through and we've really no choice."

"There has to be another way," Harriet said. "I simply do not like this plan."

Sophia blinked. "Why not? I think it's a perfectly good plan. And you have the best part of all! That of 'fiancée in love.'"

"I don't wish to be a 'fiancée in love.'"

"There!" Sophia looked eagerly at their mother. "I told you Harriet wouldn't agree to this! Perhaps we could tell people that the captain is really engaged to *me* all along and that I'm the one he really—"

"No," Mother said firmly, eyeing Sophia severely. "I've already told you that would not work. We have to stick to the same story."

Sophia sniffed. "Oh very well, though I doubt

Harri can pull it off. She's awfully stiff on stage. Remember when we asked her to play Falstaff last year? A perfectly delightful part, and yet she managed to murder it with every sentence. No one laughed a bit."

Stephen snorted. "Harriet's nothing compared to you. Remember how badly you mangled doing Lady Ophelia last Easter? That was a tragedy indeed."

"I did a fine job! Even Mrs. Strickly said so, and she's been to dozens of London plays!"

Harriet made an impatient noise. "None of that matters now! How are we going to do this?"

"Simple," Mother said. "We will just restate a few set facts."

"Such as?"

"The captain is here to see you. He has only come for a short period of time—two weeks, maybe less. He's leaving as soon as his ship is ready."

"And?"

Mother lifted her brows. "That's more than enough."

"What about what the captain told Mr. Gower in the sitting room today? That his ship was named . . . oh, something, I can't remember—and that it was being repaired in Whitby? Should we mention that, too? Or that he injured himself in a battle with pirates?"

Sophia and Ophelia both gasped. "The captain is such a brave man," Sophia breathed.

Harriet's hand curled into fists. *"He made it up!"*

Ophelia nodded. "He's so brave that he's even willing to live a lie, all to help us. Although . . . I wonder if he is remembering something in earnest and just doesn't realize it. Perhaps the captain really *is* a captain and—"

"For the love of—*he isn't real!*" Harriet burst out. "There is no Captain Frakenham, no ship, and *no pirates!*"

A short silence followed this outburst.

"Really, Harriet," Sophia said, eyeing her sister as though she'd just grown a third head, "there is no need for you to get so vexed."

"That's right," Stephen said, trying to look like the man of the house, an irritating habit that seemed to be getting worse of late. "I think you owe Ophelia an apology."

Harriet took a deep breath in through her nose. "I am sorry I shouted, but none of you seems to realize that this is a serious situation. If we are found out, the bank will waste no time in demanding their money, and we don't have it. And what will we do if the stranger remembers who he is?"

To dry the ink, Mother dusted sand over the letter she'd been writing. "We'll deal with that when it happens, *if* it happens. Remember Mrs. Billingsworth. She never remembered who she was. It's a pity she died."

"Oh wouldn't that be wonderful!" Sophia exclaimed in a dreamy voice.

"What would be wonderful?" Derrick asked, looking up from his book, a frown marring his brow. "For the poor man to die?"

"No, that he might never remember who he is. Then he would just be Captain Frakenham forever and marry Harri!"

Five pairs of eyes turned on Harriet.

She colored. "When hell freezes over."

"Harriet!" Mother frowned as she folded the note and slid it into an envelope.

"I am sorry. It's just that all of you are standing on

the edge of a cliff, cheerily planning to jump. You don't seem to realize how easily this could blow up in our faces."

"How?" Stephen demanded. "What is the worst thing that could happen?"

"What if the stranger remembered who he really is? Then where would we be?"

Ophelia pushed her glasses back in place. "We'll just have to see to it that he's never alone without one of us present to head him off."

"Good idea," Stephen said. "And if he does remember who he is, he'll just leave."

"That's what I would do," Derrick said, settling back into his book. "I might say a few choice words beforehand, but nothing more."

"Exactly," Stephen said. "In the meantime, the captain's presence will make the bank hold off on demanding the payment and we can get the shearing done."

Mother wrote something across the envelope. "Here, Sophie. Pray give that to Lady Cabot-Wells with my fondest regards, and be sure you're home by five."

Sophia glanced over her shoulder at Derrick. "Are you coming with me?"

Derrick glanced up from his book, but remained lazing in his chair. "Where to?"

"To see Lady Cabot-Wells."

He made a face. "The last time I saw her, she called me 'Donald' and asked how my cat was doing."

"She's an old woman, Derrick," Stephen said, frowning down at his brother. "She's never gotten my name right in over ten years."

"Well, I don't like her and so I'm not going to see her."

Stephen's frown deepened. "It will not hurt you to get off your a—"

"Stephen!" Mother said.

"Sorry. It's just that I cannot abide a slugabed, and Derrick has become the worst."

"I have not!" Derrick struggled to sit up, his face red. "I worked all morning and most of the afternoon in the barn, and all you can say is—"

"I think," Harriet said firmly, "that Sophia should not be gallivanting about the countryside unattended. So one of you has to go."

Derrick subsided into his chair, pulling his book back over his face.

Stephen regarded him for a long moment, then gave an exasperated sigh. "Oh very well! I'll go." He collected his crutches from the wall, then hobbled to his sister's side.

Harriet watched as her mother handed the note to Sophia. "What's that?"

"An invitation to dinner. I thought Lady Cabot-Wells should meet the captain first."

"This evening?"

"No, I thought we'd save this evening for just ourselves and the captain. We need to be certain he is convinced he is who we've told him he is. I asked Lady Cabot-Wells to join us for dinner sometime next week."

"But she's the biggest gossip on earth!"

Mother smiled. "Which is precisely why I invited her. I thought we should begin at the top and work our way down."

Sophia breezed to the door, Stephen hobbling after her. "We'll return soon, Mother." She wiggled her fingers and went out the door.

He stopped on the threshold, a thoughtful expression on his face. "You know, Harriet, if we work this right, we might be able to use your precious captain to help in other ways than just keeping the bank away."

"Such as?"

"Well . . . if he's not injured too badly, he *could* help with the shearing. All of it."

Harriet met Stephen's gaze, astounded at the thought. Good God, that would be perfect. It was difficult finding reliable workers, especially so close to shearing week, and things were getting desperate.

A slow smile began, then gradually grew until it matched Stephen's. That was an idea, the first good one she'd heard all day. One more pair of helping hands would make all the difference in the world.

"All we have to do," Stephen said, "is convince him that the captain would do it, and since he's the captain . . ."

Harriet nodded, her heart lightening a little.

"Come on, Stephen," Sophia said. "I want to change before dinner and fix my hair, and we won't have time if we dally."

Stephen sighed. "All right. I'm coming." He gave Harriet one last meaningful look, then followed Sophia out the door.

Mother beamed. "See how well things are going already? We have not only found a Captain Frakenham, but we've found another helper for the shearing. It's more than I had hoped—almost a miracle." She smiled at her children. "Sometimes prayers really are answered!"

Harriet wasn't sure that she wanted to call the dark-haired stranger a miracle any more than she wanted to call him Captain Frakenham, but she had no say in the matter at all. She'd just have to make do, put up with the man's odious, self-satisfied manner, and pretend she was engaged to the oaf. But only in public.

Meanwhile, she'd take comfort in Stephen's suggestion. If she and Stephen could contrive a way to get the stranger to help with the shearing, then perhaps some good could come of this mess after all.

Chapter 12

*Bloody hell, it's Lady Tatswell. Having just re-
turned from boring some poor unhappy* parti
*to death, she is now about to sally forth on a
fresh mission of destruction. She's—God no!
She's coming this way! Where can we hide?*

The Earl of Greyley to his wife, Anna,
at the Comptons' soirée

He had only an hour until dinner. Chase tossed
back the last bit of brandy. He closed his eyes
as the liquid warmed a path down his throat and
into his stomach. His head still ached, but the pain
was subsiding with each swallow.

Thank God he'd found the brandy decanter in the
library earlier or there would be no sleep that night.
In London, he never slept without the assistance of a
heavy dose of spirits. Not since—

He closed his eyes, his heart clutched painfully.
No. Don't think about it. Never think about it.

Slowly the feeling of taut-eyed desperation eased.
The soft sound of a clock chimed over his shoulder.
His hand shook a little as he poured himself another
glass. The last time he'd had spirits was the day he'd
been attacked. He lifted the glass to his lips, then

paused. That was probably what had caused the entire ruckus—the fact that he was drunk. The thieves must have figured him an easy mark, just as Annesley had.

Chase set the glass back on the tray, his mind suddenly clear. He'd never be an easy mark again.

Meanwhile, he'd better finish dressing for dinner. He had little doubt that it would be served at a dismally early hour considering he was residing with a houseful of sheep farmers.

Chase sighed and turned, catching sight of his cravat in the mirror. Well, it was *supposed* to be a cravat. While most of his clothing had been salvaged, his cravat linens had been sadly muddied and mangled, except for two, both of which were now being laundered. Left with no recourse, he'd been forced to accept a horribly understarched cravat linen from the household.

He tried to adjust it one more time, then stopped and shook his head in disgust. Not only was it limp, but it was a damnable nuisance trying to fasten the thing without the benefit of a decent cravat pin.

The thought of his assortment of pins—gold, diamond, ruby, sapphire—made him sigh. Gone forever, the lot of them. It was intolerable, though not as intolerable as it would have been had he lost his mother's ring.

The thought of that ring and the pocket it rested in caused his teeth to grind of their own accord.

Damn it, he'd get that ring back if it was the last thing he did. Miss Harriet Ward was about to face the St. John determination, whether she was prepared for it or not. The thought eased his spirits some, and he caught his reflection in the mirror.

He'd removed the offending bandage a half hour

earlier. A huge bruise colored his forehead. The center was still a dark and forebidding deep blue, while the edges were fading to more muted shades of purple and red with the veriest stain of yellow.

"I'm a veritable rainbow," he told himself with a rueful grin.

Chase found himself looking at the decanter once again, but he made no move toward it. Instead, he pictured Miss Harriet Ward, a disapproving look in her remarkably brown eyes, her brows lifted as if daring him to be so foolish as to appear before her drunk and witless.

That was the last thing he needed—to be witless in the presence of a woman he was beginning to think possessed an incredibly sharp mind. She would tear him to shreds before he knew what was happening.

A firm rap sounded on the door. Chase called a greeting and a mobcapped female entered, her face twisted in a look that was as welcoming as a cold stone floor in the height of winter.

She regarded him dourly as she bobbed a most unwelcoming curtsy, her disapproving gaze finding the brandy decanter almost immediately. Her expression turned even more sour. "Supper is ready. Everybody has been waitin' in the sittin' room fer ten minutes now."

Chase glanced at the clock on the mantel. "It's only a little after seven. Surely dinner is not served before eight." Even for country hours, eight was unseasonably early.

The woman stiffened as if he'd insulted her parentage. "We eat promptly at seven at Garrett Park and we're not likely to change just because ye're here."

Lovely. He was interred in a house where not only

the eldest daughter held him in derision, but so did the upstairs maid.

Chase wasn't used to such treatment. Usually when he spent a day or two at someone's country estate, his hosts were more than happy to have him about since he was an unmarried son from one of the wealthiest families in England. People didn't fawn over him precisely, but they appreciated him. Enjoyed his company. Occasionally even laughed at his jokes.

As for the servants, he was known to be generous with his vails and that had earned him some respect as well. But he could neither inform his current hostess of his parentage, nor did he have any money to pay vails—not after the robbery, anyway. All told, he was relegated to a pecuniary, disrespected level of existence, and it wasn't one that he particularly enjoyed.

He eyed the maid with some misgiving. "I suppose I am ready to go down now, Miss—"

"*Mrs.*," she snapped, as if suspecting he was attempting to flirt with her. "It's *Mrs.* Maple. I'm the housekeeper."

"Ah. May I say that Garrett Park is a lovely house? I daresay you must work hard to keep it up."

Her gaze didn't soften one bit. "See to it that you come down to dinner on time from now on. 'Tis rude to keep the family waitin', especially Miss Harriet." With that admonition, the housekeeper spun on her heel and marched off, indicating with a glare that he was to follow her.

Chase did as he was bid, hiding a rueful smile. So Miss Ward was not the only prickly character in the house, was she? It seemed that some of the servants were likewise afflicted. Perhaps it was the water.

It was a good thing he'd found that brandy decanter.

The housekeeper stopped beside the door of the same room where Chase had met Mr. Gower just that morning. She threw open the door, made a harrumph sound by way of announcing him, then stepped aside and gestured for him to enter.

Before Chase took two steps into the room, the door was smartly closed against his heels. Every eye fastened on him as the hum of conversation died an immediate death.

It was the first time Chase had been blessed with seeing the entire Ward family, and he was immediately struck by how handsome they were. There was a look of quality to them all, of grace and health. Chase felt a little guilty for having thought of them as sheep farmers.

On his entry, Harriet turned from her sisters with a genuine smile on her lips, her eyes sparkling with something other than annoyance or suspicion. It was a look Chase had yet to enjoy—unalloyed mirth. Her lips were parted to reveal even white teeth, her brown eyes shone with life, and her entire expression was winsome.

Mrs. Ward quietly moved forward, a lovely matron in an ice-blue gown, a modest bit of lace at her bosom. "Captain Frakenham, I hope your room is proving adequate."

Chase bowed. "It's more than adequate. Quite lovely, in fact."

She smiled. "Excellent. Since your memory is a bit spotty right now, I thought perhaps I should reintroduce the family. I daresay you don't remember all of them."

He flicked a glance about the room. "You have quite a number of children."

"Yes. I have five."

Chase had four brothers and one sister, but he wisely refrained from saying so. "That's a large family indeed."

She patted his arm. "Allow me to reintroduce them to you. This is Stephen, my elder son." She gestured to a tall, slender young man who leaned on a pair of crutches.

The young man grinned widely as he nodded a greeting. He was very broad shouldered, his hands as large as ham hocks. Chase noted the halfling's skin was as tanned as Harriet's.

"And this," Miss Ward continued, gesturing to her other son, "is Derrick. You met him earlier, in your room."

"Of course," Chase said, bowing.

Derrick glanced up from the book he'd been reading while leaning against a chair. He returned Chase's slight bow, his gaze flickering over him a quick moment before he went back to his book.

"Derrick is something of a bookworm," Mrs. Ward said by way of explanation. She gestured toward the two girls who were sitting side by side on the settee. "These are my younger daughters, Sophia and Ophelia."

The two girls gleamed up at him, the more fair of the two even daring to simper a bit. Of all the Wards, Chase decided that Sophia and Stephen possessed the most conventionally accepted idea of beauty. With their golden brown hair and blue eyes, they would have been noticed at any function in London.

The others were equally as attractive, though in a quieter way, like the intriguing Miss Harriet, who faded from view until roused to ire when she'd burst upon the senses like a scorching fire.

"Oh, Captain Frakenham!" Sophia bounced in her chair, her golden brown curls springing to life. "I'm so pleased to meet you! I mean—I'm glad to meet you *again*. We've known each other for oh, so long. In fact, I daresay you remember the time you and I—"

"Sophia," Mrs. Ward said in breathless tone, "let the poor man alone. He has just risen from the sickbed and will not benefit from all of your recollections."

Chase was certain that since he had absolutely no recollections of Miss Sophia whatsoever, Mrs. Ward was quite correct in her belief that he wouldn't benefit from any memories the girl planned on dredging from her imagination. Still, he managed a pleasant smile. "I'm certain Miss Sophia can remind me of our past times together over dinner."

He bowed to the youngest Ward girl. "Miss Ophelia, how nice to meet you again. I fear I don't remember you well after—" He touched his head ruefully.

She giggled, her brown eyes magnified by her spectacles. "Thank you, Captain Frakenham. I am pleased to meet you again, as well."

Mrs. Ward smiled her approval. "That only leaves Harriet, whom I'm sure you remember from this afternoon."

"Indeed." Chase bowed to Harriet, who stood to one side, her expression so far from the unalloyed mirth he'd witnessed on her face when he entered the room that he wondered if he'd imagined it.

She bowed in response—prim, proper, and uninterested. "Good evening, Captain Frakenham."

A chilled frost was flame-hot compared to the icy air that hung about Miss Harriet Ward. Chase was glad he'd had the brandy to warm himself before attempting to dine with this particular little ice maiden. From what he'd heard, frostbite was a horrible experience and not one he'd really desired to experience.

Still, fortified by the brandy, he managed a smile. "I am sorry to keep you waiting. I must still be on London hours."

"London?" Harriet's smooth voice interjected. "I didn't know Captain Frakenham had ever been to London. Have you? If so, pray tell us all what you *remember*."

Everyone stared at him, silence abounding.

Chase almost winced at his mistake. Damn it! He would have to guard his tongue with Miss Harriet about. "I don't know if I've ever been to London. Perhaps I have, since I seem to know that expression." He met Harriet's gaze steadily. "Or isn't it a common expression?"

Mrs. Ward waved a hand. "Baron Whitfield says it all the time. Shall we retire to the dining hall? Stephen, you may escort me. Derrick, you may take Sophia and Ophelia. And Captain . . . why don't you escort Harriet?"

Chase was certain Miss Harriet would hate to be so importuned, so he immediately went to her side and proffered his arm.

She looked down at it as if it were a snake, and only at the last possible moment did she lay her hand on his arm. Even then, she maintained an unusual amount of space between them.

Chase led her around a small chair on the way to the door, lengthening their journey by four or five steps. The maneuver allowed Stephen and Derrick to escort their charges first, while Chase and Harriet followed. As soon as the others were out of sight, Chase drew to a halt.

Harriet frowned. "Just what do you think you are doing?"

"Waiting for the others to go ahead."

"They are ahead."

Indeed, no one remained in the room but Chase and Harriet. He decided that he rather liked that. "We will catch up to them in a second. I wanted to ask you something."

"What? Everyone will notice we aren't with them."

"I daresay. But by the time they've noticed, you'll have answered my question, and we'll be well on our way to joining them."

"I don't like this one—" She frowned, then suddenly leaned forward and sniffed. "Brandy. I should have known it."

"I'm a sailor. Brandy is mother's milk to me."

"You are not a sailor," she said loftily. "You are a captain. That's different."

"How?"

"Well you"—she gestured vaguely—"order people about."

"And?"

"And you sail the ship. But from the main . . . deck part. Whatever that is."

"Hm. Your grasp of the technical aspects of sailing is quite limited."

"And yours is better?"

Actually it was. The St. Johns owned a rather large

yacht, and Chase and Devon sailed it frequently. "I know starboard from port."

"So do I. Starboard is left and . . ." Her brow puckered. "No, wait. I think that's wrong. Starboard is right and—"

"Miss Ward, may I ask you a personal question?" The brandy he'd consumed earlier combined with the exhilarating effects of one Miss Harriet Ward was making him brave, a feeling he decided he quite liked. "It's a very personal question."

"I don't know—"

"If we don't hurry, the others will soon return."

She bit her lip and he could see her curiosity warring with her tendency toward prudence. Curiosity finally won and she sighed, then asked, "What?"

"Do you want children?"

He'd thought to startle her, to rattle her fine composure. And he'd been right. The abrupt question left her with stained cheeks and wide eyes.

"Wh—I—I never thought about—that is—" She snapped her mouth closed for a full minute while Chase watched. "Captain Frakenham, that is not a proper topic of conversation, even for an engaged couple."

"How can you say that? Who other than an engaged couple would discuss—"

She whirled and marched to the door and on to the dining room.

Chase followed along, noting with growing pleasure the fine, firm lines of her back and the curve of her rump through the thin material of her dress.

Oh yes, it was good to be a sea captain. Very good indeed.

Chapter 13

Love, the kind the poets dream of with starry eyes and pounding hearts, always seemed to me to be rather uncomfortable. Rather like the feeling one gets sitting too close to the fire.

The Countess of Greyley to her friend,
Miss Lily Treventhal
while riding in Hyde Park
one pleasant afternoon

Chase allowed Harriet to herd him into the dining hall. He supposed their tête-à-tête was over.

Mrs. Ward turned toward them with a relieved expression. "There you are! We were beginning to wonder if you'd gotten lost."

Chase smiled. "Hardly that. I stole a few moments with your charming daughter."

Mrs. Ward looked at Harriet and apparently read her own meaning into Harriet's flushed cheeks and thin-lipped expression. "Well!" Mrs. Ward said in a hurried voice. "We should eat. Captain Frakenham, you sit there. And Harriet will sit beside you."

"Excellent." Chase made a show of holding Harriet's seat, which seemed to delight her sisters.

Ophelia beamed approvingly, while Sophia sighed as if he'd done something quite romantic. Chase made sure to let his hands brush Harriet's very upright shoulders before he took his own place beside her.

She shot him a wary look, as if uncertain he'd touched her on purpose. Chase just smiled blandly back, though he wondered at the silken feel of her skin beneath his fingertips.

Almost immediately the first course was served and soon a pleasant babble of conversation broke over the table. Chase found himself relaxing as the meal progressed.

Normally, at a formal dinner, one conversed with the person to either one's left or right and never across the table or down it. The Wards, however, much like his own family, eschewed this rather rigid conventionality, at least in the comfort of their own home.

Which was a good thing because with Derrick sitting to one side, apparently deep in thought as his gaze never left his plate, and Harriet stiffly sitting on the other, Chase would have had no conversation at all.

As it was, Sophia and Ophelia made several attempts to pull him into a conversation, all of which he avoided with great skill. He began to realize that playing the part of a man with no memory made casual conversation a rather difficult chore.

Eventually, they ceased trying and turned their attention to Stephen, who sat at the head of the table, his posture a bit arrogant. Chase supposed the whipster had taken his father's place as was appropriate, much to the chagrin of his siblings.

Chase smiled to himself. There was a warmth to

the Wards that reminded him of his own family. He and his brothers and sister didn't see so much of one another any longer of course, since two of his brothers and his sister were married. But still, they'd had many a laugh over the dinner table growing up.

Sophia leaned across the table. "Captain Frakenham, do you know the waltz? I hear they are dancing it all over London."

Chase opened his mouth to respond, then caught sight of Harriet's dark brown eyes as they rested on him, watchful as ever.

He knew how to waltz. In fact, he loved the dance. But he made himself shrug. "I'm afraid I don't remember. But if it should come back to me, I would be delighted to teach you all, with your mother's approval."

She waved a hand. "If they're doing it in drawing rooms all over London, I'm certain it would be fine to attempt it at Garrett Park."

Sophia gave a happy bounce. "Oh! That would be lovely!"

"Captain Frakenham"—Ophelia leaned forward eagerly—"what about the Sir Roger? Do you know that dance as well?"

Harriet shifted in her chair. "Let the man eat. You may speak to him another time."

"Oh, let them ask me what they will," Chase said magnanimously. "I've nothing to hide." Just things he couldn't mention.

"Of course you have nothing to hide. And even if you did, you wouldn't remember it, anyway," she said with some asperity.

"That's true." He pursed his lips together. "I suppose it is possible that I committed some dire deed on my way here."

"How do you know you didn't commit a dire deed before that?"

"Because if I'd committed a sin prior to that, I'm sure you would never have made me welcome to begin with."

Harriet glanced sideways at him and said under her breath, "I'm not so certain we should make you welcome now."

He picked up his water glass and replied, "You are certainly cruel to someone whom you are supposedly in love with."

"Perhaps I accepted your hand for your wealth. We are certainly in need of it now."

Chase's lips twitched. Harriet Ward pulled no punches. He rather liked that. "Wealth? But I am a sea captain. Do sea captains *possess* that much money? And if so, where do they get it?"

"From their trade." Harriet used her fork to spear a bit of lettuce. "Captain Frakenham is a very wealthy man. We told the bank he was waiting on a payment from a shipment he'd made of Chinese silks."

"You told the bank?" Chase lifted his water glass to hide his smile. "Strange. You make it sound as if I didn't know about this supposed payment. Did you make it up?"

Her lips folded in apparent irritation. "You misunderstood me. We didn't make up anything at all. Captain Frakenham—you—are very well off."

She was so damned prim. His head wound must have muddled him worse than he thought, for he couldn't help but think of ways to shake her from her complacency. Ways involving his mouth on hers, his hands on her trim waist. His body reacted to the startlingly heated idea.

"You intrigue me, Miss Ward." He slid slightly to one side in his chair so that his knee grazed hers.

She jerked at the touch, nearly upsetting the gravy bowl. "Oh piffle!" she snapped. "Stop that, will you?"

"Harriet!" Mrs. Ward said, blinking in astonishment. "There's no need to be upset. You didn't spill a thing."

Harriet's cheeks turned scarlet. "Sorry," she mumbled, shooting a venomous gaze at Chase.

He returned the look innocently enough as he cut the mutton that had been set on his plate.

"Captain Frakenham," Stephen suddenly said, from where he sat down the table. "It's jolly good to have you back."

"Thank you." Chase eyed the boy curiously. Though Stephen had addressed one or two comments his way, he'd hardly been enthusiastic in his welcome.

Now, however, Stephen's smile was almost blinding. "I daresay you'll be glad to see the improvements in the barn since you were last here." His eyes twinkled. "You remember the *barn*, don't you?"

Chase frowned. "The barn?"

"Oh yes," Stephen said. "You've always liked the barn." He gave a significant look at Harriet. "Hasn't he?"

Chase glanced her way and caught the veriest hint of a grin. What was this? Captain Frakenham liked the barn? What were these two up to?

"I don't remember being partial to the barn . . . Of course, I don't remember much of anything. Did I spend much time there?"

"Oh yes," Stephen said. "Nearly every day."

Harriet nodded. "You were quite, quite fond of the barn. We couldn't keep you away from it."

"And the sheep," Derrick added smugly, looking up from his plate for the first time.

"All told, Captain, it's a good thing you're here," Stephen said cheerily, waving his fork in the air. "We could use your help with the shearing, especially since I hurt my leg."

Chase paused, his fork halfway to his mouth. "I beg your pardon. Did you say 'shearing'?"

Harriet nodded, her face wreathed in a smug smile. "Sheep. It's what we do here at Garrett Park, we raise sheep, shear them, and sell their wool. And now that you're here, you can help."

Chase wasn't entirely certain what shearing entailed, but it certainly sounded onerous. A hot, dirty task, he would assume. The Wards had to be mad to think he'd do such a thing—shear sheep indeed. It was one thing to pretend he was a sea captain, another to forget altogether who and what he was. And a St. John would never stoop to sheep shearing. Not this St. John, anyway.

Chase caught Stephen and Harriet exchanging a grin. They both looked as if they'd accomplished some fabulous trick. After a moment's thought, Chase's jaw tightened, and he reluctantly decided that they had indeed accomplished something quite unusual.

If the Wards said Captain Frakenham liked shearing sheep or digging ditches or wearing his cravat tied backwards, who was he to argue? He wasn't supposed to remember anything, blast it. He couldn't even defend himself. Well, he was pretending to be Captain Frakenham, wasn't he? Surely it wouldn't be too difficult to pretend to enjoy shearing sheep.

Still, such coercion deserved retribution. He set down his fork. Captain Frakenham might not have a memory, but he sure as hell had a brain.

And if there was one thing Chase had learned from his brothers and sister, it was that turnabout was fair play. "It's funny how I have no recollection of shearing, but I do seem to remember the barn. I *was* fond of it, wasn't I?"

Stephen seemed surprised at Chase's acquiescence, but nodded. "Very."

"I seem to be somewhat unclear on the details."

"Oh. Well, after dinner, I'll take you there so you can see it again."

Chase leaned toward Harriet and smiled down into her eyes. "I daresay *we* were fond of the barn, you and I."

Her eyes widened. "What?"

"I seem to remember . . . ." He stopped and pressed his fingers to his forehead. "I do remember . . . a woman. In the hay."

Stephen, who had begun to take a drink, choked loudly.

"Yes," Chase said. "The face is blurry. But everything else . . . ." He allowed his gaze to drop from Harriet's face down to her bosom. "Everything else fits perfectly."

"My goodness!" Mrs. Ward, her face bright red, hurriedly said, "Someone . . . please pass the butter!"

Sophia, eyes wide, never removed her gaze from Chase and Harriet, as she absently handed her mother the butter.

Harriet's mouth opened, then closed, then opened again. "How . . . I can't believe you . . . What do you mean—Don't!" She held up a hand when he opened his mouth as if to reply. "We will talk about this elsewhere."

"Elsewhere?" Ophelia leaned forward, her brow furrowed. "Why do you need to discuss it elsewhere? All he said was that he remembered the barn."

Sophia shook her head, her eyes sparkling with mischief. "Later, Oph. Not now."

Ophelia stiffened. "Do not call me that! My name is Ophelia, not Oph." She turned a resentful gaze on the captain. "I do not mean to complain, but I do wish my parents had spent a little more time considering the burden of having such a name. It was not at all considerate."

Mrs. Ward grabbed the turn of conversation, smiling brightly. "Dear, I've apologized for that at least a thousand times. It was your father's turn to name the baby, and you know he was sadly addicted to Shakespeare. He happened to be in the middle of reading *Hamlet* when you were born and there was simply no reasoning with him."

Stephen dusted his fingers with his napkin. "Just thank the stars he didn't name you Cleopatra."

"Or Puck," Derrick added around a mouthful of asparagus. "That would be worse."

Sophia curled her nose. "Ugh! Puck would be a horrid name. Ophelia, if you want another name, I suppose we *could* call you Puck."

"I like that!" Derrick said. "Pass the mutton, will you, Puck?"

"Just stop!" Ophelia snapped. "You are *all* horrid!" She turned to her oldest sister. "Harriet, please make them stop teasing."

All eyes turned to Harriet. Chase noted that even Mrs. Ward waited expectantly, as if it was not at all unusual that her eldest daughter was being called upon to solve a dispute rather than herself.

Harriet put down her fork, the tines clanging lightly against the edge of the china plate. Chase rather expected her to lambaste her brothers and sisters for their levity, delivering a homily on the necessities of civility. Certainly that is what Marcus would have done.

But instead, Harriet's lips quivered ever so slightly and she said, "Ophelia, as much as I would like to commiserate with you on the ignominy of having a literary name, I cannot. My own lamentably boring name prevents me from doing more than sigh with envy."

"There is nothing wrong with Harriet," Ophelia said, her plump chin firm. "I would rather be called Harriet than Ophelia."

"Yes, well—"

"And anything is better than Oph."

"Ophelia is your name, and it's all you have, so you had best learn to enjoy it."

Ophelia's gaze narrowed. "That's not possible. Not when everyone makes fun of it."

"I'm certain not everyone thinks it humorous. Why, just ask the captain. I daresay he's heard far more unusual names."

All eyes turned on Chase.

"Well?" Ophelia asked in a rather daunting tone.

"Well what?" he responded lightly, wondering what the chit expected from him.

"What do *you* think of the name Ophelia?" She spoke stiffly now, her chin high, as if she were taking a horrible risk and she knew it, but her pride would not allow else.

Good God, why had she asked him that? Chase picked up his glass and took a sip of water in a lame effort to gain some time. If he said what he thought—that the name was indeed ridiculous—he would be damned. And so would she. He could see it in her eyes.

But if he did more, flattered her that the name was as lovely as she herself was, then he was lying to her, and surely that was an ill choice, too.

Perhaps if he just ate, kept his mouth too full to talk, she'd look elsewhere for reassurance. He resolutely cut a large piece of asparagus into two pieces and stuffed one in his mouth.

Ophelia tossed up her chin, her eyes bright with mischief. "Captain Frakenham," she said loudly.

Chase paused, the second bite of asparagus already halfway to his mouth. There was no hope for it. He had the impression she'd wait for each and every bite.

He cast a regretful look at his fork and set it on his plate. "Yes, Miss Ophelia?"

"What do you think of my name?"

He pretended to ponder this. "It's very original."

"And?"

Bloody hell, what more does she want? He was not used to being questioned. And he definitely wasn't used to being taken to task for having an opinion.

Chase tossed his napkin onto the table. "I don't know what I think about your name! I suppose you're right and it's a rather sil—Oof!" He glared down at Harriet. "You kicked me."

"I did not," she said, her gaze not on him, but on Ophelia.

Ophelia's lips quivered uncertainly. "You think my name is sil—Were you going to say silly?"

Chase moved his foot carefully, hoping some feeling would return before morning. Couldn't anyone take a joke? "Of course I wasn't going to say that! What I said, was that I thought your name was rather *silky*, like good ah, silk."

"Silky?"

"Yes, sort of feminine and soft and . . . shimmery." His brow was damp with the effort, but he managed.

"Ophelia! That is the prettiest compliment!" Sophia gave an excited bounce. "That was *very* well done, Captain. In fact"—she shot a glance at Harriet from beneath her brows—"I think that's the prettiest thing anyone has ever said."

Harriet snorted. "That's what you said when one of the Ferrell twins likened your eyes to the stars, which was not very original, I might add, or very apt considering your eyes are blue and the stars are all yellow."

Sophia stiffened. "It was not one of the Ferrell twins, but Viscount Northrake's eldest son."

"Whoever it was, it was the poorest attempt at poetry I've ever heard."

Sophia's face turned red. "Oh! How can you say that? You have no appreciation for romance. None at all! Why when I think—" Sophia suddenly stopped, her gaze moving from Harriet to Chase. A sly smile crept across her lips.

Harriet recognized the signs immediately, alarm making her stiffen. "Sophia, don't—"

"Captain!" Sophia leaned across the table toward the man. "I daresay you don't remember this, but you and Harriet were quite fond of the barn. In fact," she said, seeming to grow braver by the moment, "we were forever finding the two of you in the hay. Just as you remember."

Harriet wished the ground beneath her would open up and swallow her whole, but it was not to be. The floor remained hideously firm, and all she could do was paste a smile on her lips and avoid looking at the captain.

She was certain the fool would be grinning, and she simply could not face such mockery. Harriet cast a wild glance at her siblings, seeking assistance, but none was to be had. Stephen was far too busy holding back a huge grin, while Derrick shoved a roll into his mouth to stifle a guffaw. Sophia was pretending to have something in her eye, so she was turned away, but her shoulders were shaking with laughter.

Only Ophelia wasn't laughing . . . she was frowning, her head tilted to one side. "I dislike the barn myself. Too smelly by far."

Derrick swallowed his roll. "Depends on how distracted you are when you're there."

"Distracted? By what? We've only two horses now. The rest of the place is empty."

Stephen choked. "I ah, think that was the point."

Ophelia's brows lowered. "The point? How can an empty barn be any different than one that is in use—Ohhhhhh!" Her expression cleared even as her cheeks pinkened. She looked in awe at Harriet. "Oh my!"

"For the love of—" Harriet began, only to catch "Captain John's" gaze. His blue eyes gleamed with amusement, his lips curved in a faint, challenging smile. Harriet's jaw tightened. He was enjoying her embarrassment, the wretch. She sent him a quelling glare.

Normally, her quelling glares served their purpose and could silence an unruly sibling in seconds. But somehow, they seemed to have no effect on overly handsome men with large bruises on their foreheads.

"Harriet," Mother said, her soft voice distressed.

"Yes?"

"Would you ... could you ... please pass me the butter."

"It's right in front of you."

"Oh! So it is. Well, then. I shall need some more bread."

Harriet reached for the bowl, unaware that the captain was doing the same thing. To Harriet's shock, his fingers brushed hers, lingering a moment.

She sent him a startled look, then noticed he wasn't looking at her, but at her hand. She followed his gaze and realized that he was looking at the ring.

Oh piffle! She pulled her hand back so quickly that the bowl tilted and dropped to the table, the contents tumbling to the wooden surface.

"Goodness, Harriet," Sophia said, reaching over and collecting the bread and replacing it in the bowl. "What's wrong with you? I've never seen you so nervy."

Harriet picked up a roll and handed it to Sophia.

"Thank you, I—what's that?" Sophia's gaze was on Harriet's hand.

Harriet quickly tucked her hand into her lap, but it was too late.

Ophelia leaned forward. "I want to see it again!"

"No, no. It's nothing," Harriet said quickly, tugging on the ring under the table and praying it would come off.

Mother frowned. "Where did you get that ring? It looked quite ancient."

"I gave it to her," came a deep voice at Harriet's side.

Harriet sent a startled glance at the captain.

He glinted a smile down at her, telling her without words that she would owe him for this little favor. "It was found near my things in the forest and I asked her to wear it for safekeeping."

There was silence as everyone digested this, then Mother said brightly, "Oh, well then! That's very nice of Harri to take such good care of your things."

Stephen, apparently feeling sorry for his sister, took the opportunity to engage Derrick in an argument about who had worked the hardest on the fence in the east pasture.

To Harriet's relief the rest of the meal passed in relative calm, except that she was uncomfortably aware of the man sitting next to her.

It was strange, the way she could almost feel the presence of the man beside her, even when she wasn't looking at him. And if she closed her eyes, she could feel his lips on hers. She considered that. Why did he affect her so? Perhaps it was because she didn't have a lot of experience with such things.

Yes, that must be it. Whoever Captain Frakenham really was, he was definitely a man of the world. His touch was magical, igniting feelings she'd never had, but so would the touch of any man with so much worldly experience.

Dinner finally ended and Stephen stood. "Captain Frakenham, would you like to join me in the library for a touch of brandy?"

The captain stood almost immediately. "Of course. I hope, too, that you might provide me with a tour of the barn since I'm held to be so fond of it."

"We shall do so first thing in the morning. I'm certain Harriet will be glad to accommodate you."

Harriet sent her brother a flat stare, but he was too busy playing lord of the manor to notice.

The captain took her hand and pressed a kiss to it, right where the ring rested. His gaze lingered on the ring before he released Harriet's hand. "I look forward to touring the barn, Miss Ward. I'm certain it will open all sorts of interesting memories."

Harriet's finger tingled warmly as she looked up into "the captain's" blue eyes. It was strange, but she'd never before noticed how very long his lashes were. They swept down at the corners and tangled a bit. A slow shiver went through her.

"Come, Captain. You may ogle Harriet tomorrow while we're gathering the sheep." Stephen grinned and then retrieved his crutches.

The captain released Harriet's hand. "Good evening, Miss Ward." He bowed to the other women at the table. "Mrs. Ward. Miss Sophia. Miss Ophelia."

The second the door closed behind him, Sophia slumped in her chair. "Harriet! What a delightful man! You are so lucky. Mother, are you certain we cannot pretend that I am the one Captain Frakenham is engaged to—"

"Sophia, if you suggest that one more time, I will

have you clean every rug in the house." Mrs. Ward stood, her face pink-tinged. "Harriet, when this all came about, I had not thought—that is to say, I hope you do not allow the captain to take advantage of you in any way."

"Mother!" Harriet frowned. "I am not a green girl of sixteen. I can handle Captain Frakenham."

Mother didn't look too certain. "I hope so. He seems dreadfully decisive. But it's only two weeks. And then he'll be gone."

For some reason, the words did nothing to calm Harriet's riotous heart. Two weeks was not that long a time. But then again . . . Catching her mother's anxious gaze, she managed a fairly firm smile. "Two weeks. And then we'll be free of him *and* the bank."

Chapter 14

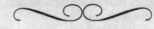

It is not that I do not know how to manage my money. It's that my money does not know how to manage me.

Miss Lily Treventhal to her brother,
Viscount Rose, while trying to explain why
her accounts did not balance—yet again

Harry Annesley turned, the gentle breeze ruffling his cloak and stirring the fetid scents that wafted down the street. "I beg your pardon?"

The man facing him wrung his felt hat even harder, his thin hands trembling. "Sorry to bother ye, guv'nor, but can ye spare a pence fer a bloke as is down on his luck?"

Harry stared at the man, noting the grime and filth that crusted his collar, chilblains marring red and gnarled hands. Harry pulled his own sumptuous cloak about him, careful that the edges didn't flutter out and touch any part of the filthy steps upon which he stood. "What I have, I've made myself, and I'll be damned if I'll share it with the likes of you—"

He stopped, aware that a faint hint of his former accent was creeping into his voice, into his mind.

Damn it, he was no longer a member of the swill that lived in the East Side. Not any more.

Harry directed his irritation at the contemptible stick of humanity that stood before him. "Be gone. I have nothing to give you."

The man's eyes blazed. He darted a quick look at the coach that sat across the street, then spat. "Full o' yerself, ain't ye? Yer pretty little coachman ain't close enough to help ye if oiye decides to take what oiye wants."

Harry's thin hold on civility cracked, slipped, shattered to the ground. He grabbed the man by the throat and hauled him forward, a dangerously thin knife appearing from the depths of his cloak. "See this 'ere pike?" Harry snarled. "One more word outta ye, and oiye'll split yer gullet here 'n' now."

The man's eyes seemed in imminent danger of popping out of his head. "Th—there's no need to get wisty, guv'nor! Oiye didn't mean nothin'—"

Harry shoved the man from him. The would-be thief stumbled backwards, then fell. He quickly regained his footing and skittered off, disappearing down an alleyway after one last frightened look. Harry secreted his knife back in an inner pocket. It would take three baths just to get the stench of this place from his nose.

He hated coming to this part of town, but there were resources here that no one could fathom. Resources he needed.

For the last week, he had been noising it about town that Chase St. John had given him a promissory note, then disappeared—a shocking breach of honor. Soon, Chase's name-conscious brothers would rush in and offer to pay the forged note just to silence Harry's assault on the beloved family

name. The problem was that they were being ridiculously stiff-necked about the whole thing. And each
day that passed, Harry feared something might go
amiss.

He desperately needed the assurance that Chase
St. John would not come sauntering back into town
and ruin all. Once the St. Johns paid the note, their
pride would keep them silent about his trickery. No
St. John would publicly admit to being bested. But if
Harry was caught beforehand and Chase was present to denounce the forgery . . . Harry decided not
to think about that unpleasant scenario. He simply
would not allow that to happen. This money was the
key to all of his problems; it would set his future and
establish the Annesley name.

At this very moment across town, in a pink-and-
green-papered sitting room within one of Mayfair's
largest residences, sat Miss Letitia Johnson-Smythe.
Cousin to an earl, her father had amassed a fortune
in shipping, which left Miss Johnson-Smythe with
that rare combination of good breeding and money.
Shy, quiet, and painfully plain, she suited Harry's
purpose perfectly.

He had been slyly working his magic on her, attending every event at which she was present, whispering in her ear about her beautiful eyes, writing
secret love notes to her, and bribing her maid to allow him to meet them in the park. He was beginning
to see some signs that she was smitten. With some
funds in the bank to prove to Papa that he was not a
fortune hunter, and with Letitia's own bleating to be
allowed to be with her Dearest Harry, the future was
looking bright indeed.

The only hurdle thus far had been with Chase's
brothers. They seemed to believe that their beloved

brother would turn up at any moment. That was a false hope that already should have been dashed to the ground since Chase had said that, the moment he reached his destination, he would send his brothers word that he was never returning.

Harry was somewhat perplexed. He'd been carefully watching the St. John establishments, and there had been no flurry of visits, no long, serious talks as were wont to happen in a family emergency. Every time Harry met with one of the St. Johns, he looked for signs of distress or disturbance, but none was forthcoming.

It was most vexing.

Which was why he was here today. In Harry's estimation, fate was never fair—she smiled on those who had already possessed her and remained elusively out of touch for those who desired her more than life itself. He picked his way down the street to a dingy pub, glanced around, then entered.

Five minutes later, his pockets much lighter, he emerged and made his way to his carriage, satisfied that he'd given fate the nudge she needed.

It hadn't been all that difficult, really. Harry had simply greased a few palms and information had come tumbling out. St. John never traveled without a change of horses, so it had been simple to discover which roads he'd taken. And it had been equally easy to see if St. John had yet left the country—he hadn't. The private cabin that had been reserved in his name had been empty when the vessel had set sail.

Which meant that Chase St. John was somewhere in England, perhaps close to London. And that was not a good situation for Harry at all.

And so here Harry was . . . in a part of town he deplored, hiring a man he detested, to do a job that he wished didn't have to be done.

He hadn't made any suggestions as to how the deed was to be accomplished. He had no desire for the dirty details. Let other, less sophisticated men deal with that sort of thing. All he'd asked was that Chase St. John not return to London anytime in the near future. Or ever, if need be.

The coachman opened the door and stood aside. Harry climbed inside and nodded. The door was closed and within seconds, they were rumbling down the narrow, squalid street, toward the bridge where fresh air and genteel amusements awaited.

Harry settled back in the corner of his coach, smoothing a hand over the velvet seat, breathing deeply of the scent of waxed wood and polished brass.

The fetid stench of the street where he'd been born faded with each cleansing breath.

"Time to rise, Captain!"

Stephen's jovial voice rang hollow in Chase's ear, dispersing a lovely dream wherein the intractable Miss Harriet Ward was being neither prim nor proper, but had somehow turned into a lush siren with a wealth of rich brown hair and the supple body of a dancer.

"C'mon, Captain! We've work to do."

Chase reluctantly opened one eye. Bloody hell, it wasn't even dawn. And what did Stephen mean about "work"?

There was no way Chase was getting up. Not at this ungodly hour of the morn. He rolled over and pulled the covers over his head.

But Stephen was a Ward, and unfortunately that

horrid name seemed to indicate a preponderance of stubbornness. Within what seemed like seconds, Chase's blankets were yanked away and a candle rudely thrust into his line of vision.

"Captain," Stephen said cheerily, "whatever is wrong? Not ill, are you? Come, the sheep awake."

Chase snatched his blankets back. "I will come and tour the barn after I've had some sleep."

Stephen yanked Chase's pillow from beneath his head and tossed it into a chair by the window. "This is no tour, but work. You're to help with the sheep today, remember?"

Chase threw an arm over his head. Had he really promised such a thing?

"So up! You've had some sleep. A good nine hours of it by my reckoning."

Chase blearily opened one eye. *Nine hours, hell*, he thought. *More like nine minutes*. After he and Stephen had shared a very small glass of brandy in the library, the time had come for the household to retire. As he would have expected, the Wards went to bed at a ridiculously early hour—a time of night when Chase would normally just be getting ready to partake of a bit of dinner.

So it was that while the household slept, he was wide-awake. As soon as he was certain everyone was asleep, Chase slipped downstairs and into the library, in search of more brandy. He found it at once, sitting in regal splendor on a tray on the library desk.

He hadn't hesitated, but had found a glass and opened the decanter. There he'd been, stopper in one hand, a glass in the other, when for some unknown reason, he'd suddenly imagined Harriet

Ward's expression if she were to see him at that very moment.

"I am only going to have one glass," he'd muttered to the apparition.

She had not appeared the least impressed.

"It won't hurt anyone."

She'd raised her brows as if to remind him of all the damage that drinking had already done in his life. And drinking had caused irreparable harm. It had cost him his dignity, his honor, his pride . . . and now, his family.

Chase had looked down at the decanter, the liquid gleaming warmly. Then, with a sigh, he'd replaced the stopper and returned the glass to the tray.

Perhaps another night. Of course, that had left him wide-awake and with no amusement at hand. Chase had been forced to do something he rarely did—read. He decided that it was an embarrassment to the Ward family that one of their guests was so importuned, but there was nothing Chase could do about it. If reading was the only amusement available, then he'd see what books were at hand.

After an aimless search, he chanced upon a tome describing the sailing ventures of a questionable gentleman in the late sixteenth century. While Chase was of the opinion great quantities of the story were fabricated, he thought some of the tale might come in handy in his rendition of Captain Frakenham. Thus the candle was low before he managed to sleep.

"Rise, slugabed!" Stephen said, reminding Chase that late night or no, he was going to have to get up.

Chase opened his eyes to find Stephen grinning above him. "Blast you to hell."

Stephen's grin widened.

Chase sighed and sat up, pushing the hair from his forehead. He hadn't seen this side of the morning in years. Oh, he'd been *awake* at the crack of dawn. But he'd never been *awoken* at the crack of dawn. "All right, all right. I'm up."

"Excellent!" Stephen paused by the nightstand to light the candle with his own. "I shall await you in the breakfast room."

"Excellent!" Chase muttered in a mocking tone, as Stephen closed the door. Good God, who in their right minds would choose to get up at this hour?

Chase sighed and stretched, then climbed out of bed, shivering a little in the predawn chill. Rubbing his arms, he crossed to the washstand to splash water on his face.

Why couldn't he have been saved by a family of lazy gypsies? Or some worthless ne'er-do-well drinkers? Anyone who might understand the importance of morning sleep.

But no. Chase had to be kidnapped by a family of sheep farmers who took great delight in torturing him with their healthy, fresh ways. It was sickening.

He made his way to the wardrobe and found his clothes, dressing in the semidark. His fingers seemed to still be asleep, and he fumbled with his cravat. Finally, too tired to care, he just knotted the blasted thing à la Belcher, a ridiculous fashion aspired to by the younger dandy set. Thank God he was buried in the country and no one he knew would see him.

Mumbling to himself, he made his way downstairs where he could hear the family gathered in the dining room, talking with a great deal too much vivacity for so ungodly a time of the morning.

He pushed open the door and was immediately assailed with the rich smells of a large breakfast. Situated on the large sideboard were platters of eggs, ham, bacon, pheasant, and toast. He blinked at the abundance of it, then turned to find himself looking down at Harriet.

She was dressed in an old gown of faded blue cotton, the skirts a little shorter than was accepted so that the ankles of her boots plainly showed. Chase realized with a faint sense of astonishment that the plain gown she'd worn the previous day must have been one of her best.

"Good morning," she said pleasantly.

Chase found his tired lips curving into a smile. She appeared fresh and bright, her brown hair braided and pinned about her head. She smiled, her teeth flashing white and even.

"I hate to complain," he said with a sigh, "but must you be so awake?"

"What else would I be at this time of the day?"

He glanced over her shoulder at the still-gray dawn that was just rising. "Day?"

Her lips quivered. "Morning, then." Her gaze drifted to his hair. "I see you had to comb your hair in the dark."

"I don't like your hair, either," he retorted easily. He didn't. The too-plain style was far too severe for her face, which seemed all angles and eyes in the dim light.

A faint color brushed her cheeks as she touched her braids, then caught herself. "A pity, that, because the sheep like my braids and I'm much more concerned with how they feel about it than you."

Sophia stood at the sideboard, a plate in her hand. "Harriet, don't monopolize the conversation! Captain, what will you have? Some eggs? A pheasant? How about some ham? Baron Whitfield brought it to us just last week and it's quite delicious."

"No, thank you." Chase didn't think he could face such a magnitude of food so early in the morning. "Perhaps later, at ten or so when I'm more awake."

"There won't be any food left by then," Harriet said matter-of-factly. "You'll eat now or you won't eat at all. We can't afford to serve breakfast three times a day."

"Better eat now," Ophelia said cheerily.

"I would eat a lot if I were you," Stephen said with unimpaired calm from where he sat, digging into a plate piled high with eggs and ham. "You won't get another chance until noon or perhaps later. And trust me, you'll be ravenous enough as it is."

Chase curled his lip. "I'll wait. I cannot stand to eat at this time of the day."

Mrs. Ward tsked. "Stephen, please keep an eye on the captain. I don't want him getting ill or over-heated. The doctor would not be pleased if his patient was to suffer a relapse at our hands."

Derrick lifted his gaze from the book he had opened beside his plate. "What about me? You never tell Stephen to see to it that I don't get overheated."

Mrs. Ward patted Derrick's hand. "If you'd just risen from the sickbed with a knot on your head, I would indeed say the same thing of you."

"I doubt it," Derrick mumbled, looking as apathetic about the whole venture as Chase felt. "I wish I could stay inside today. I am halfway through the *Iliad*."

Chase poured himself a cup of tea, strong and almost black, steam curling from the cup and into the air. He glanced resentfully at the unlit fireplace that graced the room. Surely the Wards could afford some firewood or a little coal.

But apparently not. Perhaps his blood was thin; certainly none of them seemed affected by the chill morning air.

He pulled a chair from the table and turned it sideways so he would be facing the only empty seat . . . the one Harriet would have to take.

B'God, he'd get some amusement of this day, even if it killed him. The family wanted to pretend he was Harriet's beau, and play it, he would.

She came to take her seat, pausing when she saw him, her eyes narrowing suspiciously. "What are you doing?"

"Drinking my tea and waiting for you."

"That is very romantic," Sophia informed Ophelia with a great deal of satisfaction.

Harriet didn't move, her plate clasped in her hands, steam drifting from her eggs and ham. "I don't want you there."

"Where else am I to sit? It's the only empty chair."

"You plan on staring at me while I'm eating, don't you?"

Despite the early hour, a smile tickled his lips. There was something delightfully refreshing about this woman. "Yes, I do. I plan on watching you eat every single morsel. I shall even comment upon the amount you are able to consume and wonder aloud how you stay so trim."

Stephen chuckled. "I say, Captain, you're in good spirits this morning!"

"Only because Harriet is to sit with me at breakfast."

Harriet turned toward the wide door leading outside. "I believe I'll eat on the terrace."

"You can't do that!" Mrs. Ward said, blinking. "It's too dark and far too damp."

Chase stood and took Harriet's plate and set it on the table at her chair. "I promise to look away now and again. And I'll have to get more tea eventually. You could possibly poke in a few bites at that time."

Her chin firmed.

"Harri, sit down," Stephen said. "The captain is just being attentive."

She sniffed and took her chair, almost flouncing into place. "I don't like attentive men."

Chase raised his brows. "You'd wish me to be *in*attentive? How very, very odd. Most females would argue against such treatment."

Her gaze fixed on him with cool triumph. "Really? How can you remember how most women would react to anything? You've no memory."

He curled his fingers about his cup, letting the warmth travel through him. "I know it the same way I know how to put on my boots or whether or not I like eggs. Some things just seem to come to me while others remain blank."

Mrs. Ward nodded. "It was the same way with my friend, Mrs. Billingsworth. Couldn't remember that she had a sister, but knew word for word her recipe for calf's-foot jelly."

Harriet grimaced. "Mother, pray do not keep bringing up Mrs. Billingsworth. I'm certain her case was nothing like the captain's."

Harriet scooted in her chair a bit so that she faced away from Chase, then she picked up her fork and attacked her breakfast with an inordinate amount of relish. Chase was left smiling at her back, which was fine really. Her thin dress outlined her figure perfectly, drawing his eye to her narrow waist and rounded bottom.

Chase barely had time to enjoy her proximity for a moment later, the door opened and the housekeeper appeared. "A letter for you, Mr. Stephen."

Stephen straightened, took the letter and glanced at it, his eyes suddenly ablaze. He unfolded a small, delicately colored note and began to read.

"I wonder who it could be from?" Sophia said to Ophelia, both of them staring at the note.

"I wager I know," Ophelia answered. She buttered her toast, a smirk on her lips. "I wager it's from Miss Str—"

"Hush, you two," Harriet said, frowning at Stephen.

His expression had undergone a change. Within one moment, he went from excited to crestfallen, refolding the note with hands that trembled just the slightest bit. Chase watched, wondering what was happening.

Stephen crumpled the note in his hand and stood, his face set and pale. "We had best get to work."

"As soon as you finish your breakfast," Harriet said calmly. She eyed him as she cut her ham. "But first, there is one thing we must see to. The captain's clothing is far too fine for the fields."

Stephen rubbed a hand over his brow, then abruptly sat. "Yes, yes. I can lend him some of mine." His gaze flickered over Chase. "We're of the same height."

"How nice of you, Stephen." Sophia took a sip of her tea. "He'll need boots, too."

Chase stretched his feet before him, his boots so shiny that he could see his own expression. "What's wrong with these?"

"Nothing," Sophia said. "It's just that they might get dirty."

"And scratched," Derrick offered from the depths of his books.

"Among other things." Harriet held out her own feet. She wore half boots of an indiscriminate brown that had seen far more than their fair share of wear.

Chase wrinkled his nose. "Those aren't fit to wear."

"Neither will yours be if you try to stomp through the fields with them. They weren't made for such wear. But never fear, we'll get you booted and suited for the sheep."

For some reason, Chase found her words less than reassuring. He was right. Within ten minutes of breakfast's being over, Chase found himself standing beside an old farm cart where two farmhands of dubious age and ability sat snoozing. They were dressed in faded and worn clothing, much like the ones Stephen had given to Chase.

He looked down at his own clothes. He suspected that the shirt at one time had been blue but was now a murky gray. The pants were dyed an indiscriminate black and were a trifle short. Worst of all were the boots. Though of leather, they were so worn and old that they sagged about his ankles in a preposterous manner.

He grimaced.

How had he gotten himself into this mess? Had he known that helping the Wards would mean such a total loss of his self-respect, he would never have volunteered to stay and pretend to be Captain Frakenham. But it was too late now. Though Harriet might wish to pretend otherwise, it was obvious that things were desperate.

He sighed and rubbed his neck. They were waiting on Stephen and Harriet, who had disappeared into the barn. Chase spent a few moments with his horse before coming out to the wagon. The black gelding was in fine fettle, but badly needed to stretch his legs. Perhaps this evening, before the sun set, Chase would take the animal for a quick gallop.

A ponderous bark filled the air. Chase turned to see a huge dog lumbering across the yard in his direction. The dog . . . it was the same one that had saved him in the forest. Chase took a step forward; the dog saw him at the same time and came bounding across the yard.

Chase was over six feet tall and no lightweight. But neither was the dog, who had the favor of momentum on his side. Chase landed on his rump, a wet tongue laving his mouth and chin, while two huge paws pressed down his chest and made it difficult to breathe. With a joint cry, Sophia and Ophelia came to his rescue, struggling to remove the dog who took their efforts as encouragement and licked Chase's face all the more furiously.

For an instant, Chase knew what it was to die of both compression and drowning. Derrick was finally roused enough to put down his book, climb off the wagon, grab the dog by his collar and pull him off Chase.

Chase wiped his wet face on his sleeve and rolled to his feet. "What the hell is *that*?" he asked, eyeing the horse-dog and trying to swallow his irritation.

"We don't know exactly," Ophelia said, pushing

her spectacles back on the bridge of her nose. "But he does well with the sheep."

"Max is an excellent sheepherder," Sophia agreed. She waited until Derrick had pulled the dog into the back of the wagon before she removed a huge straw hat from behind the seat and handed it to Chase. "You'll need this since we're to be in the sun today."

He took one look at the fanciful ribbons and faded silk flowers that decorated the brim and handed it back. "No thank you."

"You'll sunburn."

"There are flowers on it."

"That's because it's Harriet's. Stephen doesn't have an extra hat, but Harriet said you could wear hers."

Somehow, Chase did not doubt that one bit. "I am not wearing this hat."

"Oh, no one will see. Just us. Besides, I just added the sprig of forget-me-nots last week. Do you know how long it took to get those on there?"

Chase ground his teeth. He would not be caught dead in that blasted hat, come rain or snow. "I'm certain it must be too small for my head."

Ophelia shook her head, adjusting the ribbons of her own straw hat under her chin, then climbing into the back of the cart and making herself comfortable in the straw. She and Sophia were going to pick berries while the others gathered the sheep. "Harriet's hats are all large because she always wears braids. I daresay it will fit you perfectly."

Chase sighed, glancing at the sun barely showing on the horizon. It was difficult to imagine that it would be warm, but Sophia was probably right.

Sighing, he slapped the hat on his head, turned, and found Harriet's gaze from across the yard. She was standing beside a solemn-faced Stephen, her hands resting on her hips. Even from here, he could tell that her eyes were alight with laughter.

It took him a moment to realize the truth; she was laughing at *him*.

"Damn it!" He yanked the hat off his head and threw it into the back of the cart, then climbed in himself and took his place on the seat beside Derrick, who was still buried in his book.

Bloody hell, look at how far he'd sunk. But perhaps it was fate's way of mocking him as well. Hadn't he violated the St. John honor with his reckless behavior? Hadn't he humiliated his family name? Perhaps this was retribution of some sort.

He straightened his shoulders. Whatever life had in store for him, he'd face it. No more hiding. No more trying to drown his troubles. He was a St. John and no matter the circumstances, it was time he remembered it.

His gaze roamed over the yard until he found Harriet. She placed her hand on her brother's arm and spoke earnestly. Stephen must have disagreed with what she had to say, for he shook his head violently and, when she continued to speak, finally pulled away, turned, and then went into the barn as fast as his crutches would allow. Harriet watched him go, a strangely hollow look to her face.

Chase promptly forgot his own troubles. "What's wrong with Stephen?" he asked Sophia.

"He's in love."

Ophelia nodded. "With Miss Strickton. But she won't have anything to do with him."

"He's young," Chase said. "He'll get over it."

"I don't know about that," Sophia said, tilting her head to one side. "He's loved her for a long time. Since he was seven."

"Seven?"

Ophelia nodded. "And she's always been fond of him. Until this year, of course. Her father took her to London for the season and I think it quite turned her head."

Harriet joined them, her expression closed. Chase wanted to say something to ease her mind. But he couldn't seem to find the words. What right did he have to offer comfort, anyway? She was surrounded by her family, her loved ones, all of whom looked up to her and admired her. What could he offer that she didn't already have?

The thought left him feeling alone and out of place. He forced himself to swallow the words of support he'd thought to utter. Instead, he turned away, unaware that as he did so, Harriet's gaze followed him, her expression growing even sadder.

"Time to get to work," Harriet said. "Stephen will stay here and assist Mother." She climbed into the back of the wagon and made a seat on a barrel. "Jem, we're ready."

"Yes, Miss Ward." The older of the two farmhands untied the reins. Soon they were jouncing along, the wheels squeaking down the rutted path.

Chapter 15

If I could have one wish, it would be to become fantastically wealthy. If I could have two wishes, it would be to become fantastically wealthy and stay that way.

Viscount Rose to Mr. Giles Standish
as the two glumly watch Viscount Rose's
prize bays go up for auction
in a last-ditch attempt to settle his debts

Sheep, Chase decided on the third day of his incarceration (for he refused to think of it as else), were not the mild-mannered animals one might have been led to believe from nursery-rhyme lore.

Oh no. Despite their large brown eyes and soft woolen exteriors, they were imminently capable of capricious behavior that could only be described as malicious, malevolent, and mean.

Something as simple as herding the stupid creatures from one field into the next was tantamount to climbing the icy summits of Mt. Olympus and fighting off an army of Cyclopses while wearing a tattered loincloth and carrying no weapons other than a rock and a very small slingshot.

He'd been working with the Wards and their two

hired helpers for three whole, endless days, each one longer than the previous. And now, on the dawn of the fourth day, he could barely move, his entire body was a mass of bruises, aches, sunburn, and blisters.

The sad thing was that the shearing hadn't even begun. All they had done so far was move the sheep to the field beside the barn and repair some fencing along the way.

Of course, that had taken plenty of time, energy, and fortitude since the sheep seemed determined to thwart them every step of the way. They attempted to break free at the first sign of weakness, the largest rams taking every opportunity to run down any unsuspecting worker who might make the error of turning his back. Sheep were vicious, vindictive creatures and Chase had the lumps and bruises to prove it.

He leaned against the wagon, watching the sun rise over the gentle hills. To his surprise, he found he rather liked this time of day—the hour after dawn when everything looked clean and fresh, a covering of creamy dew gilding the grass and trees. He lifted his head and took a deep breath of fresh air, feeling some of the tension leave his shoulders. It was so easy to lose oneself in London. But here, everything seemed . . . easier. Simpler.

"Captain?" Stephen's voice intruded.

Chase straightened, then groaned.

Stephen quirked a brow. "Does your back hurt?"

"My entire body hurts. Even my hair."

Stephen managed a faint smile. "Could you and Jem get the new gate built today?"

Chase looked at the boy, noting the circles beneath his eyes. Gone was the cheery voice that had awoken

Chase on the first day. Stephen had barely smiled since then. "I'm sure Jem and I can build the gate."

"Good. Derrick and I will go with Harriet to see to the gap we found in the fence in the south pasture. The others are going to clean out the barn."

"Work, work, work."

"It's not usually like this. Once the shearing is done, things will settle back to normal."

"Will we have to get up at dawn?"

"No."

Chase would have never thought just lying in bed was something to be savored. But that had been before he'd become Captain Frakenham, or, as Chase was beginning to think of himself, The Poor Bastard. "I can't wait."

Stephen nodded, then went off to consult with Jem about the quantity of nails available.

Chase flexed his shoulders, looking about for Harriet. She hadn't appeared yet, which was unusual.

Every morning began the same—he was rudely awakened before dawn, followed by a hurried dressing in the dark in clothing best not thought about, then on to a hideously large and boisterous breakfast, something Chase had learned was vitally important unless he wished to expire of hunger before lunch was served.

If you could call it luncheon. Where breakfast was a multiplattered affair, lunch was hard bread, cheese, some apples or pickles, and all the water Chase could want.

"Water," Chase scoffed to no one in particular. It had been three days since he'd had anything worthy to eat or drink after the ungodly hour of six in the morning. Three entire, endless, painful days.

Had he any sense, he would pretend suddenly to remember who he was, pack his bags, and leave. But to do so would be to leave the Wards, and especially Harriet, to Gower's mercy.

Chase scowled at the thought. He didn't trust the banker any farther than he could throw him. The jackass rode up every day or so just to rankle the family, and Chase was fairly certain that though the man pretended otherwise, he didn't always come on bank business. Indeed, there was something very personal about the way he looked at Harriet.

Chase stirred restlessly, wincing when his shoulders protested. Apparently Captain Frakenham was not made for building fences and fighting rambunctious rams. From the very beginning, he should have loftily informed the Wards that sea captains never herded sheep. Never wrestled with sheep. And never, ever ended up with sheep excrement on their boots.

Several times, he thought of saying just that. But seeing Harriet dressed in her old gowns, her hair falling out of her braids as she dragged split rails from the back of the wagon, carried buckets of water out to him and Derrick and the other farm hands, or any of the other hundreds of chores that she performed, made him hesitate. She was working her heart out and so, for some reason, he found he could do no less.

Harriet and her family were remarkable and he found his ragged heart responding to their valiant fight. As if, in seeing them triumph over their troubles, he would somehow find the strength to triumph over his own. He'd never before witnessed a family quite like the Wards. Never met anyone quite like Harriet.

He glanced around the barnyard. "Where is Harriet?" For the first time since he'd been at Garrett Park, she had missed breakfast.

Derrick looked up from where he sat in the cart seat, a book in his lap. He blinked mildly. "I saw her in the hallway not ten minutes ago. She said something about getting the food from Cook."

And she would appear at any moment, carrying a basket that weighed as much as she. Chase turned and walked toward the house.

He went first to the kitchen, but Cook was busy adding the last few items to the basket. She hadn't seen Harriet yet.

Chase found that disturbing, but what could he do? He turned to go back outside, but then paused at the foot of the steps.

Some imp of madness tickled his fancy and he found himself looking up the steps at the doors that lined the landing. Hmm. Which bedchamber was it?

Moments later, he was walking down the hallway, when he spied her through an open doorway. She was standing in front of her bed, one foot in her boot as she hopped around, trying to get it over her ankle. She was completely dressed, though there was some sign that she'd braided her hair in far too much of a hurry.

Chase leaned against the doorframe, watching her with some amusement.

She stopped hopping around, the boot only half on her foot. "What do you want?"

"I came to see if you needed any assistance."

"Putting on my boots?" she scoffed. "I believe I can manage."

Chase grinned. "You weren't at breakfast."

Her cheeks blossomed with color. "I fell back asleep."

"So did I, but Stephen was not about to allow me the luxury of actually enjoying it. You'd better get yourself something to eat, or you'll be starved."

"I'll eat some bread and cheese on the way to the field." She plopped on the edge of her bed and grabbed the boot and began tugging. "I don't know why this won't go on."

"Let me help." Chase moved toward the bed, but something sparkling in the open wardrobe made him pause. "What's that?" He walked to it and pushed the door farther open. On the bottom shelf sat a pair of shoes. And not just any shoes, but lovely beaded silver satin ballroom slippers. He picked one up and looked at Harriet.

She tossed the boot on the floor and crossed to his side. "They're from my father. He gave them to me on my seventeenth birthday." She traced a finger down the shoe, lingering on the beads. There was a wistful gleam to her eyes, a sadness, too.

Chase turned the small shoe over in his hand. "It's never been worn."

She shrugged and turned away, her expression shuttered. "Where would I wear that?" Her fingers brushed her skirts. "And with what? Father was not a practical man. Just a dreamer."

"Dreaming is important."

"Not when it prevents you from dealing with reality," she retorted, sitting back on the edge of the bed and picking up her boot. "He always wanted the good life. So he pretended. And now, we're all paying for it."

Chase looked down at the slipper, wondering how many years it had rested in the bottom of the wardrobe. He looked at the shelf, then collected the mate. "Here. Put these on."

She paused. "What?"

Chase came to stand in front of her. "Put these on. I want to see you wear them."

"Why?"

"Maybe because you never have."

She set the boot back on the floor. "I've worn them once or twice."

He looked at the perfect, unscuffed soles. "Where? In here?"

She nodded.

Chase shook his head. "That will not do." He knelt before her.

Harriet stiffened. "What are you doing?"

"I am going to put these shoes on your feet."

"Why? Captain, I'm already late and—"

"Five minutes won't matter." He glanced up at her. "Put them on. For me."

"For . . . why would I do that?"

"Why not?"

She bit her lip and he could see her mulling the thought, considering it from every angle. "I suppose—"

"Good," he said, not giving her time to reconsider. "Take off your stockings."

"My—whatever for?"

"Because these slippers will never fit over such thick woolen stockings."

She sighed, but to his surprise, she did as she was told, rolling the gray stocking down her calf, unwittingly giving him a bare flash of a nicely rounded leg. The sight heated him in ways a mere rounded leg never had before.

He took her foot in his hand. Her foot seemed tiny, delicate even, against his large palm. "You deserve to wear shoes like these."

"Deserve?" she said, rather breathlessly.

"Deserve," he replied firmly. He slipped the shoe over her foot, then did the same with the other one.

Harriet held her feet before her and regarded the shoes solemnly. "They're quite pretty, aren't they?"

"They're beautiful." He met her gaze and smiled. "You have lovely ankles as well."

Harriet's heart skipped a beat. She'd been having a horrid day up until then. She'd awoken late, her hair wouldn't stay in its braid, she'd hit her shin on a stool, and the knob to her wardrobe door had broken, which was why the door had been standing ajar. Added to that, her blasted boots had been determined to stay off her feet.

She looked at the delicate slippers, so incongruous against her faded skirts. "They fit so well. As if made for me."

He glanced up at her, his eyes shadowed by the fall of hair over his brows. There was a hint of mischief in his gaze, something seductive and wild. Harriet's heart leapt as if in response. "I—I—" She what? She loved the shoes? Loved having him sitting so close? Loved the feel of his hands on her ankles?

Heat flooded her face, and she cleared her throat. "I suppose everyone is waiting on me."

"We can't be long. Derrick seemed to think you'd returned to get the lunch basket."

"And you were going to carry it for me? I'm honored."

He grinned. "Don't be. I just wanted to steal some cheese before Derrick could get to it."

"He's a growing boy."

"He's a greedy menace."

"That too."

He stood. "May I ask you something?"

"Of course."

"Why do you work so hard?"

She blinked. "Because there are so many things to do and so . . . I do them. Besides, work is good for the soul."

"Perhaps it is," he said musingly. He reached down and took her hand, then pulled her to her feet. "What would you do if you weren't tied here, to Garrett Park?"

"I don't consider it tied. I love my home. But if I had the money, I suppose I'd like to travel."

"Where?"

She thought a moment, her gaze finding the tips of her slippers. "To London."

He raised his brows. "That's not that far from here. A day's journey, if that."

"I know." She held out one foot and then the other. "I always thought to take these with me for my season, but by then, Father had overspent the investment funds and there was no money for such things. But one day . . ."

"One day?" he prompted.

She caught his gaze and smiled. "One day I shall wear these shoes and dance with—" She broke off, her cheeks heating.

"With?"

"With someone other than my brothers." She chuckled. "Neither one can dance at all. Stephen is forever stepping on my feet, and Derrick forgets he is even dancing and frequently comes to a complete stop."

Chase looked down at her, amazed at her spirit. Even through her wistfulness, there was an air of contentment, of satisfaction with who she was and what she wanted. More than he, who'd had every luxury, every advantage, had ever felt.

He looked about the room. "All we need—" he muttered to himself. He moved a stool and a small chest of drawers to the wall, effectively clearing the floor. "There."

"What are you doing?" She sat down on the edge of the bed and reached for one of the shoes. "We need to get to the carts. Everyone will be waiting and—"

Chase took her hands and pulled her to her feet. "Leave your shoes on."

"Why?"

He led her to the center of the room. "You are going to get your dance."

She blinked. "Here?"

"And now." He held her hand in his and clasped her gently about the waist. "Allow me to point out that I am not one of your brothers."

"I—how can—with this dress?"

He grinned. "You can take it off if you wish. Actually, I think that is an excellent idea."

"B-but there is no music."

"We'll pretend. I've noticed that your entire family is good at pretending. This shouldn't tax your abilities in the least."

She shook her head. "I don't think—"

"Don't think, Harriet. Pretend. Pretend you're at a ball. Pretend you're wearing a gown that goes with these shoes. Pretend you're surrounded with soft music, flickering candlelight, and the glitter of jewels."

She smiled, her eyes closing slightly. "Mmmm. A full orchestra. And the Prince is in attendance."

He smiled down at her. "As you wish, m'lady."

He tightened his hold on her waist. "May I have this dance?"

She lifted her wrist and consulted an imaginary dance card. "Let me see. I danced the quadrille with the Duke of Devonshire and the country dance with the Prince Regent. I suppose we can dance the last—"

He pulled her tight, her body firm against his. "The waltz. It's just beginning."

She colored adorably. "I—I don't know that dance."

"Then I shall have to teach you."

Her eyes sparkled. "Could you? I saw it danced once at the assembly rooms in Harrowgate and it looked excessively elegant."

"It is. Now, put your hand like so, and rest your other hand here . . . there you go. Now, relax and just follow me." He began to hum, swaying ever so slightly.

She followed him, naturally graceful. Her steps matched his so perfectly that he quickened the pace. She never faltered. He hummed a little louder, increasing the tempo. Her skirts flared out, her slippers glinting like dewdrops on the faded rug.

"How wonderful!" Laughter gurgled in the back of her throat as they spun around and around. "It's even more enjoyable than it appear—"

"Harri!" rang a call from the foyer. "Are you ready?"

Harriet came to a complete stop. "Oh dear! That's Stephen. They must be ready. And I don't even have my boots on!" She whirled away, her skirts brushing his legs, before she plopped onto the edge of the bed and removed the silver slippers. She yanked her thick woolen stockings back on.

Chase watched, feeling strangely bereft. Of all the women he'd known, none had intrigued him so thoroughly or as quickly as the slip of a woman on the edge of her bed. He sighed. "I'll go and get the basket from Cook."

Harriet nodded. "Please do! And pray tell Stephen I'll be right down."

"Of course." Chase turned to leave.

"Captain?"

He paused. "Yes?"

"Thank you."

Chase glanced back and saw a soft smile touch her lips.

She lifted the shoes and looked at them, a glow in her eyes. "I and my shoes thank you."

Chase tried to think of any woman of his acquaintance who would be sincerely grateful for such a trifling thing as a dance in an empty room without the benefit of an orchestra or champagne or any of the trappings most females prized.

Harriet stomped her booted feet to the floor and went to the wardrobe. She replaced the shoes on the bottom shelf and then stood back and regarded them with satisfaction. "Now no one can say they've never been worn."

"No. No they can't." And with that poor rejoinder, he left. What was it about Harriet Ward that fascinated him so? He wasn't sure what it was, but he was damned well going to find out.

Chapter 16

No cod for me, please. Makes me dream the most horrid things. Last time I ate some, I dreamed that my mother-in-law had come to stay, broke her hip on our front landing, and never left.

Mr. Giles Standish to his brother,
Mr. Lembert Standish as the two sat down
to dine at White's

Mother's soft voice traveled through the door. "Harriet?"

Harriet rolled to her side, cuddling deeper into the cocoon of warmth she'd made in the night. "Yes?"

"Time to wake up, dear."

Harriet wasn't sure she'd ever really been asleep. Her thoughts had churned restlessly last night, just as they had every night since the captain had found his way into the Ward household. Especially since the day before, when he'd danced with her.

She opened her eyes and looked around her room. It looked the same . . . yet it didn't. Something magical had happened. Something that had shaken her to the very core.

Worse, every time she closed her eyes, she found herself wearing her sparkling shoes, waltzing in his arms once again, over and over, as if her heart couldn't get enough of the sensation.

She closed her eyes, remembering the feel of his arms about her, the warmth of his breath on her temple, the deep sound of his voice against her ear—

"Harriet? I don't hear you moving."

"I'm awake," Harriet said, bouncing a little in the bed so that the rails would creak.

"Good. I'm going to help Jane set out breakfast."

Harriet sighed. "I'll be down as soon as I'm dressed."

"Very well, dear. I just didn't want you to fall asleep again." Mother's footsteps faded down the hallway.

Harriet turned onto her back, careful to keep the covers tucked beneath her chin to hold in the warmth, and wondered what made the captain so . . . fascinating.

Oh, it was true that she'd never seen a more handsome man—the combination of black hair and piercing blue eyes was enough to make anyone take notice. But added to that was a sensual smile that could send a shiver down one's spine, a set of hard-carved lips that seemed made for kissing, a rather lively sense of humor, and a definite streak of . . . reluctant chivalry, she supposed it was, for lack of a better phrase.

But there were a few other things, as well. Broad shoulders, a tapered waist, and a very firm posterior.

Not that she'd been looking at his posterior, mind you. Harriet was quite certain she wouldn't have noticed anything about the captain at all if she hadn't been forced to endure Ophelia's and Sophia's constant musing on the subject.

Every day, they watched, commented, debated, and argued about which of the captain's features they liked the best. Sophia was very fond of his blue eyes, shadowed as they were by coal black lashes so long that they curled just a bit at the ends. Ophelia rather thought she liked the way his muscles rippled beneath his shirt while he was working. The only thing the two were in complete agreement on was the captain's rump. They both thought it was a thing of godlike beauty.

To be honest, his posterior *was* rather impressive. Especially arrayed in Stephen's slightly too-tight breeches. Harriet smiled. There were some advantages to working in the fields. Mainly, you had the opportunity to watch your more interesting companions for lengthy periods of time without their being aware of it. Until four days ago, Harriet hadn't been aware of that particular benefit to field work.

Not that any of it mattered. It was a complete waste of time to dream over a man who was bound to leave. Fortunately for her, Harriet had long since learned to waste neither her time nor her life dreaming about things one could never have.

Father, of course, had believed differently. He had been a dreamer. She could remember him saying that their only chore was to enjoy life to the fullest and to let tomorrow take care of itself. But his determination to live in a manner he could ill afford had, on his death, left his family deeply in debt. Harriet had learned that the only time one could really enjoy tomorrow was after one had taken care of today.

She thought about her brothers and sisters. About

Stephen, who worked so hard that his hands were already callused and rough; about Sophia and Ophelia, who fetched and carried and cleaned; about Derrick, who'd lost the chance to attend Eton; and especially Mother, who worried about them all, more than she wanted anyone to know. Harriet had to force away a very real flare of anger at her father for his shortsightedness.

A noise outside of Harriet's door drew her attention to the clock. Piffle! If she didn't get busy, she'd be late again. And all because she'd lain in bed too long.

Harriet took a deep breath, pushed aside the mound of blankets and jumped to the floor, the cold chattering her teeth. Hugging herself, she ran across the room, threw open the door to the wardrobe, grabbed her clothing from a peg and ran back to bed.

She tossed the clothes onto the bed and then dived under the covers, luxuriating in the cozy spot she'd just left. It was warmer in the house during the winter, when it was so cold they had to have the fires lit. But in the spring, when it was warm in the daytime, they made do without the fires, which left the mornings a bit frosty early in the season.

Harriet snaked out a hand from beneath the covers and grabbed her gown. She then began the laborious process of putting it on while staying warm. Years of practice held her in good stead, and she soon had the gown in place and was ready to face the chill morning air.

Harriet stood in her stocking-clad feet and fished her boots out from under her bed, yawning away the effects of too little sleep. What was she doing, losing sleep over a man who was destined to leave?

She seemed to have no control over her thoughts of late.

It seemed that as soon as her head hit her pillow, no matter how tired she might be, her mind immediately began to dwell on Captain Frakenham. There was something about him, about the way he smiled, about the flashes of sadness she saw in his eyes at unexpected moments, at the little acts of kindness that he committed when he thought no one was looking—like asking her to dance. Or the times he helped Ophelia or Sophia with a bucket that appeared too heavy. Or—oh—a dozen other kindnesses.

She closed her eyes and for an instant, she was back in his arms, twirling across the bedroom floor, her magic shoes on her feet as they swooped and swirled until Harriet was quite sure she could fly.

Her heart warmed at the memory, banishing the cold, and she held her arms out and danced a few steps in the empty room, her skirts swirling about her legs. As she turned, she caught sight of her reflection in the mirror over the washstand. Her eyes were shining, her lips curved into a bemused smile. She looked like a woman in lo—

She dropped her hands to her side, her gaze widening. Blast it, that was no way to feel about a man who would soon leave, even if he did know how to dance. She would not be so silly as to allow herself to feel anything for him. She was not her father, ready to throw away her future and the future of those she loved for something she could never have.

"Piffle," she said aloud, to further stifle her unruly imagination. For the thousandth time, she wondered at the captain's true identity. And why he'd elected to stay here, with them. Whatever it was, Harriet decided she had better find out. She hated a mystery almost as much as she hated empty, wasted dreaming.

Firmly putting the waltz tune out of her mind and restoring her heart to its normal location in her chest, Harriet put on her boots and left her room.

He was drowning in a sea of wool. Baaing sheep surrounded him on all sides, black-faced ones, and white-faced ones, and large spotted ones. They stood all around him as far as the eye could see, as deep as the ocean itself.

Try as he might, he could not break free. All he could do was flounder helplessly as muffled waves of wool enclosed him, pressed upon him, dragged him under until he could not breathe. He struggled furiously, fighting madly, desperate for breath as he tried to break to the surface—

Chase awoke with a start, facedown in his pillow. He yanked it away and gulped in the cold morning air, his body drenched in sweat. Bloody hell, what a nightmare.

But it was no wonder—he was inundated with sheep. Chase tucked the pillow back under his head and rolled onto his back, blinked groggily into the darkness as he waited for his breathing to return to normal. He'd never worked so hard in his life, though to tell the truth, as more and more days passed, he found that he was beginning to enjoy it.

Well, some of it. There was one particular ram who detested Chase on sight, a sentiment Chase found that he could return with his full compliments. Every opportunity the ram got, he would lower his head and attempt to knock Chase into the mud.

In all truth, far worse than the work and the cantankerous ram, was the constant trail of visitors that had descended on Garrett Park. They came, they saw, they gawked. Each night, Chase would drag himself in from the fields, take a quick gallop on his poor horse, who no doubt was feeling as cooped up as Chase himself, and then put on his London clothes and pretend he wasn't nigh dead with exhaustion at dinner.

That night promised to be the worst night of all, for Lady Cabot-Wells was reputed to be attending. Mrs. Ward had announced with some glee that the woman was the busiest gossip this side of Dorset.

Chase rubbed his neck and stretched, wakening more each passing moment. The more he saw of the gossip chain that operated in Sticklye-By-The-River, the happier he was that he hadn't blurted out his name when he'd first arrived.

In one more week, all would be finished. The wool would be gathered, the bank paid, Garrett Park saved, and Chase St. John would be on his way. He rolled to his side and looked about his dark bedroom, wondering why the thought made him feel so bleak.

Didn't he want to protect his family from his own errors? Of course he did. And leaving was the best way. He was sure of it.

Almost.

What, he wondered, would Harriet do in his case? He saw her as she'd looked in his arms, dancing with such a joyous air.

Of all the women Chase had known, Harriet Ward was the most honest, genuine of all. He liked how she faced life's difficulties with her chin in the air, still able to laugh and enjoy a moment of frivolity without playing the martyr. He thought of her shoes and the joy she'd taken in wearing them.

One day, when all this was over, he would order a dress for her, one that would match those shoes. One that would fulfill every daydream she'd ever had.

The thought pleased him and he lay in the darkness, smiling.

"Captain?" Stephen threw open the door. "It's another day."

So it was. Chase kicked back his covers and sat up, stretching in the dark. The second the sheep were shorn and he was certain Garrett Park was saved, it would be time to leave. Time to resume his journey. But today was not that day.

For some reason, that small thought soothed him and it was with a lift to his step that he dressed and went to breakfast.

Harriet pushed her hat off her head and wiped her brow. These were the last of them. Beginning tomorrow, they would start the shearing.

She leaned against the fence, her neck and back aching. Thank goodness for Max. He herded the sheep almost effortlessly, crisscrossing back and forth, nipping at a heel here, a rump there. The sheep, though nervous around him, seemed to understand he meant no harm and they jostled along in the general direction he provided.

"Are we done?"

Harriet glanced up at the captain. He leaned against the fence, his shirt undone at the neck, his sleeves rolled up. A wide-brimmed straw hat was settled on his black hair, shading his eyes from the sun. He'd not worn a hat the first day, and the bridge of his nose and the tips of his ears were a pleasant shade of pink.

After seeing him glowing red at the end of the first day, Harriet had demanded that Stephen provide him one of his straw hats. The hat, old and frayed, wasn't one of Stephen's better ones, but on the captain, it seemed different somehow. Bolder. More . . . noble or something.

The captain glanced down at her at that moment, his brows lifting. "What?"

She looked away, irritated he'd caught her staring at him. "Nothing. I was just seeing if your sunburn was better."

"Oh I hardly feel it at all. Of course, that could be because the rest of me is so pained that I barely notice the sunburn, but . . ." He shrugged.

Her lips twitched. "You know, I'm surprised you are sore at all. It's almost as if you'd never done a day's labor in your life. A strange thought, that. You'd think a sailor would be more used to hard work."

Chase glanced down at the wretch. She was teasing him, he was sure of it. Always dancing on the line of the fantasy she'd forced on him, while waiting for him to reveal himself.

Well, he didn't have to reveal a thing. And while it behooved him to pretend to be "Captain John," he didn't *have* to be nice about it. He owed this little slip of impudence a lesson or two. A lesson about toying with the minds of men far greater than she.

He was a St. John, dammit. Perhaps the least of the St. Johns, but a St. John nonetheless. He turned, leaning his back against the fence so that he could more fully face her. "Strange that you should mention the sea. I wonder that I do not have any memory of that. Not even a little."

"No? I heard you tell Miss Stanhope all sorts of sea tales just the other day."

"I stole them out of a book from your library."

She appeared much struck. "Did you?"

"Tales of a Foreign Born Sailor."

"I'm impressed that you've gone to such lengths."

"You should be," he retorted. "I just find it strange that I don't have any clear memories of being at sea. I remember other things, but not that."

"Other things? Like what?"

"Like kissing. And touching. And—"

"I see," she said hastily, her color high. "You know, the doctor did say that it is not unusual for someone with an injury such as yours to remember the incidentals in life, but not the details."

"Yes, but . . . you'd think I'd remember something. Anything." He looked at the sky, and knit his brow, trying his hardest to look bemused and sad. "I certainly wish I could."

"There, Captain." She placed her hand on his arm and looked earnestly at him. "I've no doubt that one day your entire memory will pop right back into your head."

If he was a good actor, then she was a splendid actress. But he was up to the challenge. He placed one of his hands over hers and leaned down to gaze into her eyes. "What surprises me the most is that I do not, at least, remember you."

She tried to remove her hand, but he wouldn't allow it.

He further pinned his quarry with a smile. "Of all the things a man should never forget, the woman he loves is foremost. He would remember a number of things beyond her name. The curve of her cheek. The feel of her lips on his. The taste of her."

Her gaze dropped down to rest on the tips of her shoes. "Ah. Yes. Well."

Chase nodded as if thinking. "I wonder . . ." He waited.

She lifted her gaze, her color still high. "What?"

He stepped forward, closing the space between them. She stood before him, her head barely reaching his shoulder. She was a tiny thing, all bone and brown hair.

But her eyes . . . they saved her from plainness and more. Wide and finely shaped, fringed with thick black lashes, they shone with intelligence, brimmed with irritation, and flashed with humor.

In the brief time he'd known her, he'd seen all that and more.

Chase glanced at the others, but they were on the opposite side of the field, fixing the fence. Smiling down at her, he lifted his hand and brushed it down her cheek. Her skin slid silky smooth beneath his, and a tingle of awareness shot through him like lightning across water.

Chase almost pulled back his hand. He knew the feeling of attraction, of heated lust that precluded every chase. But this . . . this was something more.

Suddenly, he no longer wished to kiss her just to tease her. The kiss would be for him, to put to rest this irritating attraction he felt. "Tell me something, Harriet. Tell me something about you." He lingered over her name, tasting it thoroughly.

From beneath the brim of her hat, her face flushed a shade darker. "What do you want to know?"

"How intimate were we?"

She swallowed, the line of her throat surprisingly graceful. "I'm sure I don't know what you mean, Captain. Indeed, I hope you aren't—"

"John. Strange that not even my name rings with any resonance."

Her gaze flickered, her brown eyes uncertain, though she spoke with authority. "You hit your head rather hard."

"Did I?" He rested his hand on the rail beside her, uncertain as to what emotion he felt foremost . . . Irritation. Frustration. Amusement. He stopped. He *was* amused. This little wren had decided she needed him—Chase St. John, scion of one of the most powerful houses in England—for her plots and toils. And he'd willingly succumbed, wearing the mantle of sheep farmer and whatever else she required.

Worse, he had the irritating suspicion that even if she knew who he was, she wouldn't care. All she wanted was a man, any man available, to play the part her family had assigned.

What truly amused him was that she stood before him, met his gaze as calmly as a statue, and lied through her teeth as if born to such low deeds when in fact she was so filled with goodness and purity that she almost shone with it.

She slid a glance at him, then away. "Perhaps your memory is returning. You certainly remember how to waltz."

He smiled. "Yes I do."

She caught his gaze and, to his amazement, a smile quivered on her lips, then broke through like sunshine piercing a cloud on a rainy day.

Chase was entranced. She had a beautiful mouth. White and even teeth, perfectly set off by a pair of plump, moist lips that were the fresh pink of a new rose. Strange how he'd never noticed that before. Perhaps the plain brown wren wasn't a wren after all, but a juicy robin. "You know," he said slowly, moving even closer, "I think I do remember this . . ."

"What?" she said, her low voice suddenly breathless.

He slid his fingertips across her cheek. "I remember touching you."

"How could—you never—we never—"

"But we must have. I think . . . no, I'm certain that I remember it well."

She eyed him suspiciously. Chase had to hide a sudden inclination to grin. She was all fire and brimstone, starch and oversewn ruffles.

"You cannot remember any of that," she finally said. "It did not happen."

"Didn't it?" He leaned forward, his breath fanning her cheek, sending a ripple of heat down her spine. "I remember this . . . and more."

Harriet swallowed. Dear God, he was going to kiss her, she could see it in his eyes, feel the rapid thud of her own heart. "You are mistaken if you think you remember kissing me."

"I would never forget a woman like you."

A pang of wistfulness hit Harriet squarely in the heart. Every woman wanted to hear those words. Every woman wanted to feel special, to be thought of as unique. It was a pity then, that common logic forced her to argue. "But you did forget me. And when you leave, you will forget me again."

The words stung as she said them, but she refused to betray herself.

This was a most inappropriate conversation. They really shouldn't be talking about such things as kisses even though the memory of their previous embrace still had the power to send an illicit shiver through her body.

Harriet blinked. Good heavens, what was wrong with her that she was thinking about kisses from a strange man? Well . . . not that strange. He was, in a way, her fiancé.

Wasn't he?

He lifted a finger to her cheek and brushed a line from her cheek to the corner of her mouth, his touch sending a fury of tremors through her. "I remember that your lips were my first contact with consciousness after I was wounded."

Piffle. The man had a memory like a trap.

"But the circumstances of our other kisses . . ." He shook his head. "We can do better. Much, much better."

Harriet was suddenly certain they could. She found herself unable to move when he stepped closer, placing his hand on the fence at her hip. He had her boxed in, trapped against the railing, his arms to either side, his hips even with hers.

She should protest, she supposed. But why? She rather enjoyed the feel of him surrounding her. She looked into his eyes and almost sighed. They were so blue that Harriet could only stare. It was sinful to see a man with such long lashes. She thought about her own brown lashes and had to repress a sigh of envy. Drat the man, making her feel as if she was inadequate in some way.

She shook herself mentally. "Look, Captain—"

"Call me John. I am your fiancé, after all."

"Yes, but I—"

"I want to hear my name from your lips." He

stood so close his knees brushed her skirts. "In fact, I demand it."

"Demand?"

His eyes glinted. "Call. Me. John."

She could see that he was going to be difficult. "Oh, very well. Have it your way. Though why it would matter—"

"Perhaps the sound of my name on your lips will refresh this damnable memory of mine."

"You shouldn't curse."

"Sorry. Must be my time at sea. I daresay I know quite a few more curse words, just by dint of being a sailor."

She never thought she'd hate the word "logic," but it was truly beginning to grate on her nerves. "Oh, very well," she said, sighing. "Jo—"

Chase kissed her. He would never be sure afterward if it was her audacity in continuing the farce, his irritation in being so maneuvered, or simply the sight of her perfect lips making the most delicious "j" of his entire life. Whatever it was that sent him over the edge, he recklessly plunged forward, capturing her to him with a force that echoed his exploded control.

He wasn't sure what he expected. Resistance perhaps. Or outright anger. But what he got was something entirely different. She stiffened, but only for a second, and then something happened. She responded. Only not in a genteel, careful way as one would expect from such a starchy paragon of virtue, but in a hot, hands-clutching way that aroused Chase more thoroughly than any kiss he'd ever received.

Still, as heated as it was, it wasn't a particularly

good kiss. It was inept and strangely endearing. He pulled back and said in a low voice, "Easy, sweetheart. Not like that."

She stiffened, her face flooding with color. "What do you mean 'not like that'?"

"Apparently I've been remiss in my duties as your fiancé."

"Duties? Kissing me is a duty?"

"Not at all. I enjoy kissing you. And you, my little wren, love every moment. Or you did until I suggested there was a better way to do it."

She opened her mouth as if to berate him, then stopped, rampant curiosity on her face. "What other way is there?"

He pulled her toward him, then cupped her chin and tilted her face to his. "First, don't hold your lips so tightly together."

She eyed him for a long, serious moment. He could almost hear the rumble of her weighty thoughts. Finally, she said, "I suppose one kiss wouldn't hurt."

He bent and softly placed his lips on hers. She stood stock-still beneath his touch, the heat from her lips warming his, the scent of lemons and hay drifting over him. She was as sweet as a summer breeze, as seductive as a harvest moon. And she didn't realize it at all.

Chase brushed his lips over hers, nipping at her soft, plump lips. Again and again, he tasted and teased, each time opening her lips a little more. She remained where she was, face upturned, eyes closed. Chase captured her mouth beneath his, sliding his tongue across her bottom lip.

She started and almost pulled back, but he held her and did it again, tasting her more deeply, more intimately. This time, something changed. She melted beneath his touch, opened herself to him naturally as she threw her arms about his neck and pressed her slender body to his.

Chase's body reacted instantly, tightening with a flood of passion. Her mouth opened beneath his, and to his delight, her tongue touched his.

By God, but for all her purity she was as hot as any fancy piece—more so because her reaction was as natural as breathing. It was as if her quiet, pale demeanor hid a pulsing heart that beat so wildly that none would ever credit it.

He could not turn away. Indeed, his hands gripped her arms beneath the edge of her sleeves, his fingers splayed over her heated skin. She moaned into his mouth, the sound so erotic that he pressed against her, rubbing his hips across hers.

Somewhere far away, Max barked in abandon, the sound penetrating Chase's heated thoughts. If he didn't have a care, he might lift her skirts and take her there, in front of God and country.

Breathing erratically, he broke the kiss and lifted his head, catching Harriet's bemused gaze. Sometime or another, both of them had lost their hats. Harriet's hair had come unpinned, and long thick strands hung down her back and to either side of her face, softening the angular corners.

It was curious, but with her hair loosened, she looked more vibrant, more sensual. Without realizing that he did so, Chase touched her hair, the silken strands clinging to his hands.

She caught at his fingers and pulled his hand so that she could see his palm, her gaze widening. "Your poor hands! Why didn't you say something?"

He looked at his blistered palms and shrugged. "They are better today."

"They are bleeding!" She turned and marched toward the wagon.

"It's nothing, really," he said, following her. "They don't even hurt that—"

"Do you know what could happen if this got infected?" She reached under the seat of the wagon to pull out a small box. "Hold out your hands. Both of them."

Chase did as instructed, a little amused at how determined she seemed to be.

Harriet opened the box and took out a small vial. "This should do the trick." She uncorked the vial and a strong whiff of something indescribable hit Chase.

He took an involuntary step back but she was too quick. She caught him and poured an oily substance into his hand. Then she capped the vial. "Rub that in."

His nose curled of its own accord. "You have to be jesting—"

"Rub it in."

"I don't want to."

"It will make your blisters heal faster."

"But it smells atrocious."

She dropped the vial back in the box and replaced it under the seat. "Captain Frakenham, I—"

"John."

She turned to face him, hands on hips. "John, then. It is very important that you don't get an infection. Rub that in."

Holding his hands at arm's length, he briefly rubbed his hands together, then bent to wipe them on the grass. It hurt, but he'd have done much worse to get rid of the nasty stuff. "That is the most vile-smelling stuff."

"Yes, it is. You should have seen poor Derrick when he slid out of the loft and scraped his entire back nearly raw. Mother practically bathed him in it."

Chase lifted one of his hands and then rapidly held it away. "Bloody hell! This smells worse than the potion my mother gave me when I was twelve." He grinned at the memory. "I pretended to have a fever so that I wouldn't have to take a bath."

The words hung in the air between them.

Chase closed his eyes. He'd just given himself up. In one lousy unguarded moment, he'd lost the game.

He sighed, then opened his eyes.

Harriet stood stiff and immobile, regarding him with a frosty rage. *"Who are you?"*

Chapter 17

A short courtship is the way of it. If you let things drone on and on, then you'll have spent all your topics of conversation before the wedding day and will have nothing more to say. Marry within two months of proposing, then you'll still have something left to talk about at the breakfast table.

Mr. Lembert Standish to his friend
and mentor, Edmund Valmont
as the two stood outside of Hell's Door,
a fashionable gaming establishment

Harriet didn't know whether to slap the stranger for his audacity or crow with triumph at his slip of the tongue. Her mind swirled with emotions—shock, exuberance at being right, confusion at the realization that he'd knowingly misled them—misled her. Her brow lowered at that. The man had *lied.*

And she was not about to give the jackanapes any quarter. She crossed her arms over her chest. "Well?"

He removed his hat and raked his hair from his

eyes, then yanked his hand away and stared at it as if disgusted. "Bloody hell, now my hair will smell like—"

"Oh piffle! I don't care what your hair smells like. *Who are you?*"

He replaced the hat, the brim shading his eyes. "It doesn't really mat—"

"Your name, sir."

His brow lowered as if he might challenge her. Harriet waited, eyes narrowed. If he thought to withhold such information now, he was sadly mistaken.

She wasn't sure what she'd do if he refused, but there would be hell to pay, make no doubt.

Some of her thoughts must have shown on her face, for he exploded into a sigh. "You're determined about this, aren't you?"

"I deserve to know what manner of man we've been housing."

"Yes. I suppose you do at that. Very well. My name is Chase St. John."

Harriet's finger itched, right at the band of that silly stuck ring. She absently rubbed it. He said the name as if it should mean something. Harriet tried to remember if there were any St. Johns about, but none came to mind. "I don't know of your family. Where exactly do they live?"

"We have homes in London, Herefordshire, Yorkshire, Devonshire, Strat—"

She laughed then. Of course the man who stood before her, smelling of sheep ointment and wearing her brother's old clothes, had houses in all those places. "So many homes! Goodness, how do you manage to keep them all up?"

He shrugged as if he had never really considered the question. "Servants, I suppose."

Her amusement faded before his casual shrug. "You suppose?" He was serious. She swallowed. "How many servants do you have?"

"I don't know."

"How could you not know?"

"I just haven't thought about it." He leaned against the wagon, neatly crossing his booted feet at the ankles. "Servants just . . . are."

Harriet thought of her own servants, four in all, and of the way she'd struggled to find just one more set of hands for the shearing. Yet here before her stood a man who had so many servants, he wasn't really sure of the number.

The thought rankled. "They just are. How very nice for you. So you're chock-full of houses and servants. I daresay you're also related to the King."

"As a matter of fact, we are."

Of course they were. Harriet's stomach tightened. He wasn't just wealthy, he was one of *the* wealthy. The man was not of her world, never had been, and never would be.

Harriet knew many things about life. She'd been on her own far too long not to have garnered a few bits of wisdom here and there. Her laughing, smiling father, who teased and joked and never seemed at a loss, had left his family with mounds of debt and nothing else. All from trying to be what he was not.

Harriet would never make that mistake. "How long have you known your true identity?"

He sighed, and rocked back on his heels. "I don't know how that's pertinent to—"

"How long?"

"I've always known."

Her irritation threatened to blossom into something more. All of her suspicions had been true. "May I ask why you've lied to my family?"

His gaze hardened. "From the moment I awoke, your mother was there, telling me I was Captain Frakenham. Who lied to whom?"

She lifted her chin. "That may be. But why did you go along with it?"

"Why not? It seemed as if you needed a Captain Frakenham, and I, quite frankly, had nothing better to do."

She couldn't answer that. They *had* needed a Captain Frakenham and, as much as she hated to admit it, he'd become quite adept at his part. "I find it difficult to believe anything you say, considering the charade you've perpetrated."

"Speaking of charades," he retorted easily, "there is no Captain Frakenham, is there?"

For a mad moment, she briefly considered continuing the lies. But there was no help for it—he would divine the truth sooner or later. "Oh very well. I suppose you deserve to know. Mother made up the captain."

The lout didn't even have the decency to look surprised. "To protect your interests at the bank."

"Once Mr. Gower arrived, there was no gainsaying the bank. We are so close to coming about. All we have to do is sell the wool, and we're done with them. We just needed two more—"

"—weeks. I know." He tilted his head to one side, and he regarded her through his remarkable blue eyes. "I suppose it all comes down to this: you and I have lied to each other since the first day we met."

In that moment, it was as if the magic of their one,

solitary dance, the passion of the few kisses they'd shared, the warmth of companionship that had been steadily growing, suddenly dissipated like the morning mist.

He was right—they *had* deceived one another from their first meeting. It was not a propitious way to begin a relationship.

Not, of course, that she wanted a relationship with such a pompous jackstraw, it was just that she was only now beginning to realize how much she enjoyed him and his kisses.

In fact, just thinking of that last kiss, when his tongue had touched hers ever so suggestively—she shivered, then caught herself, somewhat shocked at how hard her heart was racing.

"Why were you willing to assume Captain Frakenham's identity? You even agreed to work here, in the fields."

He crossed his arms over his chest. "I was on my way out of the country when I was attacked. I thought that if I became Captain Frakenham while recuperating, not only would it assist you, but it would also stop the local gossips from tattling to the world about my real identity."

"Why would that matter?"

"Because my brothers would not look kindly on my leaving the country without notifying them."

She raised her brows. "Surely you had more reason than that?"

"No. They would try to talk me out of it, but—" He stopped, a bleak expression resting on his face. "I've caused enough havoc in their lives as it is. In order to make things right, I must leave."

Harriet suddenly realized that she'd seen that desolate expression before, that it visited him often, even beneath his usual blithe smile. The expression caught at her heart, for she didn't think she'd ever seen so much pain on one face. "Make things right?" Her voice softened. "What did you do that was so wrong?"

He shook his head, his expression shuttered once again. "You don't need to know more."

But she did. "You were right in thinking that your real identity would have been gossiped about far and wide. Sticklye-By-The-River is a small village and everyone knows everyone else's business far more than they should."

"I've noticed," he said dryly, no doubt thinking of the parade of visitors who came every evening to meet the "captain."

"And since we're located on the post road, everything that happens here is heard for miles around." She tilted her head to one side, regarding him steadily. "I can't imagine there are many crimes that are so severe that would require you to leave the country to make amends."

Hard white lines appeared down both sides of his mouth. "I will not tell you more."

That was certainly blunt. "Perhaps you owe a great deal of money?"

He didn't answer.

"Or mayhap a woman is involved . . ."

"No." His gaze became flint bright. "I'm not going to answer any more questions, so don't ask."

He was being rather rude, but then so was she, prying into his personal business. "Where were you going?"

"Away. Perhaps to Italy."

She tsked. "You don't seem to have a very specific

strategy, which means you would have failed. If you wish to accomplish something, then you need a plan of action."

He let his breath out in a hiss. "Look, Harriet. I had a plan of action—to get out of the country as quickly and quietly as possible. That was all the plan I needed."

She gestured around them. "Does this look like Italy to you?"

"I was waylaid by thieves or I would be there now."

"I can see why you stayed at first—your injuries. But later? Mr. St. John, why are you here now?" She didn't know what she was looking for—what she wanted to hear. But for some reason, she was holding her breath, waiting for his answer.

His jaw tightened. "You and your family have a lot riding on this venture with the sheep and I thought, since I didn't have anything better to do, that I'd stay for a day or two."

"And then you were going to disappear." It wasn't a question. She knew his intentions as plainly as if he'd spoken them aloud. "You don't want to leave England, do you?"

His gaze went past her, to the gently rolling hills and the sway of the green grass. "No."

Harriet's throat tightened at his expression. Whatever he had done, he felt it was unforgivable. She tried to imagine what it could possibly be, but looking at him, the sun shining on his broad shoulders, knowing that he possessed enough heart to stay to help her family even when his own problems seemed large and painful . . .

Harriet bit her lip, her eyes moist. She simply

couldn't imagine him committing any crime so serious that it would be necessary for him to banish himself from his own home.

Chase caught her expression. Damn it! He didn't want anyone's pity, especially not Harriet Ward's. "Now that the game is up, you will wish me to leave. I'll go this evening and—"

"You can't."

He frowned. "What?"

"You can't leave. Lady Cabot-Wells is to come this evening. What would you have us tell her?"

"That I was called back to sea."

"Then the bank would immediately demand payment. We need you, Mr. St. John. You cannot leave."

"Cannot?" he asked softly.

"You cannot leave," she repeated. "Not yet."

Chase absently rubbed his neck where it had begun to ache. If he had any sense, he'd be gone with the first ray of dawn.

That was what a sane man would do. But apparently Chase was no longer sane. Charading as the captain and working knee-deep in sheep muck had turned his brain to mush. "I suppose I could continue to be the captain for another week or so—"

"I knew you would do it!" She beamed at him, her earlier irritation melting away like snow before the sun. "That would be so lovely."

Yes, he realized with some surprise. It could be lovely indeed. Or it would have been, if he wasn't aware that he was going to have to leave, and soon. A pang shot through him.

"I don't know what to say except . . . thank you." Her brown eyes met his, warmth and light shining through.

Light that would disappear the instant she discovered his sins. "I will stay one more week but no more."

"Excellent! And while you are here, perhaps you should think things through. I can't help but wonder if—"

"I have thought things through. I cannot go back to London."

"Never?"

"Never."

She sighed. "I could help if you'd tell me more."

No one could help. This time, Chase was going to have to help himself. "You are not responsible for me, Harriet Ward."

"You are just like Stephen. He won't listen to a word I say, either." Exasperation tinged her voice.

Chase almost smiled. "You have never met a problem you couldn't solve, have you?"

"Never." She regarded him for a long moment. "I suppose we are even, you and I, for our first meeting. A deception for a deception."

"We are indeed even, thou and I." His gaze dropped to her mouth. "And well matched, too."

A faint flash of color touched her skin. And he was aware of an instant thrum of desire. Of all the beauties he'd met in London, he'd never beheld one who was as beautiful inside as she was outside. The combination was heady and he wished with all his heart that things had been different. But they weren't.

"There you are!" Derrick ambled up, Max hard on his heels.

The dog came to a sudden halt, lifted his head, sniffed, blew through his nose, then turned back the way he'd just come, though at a much faster pace.

"Max!" Derrick scowled. "Max! Come back here!"

The dog's ears and tail lowered, but he kept going.

Derrick blew out his breath in disgust and turned to walk back toward Harriet and the wagon. "I don't know about that dog. He's a wonder at herding, but at everything else, he—" Derrick slid to a stop, slapped a hand over his nose, and said in a strangled voice, "Good God, which sheep needed ointment?"

Chase started abruptly. "Sheep?" He glared down at his hands. "That was sheep ointment?"

"It works on people, too," Harriet said defensively. "Ask Derrick."

But Derrick was already walking briskly back the way he'd come, his shoulders shaking as if he was laughing too hard to speak.

"Wonderful," Chase muttered. "I'm taking a bath as soon as I get back to Garrett Park."

"Please do. You smell atrocious, and I don't think we could stand having you at the table at dinner."

"You were the one who—" Chase clamped his mouth closed at her grin. Beautiful inside and out she might be, but she was also a mischievous tease. "Should we tell your family of my real identity?"

"They deserve to know. But never fear, they will keep your secret, especially once I explain how you so graciously agreed to be Captain Frakenham for another week." She bit her lip. "I—I must admit that I was feeling somewhat bad."

"About what?"

"About making you work so hard."

"You *should* feel guilty about that. It has been intolerable."

Her guilty look disappeared. "You haven't worked any harder than the rest of us."

"Yes, but you benefit from my work. I don't benefit from it at all." He looked down at his blistered hands, now oily from the smelly balm she'd applied to them.

"Haven't we housed you and fed you and tended your wounds?"

"With sheep ointment!"

"With *good* sheep ointment."

"I don't think there is such a thing as good sheep ointment."

Derrick yelled something from across the field to Harriet. Something about the last railing on the fence he and the hands had just fixed. Harriet shouted back an answer while Chase waited.

She turned to face him. "We should be able to begin the shearing tomorrow."

"It's about time."

"So we think, too. We've never done this before, though Stephen and I have concocted a system."

She was always the practical one, except for that streak of passion that shimmered just below the surface. Chase wondered what she'd do if he kissed her once more. He stepped a little closer, but yet another shout sounded from across the field.

Harriet leaned over the fence and shouted back an answer. Frustrated at the interruption, Chase had to constrain himself from yelling an answer himself—something rather unworthy.

Finally, Harriet glanced back at Chase. "What were we—oh, yes. Our shearing system." She tossed her head slightly, a tendril of brown hair escaping over one ear. "We built some narrow pens that will only hold one sheep. You just have to loop a rope about its neck and it will be held in place so you can shear it. It should be ridiculously easy."

"One can only hope," Chase replied, though he

had his doubts. "So far, nothing about the sheep business has been what I'd call 'easy.'"

Her chin seemed to jut a bit at that. But after a moment, she said in a rather genteel voice, "You are right. Mr. St. John, you have been most helpful this week. Please accept our thanks for your assistance."

Her tone was almost warm. Chase was impressed. It must have cost her pride plenty to be able to pull that off. "You are quite welcome, Miss Ward."

"It was no problem, I assure you." She peered up at him, all wide brown eyes and thick, curling brown lashes. A faint scattering of freckles decorated her nose. "I assume that since you will continue being the captain, you will also continue to help us with the shearing."

Chase almost choked. "Isn't it enough that I am willing to play the part for your nosy neighbors?"

"It's only for a week and since you, yourself, said you weren't on a schedule—" She met his gaze with a hopeful look.

But for the first time, Chase saw a flicker of uncertainty. "Miss Ward—Harriet, if you need money for the bank payment, I could—"

Harriet's shoulders stiffened. "No. I already had to pay back the bank; I will not owe money again."

Blast it all, who said anything about a loan? "Wait a moment! You don't understand. You won't owe me a thing—"

"I don't take charity, either, if that's what you are going to suggest."

Bloody, stiff-necked fool. Chase's temper began to simmer. "Look, it's not as if—"

"It's not as if we need it." Her mouth thinned with displeasure. "Do you think we are not capable of making the final payment? For I assure you that we can and—"

A jangling sound made Harriet turn. Ophelia rode up on one of the farm horses, the old animal plodding along.

Chase gritted his teeth. Yet another interruption. Bloody hell, could no one in the family do anything without turning to Harriet for advice? It made private speech with the woman almost impossible.

Ophelia pulled the horse to when she reached the wagon. "There you are, Harri. I was looking all over for you."

"And now you've found me. What do you need?"

Chase scowled. They were in the middle of a field, for chrissakes. How *could* they get interrupted so oft?

"Something's wrong with Stephen. Mother asked him to accompany Sophia to Colonel Parker's to visit the colonel's wife, and he refused quite rudely, then stomped off to the library."

"That doesn't sound like him."

"No, it doesn't. I asked him what was wrong, but he will not say. Mother wants you to speak with him when you come home. Are you almost done?"

"Almost." Harriet appeared concerned. "I could leave now, I suppose. I really should see what's amiss—"

"Nonsense," Chase said. "Your brother is a grown man. Leave him be."

Harriet appeared offended. "Even grown men need comfort at times."

"When you've made a mull of things, it's your responsibility to fix them. Your responsibility and no one else's."

"You, sir, are wrong. If I made an error, I would think nothing of asking my family for help."

Chase met her gaze with a flat look. "We never know what we'll do until the circumstances arise."

"I know what I would do under any circumstances. And anyone who keeps secrets from his own family is a selfish wretch."

Chase stiffened, a thousand rejoinders burning a way to his lips, though they remained stubbornly closed.

"Uhm, Harriet?" Ophelia said, looking interestedly from one to the other. "Shall I tell Mother you are on your way?"

"Please do," Harriet said shortly, her gaze still locked with Chase's.

"Very well." Ophelia waited a moment more, but when nothing else was said, she gave a sigh and kicked the horse into a lumpy trot.

Chase wrenched his gaze from Harriet to see if Ophelia was yet out of range. When he turned back, Harriet was already gracing the seat of the cart, her gaze fixed straight ahead, the reins in her hands.

"I'm off to the house," she said, without looking at him. "If you wish a ride, climb on."

She said the words as if they had been wrenched from her.

Chase planted his hat more firmly on his head. "I'll walk."

"All the way to the house?" She started to say something, then stopped and shrugged. "Very well. I will see you at dinner. Don't forget Lady Cabot-Wells is coming to make an inspection of Captain Frakenham this evening. It won't do for you to arrive smelling like sheep ointment."

The harridan, ordering him about as if she owned him. "It won't do for her to see you in that gown, either," he retorted. "It's hideous."

She turned slowly and eyed him from head to foot, stopping to gaze at his sagging boots, faded breeches, and ragged hat. "It's a good thing I have such a qualified fashion advisor." She smirked and then turned away to set the farm horses into motion.

Chase watched, fuming, as she drove to the opposite field, picked up Derrick and the two hired hands and, without so much as a glance his way, headed the cart down the path toward Garrett Park.

Chase was left, standing by the mended fence, reeking of sheep ointment, and facing a long, long walk back to the house. Teeth clenched against a stream of scathing invectives, he began walking.

Chapter 18

*Never let it be said that I don't enjoy a good
bottle of brandy now and again. I don't usually
remember enjoying it, of course, but I must, for
I keep returning for more.*

Edmund Valmont to Anthony Elliot,
the Earl of Greyley, while sitting
at White's, enjoying a bottle

Selfish? How dared she? Chase threw open the
door of the house, his boots ringing loudly on
the polished wood floor. It had taken him almost
two hours to reach the house on foot. He was tired,
sore, dirty, and far too aware of the odiferous waft of
sheep salve to be comfortable.

Damn Harriet and her narrow view of things. He
wasn't selfish. Why, how many times had he come
to the rescue of his own brothers and friends? Not
that many of his friends required much in the way
of rescuing—except Harry Annesley, of course.
Chase paused in the hallway at the thought of
Harry, but he quickly shook it off. He was not selfish. The entire idea was ludicrous.

Leave it to Harriet Ward, the most obstinate, out-
landish, prone-to-exaggeration female of his ac-

quaintance to toss off an ill-conceived word like "selfish" without so much as a second's worth of consideration for his feelings.

The faint sound of girlish voices reached his ears—Sophia and Ophelia deep in conversation. Chase paused, glancing up the stairwell.

He didn't like to think of bringing anyone pain, but God knew he'd already caused far more than his fair share of it. If he closed his eyes, he could still see the white face of the woman his carriage had run down, hear the clack of the hooves on the cobblestones, feel his own rising panic as he realized she could not have escaped.

The memory of that pain held him in place at the foot of the stairs. The voices from upstairs settled into a low murmur, while golden dust motes floated through the air. The hall was silent but for those voices, a faint scent of beeswax and plaster filling his senses.

The library door swung open and out stepped Harriet dressed in a gown of cool blue muslin. She'd had time to bathe and change, and pin her hair atop her head. Except for the telltale pink of her cheeks from being in the sun and the fact that her arms and nose were sadly tanned, she looked as if she belonged in a drawing room and not a pasture.

She was closing the door, but she stopped as she caught sight of him, a guilty expression crossing her face, followed quickly by a mulish jutting of her chin.

"I made it back," he said grimly, aware that he looked and smelled atrociously. "In case you were concerned for my safety."

"I wasn't." She snapped the door closed behind

her. "Even a braying ass can walk a fathom without falling in a ditch."

The little minx. Chase closed the space between them, pinning her to the door with only an inch of space between her fresh skirts and his muddied breeches.

Her nose curled. "You smell like—"

"I know exactly what I smell like. I haven't had time for my bath. Not yet."

"Pray feel free to rinse in the trough by the barn until your bath is ready."

"You are incorrigible."

"Do you ever say anything nice about people?"

That hurt. "I was only trying to make a point. Your family leans on you far too much."

"They do no such thing. Doesn't your family mean anything to you?"

Of course it meant something to him. He had a family—a very close one, in fact. He couldn't imagine life without them. But he was beginning to be aware that part of his problem was that they had taken perhaps too good care of him. Their motives had been pure, of course—love and concern. But their actions hadn't always turned things for the better.

Now that he thought about it, whenever things went wrong, his brothers were always there and not just to support him, but often actively fixing things so that Chase didn't have to. Perhaps that was why he'd been unable to face his problem—until that one instant, he'd never had to.

He shook his head. "You aren't doing your brothers or sisters a favor when you run around correcting every difficulty they might face."

She pressed her hand against his chest. "I hate to be rude, but could you step back a little. The smell . . ."

"If I have to smell the sheep ointment, then *you* should have to smell the sheep ointment. After all, you're the one who slathered it all over me."

"Piffle! You had blisters. What else was I to do?"

"Not a damn thing. Fortunately for you, I'm too tired to argue with you more." He stepped back and allowed her room to escape.

She moved in a rustle of fresh muslin. "I'll ask Jane to have a bath drawn for you."

"Thank you."

"Don't thank me. Mother will expect you at dinner since Lady Cabot-Wells is on her way. Besides, I, for one, have no desire to sit next to you while you smell like a sick sheep." With that, she turned to the stairs and made her way up.

Chase watched her go, her trim backside perfectly outlined under her skirts. His body, tired and aching as it was, reacted instantly. Bloody hell, what was it about her that heated him as flame to tinder? He'd had so many women . . . more than he cared to count. But Harriet Ward, prim and proper and totally unlike any woman he had ever met, inflamed him to uncomfortable heights just by the simple act of walking up a flight of stairs. Damn it, he would not think about that. Not now.

Meanwhile, he'd slip into the library and retrieve the tome he'd been reading about the sea captain. He'd need some fresh "memories" of life at sea if he was to feed the rumor mill yet again.

Besides, it would be a while before his bath was ready, and it would be nice to relax with a book before he had to don his official Captain Frakenham garb and entertain the community. Chase turned to the library door through which Harriet had come, and pushed it open.

Stephen stood in the room, one shoulder against the mantel, his crutches to one side. His head was bowed, a mulish expression on his face, a glass clutched in one hand. Chase hesitated, recognizing a crisis in the making.

He really didn't want to get involved with Stephen's contretemps, but his book sat on a table just past the youth. Chase wondered if he could retrieve it without getting sucked into a lengthy conversation about whatever was paining Stephen.

He must have made some noise, for Stephen lifted his head, his gaze landing on Chase. "Oh," he said in a sullen tone. "It's you." He lifted the glass and tossed back the contents, gasping a little as he did so.

Chase caught the scent of brandy and raised his brows. "Does your sister know you are drinking?"

"Yes," Stephen said, his eyes blazing. "She is not my keeper and neither are you, sir. I am nineteen years of age and may do as I please."

Chase opened his mouth, but then stopped. Normally, he would have met such pretension with a swift and brutal rejoinder, one guaranteed to put the insolent pup in his place. But somehow, in the back of Chase's head, he heard the words "selfish wretch" spoken over and over.

Chase sighed. He really didn't have a choice. "Very well. Let's start anew. Stephen, how nice to see you."

Stephen gave a bitter laugh and turned away. His face was flushed with drink, his eyes glittering.

Chase rubbed his chin. What should he do now? Just take the book and leave? But no, that's exactly what Harriet would expect him to do and he'd be damned if he'd prove her right. "What holds you here, in the library? I believe dinner is served shortly." He ambled closer to the table.

"I don't care—" Stephen grimaced. "What is that smell?"

"My hands. I had blisters and your sister used the sheep ointment on them."

Stephen pressed a hand to his nose. "How horrid. I do hope you mean to bathe."

"As soon as the water has been heated." Chase eyed Stephen for a moment, noting how the lad's gaze rested on him with sullen intent. "Harriet told you my true identity, eh?"

Stephen nodded. "And that you've known all along who you are. Harriet seems to think you didn't act with malice and I—" He bit his lip a moment, then said, "Allow me to apologize on behalf of the family for our deception, as well. I'm sure it must seem very odd to you."

"Nonsense. It made perfect sense or I'd have never agreed to assist you. I daresay that if I'd been in your shoes, I'd have made up a Captain Frakenham, too."

"Thank you all the same," Stephen said stiffly. "You are too kind."

Chase eyed the lad curiously. Despite the boy's frigidly polite tone, there was an underlying expression of agony. What did one do when one actually wished to encourage confidences? Chase wondered what Harriet would do in just such a situation.

After a moment, he sighed. There was nothing for it but a direct attack. "Well? What's wrong with you?"

Stephen stiffened. "Nothing is wrong with me."

"Nonsense. I'm usually unaware of people's feelings and such, but even I can tell you're suffering from the doldrums."

Stephen flushed. "There's nothing—I don't—you wouldn't understand."

Chase eyed the book with a gloomy gaze. If things had worked out his way, no one would have been in the library and Chase would even now be paging through the book, looking for just the right sailing yarn to spring on Lady Cabot-Wells.

"It's a woman," Stephen blurted out.

"Of course it's a woman."

Stephen sent him a sharp glance. "What do you mean 'of course.'"

"What else would send a man into a full-thrown gloom in the middle of the day? Has to be a woman."

"I suppose," Stephen said without enthusiasm. He stared down at his hands, his bottom lip softened and then quivered ever so slightly.

Chase watched, horrified that the young man might actually burst into tears. "Here, now! See what brandy will do to you?" He sent the book one last regretful glance, then took a chair near where Stephen stood, shoulders slumped. "Tell me about this paragon of yours."

"Tell you?" Stephen's bitter laugh grated along Chase's nerves. "I can't believe this! You, who can barely set a fence rail, are offering me advice. By gad, that's rich."

Chase managed a grin. "Trust me on this; if there is one thing I do know, it's how to deal with the fair sex."

"You forget that I've seen you with Harriet."

Chase's grin disappeared. "Your sister is not an

ordinary woman. She's—" Stubborn. Intractable. Condescending when she had no right to be. And intolerably prideful. All told, Harriet Ward was impossibly argumentative. Chase caught Stephen's questioning gaze. "Your sister drives me mad."

A faint smile touched Stephen's mouth, softening his haggard look. "She has that effect on all of us. Father used to say she had an iron spine and, when disgruntled, could freeze the pond with a single look."

"Your father was a very wise man."

Stephen looked at the worn carpet beneath his feet and grimaced. "About some things. Had he had a better head on his shoulders, we wouldn't be scrambling to make this payment."

"We all have our shortcomings."

Stephen's gaze met his, hard and unflinching. "What are *your* shortcomings, then?"

The insolent tone in his voice sent a hot rejoinder flying to Chase's lips. He wasn't used to being spoken to in such a summary fashion. Especially not by a whelp who was still wet behind the ears. But just as he opened his mouth to send a sharply worded retort, he caught a glimpse of pain in Stephen's gaze.

Somewhere in the back of Chase's mind, a faint memory began to hum. He'd been fifteen, a few years younger than Stephen, and hopelessly, relentlessly in "love" with the divine Miss Leticia Overhill, a plump beauty with flaxen hair and blue eyes and the most ravishing dimples.

The fair Leticia had been several years older than he and had her sights firmly fixed on Viscount Ripley, eldest son of the Earl of Snowton. Chase had no title, and was a younger son, as well—though he was infinitely more well-to-do than the Ripleys would ever be.

Still, Leticia'd had her heart set on a title and a title she was determined to have. Chase had been devastated. Of course, now he thanked the stars for his lucky escape, though at the time he'd sworn never again to smile.

"I have many, many flaws. Not the least of which is a tendency to see things from my own stance and no one else's and a sad propensity to convince myself that certain problems will disappear if I can just outrun them." Inwardly Chase winced at how true this profession was.

Stephen eyed him with interest. "Those are grave indeed."

"I'm trying to overcome them. Besides, no one is perfect. Even my father, who was the most generous man I ever met, had his shortcomings. He loved us all dearly, but he had very little patience with children." Chase gestured to the chair opposite his. "Come. Sit. You're giving me a neck ache."

"I don't want to sit."

Chase made an exasperated noise. "Must you argue with every damn thing I say? You are far more like your sister than you realize."

Stephen's lips twitched. "Harriet would not agree."

"All the more reason to believe it's true."

Stephen sighed. "I suppose you are right." He gathered his crutches from the wall and made his way to the chair Chase indicated, stopping to refill his glass.

Though he winced to see how much brandy the lad splashed into his glass, Chase wisely refrained from commenting.

Stephen propped his crutches beside the chair and sank into it. Brandy in one hand, he eyed Chase with a complete lack of respect. "This is asinine. How could you possibly understand my situation?"

"I'm older, a male, and I was once your age."

"What does that prove?"

Good God, this helping thing was most unpleasant. Chase thrust his feet out before him, settling them on the small brass trunk that served as a tea table. Gad, but the lad was full of pride. "Stiff-necked as your sister, aren't you?"

"What if I am?"

"What indeed," Chase muttered. "Tell me what bugs have infested your lady's bonnet."

"She wouldn't like to hear you refer to her in such a manner."

"Good thing she's not here, then." Chase settled deeper into the chair, resting his head on the high back. "What seems to be the problem?"

"There isn't a problem. Not with her." All vestiges of sullenness fell from Stephen's expression. "She's an angel."

"If she's an angel, then why are you so blue-deviled?"

"Because she's above my touch."

"Who told you that?"

"She did."

Chase winced. "What a harridan."

Stephen jolted upright. "She is no such thing—"

"Calm down. All women are harridans. Every last one." Especially the brown-eyed wretch who was, he was certain, even then plotting new ways to irritate him.

Stephen's hands fisted. "I don't like your tone."

This really is not going well. He looked at Stephen's affronted expression and contained a sigh. Perhaps . . . perhaps Harriet had one thing right. Perhaps he was just the tiniest bit selfish. Just a little, mind you. He certainly could never remember asking another fellow human other than his brothers to share a problem.

Stephen took a gulp of the brandy then set it aside and reached for his crutches. "I'm sorry I said a word to you at all—"

"I'm sorry if I've offended you, but I'm not used to serving as confidant. You are my first effort."

Stephen paused. "Really?"

"Really."

"Then why did you offer?"

"Because I was told I was selfish and I was determined to prove the statement wrong."

Recognition dawned on Stephen's face. "Ahhh. You've been brangling with Harriet. That is exactly the kind of thing she would tell someone."

"I don't brangle. She brangles. I merely refuse to listen."

Stephen managed a faint grin. "I've been there a time or two myself."

To his surprise, Chase found himself grinning back. "You're an impudent whelp, did you know that?"

Stephen hesitated, replaced his crutches beside his chair. "I apologize for my short temper. I don't know what's come over me—"

"Love. According to the poets, it makes fools of all men. Or so my oldest brother has told me oft enough."

"Does he believe that?"

"Well, he thinks it applies to all men but him. So he's not infallible either. In fact, I believe that when Marcus falls in love, it will be worse than it is for the rest of us because of all the practice we've had.

We've calluses on our hearts, as it were. He, meanwhile, has nothing but pride to protect him."

"I never thought of pride as a protection."

"You should. But we were not speaking of me or my family. We were talking about your unfortunate circumstances. You are in love with a woman who says she is above you."

Stephen nodded morosely. "That's not exactly what she said, but close to it."

"What exactly *did* she say?"

"That she was . . . well—" Stephen flushed. "She said she was older. And she is, but only by two months."

Chase had to bite the inside of his lip to keep from smiling. After a moment's struggle, he managed to say in a bland tone, "The nerve."

Stephen slumped in his chair. "I warned you it was an ugly situation."

"Tell me more about this mystery woman."

"What do you want to know?"

"The usual . . . hair color, eyes . . ." Chase made a curvy gesture in the air. "All the details."

Stephen's lips thinned. "She's not like that."

Chase frowned. "Not like this?" He made another curvy shape in the air. At Stephen's stubborn scowl, Chase shook his head. "If she's not like this, then we really do need to talk."

"I, sir, do not find this at all amusing! Miss Strickton is perfection!"

The boy had no humor. None at all. "Easy, hothead. I retract my levity."

Stephen's jaw tilted to a pugnacious angle. "I know you think this is silliness. A childish sort of affair—"

"I think nothing of the sort. One of the things about love is that it always feels real. Even when it's not."

"This *is* real!"

Chase wisely did not respond. Was love just a fleeting feeling that came and went, as capricious as the moon and just as cold?

Of course, his own parents had seemed genuinely smitten, though he'd always thought their obvious affection for one another was a matter of common sense rather than crass emotion. "Have you told Miss Strickton of your feelings?"

"I tried, but she won't allow me to speak of it. Worse, ever since she had her London season, she is constantly surrounded by admirers. I can scarcely get a word alone with her."

"There's your first task, then. To get her attention. I'm certain that once you've impressed her with your sincerity and the depths of your devotion, all will change."

"So I thought. I've written her poems—"

"Everyone does that since that fellow Byron came to town. What else?"

"Flowers. But she gets bundles of them a day."

"Too common. You need something larger, more romantic. You know how women are, always gushing about this gesture or that."

Stephen bit his lip. "You're right, of course. There has to be something . . ."

Chase drummed his fingers on the arm of his chair. A long silence ensued. "I suppose jewelry would be too forward?"

"Her father would burst into flames at the thought."

Chase rubbed the bridge of his nose, then winced at the smell. He dropped his hands back to his knees. There was something very gratifying about playing the part of Mature Advisor. He cleared his throat and said in a stentorian tone, "Yes, Stephen, love is a very—" He caught the lad's apt gaze and the clichéd words dried in his throat.

Love was a very what? Annoying feeling? Irritating emotion? Chase wondered what he could say since he wasn't altogether certain that he believed in the fabled emotion anymore.

He eyed Stephen's luminous expression and checked his next words. It was possible that love, in all its infinite glory, didn't really exist. It was a myth, a fiction perpetrated by the females of the species in a vain effort to attach a man with wealth and standing to their sides forever.

In a word, love was pathetic.

Chase's brow lowered. How did one pass on such maudlin information? He really hated to see the light fade from Stephen's eyes. Everyone should have the opportunity to believe in something. At least every once in a while. "Love is a very difficult emotion to understand." There. That said it all. And yet said nothing.

Stephen latched on to it at once. "Yes! You're absolutely right! If only I could get Charlotte to understand how I feel, that it's more than mere childish affection." His brow folded in thought, and he absently sipped his brandy.

Chase watched as the brandy disappeared. "You know, I'd be careful drinking that if I were you." He held up his hands when Stephen's eyes flashed. "I'm not going to say another word, it's just that many of my own problems came from a bottle of my own choosing."

"This is only my second glass."

Which, if one never drank, was still a good quantity of brandy. But there was little Chase could say at this point. The glass was almost empty, and Stephen really didn't seem very tipsy. Perhaps the lad had a head for such things. "I don't suppose you'd welcome the suggestion that you should perhaps forget Miss Strickton for the time being."

"I cannot. You have no idea what she's like. How she smiles. The way she looks when she's trying to decide on something. The way I feel when she's near." Stephen shook his head in wonderment. "I love her and no one else."

The lad had it bad. In a vague way, Chase supposed he could understand Stephen's fascination. It was the same way he felt about Harriet.

Chase, being more mature, didn't fancy himself in love—far from it. But there were certain women who managed to raise his ire—and other parts of his anatomy—remarkably easily.

There was something special about a woman who refused to be charmed. Chase was only lately beginning to realize that fact. Perhaps it was the challenge. The simple give and take of an intelligent wit coupled with a well-turned mind.

Strange how he'd never realized the importance of such things before.

Such women needed firm handling. Direct action. "It's a pity you can't ride into a party and toss her over your saddle like that knight fellow, Loch-something," Chase said thoughtfully. "There's a lot to be said for such decisive handling."

Stephen blinked.

Chase rolled his shoulder a bit and winced. "Perhaps you could begin with something simple and build up to a grand gesture. Start with oh, I don't know . . . maybe a picnic. That could be romantic if done right." He imagined taking Harriet on a picnic. A basket of food—good food, not the work fare they got out in the field—a blanket beside a creek, and perhaps a little wine. He loved the way the sun warmed her brown hair with golden lights. And if the two of them were alone, there was no telling how many kisses he might win from her lips.

The idea held some merit. Perhaps he should—

Stephen slapped his knee, the sound breaking the silence like a gunshot. "B'God, you are right!" His voice brimmed with excitement. He snatched up his crutches and was on his feet and halfway to the door before Chase could even form a sentence.

"Stephen! What are you—"

But Stephen was already making his way out the door. His grand exit was somewhat marred by the fact that he stumbled a little while passing the tea table and had to right it.

"Stephen! Where are you going?"

Stephen grinned. "To win the woman of my heart."

Oh. Well. That sounded far more positive than the maudlin musing of the lad when Chase had first entered the room. "Good for you. I wish you luck."

"Thank you! Although, if this works—" A wide grin burst across his face. "I shall report back in an hour!" He saluted, and then left, stumbling over the very edge of the carpet as he went.

Chase was left facing the closed door. His gaze traveled to the askew tea table and then to the nearly empty brandy decanter. Though he was happy to see Stephen so revitalized, Chase had the unmistakable feeling that he'd missed something. Something significant.

He mulled that thought over for a moment, then shrugged. Whatever happened, he'd cheered up the boy and that was certainly worth something. Why, as soon as Harriet found out, Chase was certain she'd be abject in her apologies for ever calling him selfish.

Feeling very altruistic, Chase pushed up from his chair and made his way out of the library to see if perchance his bath was ready.

Chapter 19

They say that love is the grandest passion of all. Except, perhaps, passion itself.

Anthony Elliot, the Earl of Greyley,
to his wife while on the way to visit
the earl's half brother, Marcus St. John,
the Marquis of Treymount

Devon ran up the wide steps, his booted feet making a ringing announcement of his presence. Located in the heart of Mayfair, Treymount House was an awe-inspiring manor, filled with antiquities and treasures, yet blended with the most modern of conveniences.

Even in London's most exclusive neighborhood, the house caused much comment, from its towering height to the outstanding quality of stonework that graced the entry. Even the shrubbery that lined the drive was painfully perfect. Marcus, of course, would have nothing less.

To many, it seemed cold and somewhat overbearing, but to Devon, who had slid down the stair railings untold times and had frequently jumped out the lower windows while escaping from Cook after stealing a hot pie, Treymount House was just home.

Or had been until he'd moved out at the age of nineteen into his own lodgings.

"Sir," the butler said, smiling a little on seeing who had been hammering on the door. "It has been a long time."

"Hallo, Jeffries. It hasn't been that long. Two weeks, no more." Devon stepped through the door and handed his hat to the butler. "Is his lordship up and about? I feel the need to upset my brother's peaceful existence."

"I would hardly call the marquis's existence peaceful. And he has been up since dawn. In fact, he has already met with his man of business, one of his solicitors, as well as two new investors."

"Showing us all up, is he? All I've managed to do today is eat breakfast and tie my cravat."

Jeffries bowed appreciatively. "I cannot speak for your breakfast, but your cravat is without compare."

Devon grinned. "Damn! I wish you'd let me steal you away from Marcus. I'd pay you twice what you're worth and you'd never have to answer that heavy door again."

"Thank you, sir. I shall keep your offer in mind. His lordship is in the library. Shall I announce you?"

"Lud, no. I'll announce myself." Devon walked toward a wide door at the end of the hall, then stopped, staring up at a huge tapestry that now adorned the wall over the impressive curving stairs. The thing depicted a battle of some sort, with warriors in strange garb swinging huge swords. Here and there were slain enemies, their heads chopped off and lying in pools of blood. "Where in bloody hell did my brother find that?"

Jeffries paused, a faint shimmer of disapproval on his face. "I believe it just arrived from India, sir. The workers took almost three entire days to hang it to his lordship's satisfaction."

"They should take it back. I've never seen anything so hideous in my life."

"Lord Greyley had the same reaction, not ten minutes ago."

Devon turned to look at the butler. "My half brother is here as well?"

"Yes, sir. And the countess, with one of their children. I believe they came to town to consult a physician, or so I heard the countess say."

"I hope nothing is amiss. Thank you, Jeffries." Devon made his way to the library, his heels ringing on the cold marble floor. It was a good thing Anthony was here. He had a calm, logical way about him that might be of assistance.

With a light knock on the library door, Devon let himself into the room. Anthony leaned against the mantel, his huge frame dwarfing even that monstrous affair. His hair, unlike his half siblings', was a golden brown. He always reminded Devon of a bear—large and growling.

But there was no harm to Anthony. His worst fault was an overly sincere desire always to be right. Though he hadn't been born a St. John, it was the one characteristic that bound him the most closely to his brothers and sister.

His wife, Anna, was seated on a nearby chair, her reddish hair warm in the morning sun. One of their many children sat beside her, fiddling with the tassels on a pillow.

Less than a year ago, Anthony had inherited five children, and Anna had come to the house as governess. But the sparks that had existed between the two had been undeniable and within a remarkably short time, they had fallen deeply in love. Devon tried not to remember that Anthony had had that blasted talisman ring in his possession at the time.

"Devon!" Anthony said. "What brings you here? Not out of funds, are you?"

"Me? I'm never out of funds," Devon said, walking forward to greet his half brother. "I'm the lucky one, remember?"

"Ah, yes. The one who never loses. How could I have forgotten?"

"I have no idea, for I've reminded you oft enough. What brings you to London?"

"My son, Richard," Anthony said, nodding toward the boy who sat beside Anna. "Anna believes he cannot hear well, which is why he does not speak as he should."

Anna smiled over the boy's head at Devon. "Marcus went to consult with his man of business for the name of a physician who specializes in such things."

Devon came to stoop before the small boy. "Hello, Richard."

Richard looked up, his eyes brightening when he saw Devon. The lad's grin revealed a shocking number of lost teeth.

Devon chuckled and ruffled the boy's hair. "I hope you grow some new teeth soon or you won't be able to eat anything but porridge."

Richard's grin widened. He reached into his pocket and pulled out a top and a piece of string. After carefully winding the top, he yanked on the string and sent the toy spinning across the smooth surface of the table.

Devon laughed as the top neared the edge and Richard leapt to catch his toy before it hit the ground.

The door opened and Marcus appeared, a neatly written letter in one hand. Devon stood immediately.

"Well!" Marcus said, eyeing Devon with an inquiring gaze. "What's brought you hither?"

Though not as large as Anthony, Marcus exuded a raw power that instantly made him the center of all attention. Most men responded to that air of command by unconsciously stepping back. Except Chase, of course. Chase had always had more bottom than sense.

Devon nodded to Marcus. "It's a pleasure to see you, too. And do not fear, Anthony has already ascertained that I'm not here to ask for a loan."

The hard line of Marcus's mouth softened into a faint smile. "You've never borrowed money from me, though I've offered time and again."

"I'd rather eat a hot coal."

"Well. I can see you're in your usual good spirits."

"Perhaps. I came to ask your advice about something." Devon glanced at Anna and then back. "But it will wait."

Marcus's gaze sharpened. He nodded once. "Very well." He turned to Anna and handed her a letter. "Here, my dear. A letter of introduction. If there is anything to be done for Richard, the doctor will make certain that it happens with all possible speed. He is expecting you now."

"Thank you," Anna said, smiling. She tucked the letter into her reticule and then bent to Richard, who was still playing with his top.

She touched his shoulder. He looked up at her inquiringly. "Time to go," she said softly.

The boy nodded and rose.

"Shall I come, too?" Anthony asked.

"Oh no, my love," Anna said. "Stay here and keep

Marcus company. It has been several weeks since the two of you have had time to chat. I will return in a trice." She took Richard's hand and led him to the door. "Bye, Devon! Will you be here when I return?"

"Probably not, but I will stop by Greyley House tomorrow to visit."

"See that you do," she said with mock severity. "I would hate to have to travel all the way to St. James's to find you."

"You would storm White's, would you?"

"I would at least stand outside on the street and ask for you over and over in a very loud and disconsolate tone." She grinned. "I daresay you'd come running out then."

Anthony tsked. "Anna, pray do not threaten Devon so. He leads an exemplary bachelor life and doesn't understand feminine teasing."

Devon shook his head. "You mistake. Feminine teasing is all I am familiar with."

Anna chuckled. "Poor Devon! I shall expect you tomorrow. Marcus, thank you once again." She nodded pleasantly and was soon out the door, Richard following behind.

As soon as the door closed, Marcus took his place at his desk, shooting a dark glance at Devon. "Have you decided to take my advice and join me in that shipping venture?"

"Hardly that." Devon took the chair before the desk and stretched out his legs, the lamplight reflecting pleasantly in the shine of his boots. "I came about Chase."

Anthony left his place by the mantel to take a chair beside Devon. "Chase? Is he still drinking himself into the grave?"

"I don't know. The last time I saw him, he was indeed drunk, but that has been several weeks ago. I stopped by his lodgings the other day. It was apparent he's left town."

Marcus pulled a stack of correspondence to the center of the desk and began to sort through it. "How long has he been gone this time?"

"More than two weeks."

Anthony quirked a brow. "Another actress, perhaps?"

"No," Devon said thoughtfully. "At least, I don't think so. I believe something is wrong."

Marcus met his gaze. "Why do you think that?"

"He didn't just pack his things and leave. He dismissed his valet completely. I don't think he means to return."

"Never?" Anthony asked.

Devon shook his head. "He took everything of importance, even Mother's ring."

Marcus set down the papers. "Are you certain?"

"I found his valet. Chase gave the man a generous settlement and told him he wouldn't be returning to London. Those were his exact words, too."

Anthony rubbed his chin. "It could still be a woman."

"I've asked about town and he hasn't been connected with any female in particular. Not in the last month, anyway."

There was silence as Anthony and Marcus thought this through. Finally, Marcus said, "Chase has been known to disappear before. It's not that unusual."

"No. But the visit I got from Harry Annesley was."

Anthony shifted in his chair, the delicate wood creaking in protest. "I could never stomach that man's presence. Why Chase allowed the man in his company, I will never know."

Marcus's gaze narrowed on Devon. "What of Annesley's visit?"

"I was at White's. Annesley came up and asked where Chase had gone off to. He says Chase owed him money—a gambling debt. He flashed a marker to prove it."

"Did you see it?" Anthony demanded. "Was it Chase's signature?"

"It appeared to be. Which is why I'm afraid something has happened."

"Explain yourself." Marcus's voice snapped like a sail in the wind. Many people feared Marcus. There was a force behind his controlled, calm gaze. It was as if a thousand storms had been locked away, held in place only by the sheer force of his character.

Devon wasn't afraid of those storms . . . but Marcus's force of character, that *was* something to be reckoned with. "Annesley seemed very determined that everyone at White's see that blasted note. He waved it like a bloody flag. I found that highly unusual. He also seemed determined to place the idea in everyone's head that Chase had fled town because of that debt."

Anthony made a disgusted sound. "Whatever Chase may be, he would never flee a debt of honor."

Marcus nodded. "He is stiff with pride, that one."

"Not to mention," Devon said quietly, "that if Chase needed money, he had only to apply to one of us for the funds. He knows any one of us could have stood the nonsense."

Marcus absently flipped the edge of a letter between his finger and thumb. "This does sound odd."

His gaze flickered to Devon. "What do you think has happened?"

"I believe the note is a forgery. But with Chase gone, there is no way to verify that—" Devon halted, a thought he hadn't allowed himself to think beginning to form.

Anthony's brown eyes glittered. "You believe Annesley has something to do with Chase's disappearance."

"Perhaps. I've put Annesley off, which has irritated him. I expect he will have to make some other move, and soon. Since I've proven recalcitrant, I expect he will next come here."

Anthony's brow creased. "You're right, of course. Something's not—"

The door opened and Jeffries stood in the opening. He bowed to Marcus. "My lord, pardon me. But there's a Mr. Harry Annesley to see you. I told him you were busy, but he has been most insistent."

Marcus and Devon exchanged a look. "Well," Marcus said softly. "The plot thickens."

Devon nodded. It had indeed.

The door to Chase's room slammed open, the sound echoing sharply in Chase's sleep-filled head. He moaned and pulled his pillow over his head. "Go away, Stephen. It's too early to talk any more—"

"It's still evening," Harriet said. "Lady Cabot-Wells just departed."

Chase reluctantly moved the pillow so that it didn't cover his mouth. "She was a bossy old harridan."

"You charmed her very well. Mother and Sophia believe you should tread the boards if you ever find yourself at point-non-plus."

"Sorry I didn't stay long. I was so sleepy after the bath that I could barely keep my eyes open during dinner."

"I daresay you were very tired, considering how busy you've been this evening. You and I need to speak, Mr. St. John."

The tones were frosty. Chase lifted the corner of the pillow and took a good look at the woman who had just been in his dreams.

Of course, in his dreams Harriet was not glaring at him in such a way. She was usually soft and pliant, welcoming him with open arms as she told him how she thought he was the smartest, bravest, most handsome man she'd ever met.

It was quite obvious no such words were going to escape her lips this evening. Chase sighed, pushed his pillow aside, and shoved himself into a seated position. "What is it now—"

Harriet's gaze was locked on his chest. Chase looked down and remembered something else. When he'd crawled into bed, he'd decided he was too tired to wrest on a sleep shirt, so he'd gone to bed naked.

He supposed he should find better cover than that afforded by the thin sheet that pooled in his lap. But no. He wasn't the one who had stormed into someone's bedchamber in the middle of the night, determined to wreak havoc and mayhem. So instead of pulling the cover up, he leaned back against the headboard. "Very well, Harriet. What's this all about?" As he spoke, he shifted slightly and the sheet fell an inch more.

Her gaze widened as she stared at his bare chest, her gaze dropping lower . . . lower.

Chase grinned. "You burst into a man's private

chambers and there's no telling what you might see."

Her gaze jerked up to meet his, her cheeks flushing a bright red. "This is an emergency or I would have never entered your room."

"An emergency? What's wrong now?"

"Stephen."

She said the word as if it should mean something. "What about Stephen?"

"What did you say to him in the library before dinner?"

"Say? I didn't—" Oh, yes. He had said something. Something quite brilliant. "We talked about women and—" What else? Chase couldn't seem to remember the particulars. "Why?"

"Don't try and act the innocent with me," Harriet snapped. "You know very well what you've done. After listening to you and your asinine advice, Stephen stormed over to Strickton House and attempted to abduct Miss Strickton."

Chase blinked. "He did *what*?"

"Don't act surprised. You gave him the idea."

"I did no such thing! What was the boy think—" Chase closed his eyes. That fellow on the white horse. Of course. "What a fool."

"Yes, you are. You have ruined any chances that Stephen might have had with Miss Strickton."

That seemed unnecessarily harsh. After all, most women dreamed of being swept up on a white horse and trotted off to some castle.

Chase glanced around the rather plain room. Not that Garrett Park was a castle, but it had to be a better pile than anything Miss Strickton was used to. "It does sound as if Stephen acted a bit rashly, but he didn't do anything all that serious. All he did was attempt to swoop her into his arms and ride with her into the sunset. What's the harm in that?"

"Miss Strickton did not enjoy being snatched up, dragged across a smelly horse, and then carried off like a sack of potatoes. Her gown was ripped, she lost her pearl necklet, and they had to cut brambles from her hair where she fell off the horse into a very muddy field."

That didn't sound good at all. Chase shook his head. "I hate to say this, but your brother has no finesse."

Harriet's face reddened. "Finesse? What does finesse have to do with anything?"

Chase leaned back against the headboard, adjusting his pillows to a more comfortable level. "It sounds to me as if the problem was more in the execution. As a rule, women enjoy being made a fuss of."

"You call being abducted 'made a fuss of'?" she asked, apparently outraged at the thought.

"No. Being swept up on a horse like that knight fellow, Loch-something. I told Stephen that was the trick with a woman with a strong disposition, to overwhelm her with a romantic gesture."

"Is that what you told him?" she asked grimly.

"Yes. Only I suggested he work his way up to it. I thought he should start with a picnic, but he apparently disagreed."

"I cannot believe that you would sit there and just admit that you—" The words seemed to lock in her throat, for she struggled mightily before she managed to say in a strangled voice, "I hope you're satisfied now, Mr. Chase St. John. Not only has Miss Strickton rejected Stephen most cruelly, but her father came to see Mother and demanded that

Stephen stay away from the entire family or they would call the constable. Mother was quite embarrassed and poor Stephen! It is a scandal of the worst kind and all because you—"

"Don't blame me for all of that! Bloody hell, all I did was suggest that the boy take matters into his own hands; I *never* told him to abduct the chit. If you don't believe me, ask him."

"Ask him?"

"Ask him," Chase said firmly. "He may have gotten the idea from the fact that I mentioned that Lochfellow, but I never suggested that he do something that ridiculous. And I wouldn't."

Harriet's shoulders slumped. "You wouldn't?"

"Lord, no! Do I look that wet behind the ears?"

Her gaze flickered over him, once again lowering to his lap. Chase suddenly realized how intimate the setting was; Harriet and he, alone in his room. And here he was, naked and in a warm bed. His body tightened at the thought, and he had to adjust the sheet to cover his reaction.

Her cheeks heated, and she looked away, though she remained close to the bed. "I—I suppose I should have asked Stephen to be more specific. But when he said he'd gotten the idea from you, I assumed the worst. I'm sorry."

Chase had to bite his lip to keep from grinning. "If you were really sorry, you'd show it."

Her gaze flew to his. "Show it?"

"With a kiss."

"I—you—oh! That is quite enough, Mr. St. John." Her color adorably high, she wheeled to march out of the room, but Chase was too quick.

He had her in his arms and in his lap before she could do more than gasp in surprise.

For an instant, they simply sat there, staring at one another, heat rippling between them in hurried, urgent waves. Chase's body was taut with need. He had dreamed enough nights about this woman. Finding her here, in his naked lap, was almost more than he could stand.

"Let me go," she said, her voice soft and breathless.

"No."

Her eyes sparkled with irritation. "I'm sorry if I wrongly accused you. But if you'd seen Stephen when he'd returned—"

"I'd have told him to get his chin up off the ground and be a man about things."

"Oh! What do you know about picking your chin up off the ground? You, with your thousands of servants and hundreds of houses?"

"More than you know," he said, the line of his mouth suddenly grim.

Harriet paused, her irritation melting away before a sudden surge of hot curiosity. Every once in a while, she caught a glimpse of a different Chase St. John than the one usually presented to the world at large. It was almost as if beneath his arrogant, self-satisfied swagger, there was a river of emptiness, of sadness. He was a conundrum, this startlingly handsome man.

Brash and bold on the outside, seemingly interested only in himself, he was nonetheless capable of great kindness and caring. She found her gaze drawn to him; to the tempting line of his mouth, the masculine strength of his throat. To her surprise, a flash of heat burned through her. She could feel the warmth of his bared skin against her arm.

Heavens, but he was enticing. But as tasty as he

appeared, he was not from Sticklye-By-The-River. And he was definitely not a part of Garrett Park. She had to remind herself that he never would be.

His gaze met hers and in that instant, something shimmered deep in his eyes, a sparkle that was answered in her own heart. In that moment, something changed, shifted, went from abstract thought to intense action.

"Harriet," Chase murmured. Then, to her surprise, he pulled her to his bare chest and kissed her.

Chapter 20

Love does not come in a neat package, tied with a bow, and delivered to one's house. It's large and roiling, rather like a river, only noisier, infinitely messier, and far harder to control.

The Countess of Greyley
to her new sister-in-law,
Mrs. Brandon St. John,
while knitting stockings for charity

Harriet shivered and closed her eyes. It was madness. Sheer and utter madness.

But somehow, she just didn't care. She'd never felt such a flush of pure lust. Had never enjoyed the delightful feeling of being desired, passionately and intensely by a man—by any man really. But especially not by a man like Chase St. John.

"Harriet," he whispered against her ear, his hot breath stirring her hair. "I want you. I want to be with you." He nuzzled her neck and murmured against her skin, "And in you."

Harriet bit her lip, her entire body trembling. All her life, she'd been in control, had done what was right, followed the safe and sane path, taken care of others and herself. Now . . . now she didn't want any of that. She wanted to be . . . freer. Unfettered with responsibility and cares.

"Touch me," he whispered, his breath brushing over her ear. "Put your hands on me."

The old Harriet would have refused him. It was the right thing to do—to put an end to this lunacy. But the new Harriet splayed her hands over his chest, threading his crisp hairs through her fingers.

It was heavenly. His skin was warm and inviting, his muscles taut. She heard herself say his name ever so softly, "Chase." The name slid through her teeth, satin tied with a velvet rope. Her ability to refuse him melted with the sound.

She'd been so aggravated with him when she'd first come to his room. But he'd been right—Stephen was responsible for his acts, not anyone else.

Harriet suddenly wondered why Chase had even bothered to help her brother in the first place. "Why did you—"

He kissed her, his mouth covering hers, his tongue sliding between her lips. Hot and delicious, he overwhelmed her senses, made her forget everything but the feel of him.

He pulled her closer and she grasped his shoulders, his bare skin warm beneath her fingertips. His hands roamed over her back, down to her hips, then up her sides.

Harriet moaned softly just as he cupped her breasts through her gown. Sensuous shivers flashed through her.

"Ah, Harriet," he whispered again, nipping her chin, her throat, her shoulder.

Never had her plain, rather unsatisfactory name seemed so seductive as when he breathed it through his lips like a prayer of thanks. His hot mouth left a trail of delicate fire everywhere it touched.

She tilted her head back and gave him silent permission to explore the hollows, gasping in pleasure as his breath fanned over her skin.

"Mmmm," he said in a slightly raspy voice. "You smell of cinnamon and apples."

"I—I helped Cook with the pies. I think they'll be very good when—"

"You. Are. Delicious." His lips touched her throat with each word, and a series of tremors raced through her.

His free hand found her knee and he slowly pulled up her skirts. The thin material slid along her leg, inching past her calf, until he finally slipped his hand beneath. His fingers were unnaturally warm as they skimmed her leg, her thigh.

Harriet gasped. He was bold and brazen, taking and teasing. His fingers brushed the top of her pantaloons, pushing them aside until his bare fingers slid down her stomach.

Panic flared. She caught his wrist. "No."

He looked at her then, his eyes so dark they appeared almost black. "Why not?"

Why not? She could think of a thousand reasons why not and only one why—because she wanted him. Wanted him to touch her, to kiss her, to make her mindless with passion. For once in her life, she wanted to lose control and just live.

Her gaze locked on his, she released his hand. "Why not indeed."

A faint smile curled his lips, his gaze wandering over her face, touching briefly on her eyes, her nose, her upper lip. He bent and placed his lips on hers, holding still, allowing the moment to linger and swell.

Her whole body shivered awake. His hand slid lower then, over her stomach, down between her legs and he touched her in the most intimate of places.

She started then, jerked out of her desire-induced trance. "I ca—"

He kissed her, harder and more demanding than before, overwhelming her protests, overcoming her fears. And all the while, his fingers were never still. He found her most secret place, stroking and touching her, building her desires until they burned and she arched against him, her inhibitions gone in the flash of a moment.

Heaven help her, but she was on fire. She yearned for him, ached for him deep within. He kissed her cheek with the softest of touches, his mouth leaving a damp trail as he traced a line to her ear. His breath fluttered against her earlobe and sent a deluge of delicious tremors through her.

He was slow, deliberate, his intent all too clear—he meant to make her crazy with desire before seducing her in full.

And why not, Harriet decided. She was a woman grown. And in all her years, she'd never met a man like this, one who wore his sensuality like a fig leaf on an ancient statue. She knew what was behind that blasted leaf—she hadn't lived on a farm for all these years for nothing. Nonetheless, her fingers itched to remove everything that stood between her and him, so that she could get a nice, long look at what lay beneath.

What was a true revelation was how many other weapons of seduction the man had at his disposal.

Not only were his hands roaming freely, but his mouth never ceased delivering shivery kisses and delicate nips. His breath sent a flutter of heat down her spine. His skin burned beneath her fingertips, begging to be touched even more.

Harriet was lost. Her body tightened in response to each and every new delight. How she wanted this man.

She could feel his fingers busily unlacing her gown. And before she knew it, he was pushing the neckline free, shoving it down, over her shoulders, to her waist. Mindless with the need to taste him, to feel him, she pulled her arms free of the gown, and wrapped them about his neck.

He pressed a passionate kiss to her neck, his hands cupping, kneading her through the thin material of her shift, driving her wilder.

"Remove it," he murmured against her ear.

"What?" she asked breathlessly, shifting restlessly, aware of a deep ache within. She wanted more, needed more.

"Your shift," he said, placing wet kisses along her cheek and neck. "Remove it."

It was an order, softly made, yet insistent. Harriet didn't even question. She wanted this, wanted him. She tugged the lace that tied her shift free, and somehow, she never would remember exactly how, she was soon naked and pliant on the bed beneath him. He bent over her, resting on one elbow as his mouth continued to trace a heated path from her neck to her ear and back.

It was erotic, the feel of their limbs entangled with nothing between them. Harriet ran her hands over his broad shoulders, kissing his throat, his chin.

He cupped her breast, his thumb flicking over her

nipple and causing her to drop her head back and close her eyes. "Harriet, look at me."

She opened her eyes and met his gaze. He was so incredibly beautiful, his skin damp with perspiration, his blue eyes vivid, his black hair falling over his brow. Holding her gaze, he dropped his mouth to her breast and laved the peak, his hands now stroking higher, up her thigh, returning to the taut core of her womanhood.

She gasped, her head thrown back, her hair coming unbound. Chase soaked in the sight of her face as she gave herself to the passion. Her face flushed, her eyes glistened, her face softened with wonder. No vestige was left of the plainspoken, logically bound Harriet that he'd come to admire. In her place was a tempting siren with lush brown hair, a kiss-swollen mouth, and eyes that shimmered with desire.

He had to have her. *Now*. Never had he lusted for any woman, especially not an innocent. The thought held him for a moment. She was an innocent, but she was also in his bed, her face awash with pleasure, with need. Everyone at Garrett Park looked to her for their comfort. Perhaps it was time someone looked to hers.

With a renewed vow to make this moment the most incredible of her life, to show her how wonderful, how beautiful he found her, he covered her mouth with his and kissed her softly, deeply. He put every bit of himself into that kiss, mingling his soul with hers.

She responded without hesitation, opening, writhing, clutching at his shoulders. Finally, panting heavily, he broke the kiss and lifted on his elbow to look at her.

Chase couldn't move. He'd known that beneath

her plain gowns, Harriet was an attractive woman. But seeing her now, completely naked, her delicately made, but strongly wrought, body outlined against the sheets, was almost more than he could bear. She was beautiful, perfectly made.

Her legs were curvaceous, her waist narrow above her slender hips. Her small breasts were tipped with rose-colored nipples that drew his gaze and made his mouth water.

"You are beautiful," he breathed. "So beautiful."

In answer, she lifted up on her elbows to tilt her face to his. Her thick brown hair flowed about her shoulders and clung to the shadowed hollows of her neck. She grasped his neck with one hand and pulled him closer, the warmth from her palm sending a tingle of heat through him.

He splayed his hands over her shoulders and arms, marveling at the seductively carved collarbone that was displayed there. She was no soft, overfed miss, but a woman of strength, of delicately made muscles and finely wrought sinew.

His body tightened almost painfully. He could no longer think coherently about anything. Anything but this woman and her creamy thighs. He had to have her. Have her and make her his. The desire to brand her, to mark her as his own and no one else's, raced through him and all coherent thought fled at the onslaught of primitive emotion.

Chase lifted himself and poised above her, his hands tangled in her hair. "Love me, Harriet. Let me come in."

Her thighs widened and she gripped him close. Chase lowered himself into her slowly, so slowly that she stirred impatiently, shifting beneath him as if trying to pull him into her.

He held still, savoring his entry, reveling in the heat and tightness. Suddenly, he could take it no more and he pushed deep within.

She gasped, her eyes widening.

Chase could have killed himself then and there. She was a virgin. Somehow, in the erotic dance that had held them in thrall, he'd allowed himself to forget that fact.

He pulled her close and whispered softly in her ear, "Easy, love. Easy."

Slowly, she relaxed beneath him. Chase kept whispering, long strings of soft words, of warm sentiments, of heated promises. He kept his hands busy, stroking her here, soothing her there. Within moments, she began to stir restlessly, to press against him, her pain forgotten in the onslaught of desire.

Ah yes. She was a passionate woman. He could see it in the way her chest rose and fell, her small breasts puckering as if begging for a touch. He leaned forward and pressed his mouth to first one nipple, then the next, pulling gently while she gasped in pleasure.

Slowly, ever so slowly, he began to move inside her. He let her set the pace, her lithe body growing more moist, more demanding. God, but she was a sweet piece, hot and lush, more desirable than any woman he'd ever known. Chase gritted his teeth and fought to maintain control. It was the most erotic moment of his life, the feel of this woman beneath him. For the love of Hera, but he'd never experienced such a heated encounter.

How was it that a country chit completely devoid of experience could make him crazed with desire while countless women with other, far more exotic notions, left him less than inspired?

What was it about Harriet Ward that made her bolder, more colorful, more intriguing than any London-born and -bred mistress?

Whatever it was, it was intoxicating. Fascinating. Scintillating. He reveled in her nearness, in the strength of her body, in the lithe grace of her form. He cupped her closer to him, losing himself inside her silken softness.

She was lost, eyes closed, gasping for breath as her body moved demandingly, hips thrusting, feet firmly planted on the mattress. She was magnificent, her unalleviated passion pushing Chase to the edges of his own control.

Suddenly, her eyes widened and she gasped, her body clenching about him, the silky tug yanking him over the edge. Chase ground his teeth, but it was too late. His body reacted before he could withdraw and he climaxed deep inside her.

For several moments they remained where they were, entangled, arms about each other, his face pressed against her hair, her legs still tight about his waist.

It was achingly sweet, that moment. And Chase, for the first time in his life, didn't feel an overwhelming compulsion to jump up from the bed and make good his escape.

All he wanted to do was stay right where he was, holding Harriet as their bodies quieted. He was agonizingly aware of her slender hips beneath his, of her breath on his shoulder, of her hair tangled on the pillow, of the smell of her silken skin.

All of it seeped through him and made him wish they could stay just like this, hidden and warm, safe and sated for the rest of their lives.

After a long moment, Harriet shifted against the

pillows, her sigh warm on his neck. "We must get up."

"I know." Chase caught her hand in his and looked at it for a minute before he bent to kiss her finger where the talisman ring lay. It fit her slender finger perfectly, which was strange, for Chase would have sworn the ring was larger. He ran his thumb over the strange surface, a shiver of heat filling him.

Somehow, instead of looking at the ring, he found himself looking into Harriet's eyes. Drowning in the warm brown depths, the ache that was always deep in his soul, easing for a moment. She shivered.

"Cold?"

"No. I was just—" She looked down at her hand where the ring rested. "I must dress."

"Yes." But he made no move to get up. Instead, he kissed her fingers, first one and then the next.

A noise sounded in the hallway.

Harriet's eyes flew open. "Did you hear that?" she whispered.

The noise sounded again.

"Oh no!" She struggled beneath him. "We must rise."

Chase obligingly moved to one side and smiled down at her, secure that she wouldn't hop out of bed too quickly since her hair was firmly beneath his elbow. He felt amazingly invincible. Strong and powerful.

She tried to lift her head. "You're on my hair."

"If you rise, they will only catch you standing nude in the center of my room." Not that that was a bad thing. Chase rather liked the thought of Harriet standing naked in the center of his room, her thick chestnut hair falling over her shoulders, her firm bottom within reach.

"We can't stay here forever."

He bent and kissed her chin. "We can try. Stay where you are and when they knock, I'll send them away. If I use a large enough voice, they won't dare come in."

A soft knock came at the door. "Mr. St. John?"

Harriet looked up at Chase, her eyes wide. "It's Sophia," she whispered.

"I know," he whispered back, a little amused by the alarm in Harriet's normally calm gaze.

"Mr. St. John?" Sophia asked again, this time rattling the doorknob.

Harriet gasped.

"*Who is it?*" Chase growled the words rather than said them, as if he was a pirate. "I'm just getting dressed for bed." He paused, then added, "I'm naked."

There was an audible gasp outside the door, so comical that Harriet pressed a hand over her mouth, her eyes crinkled as she fought back a laugh.

Chase grinned at her and winked.

"Oh dear," Sophia was heard to say. "I didn't mean to interrupt you. And I wasn't going to open the door or anything—I just wanted to see if Harriet was about."

"She's not in here, if that's what you mean."

"Of course I didn't think—that is, I was just trying to— Oh, bother!" Sophia sighed loudly. "I must find Harriet."

They never let the poor girl alone. Chase was aware of a strong desire to fix that, to take some of the burden off Harriet's slender shoulders.

But meeting her gaze, he realized that she would not thank him for such interference. He bit back a sigh.

He smoothed back a thick strand of Harriet's brown hair from her cheek, noting the silky texture. The light from the lamp glistened on her chestnut locks, bringing out hints of red and gold. She glinted a faint smile up at him, her lips quivering slightly.

Sophia's voice sounded again, this time closer as if she was pressing her cheek to the door. "I'm sorry to bother you at all, Mr. St. John, but it's important. Harriet must come downstairs right this moment."

"This late? It must be ten o'clock."

"I know. But Mr. Gower has arrived and he says he must speak with Mother immediately. The bank will not wait another day for their payment."

Chapter 21

Gambling comes in many forms. Some people wager on cards. Some on horses. And some on their own hearts.

Mrs. Brandon St. John, newly returned from her honeymoon, to her husband, as they made their way to Treymount House for an emergency family meeting

A short time later, Harriet paused outside the sitting room and looked at herself in the mirror. She looked as she always did, except a trifle flushed.

Perfectly plain and proper, her gown smooth and unruffled, her hair pinned neatly on top of her head. No one would look at her and know that she'd just been seduced by the most handsome man in the world.

Well, the most handsome man in Sticklye-By-The-River, anyway. Who was to say that there weren't more handsome men out and about?

She thought of Chase's blue eyes, of his thick black lashes, of the way his hair fell over his brow, of his muscular arms and shoulders . . . she shook her head ruefully. What was she thinking? There simply could not be a better-looking man in the entire world.

"Harriet!" Mother bustled up, a worried expression on her face. "Thank goodness we found you."

Sophia joined them. "There you are, Harri! Where were you? I looked everywhere."

Harriet offered a casual shrug. "I was in my room doing some mending and I forgot the time." There. That sounded plausible.

Sort of.

Sophia frowned. "No you weren't. I looked there. I even looked in your dressing room and in the kitchen and in the barn and in the—"

"Oh for heaven's sake," Mother said as if exasperated, "it doesn't matter where she's been. All that matters is that she's here now."

Harriet frowned at her mother's concerned tone. "Why the uproar?"

"It's Mr. Gower." Mother's eyes were troubled. "Harriet, I believe he has proof that our guest is not the captain."

Harriet's throat tightened. "Has he said something?"

"He began to, but I told him you really needed to be present and then I left him to find you."

That was probably a good idea. Mother didn't have the calmest disposition under pressure.

"Gower didn't come alone," Sophia added. "He has two members of the board of directors with him. They look as solemn as Sunday."

Harriet's heart sank. "Oh no."

"My thoughts exactly," Mother said. "What a horrid night. First Lady Cabot-Wells grilled the poor captain over dinner, then Mr. Strickton comes roaring in about Stephen, and now this."

"I spoke to the captain about Stephen. Apparently my mutton-headed brother mistook something that was said about Lochinvar as an invitation to behave like a barbarian."

"Lochinvar?" Sophia's mouth dropped open. "I never thought—why that *is* what Lochinvar did, isn't it? He rode right into the gates of the castle and stole his beloved away. Only not on a plodding farm horse. And I rather doubt he lost his grip and dropped her on her head into a muddy field."

Mother's mouth folded with disapproval. "Your brother has no sense whatsoever, especially when it comes to the fair sex. I'm only sorry that the Stricktons had to witness Stephen's outrageous folly."

Harriet smoothed her skirts, "I cannot believe Mr. Gower would visit so late in the evening. It is quite rude."

"So I thought," Mother said. She hesitated, biting her lip. After a moment, she said, "Do you think we might prevail upon Mr. St. John to—No, of course not. We couldn't ask him. He's done so much already." Her cheeks touched with pink. "I didn't mean to cause him any pain, and I hope he's aware of that. It just seemed that, since he'd already lost his memory, it wouldn't hurt if he thought he was someone important, even if—"

"Mother, Mr. St. John never lost his memory," Harriet said.

Mother blinked. "Never? Then why did he agree to be the captain?"

"I think . . . I think he thought to help us. He was on his way out of the country when the attack occurred, leaving some unpleasant business behind."

"My goodness!" Sophia said, her eyes bright. "What unpleasant business?"

"I don't know. He hasn't offered to tell me. But he has been so kind as to agree to stay and play the part of the captain until the shearing is finished." And then he'd be gone. Harriet's heart ached at the thought.

"How kind of him," Mother said. "Whatever Gower has to say, it will seem far less relevant while there is a live, breathing man standing before him, at least claiming to be the captain."

"Precisely." Harriet straightened her shoulders and glanced at her mother and sister. "Are you ready?"

Mother patted her white hair while Sophia smoothed her skirts. "I think so," Mother finally said.

Harriet went to the door and opened it.

Mr. Gower immediately turned from where he was standing in conversation with two other men. "Miss Ward." He bowed. "Mrs. Ward. And Miss Sophia. Allow me to introduce Mr. Picknard and Mr. Silverstone from the bank."

Harriet curtsied, as did Mother and Sophia. "What a lovely surprise," Harriet said, though it took all of her persuasive powers to keep her expression pleasant. "To what do we owe the honor of this visit, late though the hour?"

"I'm sorry about the time." Mr. Gower seemed to grow taller as he glanced at his two companions from the bank. "There is a problem with the extension."

Mr. Picknard shifted uneasily. "Yes, ah . . . as you know, the extension was granted based on Miss Ward's supposed fiancé, Captain Frakenham."

"Supposed?" Mother said, blinking. "What do you mean 'supposed'?"

Mr. Picknard rubbed his red nose. Large and heavyset with reddish hair and a large, drooping moustache, he resembled an untrimmed sausage stuffed into a black coat. "By supposed we mean to say that there are some questions as to just who and if Captain Frakenham actually exists."

Gower's expression gleamed with triumph. "*Someone* has been guilty of fraud. *Someone* has attempted to trick the bank by falsifying reports. *Someone* has—"

"Oh for the love of God," puffed Mr. Silverstone. Taller than either of the other men, and dressed with quiet distinction, Silverstone appeared far better bred than either Gower or Picknard.

In fact, Harriet had the impression that here was the man who made all the decisions at the bank.

He shot a hard look at Mr. Picknard from beneath heavy gray brows, then turned back to the ladies, paying special attention to Mrs. Ward. "I hope you will pardon our intrusion this evening, but Mr. Gower has uncovered a seeming discrepancy in the stories we've been hearing about this Captain Frakenham. I'm certain you can straighten this all out. I thought perhaps we should wait until tomorrow, however"—he shot a sharp glare at Gower—"I was informed that it would be foolhardy to let this situation go on another day as certain individuals could disappear."

Harriet smoothed her damp palms on her skirts. Everything was at stake. "Mr. Silverstone, I assure you that no one has attempted to defraud your establishment. Indeed, within the week, we should have the money for the payment and—"

The door opened. Mother gave a sigh of relief. "Captain Frakenham!"

Chase bowed. Only it was not the man Harriet had grown used to seeing these last few weeks, wearing Stephen's discarded clothing and a floppy brimmed hat. Chase had gathered his own garments and now stood before them dressed exactly as he really was—a London gentleman of fashion. And not just any gentleman of fashion, but obviously one raised amidst untold wealth and privilege.

For some reason, the sight made Harriet's heart sink.

Oblivious to her feelings, he smoothed his sleeve as he walked forward. It would have been difficult to suggest an improvement on the man before them—his blue coat was perfectly cut, smooth across his broad shoulders and tapering to his narrow waist. His buff breeches fit his long, muscular legs, his black boots were shined until they resembled glass. His snowy white cravat was knotted and tied in a way Harriet had never seen, but she recognized the touch of a master when she saw it.

"There you are, Captain!" Mother said, breaking the awkward silence as she bustled forward.

He took her hand and bowed over it. "Indeed. I was just enjoying a glass of port in the library when I heard that you had guests."

"Indeed. This is Mr. Gower, whom I believe you've met. And this is Mr. Picknard and Mr. Silverstone. They're from the bank."

Harriet noticed that even Mr. Silverstone stood a little straighter when Chase nodded briefly in his direction.

"Gentlemen," Chase said in a bored tone. He looked back at Mrs. Ward and offered a glinting smile. "I hope I'm not intruding."

She laughed nervously. "Of course not! We're always glad to have you with us, Captain."

"Indeed," said Sophia, casting a sly glance at the

bankers. "I don't believe we will be detained much longer now that you've arrived."

Mr. Gower stepped forward, his gaze on Chase, a superior smile curving his wide mouth. "I would greet you, as well, but you are not who you say you are. There is no Captain Frakenham."

Harriet held her breath, but Chase merely lifted his brows. "What do you mean by that?"

Mr. Gower's superior attitude thickened. "I did some research. There is no record of a Captain Frakenham or of a ship coming to port in Whitby. None."

Every eye turned to Chase. He shrugged. "No?"

"No."

"What exactly are you suggesting, Mr. Gower? That I am an apparition?" Chase held out his hands. "Do I look like an apparition?"

Silverstone cleared his throat. "Mr. Gower, perhaps there is a better way to—"

"Who are you?" Gower said, his sharp gaze on Chase. "Tell us now."

Chase laughed softly, genuine amusement in his voice.

Harriet relaxed at the sound. He wasn't the least intimidated and she took comfort in that fact.

Gower scowled. "Damn it, sir! This is not a cause for levity. You are not who you say you are."

"No?"

"No."

Chase tilted his head to one side, a smile still warm on his lips. "Perhaps I should ask you the same question—who are *you*?"

"I am a banker, sir. My credentials are impeccable."

"And I am a sea captain. Until proven otherwise."

Triumph flickered across Gower's face. "It *has*

been proven otherwise." He reached into his pocket and pulled out two folded sheets of paper. He held out the first one. "I wrote to the harbormaster at Whitby. He has never heard of your ship, nor you."

Chase took the paper and scanned it. "Harbormaster? By the name of Crenlin? You've been fooled, Mr. Gower. The harbormaster at Whitby is a Mr. Johnston."

"That cannot be."

"I hope you didn't pay this man for his information." Chase fixed his gaze on Gower's face. "Did you?"

Silverstone and Picknard waited. Gower turned deep red. "I only gave the man two shillings to pay for post—"

"Tsk. Tsk. I fear you've been taken for a fool, Mr. Gower. I daresay this man is a resident of one of the pubs along the waterfront and takes great pleasure in thieving from men making inquiries." Chase shook his head. "Just look at the poor spelling in this missive."

"Spelling? What difference does that make?"

Chase held the ragged letter up to the light, a look of distaste on his face. "It is horridly stained, too. No doubt by cheap gin of some sort." He held the letter out to Gower, who almost snatched it from his hand. "I would not believe a word I received from this man, whoever he is."

Silverstone and Picknard appeared uneasy.

"Captain," Harriet said, "please do not take offense. I'm certain Mr. Gower did not mean to imply anything unsavory about you."

Silverstone held out his hand. "Gower, let me see that missive."

Face red, Gower handed the letter to the banker.

Silverstone peered down his nose at it, squinting in the dim light thrown off from the three lamps that illuminated the room. After a moment, he sent a steely glare at Gower from beneath his bushy brows. "Did you meet the man who sent this?"

Gower mutely shook his head.

"A sad business, this. I'm afraid I have to agree with the captain." Silverstone handed the missive back to Gower. "I hope you have some other proof that the captain is not who he says he is."

Gower's face turned so red that for a moment, Harriet thought he might explode into a boiling mass of invectives. Instead, he stuffed the missive into his pocket and held the other one out to Mr. Silverstone. "Of course I have more proof. I think even you will believe this one."

Silverstone took the letter and read it, his lips moving slightly. Harriet's heart sank when she noticed how the man's brow lowered with each word.

After a moment, Silverstone looked at Chase, a considering expression in his eyes. "This letter is from Admiral Hawkins-Smythe. He states that he is familiar with every captain in the naval service and that he has never heard of you."

Picknard snorted. "Well, there you are! The admiral lives not ten miles from here and is very well known. He served almost forty years in His Majesty's service and knows every ship that England has ever put to sea."

Harriet rubbed her brow. What a mule. She knew the admiral well and she was certain he could discredit Chase.

Undeterred, Chase shrugged. "The admiral has never heard of me, and I have never heard of the admiral."

"What?" Silverstone asked.

"I captain a merchant ship, owned by a private company. The only way your admiral would know me is if he had, at some time, boarded my vessel to search for contraband or some such nonsense. Which has never happened to a ship under my command."

Silence fell on the small group. Finally, Silverstone sighed. "He's right." The banker sent a hard look at Gower. "I think we've taken enough time away from these good people."

"Yes, but what about—"

"Do you have any more evidence?" Silverstone asked, his lip curled with distaste as he waved the letter in the air. "Something more than this."

Gower's mouth whitened. He struggled as if to say something, but no words would come out.

Harriet almost pitied the man. Almost. "Mr. Silverstone, Mr. Picknard, I'm so sorry you wasted your time this evening."

Mother nodded, her white hair shimmering softly in the light. "I hate to see you leave so quickly. Perhaps you would like to stay for some port? My oldest son could—"

"Thank you, but no," Mr. Silverstone said. "I apologize again for interrupting your evening. We will see you in a week when the payment is due." He sent a glare at Gower. "Well, sir. Are you ready to leave?"

For a moment, Harriet thought that Gower would argue, but he gave a sharp nod instead and stepped back to allow the two older men access to the doorway.

Mother and Sophia led the way out into the hall, Silverstone and Picknard following close behind.

Gower remained in the center of the room, his eyes narrowed on Chase.

Chase, of course, didn't back away. Instead, he stepped forward until the two were almost toe to toe.

Harriet sighed. They looked like two rams, blowing steam out their nostrils as they circled one another in a field. "Mr. Gower—please. I think you've done quite enough tonight without—"

Chase waved a hand. "Beloved, allow the man to speak. I can tell he has something of great import to say to us both."

Gower had stiffened at Chase's endearment. His jaw tightened and he said through clenched teeth, "I do not know who you are, but you are not Captain Frakenham."

Harriet managed a pleasant smile, though she felt far from such a thing. "Mr. Gower, I'm certain that in time all of this will—"

"Listen, Gower," Chase said. "I don't know what you hope to gain by this, but leave the Wards alone. If your complaint is with me, then we will settle it as men."

Harriet closed her eyes. Didn't Chase realize that her future, the future of the Wards, the future of Garrett Park, quite possibly rested in this man's hands?

She sneaked a peek at Gower, her shoulders slumping when she saw that his hands had tightened into fists.

"You, sir, are a charlatan. And I will not rest until I discover who and what you are."

Chase's smile was not pleasant. "Try your damnedest, Gower. Just do not be surprised if what you find is not to your liking."

Harriet tried to intercede once again. "Mr. Gower,

please excuse the captain. He's just a little upset about the allegations——"

"I am not upset at all," Chase said smoothly. "In fact, I welcome the challenge. Gower, feel free to investigate me in any manner at your disposal. I have nothing to hide and I wish you the best of fortune in discovering exactly who and what I am."

Gower's neck was by then as reddish as his face. "Be careful what you wish for or you may well get it."

With that, he turned on his heel and stomped from the room, stopping only to give Harriet a scathing look.

"Oh dear," Harriet said as she heard the front door slam shut.

Mother and Sophia entered almost immediately. "What happened?" Sophia asked breathlessly.

Harriet sighed. "Captain Frakenham was doing a lovely imitation of a rooster." She sent him a cutting look. "What was that all about? You'd already done what you needed to do, which was cast doubt on his allegations. Getting him angry will only make him more determined to prove you wrong."

Chase crossed his arms and leaned one shoulder to the mantel, his mouth still hard. "He was rude to you. I couldn't allow that to continue."

Harriet made an exasperated noise. "Piffle! I vow, but you do not understand. We need his good graces to keep the bank from foreclosing."

Mother sighed. "Harriet is right. Silverstone has told several people in town that he believes Gower might be the man to take his place on the board one day."

"Harri?" Stephen and Derrick stood in the doorway, Ophelia peering around them. "What happened?"

Sophia took a quick, excited step forward. "Oh, it was marvelous! Mr. St. John came to our rescue and played the part of Captain Frakenham with such enthusiasm!" She clasped her hands together and beamed at Chase. "The bankers were completely fooled."

"For now," Harriet said. "But Gower will be back."

Stephen scowled. "I hate that man. What are we to do now?"

Everyone looked at Harriet. She met their gazes without expression. Chase found that he wanted to go to her, to put his arm about her shoulders. She looked so young, and far too small to have such burdens placed on her slender shoulders.

But while he was trying to find a way to say that, to say something that would take the focus off Harriet, she lifted her chin.

A look of stark determination settled on her face as she faced her family. "Tomorrow, we begin the shearing."

Chapter 22

If one of your supposed friends decided to rudely impose his will over yours, it would be considered an act of despotic familiarity. But when your family decides to do it, it is considered an act of kindness, brought on by a superior understanding of your poor nature and the fact that they possess a greater intellect than any you could claim. It's quite enough to make one wish one was an orphan.

Mr. Brandon St. John to Mr. Devon St. John,
on leaving Treymount House after
the emergency family meeting

The next morning broke cool and breezy and it was with a true sense of purpose that the Ward family, their two hired hands, and Chase gathered at the barn. Harriet ran the operation like a general and soon everyone was sent on his appointed duties. Sophia and Ophelia went to man the gates at each end of the sheep pens. Mother went to oversee a nice luncheon, to be served under the oak tree once noon arrived.

Harriet decided Stephen and one of the hired men

would help her with one lot of sheep while Derrick and Chase would be responsible for shearing the other lot.

Harriet stole a glance at Chase where he stood in the barn, wearing Stephen's old clothing. Chase's hair fell over his brow, his arms bared from where he'd rolled up his shirtsleeves. This was a man who was used to riding the best horses, dancing with the most beautiful debutantes, sharing confidences with the crème de la crème of society.

Yet here he was, dressed to work in the fields, as if he was a member of her family.

And in a way, that was exactly what he had become. When he'd first arrived he'd been arrogant and spoiled. But every day she saw him changing, opening his heart to her family, becoming more a part of them all. For the first time, she realized how difficult it was going to be when he left.

Stephen hobbled up. "There you are, Mr. St—"

"Just call me Chase, if you please."

Stephen grinned. "Chase, then."

"I've been meaning to tell you that I'm sorry things did not prosper with Miss Strickton."

Hot pink flooded Stephen's cheeks. "I'm sorry I took you so literally. It seemed like a good idea at the time."

"I daresay that was the brandy thinking and not you."

"You are probably right."

"Don't worry about it. There may be a way 'round Miss Strickton's hard heart yet."

Stephen's face fell. "No. I fear I've botched it so badly, there is no redeeming myself now."

"We'll see," Chase said.

Stephen grimaced. "She said she never wanted to see me again. And I don't blame her. I made a mull of it."

"I believe our problem is that we didn't attempt to approach the situation the way a woman would."

"What?"

"What do you think would impress Miss Strickton? What does she seem to be drawn to?"

"Sir Roger Blevins," Stephen said glumly.

"Who is that?"

"A completely pompous ass who makes as if he's a swell of some sort just because he's been to London a time or two. I think he's a damned mushroom. A complete cit with no breeding. But to hear him tell it, he practically grew up riding with the Prince and shooting billiards with lords and ladies."

Chase frowned. "Sir Roger Blevins, you said? I've never heard that name and I can tell you for a fact that he's not a member of White's."

"I wish someone would tell that to Miss Strickton." Stephen brightened. "Say! Could you—"

"No, no. You're mistaken if you think discrediting your opponents will win you anything. What you need to do is outshine the fellow, make her forget all about him. How does this Sir Blevins dress?"

"Wide collars, shirt points up to here, huge cravat. He can barely turn his head, yet Miss Strickton acts as if she'd never seen anything more beautiful."

Chase rubbed his chin a moment. "Yes. I think I know just what you need to do. After we finish today, you will go to town. Will Miss Strickton be there?"

"She should be. Her father's house overlooks Sticklye, and she rides through often." Stephen frowned. "But what would seeing Miss Strickton again do? She will only wish me to the devil."

"Not this time, she won't. You'll see."

Harriet wondered what was going through Chase's mind. She didn't know if she liked his smile or not—it seemed to be a sort of scheming smile.

Harriet's finger itched and she absently rubbed the talisman ring. Every day for a week, she had tried to remove the blasted thing, but to no avail. Now, of course, she was used to it.

She glanced down at the ring and noticed how delicate it appeared on her finger. Her hands were red and chapped from helping with the fence rails, her nails ruthlessly pared. She wondered what the hands of the women in London looked like, then decided she really didn't want to know.

It was unlike Harriet not to face facts. She was usually the first one to denounce avoiding unpleasantness. It was always better to stand before the horrid truths of life and get on with things. But somehow, all the rules changed when they concerned Chase. Everything changed—even Harriet, in some indefinable way.

"Are we ready?" Chase asked, so close to Harriet's ear that she started. He grinned down at her.

Her body warmed to awareness and she instantly thought of how he'd looked after they'd made love, his eyes shining, his hair mussed. "Are we ready for what?" she returned in a breathless voice.

"To begin shearing, of course."

Derrick walked up. "Well, Harriet? Who does what?"

"Take Mr. St. John with you. Use the first shearing pen. I'll take one of the hired hands and Stephen. He can't herd the animals, but he can open and shut the shearing gate. Sophia and Ophelia will take care of the larger gates."

Derrick agreed. "Well, St. John. It looks as if it is you and I for this round."

Chase nodded, though his gaze never left Harriet. "You know, they say the first round is never quite as good as the second or third. That over time, things get even better."

Harriet colored faintly. She knew what he was thinking about because it was what *she* was thinking about. "Just see to it that you are careful with the shears. They are wicked and I wouldn't want you to lose anything important."

Chase's grin widened. "I've never had a problem handling my blade, thank you."

Derrick choked on a laugh as he grabbed Chase's arm. "Come, Blademaster. We've work to do and while teasing Harriet has its merits, now is not the time."

Harriet heard Chase's quiet laugh as he went outside with Derrick. Chase had wormed his way into the hearts of everyone at Garrett Park. She tried to imagine what it would be like without him, but somehow no picture would form. She only knew that having him here, with her family, working in the fields or sitting at the dinner table entertaining their neighbors with tales of made-up sea lore, was now a part of her life. An important, vital part. And she ached to think what that life would be like without him.

"He is a very intriguing man," Stephen said quietly.

She turned to find her brother regarding her from where he stood, leaning against the cart. "Yes, he is."

"He's made quite an impression on Mother and Sophia. And Derrick, too."

Harriet waited, but Stephen said nothing more, just remained where he was, looking at her.

She sighed. "I'm certain he's made an impression on everyone here. He has been most generous in a reluctant sort of way."

Stephen's gaze trailed to where Chase and Derrick stood. "Can't say that I blame him for being reluctant. I daresay people have been importuning him for money and favors his entire life."

Harriet had never thought of that, but it seemed as if it might be true. Certainly the Wards had done just that. She thought of what Chase had let slip about his former life over all their evening meals, of his homes, horses, and carriages. It wasn't really what he said so much as what he didn't say. He was of a world far removed from Garrett Park, and she knew that come the end of the week, he would leave and return to the world in which he belonged.

She took no delight in that thought. "With all that money, I'm certain he and his family have done their fair share of charity."

"Charity and generosity are not the same thing."

"That is very true." Harriet forced her lips into a stiff smile. "It's a good thing we found him, then, isn't it? I, for one, believe we've improved him immensely."

"Indeed we have. I wonder how he'll do in London with his newfound country virtues?"

She wished she could believe that he would never forget Garrett Park, never forget her. But somehow, she couldn't. She would not waste her time wishing for the impossible. Harriet picked up the shears. "We've a lot to do today." With that, she marched out of the barn, intent on working so hard that she didn't think at all of Chase St. John or his imminent departure.

Chase gripped the stick tighter, glaring at the large sheep that stood just out of arm's reach. That was the problem, the sheep had managed to remain at arm's reach for the last thirty minutes. "You blasted scrap of leather."

Ophelia pushed her spectacles back up on her nose. She sat atop the huge fence that led to the holding pen, watching the whole scene while Derrick remained in the small narrow leader pen to one side. "You can't talk to them like that."

"Why not?" Chase snapped, wishing she was anywhere but here. It was hard enough doing this with Derrick dying of laughter at his post. Having Ophelia perched on the gate like a chubby angel, offering advice every two minutes made the chore all the more difficult. "I can speak to them any way I want."

Blasted hell, this *should* be easy. All he had to do was use this stick to coerce a sheep into the narrow lead pen where Derrick waited with a looped rope. Derrick would secure the rope about the sheep's head and tether the animal to the wide board at the head of the pen. Once tied in such a fashion, the sheep was left standing and immobile, and they could shear it.

Or so the theory went.

Ophelia pursed her lips. "Don't listen to me if you don't wish to. I'm just telling you how Harri does it."

Chase glanced over to the other pen. From where he was standing, it appeared as if Harriet and Stephen, ably aided by Sophia, had already sheared three sheep while Chase, Derrick, and Ophelia hadn't managed a one.

For the love of Hera, it was ludicrous. He eyed the sheep before him, noting how the animal was eyeing him back, distrust in its black eyes. "Bloody asinine creature."

"You can't talk to them like that," Ophelia insisted yet again.

He turned to glare at her. "Why the hell not?"

"Because they'll get mad. Sheep are very intelligent creatures. They know every word you say to them."

"Nonsense. They are completely stupid. You can tell that by looking in their eyes."

"Harriet gives each sheep a name so they know she's talking to them. See how they obey her?"

Chase looked over at the other pen. Harriet stood in the center, a stick in her hand, the sheep gradually moving toward the leading pen. "Where is Max? That dog could do this."

"He's helping round up strays," Derrick said.

"He needs to be here, with me. There is no way I'm going to get this"— he pointed his stick at the huge sheep—"in there." He directed the stick at the narrow gate.

"We have to," Derrick said.

"How?"

"One at a time. Come on now, give it another go. You don't want Harri coming over here offering advice, do you? I assure you that she likes nothing better."

Like hell he wanted that. Blast and double blast. Chase gripped the stick tighter and began trying to get the sheep into the narrow gate. Each time, the sheep would get just beside the opening . . . and then, with a wild kick or a bleating cry, it would bolt to the other side of the pen.

After another twenty minutes, Ophelia sighed. "I told you to name it."

"I did," Chase said grimly.

"What?"

"Pox-Ridden Sow."

Ophelia giggled. "How lovely. What will you call that one?" She pointed at a very fat, lazy-looking ewe with a black nose and two black feet, which stood peering into the pen with obvious interest.

"Jackass."

Ophelia chuckled. "And the ram?"

Chase glanced into the other pen, where a very large and angry-looking ram stood stubbornly and silently daring them to try and get him into the leading pen. "I can't say his name aloud or lightning might strike."

"How will you call him to you?"

"I won't. I don't like him, and so I will never, ever call him. See? It all works out."

Derrick choked on a laugh. "Come on, St. John. Let's try and do at least one before lunch."

Chase rubbed his face, loosened up his shoulders, then hunched down, intent on winning the battle. This time, something went right. He waited until the sheep got close to the pen, then he dodged to the side, knowing that it would do the same in an effort to avoid being herded through the small gate. His abrupt movement startled the sheep and she bolted into the leading pen where Derrick tossed the loop over her neck and tied her tight. Pox-Ridden Sow was right where they wanted her.

Chase felt as if he was ten feet tall.

Derrick laughed and then stood, hands on hips. "You know, you may have a talent for this after all."

It was faint praise, but coming from one of the Wards, for some reason, it was great praise indeed. Chase just grinned in return and brought out the shears.

The rest of the morning passed quickly, and Chase got better and better at the process. Except for having to put up with Ophelia and Derrick, who seemed to be in extraordinarily good spirits, things went fairly smoothly. In fact, things went so smoothly that they finished shearing the sheep in their pen just as lunch was ready.

Half an hour later, Chase found himself standing beside Harriet at a table under a tree where Mrs. Ward was overseeing a feast fit for an army.

Harriet was hot and tired, her gown muddied, her hair falling from beneath the edges of her bonnet, hanging in loose tendrils down her back. But the wide grin she tossed him when she saw him was worth every bit of effort he'd expended this morning. "We're ahead of schedule already!"

He smiled down at her, noting that the sun had decorated her nose with a faint spray of freckles. Strange how he'd never considered freckles appealing, but on Harriet they were charming as could be.

Under his close scrutiny, her smile wavered. "What . . . what is it?" She rubbed her nose. "Do I have mud on my nose—"

"No. Not at all." He looked around at the sun-drenched fields and neat barn. The faint sound of laughter came from the others as they talked and teased one another. The sweet scent of cut hay filled the air, as did the faint baaing of the sheep. It was an idyllic, wonderful moment. One destined to be etched in his mind forever.

Chase looked back at Harriet. "You belong here."

That appeared to surprise her. She glanced around for a moment before saying softly. "Yes, I do. This is home."

"Do you ever see yourself going anywhere else?"

She hesitated and he could see her weighing her words. After a moment, she shook her head. "Perhaps. Perhaps not. I love this place. My parents moved here when I was six. And I've never wanted to live anywhere else. But . . . one never knows how one will feel in a year or more."

Chase tried to picture Harriet in town, dressed for dinner, or on her way to a ball. But somehow, he knew she'd be miserable. And London, with its penchant for the wealthy and the beautiful, would never stop long enough to see the true beauty in the woman before him. "I can't imagine you in London."

Her smile seemed pained, though she said lightly enough, "And I can't imagine you living in the country."

For some reason, the words caught at him. What was this? Maudlin nonsense at the thought of . . . of what? Of leaving Garrett Park? What foolishness.

To be honest, he had to admit that what he truly enjoyed was the time he'd spent with the Wards. They reminded him of his own family before everyone had grown up and left home. And perhaps he felt a fondness for Harriet that was more intense than his usual flirts, but that was to be expected. After all, they'd spent untold hours together, talking and working, things he rarely did with his flirts in London.

Chase realized that he rather enjoyed working. It was invigorating in a way, facing each day's challenge. Town life was all he'd ever known, all he'd ever thought of knowing. Farming, after all, was hardly the pursuit of a true gentleman. It was possible to dabble in trade a bit, so long as one didn't take it too seriously.

Chase yanked his hat a little more firmly onto his head and glinted a smile at Harriet. "Regardless of where I used to be and where I will be going, I am in the country now." He looked down at his muddied boots and grimaced. "Very much so."

"For the moment." She tightened the ribbons beneath her chin. "You would be discontent indeed if you thought you would be stuck here for the rest of your life."

"Harri!" Ophelia called.

Harriet turned toward the sheep pen. Everyone had left the table and was now lined along the fence where Ophelia had sat perched just a half hour earlier, giggling behind her hand.

"Harri!" This time it was Stephen. "You need to come and see this."

Harriet glanced at Chase. "What did you do?"

"Me? Nothing. Perhaps they are admiring how quickly we managed to get them done."

"Yes, but—"

"Harri!" This time it was Sophia, her voice breaking as if on a giggle.

Harriet's brow lowered. "I suppose I should see what they want." With that, she walked to the gate.

Chase stayed where he was for a moment, enjoying the warmth of the sun on his shoulders, the scent of hay and the fresh-baked bread they'd had for lunch. He felt amazingly well. There was something to be said for the simple life, he supposed. If only it wasn't quite so . . . wholesome.

Yes, that's what it was—wholesome. Something Chase most decidedly wasn't. The thought caught at his heart, and he realized that as welcoming as the Wards were now, they wouldn't be once they realized what he really was. What he'd done. His heart sank.

The sun seemed suddenly less bright. He made his way to the pen where the Wards were gathered, looking over the fence at his protégés, a lively spring breeze tugging at skirts and ruffling shirts. Chase came to stand beside Harriet, looking at his work critically.

The sheep weren't all perfectly sheared, of course. But this was his first time. Chase defied anyone else to have gotten as close or as even on their very first venture into the shearing business.

He glanced at his companions. "Well?"

Stephen raked a hand through his hair, his gaze fixed on the sheep that grazed before him. Sophia just looked stunned. Only Derrick looked happy, his face split in a wide grin, while Ophelia hid her mouth behind her hand, her eyes crinkled with laughter.

What the hell? Chase looked at Harriet. Her eyes wide, her fingers pressed to her lips, she was regarding the sheep as if she'd never before seen one.

"What?" he demanded, a feeling of unease flickering through him.

Harriet's gaze met his, laughter sparkling in her brown eyes.

"Bloody hell," he cursed. "You said the closer the better." He knew he sounded defensive, but something was not right.

"Yes, but—"

Sophia burst out giggling. "Oh, I'm so sorry," she choked when Chase whirled to face her. "It's just that . . . the sheep. They all look like poodles."

"Poodles?" Chase followed her gaze.

Ophelia tilted her head to one side, her lips quivering. "Poodles or lions. Some definitely have a lionish appearance. I thought he did a very good job on the ram."

"Chase," Harriet asked, laughter burbling in her voice, "why did you shear them like that?"

Chase grit his teeth. "Because it's what you have to do. I left the wool around their heads and tails so I wouldn't snip anything vital. Derrick said that was often the way you had to . . ." Chase's voice trailed off as he turned to look at the youth.

But Derrick was nowhere to be found.

Bloody hell! "That bast—"

"Chase!" Harriet said, grinning as the others broke into loud shouts of laughter. "He was just funning you."

Ophelia wiped her eyes with the back of her hand. "You should have heard Derrick. Even I thought he was serious at first."

Chase clenched his hands into fists. They'd made him look a fool. "I've had enough funning."

"Nonsense." She looked back at the sheep, a giggle escaping. "No one can have enough funning."

Chase thought glumly of all the work he'd done. "If I catch Derrick, I'll—"

"Oh, don't be upset," Harriet said, grinning up at him.

"We don't have time to play these games."

Her smile faded a little at that. "No, we don't. But it's not such a horrible thing, after all."

Stephen chuckled. "We can't leave that much wool on those sheep, so we'll trim them again."

Harriet nodded. "Actually, why don't we allow *Derrick* to trim them. Pray find him and tell him that I want it done before the next batch is brought in for shearing."

Stephen nodded, but before he left, he slapped Chase on the back. "I had no idea you were so talented with shears. If you've the time, perhaps you can do something with those bushes in the front of the house. A little topiary would not be amiss."

Ophelia giggled. "Since he made the sheep look like poodles, perhaps he can make the shrubbery look like sheep."

"I'll see what I can do," Chase said dryly, the beginning of a smile teasing his lips.

He looked around at the sea of grinning faces that surrounded him, aware of a comfortable feeling of belonging. "What did I do to deserve being rescued by a family of sheepherding wits? Why could I not have been found by average, normal people with no sense of humor and not a single sheep on the premises?"

Harriet lifted her brows in mock horror. "And what would you have done for three weeks without our wit or our sheep? You have to admit that you've learned some very important life lessons."

"Such as?"

"The art of rising early."

Sophia nodded. "He's still a bit surly, but Stephen no longer has to beat him about the head with his pillow."

"A lovely talent, that," Chase said. "I suppose I would never have known how to get up at such an ungodly hour without your help."

"Yes," Ophelia said, "and you've learned that sheep ointment is best used only on sheep."

"I believe I already knew that lesson. It is Harriet who did not."

"Oh, I never use it on myself," Harriet said airily. "Just on braggarts who do not appreciate the efforts expended on their behalf."

"And you've learned to be far more pleasant," Sophia said brightly. "Mother was just saying that she could not imagine dinner without your stories of town and the people there, although I still do not credit it that Lord Byron eats naught but potatoes and vinegar."

Chase sighed, though a grin tickled his mouth.

Ophelia frowned. "How will we find Derrick to tell him he has work to do?"

Stephen pushed himself from the gate railing and grabbed his crutches. "He'll be in the library, reading a book. I'll fetch him myself."

Harriet nodded and looked at Ophelia and Sophia. "Help Mother clean up luncheon. Chase and I will sharpen the shears in the barn and we'll all be back here in an hour when the next batch of sheep is brought in."

They nodded and scurried off, laughing and talking as they went.

Harriet watched them go, a bubble of laughter still in her throat. She collected the shears and walked toward the barn, aware of Chase falling into step beside her.

As they neared the barn, she stole a glance up at him. He strode beside her, his shirt open at the throat, his sleeves rolled up, his skin already tanning a light brown. The breeze played with his hair, sending it over his brow.

He looked different from the man they'd found in the woods, she suddenly realized, wondering what it was. He didn't seem so . . . sullen. Angry. "Are you happy?"

He looked down at her. "Happy?"

She hadn't meant to voice the question aloud. But since she had . . . "Yes. Are you happy? It's an easy enough question."

"I don't know. I hadn't thought about it." He pursed his lips.

Harriet tried not to watch, but she couldn't help herself. Chase's lips had kissed her, possessed her, tasted her in ways she'd never thought lips could.

He caught her glance, and his gaze immediately darkened. He bent and said into her ear, "Don't look at me like that unless you're willing to pay the consequences."

His voice brushed over her, sending a trill of shivers down her back. "I didn't look at you any particular way."

"Didn't you?"

"No."

His hand snaked about her wrist and suddenly, she was jerked into the barn, the shears tumbling to the barn floor. Harriet could only blink as Chase pushed the large doors closed and dropped the bar into place.

He leaned against the doors, a devilish smile curving his lips. "Now I have you. And right where I want you, too."

Chapter 23

We leave at first light. And I'm very sorry about your new rug.

> Mr. Devon St. John to his brother Marcus,
> the Marquis of Treymount at
> Treymount House in Mayfair

"Wh—what are you doing?" Harriet asked, uncertainty and excitement warring for expression.

"I am making sure we aren't interrupted." Chase tested the bar once, then turned and walked toward her, his boots crunching on the hay-strewn floor, his thigh muscles rippling with each step.

Heaven help her but he had the most beautiful thighs . . . the memory of those thighs between her own made her close her eyes, a heated shiver rippling through her.

He reached her side and traced his finger down her cheek. "Since that first night I arrived and your brothers and sisters tried to convince me that I had a liking for the barn, I've been wanting to visit the barn with you."

He captured the ties that held her hat. He twined

the faded blue ribbons around his fingers and then gently drew her forth.

Her eyes widened and she leaned away, one hand bracing the hat in place. "I—I don't think that is necessary."

She was hot and disheveled, her hair falling in wisps from beneath the hat and sticking damply to her neck and cheek. Her flushed skin held a dewy moisture that begged to be tasted.

In all his years, Chase had never been so close to a woman engaged in such physically demanding labor. He tugged the bonnet ties a bit harder, pulling her forward another reluctant pace.

The neck of her washed-out dress was damp, as if beads of sweat had trickled to rest there. He marveled at her. This plain little woman would practically fade from sight when dressed in white muslin, sitting in a parlor. But here, in a musty barn, damp from her exertions, her cheeks flushed, her eyes sparkling with mischief . . . she was beyond beautiful.

She was bold and lovely, loud in actions and brave in thought. She was, in a word, the most amazing woman he'd ever met.

He released one ribbon of her hat and ran the back of his finger over her cheek. "You are incredible."

The air about them thickened, deepened, as if the heat had slowed the pace of the earth. She licked her lips as if they were suddenly dry. The movement of her pink tongue was almost more than he could bear.

She glanced wildly around, as if to find rescue from the fields, or perhaps the sheep. "We—I—you—"

He raised his brows.

She flushed, deeply, the color creeping up her

neck to flood her hot cheeks with even brighter streaks of red. "We should get a drink of water." She turned stiffly on her heel and marched to the bucket of water that hung from one of the loft poles as if on her way to the guillotine.

He grinned even as a fat trickle of sweat ran between his shoulder blades. "You're right." He followed her closely, reaching past her to take the dipper that hung from the side of the barrel. "Allow me."

"I don't need assistance getting a drink of water. I am perfectly capable of getting it myself."

"I know." He plunged the dipper into the water, then lifted it clear. Water dripped from the shiny metal and pooled into the barrel below. Chase was suddenly aware of how thirsty he was. It was hot, sticky, dry work. Work he wasn't accustomed to doing. The whole world seemed covered in a haze of dust that made the water seem all the more pure. All the tastier. He began to lift the dipper to his own mouth when he caught sight of Harriet's face.

Dust smeared a dark path from her temple to her chin. Her skin was flushed and ripe. As he looked at her, she ran the edge of her tongue along her lower lip as if in anticipation of the cold drink. Chase reached over with his free hand and pushed her hat from her hair.

She blinked. "Wh—"

He lifted the ladle and poured the water on her head. It cascaded down her face, drenching her shoulders, cooling her heated skin.

She gasped, sputtering. "You—Why—"

"You were hot." He dipped out more water and poured it over his own head. The water bathed him in an instant, cooling and cleansing.

He opened his eyes to find Harriet looking at him, amusement warming her brown eyes.

"You are impossible."

He grinned in return. "I just wanted to help." He refilled the ladle and then handed it to her. "Drink."

Her gaze met his for the briefest of moments, the deep brown still sparkling with laughter. To his surprise, she didn't say a word, but reached up and cupped the cool metal in both hands and took a deep, cold drink.

Chase watched, all amusement leaving him as her soft lips closed over the curved metal bowl of the ladle. She drank deeply, unabashedly gulping the water, a thin trickle escaping her lips and running down her chin.

Chase found his hands had curled into fists. Not out of anger, but out of need. He wanted this woman, wanted her so badly that his entire body ached with the effort to hide it.

She dropped the ladle from her mouth, her eyes still closed as if in ecstasy. Chase could not breathe. He could not swallow. He could not do anything but stand numbly beside her as she sighed happily, her pink tongue tracing the last bit of moisture from her plump bottom lip.

Suddenly, Chase knew that he was standing too close to her. Too near to stop himself. Before he realized what he was doing, his hands had come unfisted and he was holding her—pulling her to him.

She melted against him, warm and willing, her mouth curved in a welcoming smile.

He wanted to kiss her. To taste her as deeply as she'd drunk the water. He wanted to devour her taste, her scent, claim her with his mouth, his tongue, every inch of him that pressed against her.

But instead, he merely held her, imprisoning her within his arms. Then he reclaimed the ladle from her limp hands and reached behind her to dip it deep in the water.

Harriet's gaze followed his arm as he held it over their heads.

She stared up at the ladle, her throat inadvertently exposed. Her gaze widened as he began to tilt it. "You wouldn't da—"

He dumped it all, the coldness cascading over their heads, shoulders and back.

Water clung to her lashes and bathed her cheeks, cooling their hot color to pink. She tilted her face up, a chuckle escaping her wet lips. "That was divine. You're worse than Stephen, you know. He is forever pouring water over poor Derrick when the poor boy least expects it. It makes Derrick furious for there are times his beloved books get a good splashing, too."

"My brothers and sister were much the same," he murmured, pulling the pins from her hair.

Her breathing came a bit quicker, but she managed to ask, "What did your brothers and sister torment *you* about?"

"I'll never tell."

Harriet knew a challenge when she heard one. "Won't you?" She leaned against him, her wet dress pressing against his soaked shirt as she traced a finger down the side of his throat. "Not even if you have inducement?"

His gaze glittered then, a sudden heat that quite took Harriet's breath away. "What kind of inducement? Would you . . . take this off for me?" His finger traced the neckline of her gown.

Harriet drew a quick breath as his fingers slid near her breast . . . then away. "In exchange for what?"

He dropped his hand from her gown. "For something my brothers and sister used to torment me about."

She considered this a moment. "How much did they torment you?"

"Every chance they got."

She eyed him uncertainly. "I don't know."

"One of my brothers even carved my nickname in the headboard of my bed. I thought my mother would explode into flames when she saw what we'd done to that bed. It was four hundred years old and had been in her family for centuries."

"Really?"

He nodded. "She was not pleased, to put it mildly."

"Whatever your secret nickname it must be something horrid. Hmm. That *is* tempting indeed." She looked down at her gown. It was a round gown. Like all round gowns, it had a large neckline through which a ribbon was threaded, pulled tight, then tied, making for a modest appearance.

All she had to do was untie the ribbon, give a slight tug, and the entire gown would fall off her shoulders. Harriet's body tightened at the thought. Chase made her feel . . . freer somehow. Rich like a plum pudding, and as decadent as ice in the middle of summer. "Tell me your secret."

"And?"

She swallowed, aware of a trembling in her limbs. "Tell me your secret and I'll show you mine."

He grinned. "They called me the Frog, which was pure mockery since I have never managed to learn to swim."

"The Frog? That's it? That's your horrid secret?"

"I was six. It seemed horrid at the time."

She had to grin.

He reached out and traced the line of her gown with his fingertips, his skin brushing hers. "Now you owe me."

"So I do. But . . . it doesn't seem fair that I might be the only one without any clothing."

He pulled his soaked shirt over his head before she could draw a breath.

Harriet chuckled. "A man of action. I like that."

Chase's grin broke through, and he leaned against one of the large poles that held the loft as he pulled off his boots. "I've never been one to linger except, of course"—he flashed a smile, wickedly intent—"in certain instances. And then I can stay till dawn."

"Braggart."

"That's for the lady to say." His gaze dropped across her, as if seeing through her gown, brushing her breasts, stomach, and thighs. Each place his gaze touched, a shimmering of heat was left behind, like a dusting of hot ash.

She shivered. The fine hair on Harriet's arms were all on end, her nipples pebbled into hardness. He was the most sensual man she'd ever met. Even something as simple as talking became a heated dance, a silky waltz of entendre and double entendre.

And she loved it. Savored it. Reveled in it. Harriet found the ribbon that tied her gown. She laced it between her fingers and tugged ever so gently. Chase's gaze followed her every move even as he threw his boots into the corner of the barn and undid his breeches.

Harriet's breath grew rapid. The air was warm and sweet, the scent of cut hay and feed tickling her nose. Every day she walked into this barn; every day she saw the piles of hay, the empty stalls, the plain plank walls. The shimmer of the tin dipper that hung from the bucket of water on the loft pole.

She saw every detail each and every day and yet she didn't see a thing. But now, after this, she had the feeling that from now on, the inside of the barn would be firmly fixed in her mind, and she'd see it with startling clarity.

Chase gave a tug and his wet breeches were off. He tossed them aside with the same careless disregard he'd thrown the old worn boots and the shirt. Now he stood before her, unclothed, his black hair falling over his brow, his blue eyes devouring her as if he was already touching her, his well-muscled body glimmering in the golden slants of light that cut through the barn.

Oblivious to her gaze, he pulled an old blanket from the tack room and tossed it over the hay. Then he turned to face her, a devilish glint in his gaze. "It's not as luxurious as I'd like, or you deserve, but it's ours."

Ours. There was something indescribably beautiful about that word. Harriet tried to swallow, but couldn't. He was so beautiful. And for this one precious moment, he was hers.

She knew as certainly as she stood before him, her fingers threaded through the ribbon that held her gown closed, that this moment was ephemeral, as substantial as the golden dust motes that trickled through the air and disappeared once they floated out of the light.

Her gaze dropped to her hand where the talisman ring glistened, a silver stripe across one finger. Harriet knew the day would come when Chase St. John, the arrogant scion of a wealthy family—perhaps one of the wealthiest in the land, would discard his Captain John Frakenham disguise forever and rejoin the real world—his world. A world that had nothing to do with Harriet or the Wards, or Garrett Park.

But it didn't matter, she decided, closing her hand tight about the ribbon, the ring pressing into her skin. All that mattered was him, the feel of him, the taste of him. Harriet tugged the ribbon and her gown loosened. She slipped it from her shoulders and let it fall to the floor, then stepped out of it.

Chase had never seen anything so beautiful. Harriet stood in the center of the barn, clothed only in her shift. It was a plain shift, with far fewer buttons and ribbons than Chase was used to seeing. The material was thin, but as was all the clothing worn by the Ward family, it was neat, tidy, studiously clean, and in this instance, driving Chase St. John wild with impatience.

There was something masterful about the way the fabric hugged Harriet's slender body. It clung lovingly to the gentle slope of her breast, fell in delicate folds to her flat stomach, then smoothed across her hips before falling to a narrow froth of white lace at her knees.

"You are beautiful," he breathed. "So beautiful."

In answer, she placed her hands on his chest and tilted her face to his, stepping closer. Her hair curled wetly about her shoulders and clung to the shadowed hollows of her neck. The warmth from her palms sent a tingle of heat through him, the hot white band where the talisman ring rested seeming to burn a mark in his skin.

Chase reached for her, his heart racing. He would never remember unlacing her shift. Or taking it off and tossing it aside. All he would remember was the feel of her beneath him when he joined her on the blanket. She reached up and pulled his mouth to hers even as she locked her legs about his hips.

Chase was lost, awash in instant heat and welcoming wetness. He closed his eyes, his entire body aflame, his muscles tightening as he moved inside her. Harriet was made for him. The thought was both a revelation and a calm, orderly fact. An icy certainty in a heated moment that cooled and calmed even as it invigorated his spirit, fueled his pounding pulse.

He would be leaving soon. It was inevitable. He simply could not stay. There was no place for him at Garrett Park, or there wouldn't be once Harriet knew of his past mistakes. There was goodness here, with the Wards, but most especially with Harriet herself. And he was far, far less than he should be.

The thought made the moment all the more sweet. And he knew that in a way, he was trying to leave her with something, a memory of himself that might never fade. He thrust into her deeply. She gasped, her legs tightening about his waist as she moved beneath him.

Chase tasted her neck, her throat, his hands never slowing, never still. He wanted her to remember this moment, this second for the rest of her life.

Suddenly, she arched against him, her cry of pleasure ringing through the air. Chase gritted his teeth as she clenched about him. God, she was sweet, but he would not release. Not yet.

After an agonizing moment, she relaxed beneath him, her breathing ragged against his neck.

"You are divine," he managed to say, feeling her breasts against his chest, her hips firm with his. She was a conundrum, this woman. Strength mixed with curves.

He bent down and kissed her, capturing her water-sweetened lips with his.

Harriet didn't move—she couldn't. For an instant, she thought her heat-sizzled mind had finally let go of the last vestiges of sanity. Surely this was a dream of some sort, induced by the heat and the strain of the last few days.

But . . . his lips felt real as they closed over hers, warm and insistent.

His hand, before gently resting on her elbows, slid up to her shoulders as he pulled her close, her chest against his.

She was encircled, captured, held in place as if spellbound. The kiss deepened, and Harriet leaned into the embrace, completely lost to his touch. A shiver of heat prickled up her spine, all thinking coming to an abrupt halt.

Heaven help her, but he was delectable. Every handsome, frustrating inch of him. She wanted this. Wanted him to kiss her. Wanted, for one moment, to be the only woman that Chase St. John thought of.

The thought spurred her on. She ran her hands up his chest, marveling at the tautness of his stomach, his shoulders. A new need grew within her. She wanted to drive him as mad with desire as he had driven her. She wanted to give back what he had already given. "What—" She bit her lip, searching for the words.

He kissed her cheek, her neck. "What's what?" he asked.

"What do you like?" Her whisper was broken, hesitant.

He stopped then and lifted his head, his eyes dark, questioning.

She placed her hands on either side of his face and drew him forward until he was looking directly into her eyes. "What do *you* want?"

A slow, masculine smile touched his lips. "With you—everything." His smile faded, his eyes burning brighter. "Absolutely everything."

He kissed her again, but this time with heart-stopping urgency. Harriet melted beneath his touch, her heart taking wing and soaring with her spirit. His lips trailed delicate fire down her throat to her neck, and lower. She arched as his mouth closed over one nipple, then the other, before he returned to her neck and the delicate spot behind her ear.

"Do you know," he asked as he nuzzled her neck, "my favorite place to kiss a woman?"

It was difficult to think clearly enough to talk with her heart racing so. "Where?" she managed to gasp.

He lifted on one elbow to gaze down at her. "You'll have to turn over."

Turn over? A raw shiver traced over her skin. Without a word, Harriet turned onto her stomach.

For an instant, she felt exposed in some way that she hadn't before. Perhaps it was because she could no longer see his face. Perhaps it was the newness of the situation. Whatever it was, her entire body trembled. She could feel him moving to one side, and then down.

His voice brushed her lower back. "My favorite place to kiss a woman . . . is here." His lips brushed her back at the base of her spine.

Harriet arched at the sensation. It was unsettling to be naked before a man, especially like this. She couldn't help but feel vulnerable, exposed. But he didn't slow down long enough to let her react to that feeling; his lips were traveling a delicately tortuous path, leaving a trail of heated kisses all the way from her lower spine up to her shoulder, to her neck.

His weight pressed against her and she could feel his hardness pressing against the backs of her legs.

"My beloved Persephone," he whispered in her ear, "I want to show you something." His lips trailed down the side of her neck.

Harriet could barely think. She wanted him so badly, her entire body was aflame now. She wanted to roll over, to lock her legs about him and let him fill her. But instead she was held, stomach down on the blanket as he tortured her with long, slow kisses in the most indelicate places.

"Lift your hips," he whispered.

Harriet frowned. "How can I turn over if—"

"Lift for me, sweet." His hands about her waist, he tilted her hips up.

She did as he asked. If she'd felt exposed before, now she was indecently lifted, her butt cheeks arched in the air.

Chase lifted himself above her and found her wetness. She was moist, swollen, squirming ever so slightly beneath him in a way that was driving him mad with lust.

He splayed his hands over her back, marveling at the muscles that were displayed there. She was beauty and feminine strength, delicacy and exotic enticement. He lifted himself and pushed into her wetness, his mouth never leaving the back of her neck as he nipped and teased.

"Oh my—Chase!" She arched beneath him, lifting her hips higher, pressing back against him. God, but she was hot and tight and ready for him. Her hot wetness held him in a velvet-sleeved grip, tormenting him mercilessly. Beads of sweat dotted his upper lip and brow as he moved into her, slid deep, then withdrew to the tip.

Harriet groaned and pressed back as if eager for him to resume his pace. He thrust again. And again. And each time she met him, writhing enticingly beneath him. He could feel the excitement building inside her, feel the tremors of her as he thrust deeply. He fought for control, but the more he fought, the more she drew him onward. Finally, with a gasp, she said his name and broke his tenuous control. She swept him with her over the edge of passion and beyond.

Chapter 24

*If we go to all of this trouble just to find Chase
snuggled between the sheets with a woman, I
will personally haul him outside and beat him
to within an inch of his life.*

Marcus St. John, the Marquis of Treymount,
to his brother, Mr. Devon St. John, as they
climbed into the Treymount coach

Chase collapsed, cradling Harriet in his arms as
he fought for breath, for the ability even to
think. In all of his days, he'd never experienced such
a sensuous woman. Never.

He pressed a kiss on her neck and then turned her
so that she faced him. She had her eyes tightly
clenched, her breath ragged between her lips.

"Harriet?" he whispered against her bare skin.

A shiver trembled across her.

Chase took her hand and threaded her fingers
with his, then leaned forward and placed a soft kiss
on the corner of her mouth. "You are magnificent."

Her eyes cracked open at that and to his relief, a
faint smile touched the corners of her lips.

He smiled and pressed another kiss to the spot below her ear. "And I think I lo—" He stopped.

Had he almost said—it was impossible! Why the hell had he almost said *that*?

She blinked, her eyes now wide open. "What . . . what did you say?"

"Nothing," he said hastily. He pushed himself upright and raked a hand through his hair, unwilling to admit how shaken he was that he'd almost let such a thing slip. "I was going to say that I . . . love the way you kiss."

She arched a brow in disbelief. "My kisses are nothing special."

"Oh yes, they are." He smoothed the hair from her forehead, noting how the sun had kissed her cheeks with even more freckles. He traced a path from freckle to freckle with the tip of his finger. It would soon be time for him to leave, and yet here Harriet would be, fighting to make Garrett Park a working, living estate for her brothers and sisters. "I worry about you."

"Me? Why on earth would you worry about me?"

"You work too hard."

Her smile disappeared. "I don't work any harder than the others. Chase, don't make me out to be a saint. I'm afflicted with far too many faults to be considered anything other than human."

"What faults do you have?"

She snorted. "Well, let's see. I'm short-tempered. I have a dislike for doing anything whatsoever inside the house; Mother despaired of my watercolors and embroidery years ago. Oh and . . ." She peered up at him, a twinkle in her eyes. "I'm apparently not a woman of virtue, either."

He winced.

"Not that I mind," she added swiftly. She placed her hand on the side of his face. "In fact, I'm glad we've had this time together. I've enjoyed every second of it. Especially today."

"Today?"

"Yes, the last round left me feeling quite . . . exuberant."

Despite his misgivings, he found himself smiling down at her. "I feel the same way."

"I know. I could tell." She eyed him for a moment. "Well?"

"Well, what?"

"I confessed my shortcomings. What are yours?"

God, what he would give to be able to answer that question. "We've all done things we're not proud of."

She glanced up at him, curiosity bright in her brown eyes. "You sound almost . . . sad."

He was sad. And sorry. He had to move, to get up. He pushed himself to his feet. "Harriet . . . I've done things I'm not proud of. One . . . one thing in particular."

She met his gaze solemnly, and to his surprise, there was no condemnation in her expression. "What?"

He opened his mouth to tell her, but no words would come out. All those months of not saying, of not facing the truth, seemed to have melted into him until he could not break free.

She lifted onto her elbows, her gaze never wavering. "Whatever it is that you did, did you make amends?"

"Amends?" He grabbed up his breeches, and yanked them on. "There was no way to make amends for this."

She sat the rest of the way up and wrapped her arms around her knees. In the indirect light, her brown hair falling over her shoulders, her eyes wide and solemn, she looked like a pixie. "But you *tried* to fix things?"

He nodded once, hating himself, hating that he was having this conversation with Harriet, of all people. Bloody hell, life was not fair. He found his shirt and yanked it over his head.

She shrugged. "Then that's all you can do."

He had just picked up one of his boots. He stopped and turned to face her. "Do you believe that?"

"If you try your best, then no one can ask for more."

Chase looked at her for a long moment. "I wish I could believe that. And maybe it's true for other people, but I'm a St. John, born with every conceivable benefit. There are no excuses for my actions."

"What exactly did you do?"

"I . . ." The words pushed at him, begging for release. He swallowed, then closed his eyes. "I killed someone."

Silence. He forced his eyes open, ready to read the condemnation in her eyes.

She met his gaze, her face pale.

"I didn't mean to," he gritted out. "I didn't. I was careening drunkenly through the streets of London in my new carriage. I ran over a woman. She . . ." He gave a helpless shrug as his eyes grew hot.

Harriet's eyes were already wet. "Oh, Chase," she whispered. "I'm so sorry."

"So am I. I was with . . . not a friend. But a person I knew. When the accident happened, I pulled the horses to and started to get out to see if the woman needed assistance. But my companion panicked and began screaming at me to drive on. I was drunk and frightened and . . . I did."

"Did you go back?"

"As soon as I was sober enough to realize what had happened. The man I was with, he helped search for her, too. He visited the hospitals and I spoke to every person I saw on that street, but we never found her."

Chase turned away from Harriet and pulled on his boots. He didn't think he could stand seeing the disappointment in her eyes. "I was on my way out of the country when I came here."

"Out of the country . . . Why?"

"The companion I was with that night has been steadily draining me of funds ever since the accident. I decided the time had come to face my demons."

"By running away?"

"By protecting my family from scandal. My brothers and sister do not know the truth. I couldn't tell them." Chase picked up Harriet's gown and shift and draped them over the edge of a stall.

"You need to tell them."

"It is better if no one knows."

She regarded him steadily. "You are the one who told me that I was not doing my family any favors by taking care of them. Perhaps you should heed your own advice."

Chase wiped a hand over his eyes. He *had* said that. And for Harriet, it made sense. But for him? "I'm not sure why I told you about it. I-I haven't told anyone."

"Perhaps it is practice, for when you face your family." There was a rustle of hay as Harriet stood and made her way to the water bucket. Water plopped in fat drips to the ground as she washed.

Chase watched her silently, noting the lush curve

of her backside, the tight muscles of her calf. She was a nymph of ancient lore, washing herself at the bucket, the slanted afternoon light that cut through the cracks in the barn walls stripping across her smooth creamy skin and touching her hair with gold. But for all that her outer beauty tantalized him, it was her inner beauty that held him, captured him, and refused to release him. The unfairness of his situation cut to his soul. Damn it, why had he met her now, when he had no choice but to leave?

Chase turned toward the barn door, his chest tight. "I should go and see if Stephen and Derrick need any help."

"What you should do," she said in a matter-of-fact voice that brooked no argument, "is pack your things and get yourself home as soon as possible. You cannot run from yourself, you know." There was a soft whisper as she pulled her clothing from where Chase had hung them and began to dress.

Chase stiffened. "I'm not running. I am—"

"Running."

She was right, and he knew it.

"You made a mistake, Chase. We all make mistakes."

"Not mistakes that cost lives."

"No. But whatever our mistakes are, they weren't performed because of malicious intent. They happened because we were careless or didn't realize the consequences of our actions."

"It's not that easy."

"Isn't it?" She came to stand before him, calmly pinning her hair. "Tell me what you've been doing since this accident."

"Doing? I don't know. I suppose I've been drinking. Trying to forget—"

"You've been wallowing in a sea of self-pity. *That* is your grossest error."

Chase didn't know what to say. She looked so damnably sure of herself. He envied her in that moment, envied her calm certainty about life, her intrepid spirit, her refusal to let life sour her spirits. He wondered how he'd been so fortunate as to have met her. "You, Harriet Ward, are an exceptional woman."

Color flooded her cheeks. "I'm nothing special," she said gruffly.

"Really? Do you not run this entire estate all by yourself?"

She laughed, the light slanting over her sparkling eyes. "No. Garrett Park is run by committee. Derrick is in charge of household repairs. He's very talented at tinkering with things. Stephen is in charge of keeping up the stables. He's always been good with horses, though we had to sell most of them three years ago."

"What a pity."

"Yes, Stephen was devastated, though he refused to admit it."

"What do your sisters do?"

"Sophia helps with the books. She's almost as good at figures as she is at playwriting." A faint smile softened the line of Harriet's mouth. "Better, in fact, though I'd never tell her that."

"And your mother?"

"Who do you think sees to it that we all have fresh linens every week? That the meat is cooked well and the floors always scrubbed? She makes sure there is enough so that we can eat through the winter, and she spoils us with clothes that she herself sews."

When he stopped to think about it, it was amazing

how this family, left in near poverty and distress, had banded together to make a success out of their seemingly dire straits. But he supposed he understood that concept—in a way, his brothers were never closer than when facing adversity. "What does the intrepid Ophelia do?"

"She sees to it that we are not remiss in our attention to our neighbors."

He frowned. After hearing of the contributions of the others, that seemed far less than important.

His thoughts must have been evident on his face, for Harriet sent him a sharp frown. "Ophelia spends a good portion of every year helping Cook with the herbs. She also makes Christmas gifts for our neighbors. She does far more than her fair share."

"Gifts? Why bother with gifts?"

She turned to fix a gimlet stare on his face. "Neighbors, Mr. St. John, are important to us all. When our plow horse strained her foreleg in the midst of spring plowing, our neighbor to the west, Baron Whitfield, sent one of his horses to take her place. When Ophelia became ill and we needed medicine, but were unable to get to town because it had snowed so deeply that our poor farm mare could not make it out the drive, Mr. Nash came to our aid. He made the trip to town himself, wrapped head to foot in wool and riding in an old farmer's cart to cut through the roads."

She eyed Chase up and down, as if uncertain whether to spit on him or kick his shins. "I can give you other examples, if you'd like."

"No. No, that won't be necessary. I had just forgotten—" He raked a hand through his hair. He couldn't forget what he'd never known. The St. Johns were the community. Not a mere part of it.

Harriet turned and made her way to the door. She grabbed the bar and lifted it to one side, then pulled the door open. Sunlight flooded the barn, turning the hay to spun gold.

Her gaze fell on the pile of shears and she laughed. "I almost forgot those."

Her eyes crinkled and her mouth curved in such a beguiling fashion. He caught her amused look and an unaccustomed heat traveled up his neck.

She straightened, her gaze suddenly fixed on the driveway. "Someone is coming. I think—oh, it's just the cart from the inn. Mother must have asked them to send some spiced wine."

Chase glanced indifferently at the cart, watching as Derrick walked up to speak to the driver. They spoke for a moment, then Derrick gestured toward the barn. The man looked toward Harriet and Chase, nodded once, then hawed the horses on.

Harriet frowned. "I wonder what that was about?"

Derrick stood in the drive, watching the cart rumble away before he walked toward them. "That was strange," he said on reaching them.

"What did he want?" Harriet asked.

"He said he'd heard about the captain and wondered if he could meet him." Derrick flickered a gaze at Chase. "He was wondering if you were the same Captain Frakenham that he sailed with two years ago."

"I doubt it," Chase said.

"That's what I said," Derrick returned, a disturbed look in his eyes. "I even pointed you out, thinking that would turn him. But instead, he seemed to recognize you."

Chase frowned. "Are you certain?"

"I think so. He nodded as if you looked exactly the way he'd expected you to. But then, when I offered to introduce you, he said that wouldn't be necessary."

Harriet sighed. "I wonder if Mr. Gower is up to his tricks again."

"I can't imagine how," Chase said. "But if so, he's too late. We'll be done with the shearing in another two days and he won't be able to do a thing to you after that."

Derrick nodded, a relieved look on his face. "That's true. Well, I'd best get back to the pens. I have some shearing to do." He grabbed a set of shears and then walked away, whistling a sprightly tune.

"I must help," Harriet said, collecting the other shears. She turned to go, but Chase caught her wrist.

Against her brown skin the talisman ring glittered as if jewel-encrusted. "You wore this to irk me."

She bit her lip. "Actually, I can't get it off. I haven't been able to get it off since the first time I put it on." She grasped it with her other hand and pulled and pulled, but the ring would not budge. She stopped and sighed. "I tried butter and oil, but it's stuck."

Chase looked down at her fingers. They seemed so slender beneath the heavy silver band. He lifted her hand in his and gently tugged on the ring. It hung for a second, as if not wanting to move. But then it released and easily slid off her finger.

Harriet's mouth opened. Then closed. Then opened again. "How did—I tried so hard! I can't believe you just—Oh, piffle!"

Chase looked at the ring. Mother had said that it would lead the possessor to his one true love. Could it be—

"Harri!" Stephen and Sophia waved from across the barn yard.

Harriet sighed. "Time to get back to work, I suppose."

"Yes, it is." At least for today. "Harriet, about the ring. Perhaps you should—"

"No. It belongs with you. I—"

Stephen and Sophia called again and Harriet sighed. "I have to go. We'll discuss this later."

Chase nodded and watched as she joined her brother and sister. Chase wondered if the ring felt as bereft as he did. His fingers curled over it.

After a moment, he slipped it into his pocket and went to help Derrick with the shearing.

This time, Chase worked as hard as he could, though his mind never stopped mulling over the thorny problem that faced him.

He was beginning to care far too much for Harriet Ward. He had to leave Garrett Park. And soon.

Chapter 25

Bloody hell, can't you get this contraption to go any faster?

Mr. Devon St. John to Little Bob,
the coachman, as they rumbled
through the dark

That day and the next, Chase worked harder than he had ever worked in his life. Derrick had at first asked what the hurry was, but had soon gotten into the spirit of things, and it was with huge satisfaction that they stood two nights later and looked at the bales of wool that filled the barn. They'd had to move the horses to the shed for the night, just to make room for it all.

They were almost finished. The time had come for Chase to leave. Sighing, Chase hung the lantern on a nail and pulled a pair of gloves from his back pocket and tugged them on.

Derrick groaned. "We don't have to stack the bales tonight."

Chase looked at the untidy bundles of wool that littered the barn. "I'm going to at least get them sorted into wagonloads."

"That will take hours."

"I haven't anything better to do."

"I have." Derrick put his hands on his hips and stretched, then groaned. "I'm going to get a hot bath, then go to bed. If I don't, I won't be able to move tomorrow."

Chase smiled. "You're going inside to read a book. Don't pretend otherwise."

"Oh, all right," Derrick said with a lopsided grin. "I was going to read a little. But I was also going to take a bath, and I really am sore."

"We all are." The sun had set an hour ago, and now all that was left was one last dinner with the Wards. For some reason, the thought of facing them seemed impossible. It would be better if he just quietly went away. His good humor slipped a notch, then disappeared altogether. "Go on to the house. I'll do what I can before dinner and join you then."

"Very well," Derrick said. He walked toward the barn door, then hesitated. "By the way, I've been meaning to say—well, you've worked hard and you didn't need to."

"Of course I needed to. We've a payment to make on Garrett Park, don't we?"

"We." Derrick smiled. "Yes, *we* do. Thank you."

"It's my pleasure." Chase watched as Derrick walked out the door. A murmur of voices in the yard and the glimmer of a lantern through the cracks in the walls told him that Harriet was on her way. She appeared a moment later, Stephen by her side.

If Chase looked weary, so did Harriet. Her eyes were shadowed, her shoulders stooped. He could almost feel the weariness seep from her.

Stephen stepped forward. "There you are, Chase.

We did well today, didn't we? Harri says we're a good day ahead of schedule."

"We did very well." Chase picked up a bundle of wool and stacked it on a neat pile by the back wall. "I daresay we won't have more than a few hours of work left in the morning. We'll have the wool ready for market two days ahead of schedule."

Stephen grinned. "I cannot wait to see Gower's face when we make that final payment."

Chase straightened, trying not to look at Harriet, who stood quietly inside the door. "Stephen, I have something for you."

"What?"

"The clothing that is in my wardrobe."

"B—but that's your clothing!"

"Indeed it is. I've been wearing your clothes, so now is the time for you to wear mine."

"But—why?"

"Wear them when you go to town tomorrow and make certain Miss Strickton sees you. If she is impressed with that popinjay you were telling me about, she'll be quite smitten with you. You can even ride my horse."

Stephen's eyes brightened. "By Jove, that's the very thing! Are you sure you don't mind?"

"Of course I don't mind. I have plenty more clothes where those came from." So many that he was almost embarrassed to think about it. Strange how things had changed. How he had changed.

"Do you mind if I look at them now?" Stephen said eagerly. "I'd like to try on your blue coat. Oh, and those buff breeches! Those are quite the thing. And the wine-colored waistcoat is—"

"Go!" Chase laughed. "You may try them all on."

Stephen turned, then stopped when he saw Harriet. "Oh! Almost forgot you, Harri. Here. I'll leave the lantern so you can see your way to the house." He handed her the lantern, then hurried off.

Chase began stacking the bundles once more, wondering what he should say. What he *could* say.

Silence hung loud and heavy, and then Harriet walked farther inside the barn. She set the lantern on the ground by the loft pole and surveyed the bundles of wool for a long moment. "We did well today."

"Yes, we did." Chase didn't trust himself to look at her. Not now. Not ever.

She was silent a moment more, watching as he piled the bundles higher. Finally she said, "I will see you at dinner."

It wasn't a question, so Chase didn't answer it. Clenching his teeth, he continued stacking the bales. God, but it would be hard, leaving her tomorrow. Leaving everything at Garrett Park. But what else could he do?

A moment later, he heard her give a soft sigh before moving toward the door. "Harriet—" The word was torn from him. He turned to face her.

She stood by the door, her back to him. "Yes?"

Her voice sifted gently to him, a whisper of silk on the silence of the night. Chase closed his eyes, his chest so tight that it ached. But what could he say? That he loved her?

The thought slammed into his heart and sucked all his breath from his lungs. He loved Harriet. Loved her so much that the thought of being separated from her made him ache with a physical pain. He loved her and needed her, but love wasn't enough. What if he couldn't get forgiveness from his family for his sins? What if he became an outcast, a pariah? He would never put that burden on another soul.

Especially not on Harriet. "Good night, Harriet. I'm not coming to dinner this evening."

She didn't move for so long that he wondered if she'd heard him. But then she sighed and nodded. The next instant, she was gone.

Chase stayed where he was for a long time. The night air grew damp and chill, the wind picked up and blew through the cracks in the barn walls. Chase wiped a hand across his face, surprised to find it damp. He cursed, then turned to finish stacking the bales.

Much later, he finished, his body so weary he could barely move. He took off the gloves and laid them on a bench by the door so that he would find them the next day. One more day . . . that's all he had left.

Chase turned to collect the lantern. As he lifted it, the nail on which it was hung came loose from the pole and fell to the floor. Chase cursed, then bent to pick it up. As he did so, he saw something in the scattered hay on the ground.

What was that? He brushed aside some loose hay and found the St. John talisman ring. How had that gotten here? Chase picked it up and turned it over in his hand. It lay in his palm, cold and dull. It must have fallen from his pocket—

A whisper of movement stirred the air behind him. Chase whirled, but he was too late. The world exploded in a blinding flash of color and pain. And then . . . there was nothing.

The clock chimed midnight when Harriet finally gave up trying to pretend to sleep. She rose and lit a candle. She was tired and aching, her eyes hot and dry. Damn Chase St. John. Not only was he stealing her heart, but he'd stolen her peace of mind, as well.

She sighed. She wasn't being fair and she knew it. He'd done far more than anyone could have asked. It was just that she wanted the impossible—she wanted him to love her, to love her and to love Garrett Park.

Harriet looked at herself in the mirror over her dressing table, grimacing at the circles beneath her eyes. She rubbed her cheeks, trying to find some color. Heavens, she was as pale as a ghost. Sinking onto the cushioned seat, she began combing her hair.

It was lamentably thick and sadly brown. When she'd been a child, she'd spent an entire summer without her hat in an effort to get some sort of color to it. She'd thought perhaps a startling reddish hint might appear, but instead, all she'd done was turn her skin a lightly toasted color that did little to alleviate the overall brownish cast of her appearance, but had added several unfortunate freckles to the bridge of her nose.

"Brown, brown, brown," she muttered with dissatisfaction at her reflection in the mirror, pulling the brush through an especially troublesome knot. Perhaps, if she'd had flaxen hair and apple cheeks and not boring brown hair and a thin face, then Chase might have fallen deeply and irrevocably in love with her. Like a prince in a fairy tale.

That would have been divine. Harriet imagined what it would be like to have a man like Chase St. John all to herself. Her heart ached at the thought.

Someone pounded on her door. "Harri!" Stephen's voice, raised in fear.

Heavens! What was wrong? Harriet hurried to open the door.

Stephen leaned on his crutches, still dressed in his nightclothes. His eyes were wild, his face white. "The barn is on fire! The wool—" His voice broke.

Dear God, no! Harriet ran to the window and yanked back the curtains. A bright reddish glow lit the predawn blackness.

Harriet's eyes filled with tears. She couldn't believe it. How could this have—"Chase!" She whirled to face Stephen. "Have you seen him?"

Stephen blinked. "No. No, I haven't. Do you think he set the—"

"No, you fool! He was in the barn. By himself. If he fell or—" Harriet brushed past Stephen and ran down the hall to Chase's room. She knocked once, then yanked the door open. It was painfully empty, the bed unslept in.

"Dear God, no," Harriet said. She would never remember running down the stairs through the foyer, or out the front door. One moment, she was looking at Chase's unmussed bed, and the next, she was standing in the yard, looking up at the barn as it bellowed huge flames. The entire structure cracked and hissed as if furious at the black sky that stretched above it.

Derrick ran up beside her, followed by Sophia and Ophelia. Ophelia had a thick robe over her nightgown, but Sophia had only a blanket over her gown-clad shoulders.

Harriet looked around wildly, her heart thumping painfully against her ribs. "Chase is inside and we have to save him. I need to—"

"*No,*" Derrick said firmly. "You can't. Just look at it."

"But Chase—"

Sophia put her arm about Harriet. "I'm certain

he's not in there. I daresay he's in the house right now. Maybe he went to the kitchen to get a drink or—"

"I checked his room! His bed hadn't been slept in! Please, we have to—"

"Maybe he's in the library," Ophelia said desperately, though her voice warbled and a tear leaked down one cheek.

"No!" Harriet cried, her heart pounding painfully. Please God, she had to find him. She had to.

"Look!" Sophia said, tightening her hold on Harriet. "Someone is coming! Maybe they can help."

They all turned and there, riding down the driveway was Mr. Gower. He pulled up at the sight of the fire. Then he turned and looked at them, meeting Harriet's gaze for a long moment.

She could feel his superior smirk all the way from here.

"I daresay he saw the flames from his house," Ophelia said. "It's only over the ridge."

"He can help find St. John," Derrick said, turning as if to go to the banker. But before Derrick could take two steps, the banker turned and left, walking his horse calmly back down the lane.

Derrick halted, his hands in fists. "That cowardly bastard!"

Harriet broke from Sophia's side and caught Derrick's arm. "We'll have to do this ourselves. Come, Derrick. Sophia, give me your blanket."

Sophia unwrapped the blanket from her shoulders. "What are you going to—"

Harriet whisked the blanket into her arms and ran to the trough by the railing. She tossed the blanket into the cold water and pushed it all the way under.

Then she picked it up and wrapped it around her, shivering as the cold water soaked her night rail to the skin.

Derrick grabbed her arm, Stephen and Mother followed behind him.

"What do you think you're doing?" Stephen demanded, almost shouting over the crackle of the fire.

"I have to help. He was stacking the wool, he'd have to be near the door and—"

"Harriet, we can't let you do anything foolhardy," Mother said, coughing as a thick billow of smoke covered them.

Derrick nodded grimly. "We'll stop you if we have to."

"Oh for the love oh—When have I ever been foolhardy? Look at the barn! The fire's mainly on one side. If we go now, we can find him. If we wait, the smoke will get too thick."

Derrick hesitated, then glanced inquiringly at Stephen. "She's right. We could possibly—"

"*No.* It's madness. I can't allow—"

"It isn't your choice." Harriet tightened the blanket about her and turned to the barn.

Mother moved to stand before her. "Dear, just listen—"

Harriet quickly stepped around her and ran.

Behind her, Derrick cursed, but then yanked off his coat and plunged it into the trough.

Harriet didn't wait. Holding the edge of the wet blanket over her mouth, she ducked low and went though the barn door.

Smoke billowed around her, stinging her eyes and sucking the breath from her lungs. Where was he?

She crouched in the doorway, trying to get her bearings and remember where he was when she'd left him.

The smoke thickened, the fire cracked and popped overhead, a live creature, devouring the ancient wood as if starved. It roared with the throaty growl of a hungry bear.

Harriet could barely hear herself think. Chase was in here, she knew it. She could feel it as surely as she could feel the dirt beneath her hands, feel the smoke that tortured her eyes.

Suddenly, she found him, sprawled on the floor. Her fingers closing over his hair, his face. She shook him, trying to wake him. "*Chase!*" she choked, catching her breath. "*Get up!*"

Derrick materialized out of the smoke, his wet coat tied over his face. He bent over Chase.

After a second, he glanced up and yelled over the roar of the fire. "We must get him out of here. Once the fire gets to the wool—"

"Take his shoulders, I'll get his feet."

Derrick did as she told him and they struggled to lift St. John. It took every ounce of strength Harriet possessed, but she managed. Together, she and Derrick staggered out of the barn, choking and wheezing as they went. They half dragged, half carried their burden to the yard and then fell into a heap, gasping for breath in the cool air.

Mother was there in an instant. She looked at Harriet and then Derrick. "If you two ever, ever do something that foolhardy again, I'll—"

"Mother," Harriet gasped. "Chase is injured. His head—" She couldn't go on.

Mother's expression softened. "I'll see to him." She glanced at Ophelia, who hovered nearby. "Bring your brother and sister some water." She turned and began to examine Chase.

Ophelia brought a bucket and dipper. Harriet sipped the water and rubbed her chest where it burned, trying hard not to think. If she thought about Chase, alone in the barn, injured and bleeding while flames crackled about him, she would cry. Cry and cry until she could cry no more. She closed her eyes and said a fervent prayer. He was so special. So dear. She loved him so much that—She opened her eyes. She loved him.

Mother rocked back on her heels, her face grave. "I can't believe it."

Harriet's heart dropped. "He's going to die, isn't he?" Her voice cracked.

"No. He's breathing. And he's not bleeding badly at all. It's this." She pulled back his shirtsleeves. "He was tied, Harriet. Both his hands and feet." She met Harriet's gaze with a frightened look. "Harriet, someone tried to kill him."

Chapter 26

The St. Johns hate as hard as they love. 'Tis the way o' them and I don't see them a-changin'.

Little Bob, the coachman, to Miss Lucy,
Lady Birlington's maid,
while meeting for a tryst

Doctor Blackthorne shook his head. "It's a sad business this."

Harriet, who had been hovering beside the couch, stepped forward quickly. "What? Is he well? Do you need some water? Or should I—"

"Harriet," Mother said, taking her daughter by the arm and leading her to a chair. "Come and sit here and let the doctor do his job."

Harriet subsided into the chair, her hands clasped before her. She said a quick prayer, though she kept her gaze fastened on Chase. He looked so pale, lying there on the couch, his clothes and face smeared with soot, his hair matted with blood. Dr. Blackthorne had said no stitches were needed, but Harriet wasn't sure she believed him. All she knew was that if Chase St. John would live, she'd never want for anything again.

The door opened and Sophia came in. "Mother! A coach just arrived!"

"A coach?" Mother went to the window. "Who could that be?"

Doctor Blackthorne reached into his bag and pulled out a small bottle. He uncapped it and waved it beneath Chase's nose. Almost immediately, Chase coughed and sputtered.

He waved his hand weakly, batting it away. "For the love of Hera, get that out of my face!"

Harriet didn't think she'd ever heard a sweeter sentence. She leaned forward and grasped his hand, holding it between both of hers. "Thank God you are well!"

Chase looked at Harriet, then looked past her to the doctor, and then past the doctor at the rest of the Wards, who were all lined up on the other side of the room, watching him with anxious expressions. His gaze wandered back to Harriet, and he took in the fact that she was wearing a bedraggled night rail, long black soot stains on the knees and streaking her face.

He tightened his grip on her hand. "Good God, what happened to you?"

She only managed a tremulous smile as a large tear made a path down her cheek, cutting a streak through the dirt and soot. "There was a fire—and the barn—you were—"

To Chase's utter amazement, she burst into tears. Not tender tears he'd previously seen, but heavy sobs that tore at his heart. Wordlessly, he reached out and pulled her down to the settee, holding her tight.

Her cries muffled against his shirt, her tears making a warm wet splotch, Chase silently held her, waiting for her tears to subside.

From across the room, his gaze met Mrs. Ward's. She, the doctor, Derrick, Stephen, Sophia, and Ophelia all stood, watching. He reddened, but he refused to relinquish his hold on Harriet. "She's crying," he said defensively.

"So we see," Mrs. Ward said, a faint smile on her lips.

"And hear," Sophia added helpfully. Her eyes sparkled with unshed tears, and there was a trembling smile on her lips.

Chase clamped his mouth closed. He was not going to get into a discussion about this. All he wanted was for Harriet to stop crying. He rested his chin on her head and rubbed her back. "Easy," he whispered. "Easy, love. I'm fine. Really I am."

She clutched his shirt and sobbed harder.

The door opened and the gaunt housekeeper stood in the doorway. "That fellow Gower has come, and with him are those two men from the bank."

Stephen squared his shoulders. "Bring them in, Jane. We'd best get it over with. The wool is lost and there's nothing more to be done."

Ophelia sighed and dropped into the window seat, her skirts billowing out about her. "All that work—for nothing." Her voice echoed hollowly.

"Nonsense," Sophia said with false cheer. "We had a lovely time and I'm certain I'll never laugh as hard as I did when I saw Mr. St. John's sheep."

Harriet hiccupped a sob, then pulled away from Chase. "G—give me a moment to compose myself. I'll talk to Gower—"

"No, you won't," Mother said briskly. "You aren't in any shape to talk to anyone. Just lie there on the settee with Mr. St. John and let me deal with this mess."

"Lie on the settee with Mr. St. John?" Harriet blinked down at him.

Chase grinned and pulled her back to his side. "Do as your mother says."

Mother beamed.

"I'll bring the gentlemen in," Jane said with a fierce glower, "but I will *not* bring them anything to eat."

Doctor Blackthorne replaced the smelling salts in his bag. "I can see that I'm not needed here. I'll be off." He glanced at Mrs. Ward. "I'll stop back by this evening to make certain everyone is well."

Mrs. Ward nodded. "Thank you so much. I will walk you out, but—"

He held up his hand. "Don't even think of it." He made his way to the door, stopping briefly by the settee. "You're going to have the devil of a headache."

Chase shrugged. "I'll live with it."

The doctor eyed Harriet, who was snuggled neatly beside Chase. "I daresay you will." With a wink, he left the room.

A moment later, Jane returned, the bankers in tow. Stephen came forward. "Gentlemen."

Gower nodded his head. "Stephen. Mr. Silverstone, Mr. Picknard, and I were just looking at the barn. It's still smoldering, but it seems a complete loss."

"It is," Stephen said shortly.

Gower smirked. "I thought it would be best to bring them out here myself so that they could see the damage firsthand."

Chase had never wanted to box someone's ears so badly in his life.

Stephen lifted his chin. "We might as well make

this easier on all of us. Mr. Silverstone, Mr. Picknard, we cannot pay the note."

Gower brightened. "There! I told you that—"

"Mr. Gower!" Mr. Silverstone frowned at his assistant. "One does not gloat over others' misfortunes. This is a sad business. These people have worked hard."

Chase looked at the Wards' faces, at the hopelessness in their expressions. He caught Harriet's gaze and gave her a comforting squeeze. "Don't despair."

She smiled then, and though it was a tremulous smile, he knew what it cost her. "I am not despairing. We will come about, one way or another. Even without Garrett Park, we are still a family."

His heart warmed. He was graced by the beauty of the woman he held in his arms. "You are the most generous woman I have ever met."

She placed her free hand on his face, her fingers gentle. "I love you, Chase St. John. And nothing is more important than that."

He couldn't speak. Not one word. His heart bounded with joy, his soul burst into song, but not a single word came forth. And he knew in that moment that he had indeed finally found the strength he needed to face whatever the world had to offer.

He captured Harriet's free hand and pressed his lips to her palm. "Harriet Ward, I love you."

Tears filled her eyes once again, but they were held in check by the huge smile that graced her lips.

"That's enough of that!" Gower said, his face red. "We are here on official bank business. I have no wish to see—"

"Goodness!" Ophelia said from where she sat perched on the window seat. "You won't believe this!"

"What?" Sophia asked. "What's happened?"

"There's a carriage and eight in the drive! Two of them! And they both have crests on the doors and footmen and—"

Jane stood in the door. "If you are going to announce the guests, then I'll go back upstairs and change the linens."

"Who is it?" Stephen asked, looking completely confused.

Mr. Silverstone cleared his throat. "Perhaps Mr. Picknard, Mr. Gower, and I should leave so that—"

"No," Chase said, pushing himself upright. He pulled Harriet with him and settled her on the settee beside him. "Sorry, sweet, but we've guests."

Harriet snuggled in beside Chase, her heart humming. But before she could speak, a shadow darkened the doorway.

A man walked into the room. He was tall—only slightly more than Chase—but he exuded a raw power that made even Mr. Silverstone stand more at attention. He was soberly dressed, yet in the height of fashion, a blue sapphire nestled in the center of his cravat.

His gaze cut across the room and found Chase instantly. Harriet was suddenly struck with the resemblance. Black hair and clear blue eyes, an aristocratic nose, a natural air of hauteur . . .

Chase struggled to his feet, swaying slightly as he did so. "Marcus!"

The man came forward immediately and grasped Chase's arm. "Bloody hell, what happened to you?"

Chase grinned. "You always said I needed a business venture, so I took up sheep shearing."

"It looks like incredibly dirty and dangerous work. You'd better sit before you fall."

Chase sat back down, immediately returning Harriet to his side.

Harriet caught Marcus's considering gaze, her cheeks heating. To her surprise, he offered her a slight, calm smile before turning back to Chase. "I'm sorry I'm late. It took us some time to discover your whereabouts."

"We?" Chase asked.

The doorway was immediately filled, this time with a younger man, though he was clearly marked by his black hair and laughing blue eyes. "There you are, you scoundrel."

"Devon!" Chase grinned. "Marcus has you running fetch and carry, does he?"

"Lud, no. That's why Anthony is here."

"You brought our half brother?"

"Oh yes. He's in the carriage now, with your present."

"Present?"

"An early birthday gift." Devon looked around the room, skimming over the bankers and coming to rest on Sophia. "Well! What have we here?"

Sophia's cheeks flooded with color and she dimpled adorably.

Chase's smile dimmed. "She's sixteen, Devon."

"Oh. What a pity." Devon shrugged. "I wish I wasn't a man of scruples."

"Chase," Marcus said softly, "perhaps you could do the introductions?"

"With pleasure. This," he hugged Harriet tighter, "is Miss Harriet Ward. Harriet, m'love, these are my brothers, the Marquis of Treymount and Devon St. John."

Harriet managed a nod, for Chase held her so tightly she couldn't rise.

Marcus bowed. "A pleasure, Miss Ward."

"Indeed," Devon said, sweeping a gallant bow.

Chase didn't give them more time. "And this is Miss Sophia and Miss Ophelia. Derrick. And Stephen."

Marcus bowed again, then eyed Gower, who stood rigidly in the center of the room. "And these gentlemen?"

"Mr. Picknard and Mr. Silverstone from the bank, and his assistant, Mr. Gower."

Mr. Silverstone cleared his throat. "It's a pleasure to meet you, my lord. I'm afraid I don't quite understand what's happening—"

"Neither do I," Marcus assured him with a cool smile. "But I'm certain my brother can explain everything."

"Brother?" Mr. Silverstone looked at Chase, his brows raised. "The captain is your—"

"No," Chase said. "I am not a captain. I'm Chase St. John."

"Captain?" Devon asked, obviously amused. "When did you become a captain?"

"I'll explain later," Chase muttered, sending his brother a quelling glance.

"Explain now," Marcus cut in, his brow lowered. "The short version, if you please."

Chase sighed. "I was attacked by footpads on the road near here. It was my fault; I was drunk and an obvious target. Anyway, when I woke up, I—"

"—kindly agreed to pretend to be my fiancé," Harriet said breathlessly. She met Marcus's glance and colored adorably. "My fiancé that did not really exist. We call him Captain John Frakenham. We made him up to keep the bank at bay."

Devon burst out laughing. "So Chase pretended

to be a sea captain? B'God, I would have given gold money to have seen that!"

"St. John?" Gower suddenly sputtered. "Wait! I read that name in Debrett's! Y—you are not telling me that—No. I will not believe it."

"You don't have to. It's none of your concern." Chase reached into his pocket and pulled out the talisman ring. He glanced at Marcus. "Though I was waylaid by thieves, fortunately this was saved."

"Thank goodness," Marcus murmured. He eyed the ring a moment. "I think."

Devon frowned. "Chase, I don't mean to pry, but you look like hell."

"I was in the barn putting up the wool when someone knocked me on the head and set the building on fire."

There was a moment of stunned silence, then Devon chuckled. "Always willing to play a joke, aren't you?"

"I am not joking."

Harriet glanced at Chase's stern expression. She placed her hand on his and was rewarded with a gentle squeeze.

Devon's smile faded. "Oh. I can believe you were attacked and nearly set afire . . . but putting up wool? You expect us to believe that?"

"Yes."

"Attacked?" Mr. Silverstone said, looking concerned. "You were attacked?"

"And tied and left to burn," Stephen added grimly.

Derrick looked at Gower. "Didn't you tell them about the fire?"

Mr. Silverstone frowned. "All Mr. Gower has told me is that your barn burned to the ground and you cannot make the final payment."

Gower waved his hand. "I didn't know anyone was tied and left to burn—"

"You knew someone was in the barn while it was burning," Derrick said grimly, "because we asked for your help, and you just turned and rode off."

Silverstone whirled on Gower, the older man's thick brows lowered even more. "Did you witness their misfortune and then turn and leave?"

Gower's face turned bright red. "I saw no need to—"

"You—" Silverstone's jaw set. He glared at Gower. "There have been several instances when I've wondered at your moral fiber. I can see my concerns were well founded. You've wanted the Wards to fail since you first came to the bank."

Mr. Picknard nodded. "I believe we've seen enough, Silverstone."

"Indeed we have. Mr. Gower, the second we return to the bank, you will clean out your desk."

Gower's hands opened and closed. "That's not—I didn't mean—but what about the Wards? What about their note?"

"That's no longer your concern," Silverstone snapped. "Leave, Gower. You are dismissed."

Gower sputtered. "B-b-but—"

"Leave," Silverstone ordered again, but in a colder voice. "Or I'll see to it that you never work in banking again. Ever."

Red-faced, Gower seemed to be struggling with his temper. Finally, he swallowed, then said, "Yes, sir." It was easy to see that he wanted to say more.

Silverstone looked Gower up and down before turning away and murmuring something to Mr. Picknard.

There was nothing left to be done. Gower cast one

last look at Harriet, slammed his hat on his head, and then turned on his heel and left.

Chase watched the man go. Had it not been for Harriet's small hand on his arm, he would have gone after that lout and shown him the true meaning of the word "honor."

Mother cleared her throat. "Mr. Silverstone, thank you very much. Mr. Gower has not been at all pleasant for us to deal with. However, he was right about one thing. Without the wool . . . we cannot make the final payment."

Harriet's heart sank. It was so unfair—they had all worked so hard, so very hard. Chase gave her hand a gentle squeeze. She looked at him and he lifted her fingers to his lips.

Mr. Silverstone nodded. "If the board would approve an extension for a month, then perhaps—"

"No," Mother said. "I'm afraid it would take an entire year to find the money."

"A year?" Mr. Silverstone sighed. "I'm afraid we could never get the board to agree—"

"What about two months?" Chase asked. "Would that be acceptable?"

"Of course," Silverstone said with a nod. "I'm certain that Picknard and I could get an extension for that length of time."

Mother frowned. "But what could we possibly do in two months?"

"I could marry your daughter." He looked down at Harriet. "If she'll have me."

Harriet's throat, already a bit sore from the fire, now seemed to close. She swallowed three times before she could even rasp out, "What—you can't want to—but you've never—"

Chase turned her to face him, his hands resting

gently on her shoulders. "Harriet, I love you, and I want to marry you. I know I have things I must do, things I have to see to, but I think, with you by my side, that I can face those things."

Harriet's heart quivered. "You are sure?"

"With all my heart."

"But you were going to leave last night. I could tell—"

"Only because I hadn't settled things in London. But I wouldn't have been gone long. I couldn't have stayed away, no matter how much I wished it. And now . . . now I realize that with you beside me, I can accomplish anything."

Tears welled in Harriet's eyes.

Devon cleared his throat. "Mr. Silverstone, I believe you have your answer. A two-month extension seems to be in order." Devon smiled at Harriet. "Mustn't keep the bank waiting, you know."

Harriet found herself returning the smile. "No. We mustn't." She turned to Chase. "Yes," she said softly. "Yes, I will marry you. And I already have the perfect shoes, too."

Chase tilted back his head and laughed, pulling her into his arms and hugging her tightly.

Mr. Silverstone smiled indulgently. "I hope we receive an invitation."

"Oh, you will," Marcus said. "Here. Allow me to escort you out. I want to tell you what I plan on giving the couple as a wedding gift. I'm sure it will go a long way to assuring you that the payment can be made, however much it is."

Marcus took the bankers outside while Harriet smiled up at Chase. "It seems I've loved you for so long. Since the first moment I saw you, I think."

He smiled into her eyes. "I'm afraid I can't make

the same claim. You stole my heart in little bits and pieces."

"Oh for heaven's sake—" Derrick dropped into a chair. "Do we have to listen to this?"

Devon nodded. "Sickening, isn't it? Personally, I prefer to do my lovemaking in private, but well . . . that's just me."

"Oh, look!" Ophelia said from her post by the window. "Here comes a very large rug!"

"A what?" Sophia asked.

Marcus reentered the room. Behind him came the largest man Harriet had ever seen. Tall and blond, he barely cleared the doorway, especially since he carried a rolled-up rug over one shoulder.

Harriet openly gaped until Chase kissed her chin and reminded her not to stare. "Sorry," she whispered.

"That's Anthony, my half brother."

Anthony stopped on seeing Chase. "Good God, what happened to you?"

"Sheep. I'll never eat mutton again."

"I can see why not." Anthony dropped the rug in front of Chase.

"What's this?"

"Your birthday present," Devon said merrily. "Open it."

Harriet looked at the rug. To her amazement, it began to wiggle. "Chase . . ."

"I see, sweetheart." Chase stood, gripped the edge of the rug and yanked. It unrolled with a thud, the disheveled figure of a man coming to rest at Anthony's large feet.

The man looked up at Anthony and visibly started. "*Argh!*"

"Don't worry, little man," Anthony said, grinning.

"There will be no more magic rug rides if you behave yourself."

"Oh, he will behave himself," Marcus said, coming to stand beside Anthony. "Won't you, Mr. Annesley?"

The man nodded, his eyes wide.

"Who is this?" Harriet asked Chase. Sophia and Ophelia were standing on tiptoe to see, while Stephen and Derrick watched with wide grins.

"This," Chase said grimly, "is the man I told you about. The one I thought was my friend, but wasn't." Chase looked at Marcus. "Before anything is said, I must speak. T—there is something I must tell you."

"We already know," Marcus said. "You were out in your phaeton and you accidentally hit a woman."

Chase winced. "Yes. I should never have been drinking while—"

"Wait." Marcus lifted his foot and prodded Harry. "Tell him."

Harry shook his head. "I am not a man to be made a fool of, Treymount! I demand—"

"That's it," Anthony said with unperturbed calm, "back into the rug you go."

"*No!*" Harry said, scooting away from Anthony. "No! I just—I can't—what the hell do you want?"

"The truth," Marcus said.

Devon leaned toward Stephen and said in a low voice, "There is an Easy Way to learn things, and a Hard Way. Some people always seem drawn to the Hard Way."

Harry sighed. "Oh blast it! I cannot believe—you know I could go to the constable and—"

"And what?" Marcus asked, obviously amused.

"Tell them we forced you to ride inside a rug for a day?"

"It was longer than that," Harry said defensively.

"We let you out to get a drink of water," Anthony said.

"And we fed you," Devon added. He looked at Stephen. "I voted against that, but Marcus has a humanitarian streak."

"Oh all right!" Annesley snapped. "May I at least stand?"

Anthony seemed to consider it. "No."

"No? Why not?"

"You might run. And while I know I could catch you, I just ate, and I've no wish to unsettle my stomach."

"I," Annesley said in a lofty tone, "will not run."

"Very well. But if you try—" Anthony balled his huge fist and slammed it into his other palm.

Annesley gulped. "There is no need for that." He clambered to his feet. "I'll tell you everything, though I think this is grossly unfair."

"Unfair?" Chase asked.

Annesley shrugged. "I owe you an apology. I should never have extorted money from you."

Everyone waited.

"And?" Marcus said, his cold gaze pinning Annesley.

The rogue rubbed his neck wearily. "And there was no . . . you know."

"No what?" Chase asked.

"No accident. Well, there was an accident, but the woman was unharmed."

"*What?*" Chase started forward, but Harriet held him in place.

Annesley sighed. "After that night, I went out and found her. She was in the first hospital I went to. I paid her ten pounds to disappear."

"Was she hurt?"

"A scrape or two. Nothing more." Annesley met Chase's gaze and gave a rueful shrug. "It just seemed like too good an opportunity to let pass."

"Tell him what else you did," Devon said.

Annesley sent a cutting glance at Devon.

Devon lifted his brows, a chill to his gaze. "Who put you in the rug the first time?"

Annesley's jaw tightened. He turned back to Chase. "I borrowed your bill from White's and used it to make a promissory note."

"For twenty thousand pounds," Anthony added.

Harriet could feel Chase's fury. She gripped his hand tightly.

"And?" Devon prompted, eyes narrowing. "There's more."

"What more?" Annesley asked, laughing uneasily.

"I know what more," Chase said. He took Harriet's hand and placed a kiss on the back of it. "Hold that for me, sweet." He approached Annesley. When he stood directly before him, he pulled back his sleeves. His wrists were raw from where he'd been bound. "Someone attacked me in the barn and tied me up, then set the place on fire. You wouldn't know anything about that, would you?"

Annesley appeared pained. "All I asked was that you be delayed. That is all. I may be a bit of a shyster, but I am no murderer."

"I disagree. You are exactly the type of monster capable of doing such a thing. It's your fault I was attacked. Your fault the barn was burned and the wool lost."

"I don't know anything about wool or—"

Chase slammed his fist into Annesley's mouth. The man turned a complete circle, then landed, face-down, on the rug.

"Well done!" Devon exclaimed. He clapped his hands lightly. Sophia and Ophelia joined in, while Stephen and Derrick nodded their approval.

Anthony rolled the rug back up and then hefted it to his shoulder. "I'll put this in the carriage, and we'll deliver it to the constable on our way through town, along with the name of the fellow Annesley hired to delay your return to London."

"Be sure you tie that rug tightly. I wouldn't want any unnecessary air to get inside."

Anthony grinned, then went out the door, letting the rug thunk solidly against the doorframe as he went.

Chase turned back to Harriet. For the first time in his life, happiness was within a fingertip's length.

Marcus moved to the door. "Devon, I believe the time has come for us to leave."

"So soon?"

"Now," Marcus said firmly.

Devon sighed. He bowed to everyone, kissed Mrs. Ward's hand, then winked at Sophia. "Fare thee well, my friends! Chase, will we see you back in town?"

"Yes. I've a wedding to plan, you know."

Devon grimaced. "Well, don't look to me for assistance. You know how I feel about weddings." He sent a fond smile to Chase. "I'm glad you're well."

Chase smiled back. "So am I."

Marcus waited for Devon to leave the room before he turned to Chase. "If you need help procuring a special license—"

"If I need help, I'll ask for it." Chase smiled down at Harriet. "That's one thing I've learned in staying here at Garrett Park."

Marcus's hard mouth curved into a smile. "Then perhaps that knock on the head was good for you." He bowed to the others. "Good day. I look forward to seeing all of you at the wedding." In a moment he was gone.

They all stood in silence as the sound of the carriages faded away.

Ophelia let the curtain drop. "Well!" she said with a beatific expression.

Mrs. Ward glanced at Chase and Harriet, then cleared her throat. "Sophia and Ophelia, could you help me in the breakfast room?"

Sophia frowned. "Breakfast room? Now? Why—"

Mrs. Ward calmly propelled Sophia out the door, Ophelia following.

"Stephen and Derrick," Mrs. Ward continued determinedly, "I believe you are needed in the kitchen."

"The kitchen?" Derrick scowled. "I was going to sit here and read—"

"Come on, Derrick." Stephen grabbed his brother's arm and dragged him to the door. "You can read in the kitchen."

"Yes, but—" The door shut behind him. Mrs. Ward soon followed.

Moments later, the room was silent and empty except for Chase and Harriet.

Chase sighed heavily and rubbed his chin on Harriet's hair.

"What now?" she asked, wrapping her arms about his waist and snuggling closer.

What now, indeed. Life lay ahead of them, bright

and shining and full of hope. Chase reached into his pocket and found the talisman ring. Then he took Harriet's hand and slid it gently over her finger.

"Oh no! It will never come off!"

Chase kissed her cheek. "Oh yes it will. On the day we marry. And if it doesn't, then we'll just be stuck with it forever."

She smiled and looked up him, her eyes shimmering softly. "Forever, my love, may not be long enough."

Epilogue

Coo 'ee, now there's a handsome man! Not as handsome as one of those St. John brothers, but that's to be understood. The earth can only handle so much handsomeness afore it splits in half.

Miss Lucy, Lady Birlington's upstairs maid,
to Madame Blanchard, the French dresser,
while eyeing the new footman

Devon St. John leaned back in the plush coach, stretching his legs into the farthest corner. The coach swayed and bounced, taking curves at breakneck speed as they flew through the countryside, going northward, toward Scotland.

Scotland, Devon decided, was safe. He would visit his friend, Viscount Strathmore, for a few weeks and then, when the way was clear, he'd return to England. But only once he was assured that the way was clear.

Life, Devon decided, was beautiful. He'd just escaped the largest trap ever to befall a man, especially a St. John. Somewhere back at a church in the tiny village of Sticklye-By-The-River, his brother Chase was getting married. In fact . . . Devon pulled out his watch and looked at it. The ceremony would be over in another ten minutes or so. Then, once the reception began, everyone would look around and see that Devon had already made good his escape. And Chase, already cursed by the ring and thus married, would realize that there was only one single St. John brother left in proximity—Marcus, the oldest. Chase would have no choice then, but to trick Marcus into taking the bloody ring while Devon cavorted merrily in Scotland.

Devon grinned sleepily. Sometimes he amazed himself with his intelligence. It really had been too easy. He snuggled in the corner, crossed his arms, and closed his eyes.

Several hours later, the coach crossed the Scottish border. Devon was awakened by the definite chill that had begun to crisp the air. He thought about asking the coachman to stop, but then thought better of it. They were making such good time.

Devon reached across the seat and grabbed the carriage blanket that was folded neatly in one corner. As he pulled the blanket toward him, a loud ping sounded in the carriage. Then another and another as something small and metal bounced along the floor and then rolled to a stop.

"No!" Devon closed his eyes, refusing to even look. Chase St. John had left the blasted talisman ring neatly tucked in Devon's carriage blanket. And now, miles and miles from home, Devon was stuck, the ring was his.

He was doomed. Doomed unless he could come up with a way to circumvent the magical impulses of the ring.

The only hope Devon had was to avoid women. All of them. He reflected glumly on what he'd been told about Scottish women, of their innate passion and flaming good looks and in that instant, he knew he was damned.

Well and truly damned.

Start the New Year with these thrilling new romances coming in January from Avon Books

MARRIED TO THE VISCOUNT by Sabrina Jeffries
An Avon Romantic Treasure

Abigail Mercer had married Viscount Ravenswood by proxy, but when she arrives on his doorstep, the dashing rogue denies their union! Now, rather than risk a scandal, the Viscount has proposed a marriage in name only, but Abigail has other plans.

DO NOT DISTURB by Christie Ridgway
An Avon Contemporary Romance

Investigative reporter Angel Buchanan has just uncovered a whopper: her deadbeat dad is actually a man famous for his family values. But legendary lawyer C.J. Jones is determined to keep Angel quiet . . . and he'll gladly woo her into submission.

NO ORDINARY GROOM by Gayle Callen
An Avon Romance

Jane Whittington wants excitement and adventure, not marriage to a fop! But William Chadwick is more than he seems. And if excitement is what Jane seeks, then he'll give her what she desires . . . one kiss at a time.

SEEN BY MOONLIGHT by Kathleen Eschenburg
An Avon Romance

Annabelle Hallston will do anything to keep her younger brother safe—which is the only reason she agreed to marry Royce Kincaid. The notorious black sheep of an aristocratic family, Royce does not believe in love . . . until Anabelle unlocks his true passion and frees his wounded soul.